BACK ON TRACK

Dear Gil and Carol,
   I t's been delightful
getting acquainted with you!
I hope you enjoy reading
this book as much as I
have enjoyed writing it!
   Dr. G. K. Marshall

BACK ON TRACK

Dr. G.K. Marshall

ELM HILL

A Division of
HarperCollins Christian Publishing

www.elmhillbooks.com

Back on Track

Published in Nashville, Tennessee, by Elm Hill, an imprint of Thomas Nelson. Elm Hill and Thomas Nelson are registered trademarks of HarperCollins Christian Publishing, Inc.

Elm Hill titles may be purchased in bulk for educational, business, fund-raising, or sales promotional use. For information, please e-mail SpecialMarkets@ ThomasNelson.com.

Publisher's Note: This novel is a work of fiction. Names, characters, places, and incidents are either products of the author's imagination or used fictitiously. All characters are fictional, and any similarity to people living or dead is purely coincidental.

Library of Congress Cataloging-in-Publication Data

Library of Congress Control Number: 2018960789

ISBN 978-1-595557704 (Paperback)
ISBN 978-1-595557735 (Hardbound)
ISBN 978-1-595557810 (eBook)

CHAPTER I

FRIDAY, FEBRUARY 28

It was a cold, snowy evening, and sitting on a log by a shed was a boy scuffing his ragged shoes in the snow and dirt. A stubborn, petulant set was on his face as he sat alone. His barely older sister approached him, walking precariously along in the ice and snow with her hands in her thin coat pockets, her shoulders hunched to preserve some warmth.

"Danny, please don't go to the snowball fight," she said. "Come home with me. Those boys are really not your friends; they'll end up turning on you, and you'll get hurt and feel miserable." The boy's expression turned fierce, but as he shifted, his sister saw tears in his eyes and knew her request was taking effect. "Come on back to the house with me," she pleaded. "We'll make some warm tea and have toast."

Reluctantly the boy stood and followed his sister, quietly acquiescing to her plans.

"I guess you're right," he said "but sometimes I feel like I want to be a part of things, and I don't want them calling me afraid and tied to your apron strings."

"If they won't treat you decently, you don't want them as friends," she replied.

"We all need friends," he rejoined, plodding along in the snow after her.

"Yes, well, we're friends," she said brightly glancing back at him. "We need each other, and we need to be friends if nothing else. Who knows how long we'll be living here, and those snowballing fellows will be history. Let's go up to the apartment and get warm."

"It's not warm in there," Danny responded. "We can't turn the thermostat above fifty-five degrees or we'll get swats!"

"Yes, but it's colder out here, and we can get under some blankets on the couch and read or something."

"I wish we had a stove or fireplace," Danny complained. "I'm cold."

The two trudged on in silence, finally climbing the three stories of steps, walking down the hall, and unlocking the apartment door to enter the chilly rooms. A weary green couch sat in one corner with frayed magazines on a small table in front of it. Dirty brown carpet with matted paths covered the floor, and there were rickety venetian blinds without drapes over the windows. Danny sat on the couch pulling his wet boots under him. His sister went into a bedroom bringing two blankets with her. When she saw the wet boots on the couch she frowned, and Danny dutifully pulled them off and scooted away from the wet patches he'd produced.

"Sissy, there's nothing here to read that's new," he said.

"Yes, I know; we can go to the library tomorrow, but I've been thinking and I want to talk," she said, covering them with the two blankets. They were both still in their coats.

"You talk and talk," he complained.

"Yes," she grinned, "I do, but this is very important! I've been thinking about us and what's going to happen to us, and I don't see things getting better. We need to be planning on how to handle things before they get worse."

"Shucks! How could it get any worse?"

"Dad could die or leave us."

"It's almost like he's not here now."

"Yes, but there's this place to live and generally some food even if he's gone most of the time," she countered.

"So what's the plan?"

"Well, I'm going to start out by saying that despite this horrid problem we're both smart, and that's one thing we've got going for us."

"What makes you think we're smart?" he asked, wanting to hear.

"We both like to read and, despite being in so many schools, we both keep up quite well. In fact, I think that's part of why you're so often picked on. Not only are you small, but you know the answers to the questions the teacher asks. Isn't that right?"

"Yeah," he agreed grudgingly, "but how can we be smart if our parents are so dumb they won't take care of us right?"

Sissy pondered this a bit and slowly released her thoughts as they materialized. "I suspect our parents may be smart, but they've been caught by drugs and drink—Mom with drugs and Dad with drink. Mom's dad was a dentist, and both of Dad's parents were teachers. They must have brains—good brains."

"Where are they all now?" he asked.

"I don't know, but that's part of what I want to talk about." She said. "First, we need to make a pact between us to always help each other out no matter what happens; then we need to work together to see if we can find either of our folk's families. We also need to do our best never to lose each other. We could be sent to separate foster homes, but I don't think the state could stop us talking to each other. Next, I think it is very important that we both stay in school as long as it is possible by any means, and finally, neither of us must allow our lives to be ruined by drugs or drink!"

"That's a lot to remember to do!" Danny exclaimed.

"Not too much," she defended. "Everything's important!"

"Let's see—make a pact to help, find our families, stick together, stay in school, and no drink or drugs—five things," Danny enumerated.

"Yes, and you just proved my point of how smart you are," she said, grinning again. "So are you in?"

Danny slowly considered then said, "What if I don't want to?"

"I can't make you," Sissy replied, "but I think you'll do it because you love me and deep down, you already see it's our only hope to have things be better."

Danny closed his eyes and realized he wanted to cry. It took him a moment to control his emotions, but then he vehemently exclaimed, "I'm in; it's a deal!"

Both youngsters then sat side by side leaning against each other in their thin coats under the blankets and were silent. The silence lengthened, and they both drifted off to sleep. A couple of hours later in the night's darkness, their father, more drunk than usual, stumbled into the room and seeing the sleeping children, went straight to his own bed, removing only his boots.

As the gray light of a new day filtered in through the blinds, Sissy woke first and was initially disoriented, but then the discussion of the previous evening came back to her. In the adjacent bedroom she heard her father snoring, and she watched her brother's face in the dim light noting his dark, curling lashes. A fierce love and sense of protectiveness rose within her as she again thought of the five points and how to remember them. A pact of help, find families, stay together, school, no drink or drugs. She rearranged the ideas in her head. *I need more vowels*, she thought. *ST—stay together, AP—a pact, FA-families, S-school, NAD—no alcohol drugs. STAPFASNADS. I wonder if we could remember that.*

Danny stirred and opened his eyes. "I'm hungry," he said. "We didn't eat supper."

Sissy quietly got up and stealthily closed the door to their dad's bedroom. Then she tiptoed to the refrigerator, tightened her lips, and looked into the pantry. "There's no new milk," she said. "But there's a box of frosted sugar flakes. Let's put some warm water on those," she offered in a hushed voice. "Today's Saturday, so there's no school breakfast."

Danny frowned but said nothing. Sissy got two large cereal bowls and filled them with the frosted flakes and ran the tap water until it was hot, adding a bit to the cereal.

"Let's stir it and let it sit a little so the hot water and sitting will make it seem a little more like it could be milk," she offered. "Let's also write a note to Dad," she said in a lower voice, "letting him know we've gone to the library. He'll likely be mean and grouchy when he wakes up."

"Let's list some food on the note for him to buy," Danny suggested. "We need milk and eggs and potatoes and more cereal."

"Sure," Sissy agreed, "but he probably won't wake up for a long time. The library closes at two, so surely he'll wake up before then. It looks cold outside, so we'll need to dress warm."

"You say 'warmly,'" Danny corrected.

"How do you know?" Sissy rolled her eyes.

"The teacher said," he defended.

"Well, you're probably right," she agreed slowly, "because it is an adverb and adverbs often have a 'ly' at the end. I'm wearing three shirts and two pairs of jeans."

"You'll look all bunchy," Danny offered, laughing.

"I'm skinny," she said, "I won't."

The children finished their cereal and donned their layered clothes and coats. Sissy wrote the note and they headed for the library.

The crisp, clear morning greeted them with bright sunshine but sharp coldness. After leaving the dark empty halls of the apartment complex, the morning seemed almost daunting with its light. The sidewalk was cluttered with brittle chips of ice and snow that crunched as they moved along. Saturday morning traffic was light and at times the streets along the several blocks to the library seemed almost deserted. The children both carried tattered spiral notebooks, nothing else.

"Man, I wish we could still check out library books; those books in our room are very old. We've read them a hundred times!" Danny said. "Why did you say we can't?" he asked.

"We'd need Dad's driver's license to get a library card so we can get them, and I've been afraid to ask," Sissy answered. "Actually, I don't know if he still has a license, and he may get mad if I ask for it and he doesn't."

"We used to have a car," Danny observed.

"Yeah, but that was months ago," Sissy said quietly, "before Dad started drinking so horribly much."

"Don't say 'yeah,' say yes," Danny corrected, obviously diverting the conversation.

"Okay, y-e-s," Sissy replied, dragging out the word for emphasis. "Now, let's start our five-point-program thing this morning by looking for the grandparents. What do we know about them?"

"Do you remember any first names?" Danny asked.

"No, all I remember is calling them Grandma and Grandpa. When we were little, Mom's last name was probably Denton since I remember people laughing about her Dad's name being 'Dr. Denton the dentist.'"

"Why would they laugh about that? All the d's?"

"Or maybe because 'dentist' and 'Denton' sound alike," Sissy offered.

"Maybe we can get on the computer and look him up," Danny said, thinking out loud. "But I don't know if children can use the library's computers."

"We'll ask!" Sissy exclaimed, dancing backwards in her excitement. "What a great idea! Let's write down everything we know and everything we find out in our notebooks. That is important. I believe Dad may be trying to stay away from all of them as much as possible because he's ashamed of his drinking. He never mentions anyone in the family at all. How could we talk about it without making him suspicious?"

"We could start out just by asking him about them, telling him we want to know about them in case something should happen to him," Danny offered.

"No, I think that's too direct," Sissy countered. "He'll act all angry and mean like he did last time and ask us if he's not good enough for us. Remember he swatted both of us and sent us to bed early and left?"

The library janitor was just unlocking the door when the children arrived.

"You guys sure look ambitious this morning!" he said. "Come in and get warm. The story reader won't be here until ten o'clock."

"Thank you," the children pleasantly chirped together in unison, avoiding being insulted by the old fellow intimating that they'd enjoy the vacuous children's books chosen by the library reader for preschoolers. They headed to the library desk manned by an extremely obese lady who was dressed in a moo moo and sported a double dose of makeup.

"Good morning!" Sissy greeted. "I'm eleven, and I would like to use the computers."

"Oh, sweetie you're far too young," the lady replied, her double-triple chins rippling wildly. "You have to be sixteen to use them on your own. You can use them only with adult supervision."

Sissy looked at Danny who was standing with his mouth gaped open staring at the librarian's jiggling chins.

"Don't stare," she whispered.

Danny grinned at her, grinned at the librarian, and said in a sad little falsetto voice, "We need to use the computer to find our grandparents."

The librarian's face settled into a comical screen of perplexity and reevaluation.

"Maybe I could find someone to help you. Go over and read for a while, and if someone comes in I'll ask them to help you."

The children moved to the reading area.

"You're such a little actor," Sissy accused Danny.

"Well, it worked," Danny replied smugly.

"What will we tell them when they ask questions about us?"

"We'll tell them Momma is gone and Dad is sick," Danny offered.

Sissy thought a bit and nodded. "Yes, I think that will work; it's actually true. Do we know where Grandpa Denton lives?"

"No, but it must be where it doesn't snow. Mamma used to say she only saw snow once in a while when she was little. I wonder if her mom and dad know where she is. I'm sure they don't know where we are."

"I agree," Sissy said. "But unless Dad allows, we can't go to them. However, it would be better to know where they are in case of problems."

"Where do you think Momma is?" Danny asked. "Do you think she's in this town?"

"I doubt it," Sissy replied. "We've moved twice since Dad said for her to leave and never come back unless she quits drugs. That was in St. Louis. But now Dad's drinking is about as bad as her drugs."

"What kind of drugs did she use?"

"Well—pot, which is marijuana, and other stuff Dad said," Sissy replied. "I think Dad moved from St. Louis so she couldn't find us, but I think he drinks because he misses her."

Danny stood by the library shelf, which was invitingly bulging with colorful children's books, but he was looking down and whispering, "What a mess."

"May I help you?" a lady in a short fur vest asked walking up to them. "The librarian said you needed to use the computer to find your grandparents."

The children looked up startled from their separate reveries, but immediately brightened.

"We wanted to use the computer," Sissy said, "but we need an adult. Are you going to help us?"

"Sure, let's go get started," the lady said. "My name is Belle Jonas, and I have half an hour to help you. Do you know anything about computers?"

"I've had classes in school for the past semester, but I don't know much," Sissy explained. "We don't have a computer at home. I was hoping we could use Google."

"What town do your grandparents live in, and what is their last name?" Belle asked.

"We don't know the town, but we don't think it snows there, and Grandpa is a dentist named Dr. Denton; we don't know his first name," Danny said.

"Well, let's see what we can find on Google," Belle said. "We might try Dogpile, too."

"Dogpile?" Danny snickered.

"Yes, a rather indecent name, isn't it?" Bell smiled back. "Is it Dentin or Denton?" she asked, spelling the names out.

"We don't know," Sissy said.

Belle entered Dr. Denton, DDS; Dr. Dentin, DDS; dentist, Dr. Denton along with dentist, Dr. Dentin into the Google search space but nothing came up.

"I don't know if it is these slow library computers or if there isn't a match," Belle said, perturbed. "Let's try Dogpile."

"Google won't even bring up Dogpile," Danny observed after several minutes. "All we can do is make the little snake spin."

"Yes, you're right," Belle agreed. "We need to use my computer, but I don't have it here. If the library has wireless, I could bring it back some other time and we could take a look. I can't stay because I have other things to do today, but I could come back for a while tomorrow afternoon. Could you?"

Danny and Sissy looked at each other and Sissy responded carefully. "Yes, if our dad will let us. Sometimes he is pretty grouchy."

"Maybe you could get a book to read to him," Belle suggested. "And then he'd let you come."

"He never reads," Danny said, "and we don't read to him."

Belle looked at the bright-faced, raggedly dressed children with increasing curiosity and some concern.

"I'll be here at 1:30 tomorrow afternoon whether you can make it or not, and if you can't come, I'll be back here about the same time as this next Saturday morning."

"Oh, thank you! Thank you!" Sissy exclaimed. "We'll really try to come tomorrow."

"We like you," Danny grinned, warming up to Belle.

"Goodbye then," she said, picking up her books and donning her coat. "You children have a good time and try to stay warm."

Danny and Sissy sat in a corner of the library. Danny's interest lay in science and action books, while Sissy enjoyed fiction, especially historical novels. They sat lost in their books until one o'clock, when Danny's stomach started growling.

"I'm hungry," he whined.

Looking up, Sissy grinned and agreed. "Boy, I am, too. Reading is so much fun, and I've forgotten the time. We'll be too hungry to stay until two o'clock, so let's go home now."

Putting on their coats and replacing their books, the two children prepared for the walk home.

"I hope Dad's in a good mood," Danny considered. "I hope there's some food."

The day had warmed a bit with the bright sunshine, but the ice still crackled under their shoes on the sidewalk. When they came within a half block of the apartment building, Danny threw out his arm to block his sister, and in a hoarse cry said, "Look, men with guns!" Sure enough, in dark ski masks were four men, pistols in hand, moving a fifth man across the sidewalk into a large black SUV.

"Is that Dad?" Sissy asked hoarsely.

"I don't know, but I think so," Danny answered. "I'm afraid to go find out."

The children watched as the SUV drove off down the street, then they hurried on into the apartment building. The door to their apartment was ajar, and they slowly entered. Everything seemed just as they had left it except their father was not in his bed. His door was open, and the bed had not been made. The blankets on the couch where they'd slept had not been moved.

"Do you think that was him for sure?" Danny asked.

"Well, he's not here, and if he's gone and there's no food, we're in real trouble," Sissy replied. "All I found was the cereal from this morning, so let's eat more of it now unless there is food he bought in the refrigerator. Our note from this morning is gone."

She looked into the refrigerator and grimaced. "There's nothing here." Danny got a bowl and reached into the cereal box to pick up a handful of flakes. He pulled out a piece of paper and looking at it, shrieked, "Look, money!!" Reaching in again, he pulled out more $100 bills.

"Gracious!" exclaimed Sissy. "Let's dump it all out." She dug in the cupboard and pulled out a large cake pan dumping the contents of the cereal box into it. The children were amazed to see the numbers of bills.

"We need to count it," Danny crowed, so they sat and counted it twice. There were two-hundred $100 bills.

"How much money is this?" Sissy queried.

"Two hundred times $100 is twenty thousand dollars. I wonder who it belongs to."

"I don't know, but here's a note," Sissy said as she excitedly sorted through the remaining flakes in the cake pan. Opening the paper she read, "Kids, this money is for you to live on. I may have to be gone for several days, Dad. P.S. Don't spend any more than you have to, it's all I have."

"Wow!" Danny exclaimed. "What are we going to do?"

"You know," Sissy said, "this is the kind of thing I was afraid of. In a way, we already have a plan. The money will just make things a lot easier, but we're really going to have to be careful not to be turned over to Child Protective Services."

"And why don't you like them?" Danny asked.

"Because they put you in foster homes, and you can't do things your own way. We need to find our grandparents."

"How are we going to take care of the money?" Danny asked. "What if the men with the guns come back and take it, too? When they search a house, they look everywhere."

"Perhaps we should keep it in our pockets. But we must not show it to anyone."

"My pockets aren't big enough," Danny observed.

"Well, that brings up something else," Sissy decided. "We need different clothes. Everything we have is worn out and too small. I think it would be sensible to go get the right clothes with pockets for money. Let's take some of the money and get some things at the used clothes shop we passed on the way to the library today."

"I'm really hungry," Danny complained. "Let's eat something first."

"I don't think I could eat now if someone tried to make me!" Sissy exclaimed in an exasperated manner. "How can you eat when Daddy is taken by men with guns?"

Danny looked at his sister soberly, saying, "I know it's scary, but I'm really, really hungry! Not eating will not make things better. I do feel all shaky inside, but I'm also hungry. Try to eat even though you don't feel like it."

Reluctantly Sissy got down bowls for the cereal. Danny placed spoons beside the bowls, placing handfuls of frosted flakes from the cake pan into both bowls. Sissy ran water in the spigot until it was hot, dumping the liquid over the flakes. They woodenly sat at the small kitchen waiting for the water to soak in a bit before they started their meal. Finally, Danny said, "We need more food."

"You're right," Sissy acceded "We also need warm clothes—coats, caps, and mittens. We each should have three sets of clothes—jeans, shirts, and underwear. We can wash two sets and still have the third set to wear. I need to check and see if there is laundry soap to wash all the things before we wear them. There's a sign in that store window that tells people to do that."

"So you've been there before?" Danny queried.

"Yes, I went in once and looked around. There are racks and racks of old clothes and shelves full of used shoes."

"We need to make the money last," Danny worried. "Won't this cost too much?"

"It will cost a little," Sissy said, "but it's a wonder we've not already become ill we get so cold. We also need to see that we have soap and shampoo to keep clean. You go check the bathroom and see if we have any. I'll find something to put the money in."

Soon the children were trundling out the door in their thin coats and with a folding shopping cart to make their purchases. They had their money in a small blue nylon bag.

"We need to hurry before the places close," Sissy considered. "I think the clothes store closes earlier on Saturday, so we will go there first. We need to get to the grocery before it closes as well."

On arriving at the used clothes shop, the children started looking for their clothing. A young bright college student saw them and offered her help.

"So you need some warm clothes?" she asked, smiling.

"Yes," Danny replied. "These things we've got are too thin and too little."

"You do know the clothes cost some money; they're not free," the young lady cautioned.

"Yes, we're shopping here to spend as little as possible," Sissy replied.

"Good thinking," the clerk said. "Let's look at the boy's clothes first. Here are shirts of your brother's size. What's his name?"

"I'm Danny, what's your name?" Danny inserted into the conversation.

Somewhat taken aback, the young lady replied, "Oh, I'm sorry. I'm Alison. What color shirts do you want?"

"I want three with long sleeves, buttons, and two pockets and made out of thick cloth," Danny directed.

"Well, you certainly know what you want," Alison commented. "Here are some flannel shirts, but none of them have two pockets."

Danny looked at Sissy.

"You can't store much in shirt pockets. I think those will do. They look warm," Sissy commented.

"Yep, they're OK," Danny agreed.

"I'd almost like a shirt like that myself," Sissy considered.

"You don't want to look like a guy," Danny directed.

"You kids keep things going," Alison placated. "Here are the pants we have. Do you have plans for pants like blue jeans?"

"No, I want cargo pants with extra big pockets and long legs with thick material," Danny again directed.

Fortunately three pairs were found; a little large, meeting Danny's specifications.

"A little large is OK," Danny said. "I'm tired of short pants. Now, where are the socks and underclothes?"

"Oh, I'm sorry," Alison informed the children, "we don't have those here. You must go to a store that sells those new. If you go to K-Mart or Walmart, you can get several sets pretty inexpensively."

"Shucks," Danny said. "I'd hoped we'd be through today, but you do have some shoes, don't you? I want brown shoes with thick soles and laces."

Alison and Sissy caught one another's eyes and grinned. The boy certainly knew his mind. The shoes were found, and Danny asked if it were all right if he wore them home. When permission was granted he took his old shoes off, and Sissy was dismayed to see a hole that went clear through the sole and both socks with the toes out. However, nothing was said.

"I need sensible shoes that don't look too frumpy," Sissy said.

"How about these boots?" Alison suggested.

"I think I'd feel funny wearing the same boots every day."

"Well, if you're wearing jeans or pants, you could wear the legs out one day and tuck them in the boots the next for a change."

"Good idea," said Sissy, "because I want pockets, and mostly only pants have pockets."

"You two really have a thing for pockets, don't you?"

"Yes," they answered in tandem, moving on to look at girl's clothing and putting the boots in the cart. They selected pants and tops for Sissy and outdoor gear for both.

"I certainly hope we're not going over your budget," Alison worried.

"No, we're OK; I don't think this will be too much," Sissy said, looking at the total of $60.00 and pulling a $100-dollar bill out of her pocket.

Looking at the total, Alison commented, "You kids probably don't know what good shoppers you both are. If you ever come into the store again, I would like to help you."

A sharp cold breeze struck the children as they left the store. The streets were alive with traffic and bustle.

"Oh, I am so hungry," Danny complained. "We must find food.

Couldn't we please just get a hamburger at McDonald's? We could get the two cheeseburgers and each have one. We could just get the burgers and nothing to drink."

"Boy, that sounds so tempting," Sissy responded, "but we've made a big dent into one of the bills already."

"Please?" he begged. "We have to go clear to the grocery and home, and all I've had is two piddling bowls of frosted flakes today. Besides I'm a growing boy, and you know I'm small; I'll never grow if I don't have some food."

"Well, you're right," his sister agreed dolefully. "You do need to eat, but except for the money we've found it's been a scary, terrible day. Some food would help."

Several blocks on, they wheeled their home shopping cart into a McDonald's and sat in a corner booth.

"I'll order, and you stay here with the clothes," Sissy directed.

"Oh, look!" said Danny, pointing out the window. "There's the SUV. It looks like the one with the men who had guns."

"There are a lot of black SUVs!" Sissy exclaimed exasperatedly.

"Not Chevy Tahoes with two aerials in the back," Danny returned.

"Really? Look, it's stopping, and guys are getting out. Do you think Dad could be with them?"

Two men dressed entirely in black with leather jackets walked into the restaurant and stood in line to order. Both had swarthy complexions and were young, well-built. The children sat frozen in their seats attempting to look as unobtrusive as possible. The men ordered and walked out with their purchases.

"Man, did you see that?" Danny asked.

"What?" Sissy responded.

"They took out enough food for six people. They may be holding Dad prisoner."

"You don't know that."

"No, I don't. However, because there was a note to us and because the money was in the cereal box, Dad probably knew the men were coming after him and he couldn't get away so he did those things in a hurry. Now here only a little later we see the same fellows buying extra food that they could be taking to feed him.

"Oooh, I don't like that at all!" Sissy exclaimed. "That sounds so dangerous—so dangerous. If we didn't have to be brave, I'd start crying right now."

"I'll stay here with the clothes. You go order the food." Danny pressed, getting back on the track of feeding his stomach. He furtively watched the cars roll by outside the window.

As evening set in, the streetlights blinked on and the cars began sporting lit headlights. Sissy returned with the burgers, and the children savored them slowly.

"We can't eat here often," Sissy said. "First, it costs too much—I spent $3.49—and secondly, I've been told before that it's not very healthy food."

"It's got to be healthier than frosted flakes," Danny countered, laughing.

"We need to buy food that is cheap but healthy and stuff that won't spoil. Since we eat at school for breakfast and lunch, all we need is suppers."

"Vegetables are healthy," Danny offered.

"But I don't know how to fix them."

"Buy them in cans; I like green beans and tomatoes."

"Well, those are healthy."

"Let's get some green beans, tomatoes, milk, bread, cereal, sugar and eggs. How about some bananas? Maybe eight—some for today, tomorrow and Monday?"

"OK," Sissy assented, "let's get going."

The children walked to the grocery store and progressed with their purchases until they came to the cereal. "Wow! Did you know a box of frosted flakes is $4.49?" asked Danny. "Here's some unsweetened store brand for half as much, and it will be a big box. We can add the sugar!"

Sissy raised her eyebrows, "I never knew that. Dad always bought it. I sure hope he's OK even if he's been so mean and grouchy. Do you remember when we were little how much fun he could be laughing and playing with us? It's as if he's a completely different person. I think it's been two years since he's not been drunk when he's home. I don't understand how he gets to work every day, and I don't even know where he works or what he does."

The children had moved with their bulky bags of clothes and newly purchased stacked items to the grocery checkout.

"Oh, what busy little shoppers you've been," gushed the elderly cashier. "Where are your parents?"

"Mom's gone, and Dad is sick," Danny informed stolidly.

The cashier peered at the children over her glasses. "I know you," she said. "You've been here with you father. He needs to drink less beer; no wonder he's sick. What did you kiddos buy?"

The children silently put their food on the counter for checkout, and the cashier rapidly ran the items through the scanner. Eyeing the clothes bags and their disreputable coats, she exclaimed, "Why aren't you wearing these nice warms coats? It's cold outside."

"We just bought them at the used clothes store, and we want to wash them first," Sissy offered.

"Good idea," the cashier agreed but looked at them speculatively. "Can coats like this be washed?"

"I checked the labels," Sissy said.

"Good thinking. You tell your dad that Sally from the grocery store says 'Stay off the bottle.'"

"Thanks!" Danny said and the children walked out of the store feeling like they had dodged a bullet.

"She's sure snoopy," Danny complained. "I don't remember her at all."

"We've only been in here a couple of times with Dad," Sissy said. "I think she probably remembers him. He probably mainly buys beer and frosted flakes and milk, and she thought that was strange."

"Maybe we shouldn't go back," Danny worried.

"Well, I don't think it's a problem. She's snoopy but friendly. Besides, there's no other grocery store nearby."

The walkway was icy, and the night was getting colder. The children hurried along and stood dancing by their cart when the traffic lights were red.

"I'm tired!" Danny claimed. "I'm going to be glad when we're home."

Entering the apartment house, they walked down the hall and saw that the door was open again.

"I'm certain I locked it," Sissy whispered. "Maybe Dad is back. What's he going to think about our clothes?"

Slowly the children pushed open the door and switched on the lights. All the cupboards were open, all the kitchen drawers pulled out, and the blankets and cushions from the couch were spread out all over the living room floor. In the bedroom, all clothes were heaped on the beds, and the dresser drawers were ajar with the contents scattered everywhere. Two pictures on the wall were askew. The rooms had been searched and torn apart.

"Oooh!" Danny breathed. "This is scary." He began to cry but tried hard to stifle his sobs. Sissy, squeezing tears back from her own eyes, said, "I'm glad we had the money with us! You were so right. Obviously they have the key to the door or else they can pick locks. See, the chain lock's cut. Was it that way this afternoon? I still don't want to call the police because if they find out that we're alone, they'll take us to child protective." Looking around she added, "Everything is messed up, but nothing seems gone. I think they're looking for the money. Let's shut the door and get this stuff put away. We can eat a banana and wash the clothes in the morning. It'll be Sunday."

Quietly the children put away the cushions, dragged the blankets back to the beds, closed the cupboards, and hung the clothes back in the closets.

"Dad's work boots are here, but his dress shoes are gone," Danny noted. I doubt if he can go back to work."

"Sissy sat on the edge of her own twin bed in the bedroom she shared with her brother and closed her eyes. "I'm so tired," she said, "but I'm so afraid. I don't think I'll sleep.

"You know, I'm guessing they won't come back. They didn't find any-thing this time, and I think we've been plain lucky. We've been gone both times and had the money with us this time," Danny said. "The worry is that we'll be here if they come back."

"But they must know that Dad has children," Sissy considered. "Our clothes and stuff are here."

"A lot of dads live alone, and their kids only visit every so often," Danny replied. "So our stuff would not necessarily mean that we live here. There's not much of it. I also think Dad probably wouldn't tell them we're here since he left the money in the cereal box. He knew for sure that we would look there."

"Well, since the chain lock's broken, let's push the coffee table in front of the door," Sissy directed.

Soon the children climbed into bed exhausted and immediately fell asleep, but in the middle of the night Sissy was awakened by screams.

"Daddy! Daddy! They're out there. They're coming in!" Danny yelled, bursting into wild, wrenching sobs.

Sissy stumbled out of bed and knelt by the side of his low bed. "Hey, hey, Danny Taylor, you wake up!" she urged loudly. "You're OK; nobo-dy's out there." She shook him and he slowly awakened looking fearfully about.

"I think you were dreaming about the gunmen coming back," Sissy prompted.

"Yeah! I mean yes!" he exclaimed. "Two of them had axes, and one had a large machine gun. They all had on black ski masks and were sneaking up the walk in the snow, but we were in a house and not an apartment; I was looking out the big window in the living room and Daddy was asleep on the couch. Mommy was standing at the kitchen door." He turned as tears formed in his eyes. "She was cooking."

"You said Daddy," Sissy remarked. "A long time ago Dad started giv-ing us swats if we called him that. I wonder why he did that."

"To be mean, I think," Danny offered. "Why does it matter?"

"I think he didn't want little children, so he was making us grow up."

19

"That's a dumb way to do it, but in spite of it I wish he was here to take care of us," Danny said.

"Wish he 'were' here," Sissy corrected. "Gotcha!" Sissy gloated.

"Not 'gotcha,' 'got you,'" Danny parried smilingly, "So, got you!"

"Well, at least you're feeling better. Do you think you can get back to sleep?"

"Yes, let's sing together and go to sleep. Like Momma did, 'Birdie in the Apple Tree.'"

So they sang:

"There's a little birdie in the apple tree
Chirping out his little song so merrily.
He's a happy birdie and I think he knows
That God is watching over him where 'ere he goes.
But that little birdie isn't half so dear;
As all the little boys and girls that God put here.
So as I watch that birdie in the apple tree.
I know that God is watching over me."

"Do you think there's really a God?" Danny asked.

"I suppose so, but I don't think He's doing a very good job watching over us."

"Well, we weren't here either time the men with the guns came," Danny said sleepily, and the children both drifted back off to sleep.

The morning arrived finding the apartment dirty but uncluttered. Danny awoke slowly and thought about the events of the day before as he listened to his sister's even breathing across the room. He wondered if his dad were still alive and felt an overwhelming sadness and fear wash over him. He thought about the new clothes and the task of washing them. He thought about seeing the black SUV at McDonald's and the slick-looking, dark, young men who had ridden in it. He wondered about not calling the police. Then he thought about being hungry and crawled out of bed to stand by his sister and say, "Sissy, Sissy! Wake up! We need to eat. We only had a banana last night. Can you fry the eggs? Can I make the toast and put butter and jelly on it?"

Sissy blinked at the onslaught of questions and yawned, agreeing, "I'll fry the eggs and you make the toast. Sunday mornings are always boring because we can't go to the library."

"Yes, but we need to wash the clothes," Danny said, "and maybe we need to wash the sheets and towels. Dad did sometimes."

"We'll put in the clothes, and if we need extra for a load we'll at least do the towels."

"This whole place seems sort of grimy," Danny said, looking around. "I don't know how to make it look better."

"Well, we don't have a sweeper, and I doubt it would help much anyway. We can use the broom on the carpet and a mop on the floor if we have time, but remember Mrs. Belle Jonas is to meet us back at the library at 1:30."

"Oh, yes, and I just thought," Danny said excitedly, "we didn't talk about looking for the other grandparents. I think we just thought a dentist would be easier to find than a teacher. Do you know any first names for them?"

"No I don't," Sissy replied. "Just Grandma and Grandpa Taylor. They were both pretty old."

"Yes, but I remember Grandpa seemed pretty healthy; he was lively and quick. Do we have aunts and uncles or cousins?"

"I think maybe there's an uncle on the Taylor side, but I think he lived a long way away, and I don't ever remember seeing him. I do think maybe there were some pictures on the refrigerator of Dad and him."

"It seems we ought to know more."

"Yes, it does, but I think our folks tried to avoid all the grandparents starting not long after you were born, and by the time I was two and a half to three years old, I don't think we ever saw them again. I think it's amazing you remember Grandpa Taylor. He certainly was lively and quick. You must not have been more than two or so the last time you saw him. Do you remember their house?"

Danny stopped to think. "No, but I think it was on a busy street because I couldn't go out the front door."

"Yeah, I mean yes," she grinned, "you're right. The street was busy and close to the house. You could always hear the traffic, and they parked their car in the back. I wonder how much more we could remember if we talked about it?"

"Not right now," Danny said. "I'm hungry."

The children set about preparing breakfast; Danny toasted the bread, and Sissy fried the eggs while they both ate another banana. After the meal, they busily swept the carpet, mopped the kitchen floor, and wiped off the table and counters before heading out to the laundry room with their 'new clothes.' They locked the door behind them.

"Did you bring the money?" Danny asked

Sissy replied by holding up the blue nylon bag. "We absolutely must not talk about this money when anyone's around," she cautioned. "Actually, we probably shouldn't even mention it in public in case anyone is overhearing us."

"Yes, I think you're right," Danny agreed. "How should we keep it—in pockets? In a billfold?"

"No, I think we need to keep it in a little plastic sandwich bag that's not very thick. The money is bulky enough. Your pockets all have buttons, and I tried to make certain mine did too." Sissy continued, "We really do need to be careful with the money."

"Yes, we do," Danny agreed, "but do you think we could have it warmer in the apartment?"

"Yes, let's at least turn it up to 65," Sissy said. "By wearing double layers of clothes while we're home that would help, and it would be a lot better than 55!"

"We still need to get underwear," Danny recalled, "I want some new long johns."

"I don't know where there's a Walmart," Sissy said. "Probably some of the other stores nearby have underwear, but prices might be higher."

"Maybe the underwear would be warmer," Danny countered.

"No, I think it is all pretty much the same. Maybe it would last better though."

There were several machines in the laundry room, and the children dumped in their various clothes followed by the soap. This task had often been done before at their dad's impatient direction, so they managed it quite efficiently.

"If we take the stuff out of the dryer right when it stops, we probably won't have so many wrinkles," Sissy stated. "Why don't you take the key and go back to the apartment and get our sheets, Dad's sheets, and the pillow cases. We forgot them."

"I—ummm—really don't want to go alone," Danny's voice faltered.

"You know I wouldn't either, but one of us needs to stay here."

"Why?"

"To take the clothes out."

"If we hurry, we'll get back in plenty of time."

Sissy, offering no resistance, hopped up from her stool, and the children raced off down the halls and around the corners. Arriving at their apartment door, they found that it was still locked and all was quiet.

"Well, shoot! I could have come alone." Danny laughed.

"But running was fun," Sissy said, puffing out of breath.

"We forgot the cart, but we can carry the sheets back."

Hurrying back with their bundles of sheets and pillowcases, they met a nicely dressed lady walking along the hall.

"She's probably coming back from church," Danny conjectured in a whisper. "What time is it?"

"I think it's about 11:30," Sissy replied. "We have two hours to finish the laundry, eat a bite, and get to the library. I think we can do it, but we can't dawdle."

"What's 'dawdle'?"

"It means 'go too slowly.'"

"I've never heard it."

"My teacher last year used it. I like the word."

"We need a dictionary," Danny said.

"People use their cell phones now."

"For real?" Danny exclaimed.

"Sure."

"I'll check at the library," Danny said somewhat doubting this bit of news.

"Don't you trust me?"

"Not when it comes to words."

Sissy laughed. "Just so we have that straight. Hey, the dryers have stopped."

The next hour and a half were spent folding clothes, finishing up the laundry, eating, and trying on their new apparel.

"Let's comb our hair and get going," Sissy said. "Mrs. Jonas was really kind to offer to come back with her computer.

With fresh clean coats, sturdy shoes, and heavy pants, the children looked at each other with approval. They divided the money and buttoned it unobtrusively in their pockets, leaving the blue nylon bag to less exotic purposes.

The day was windy and the temperature had dropped to the single digits, so they walked and trotted to the library, arriving rosy-cheeked and out of breath but much warmer than they would have been had they still worn their old tattered coats and shoes. Bursting in through the door and on through the vestibule, they brought with them a swirl of cold air and looked around for their new friend, Belle Jonas. They found her near the old card files with her computer up and running.

"My, you youngsters look great," she greeted in a whisper. "Where did you get the nice warm coats?"

"Dad gave us money," Sissy replied, "and we bought them at the used clothes store."

"Well, they look like new and so much warmer," Bell said appreciatively. "I was worried you'd be too cold to come out today, even if you were allowed. How's your dad? Is he better?" she inquired.

The children exchanged glances.

"We don't really know," Danny said, blushing. "We don't know if he's better or worse; he doesn't tell us much like that."

Looking concerned, Belle asked, "Well, is he in pain?"

"We don't know," Sissy said, taking up the ball. "He wasn't there this morning." Changing the subject, she asked, "Have you been able to find anything?"

Ms. Jonas, feeling that she had pressed enough, replied. "Well, there don't appear to be any Dentons, so we can forget that. A lot of what wants to come up has to do with dental clinics in Denton, Texas. However, there is a Dr. James Denton in Shreveport, Louisiana. Does that sound familiar? I have his office address on Line Avenue and a phone number."

"Were there others?" Danny asked.

"Yes, but they're mostly in central or northern cities or towns," Belle replied.

"He wouldn't answer on a Sunday," Belle said, "but we could call on a weekday."

"We were wondering about our other side of the family, too," Danny said hesitantly. "But we don't know their first names either. The last name is Taylor, and both of them were teachers."

"Do you know a city?" Belle asked. The children shook their heads. "I was wondering," Belle said, "if you might have some old letters around the house maybe in a shoebox or something that you could read names or addresses. Maybe some old Christmas cards?"

"There was a big shoe box by Dad's shoes," Danny said slowly, "where Dad put the bills and such. We could have looked there. I was hanging up clothes in the closet yesterday and I remember seeing Dad's work boots, but I'm almost certain there wasn't any box now that I come to think of it."

"And your Dad won't just tell…?"

"Well," Sissy said slowly, "actually we've been afraid to ask."

"Do you have any ideas what the Taylors teach?"

"I think they were teachers, but they're too old to teach now," Sissy replied. "Maybe we could look up 'husband and wife teachers named Taylor.' Would that work?"

Smiling at the thought, Belle said, "I doubt it, but I'll try it."

At that moment the fire alarm started to sound, and the obese librarian rose from her seat and announced in a stentorian voice, "Everyone stay calm but leave the building immediately."

The children and Mrs. Jonas quickly arose from their seats and grabbed their coats. Walking out with the rest of the group, they pulled on their coats, caps, mittens and gloves.

"Well, that's the end of that," Mrs. Jonas said as they arrived out by the street where sirens were blaring as fire trucks with firemen were appearing on the scene directing people back from the building.

"We need to leave the area quickly," Mrs. Jonas instructed the children. "I'll meet you again next Saturday at 8:30 if you are able to come. Bye now, children, we need to get out of here. I must call a taxi; can the two of you get home safely?"

"It's not far; we'll go now," Danny replied. "We'll be fine."

As the children regrouped their thoughts and started home, Sissy exclaimed, "Well, that was a bummer!"

"Yeah," Danny agreed. "We hardly did anything. The bell, the fire trucks, and the speakers were sure loud. They certainly didn't want anyone to stay."

"As cold as it is, we need to get right home anyhow."

While the wind had been to their backs on the way to the library, it now blew directly into their faces. After three blocks, the children dodged into a doughnut shop to get warm.

"Ooooh, this smells so good," Sissy said. "I wonder how much a glass of milk and doughnuts would cost?"

They checked on the price and for the two of them found that it would be over five dollars.

"That's as much as a big box of cereal!" Danny said. "We could eat several meals for that." So the children hurried on out and home where they ate cereal covered with sugar and bananas and then opened a can of green beans to which they added salt and pepper after warming.

"This sure isn't as good as the doughnuts, but it fills us up. I'm tired, and I'm taking a nap," Danny firmly proclaimed.

"You go ahead; I would, too, but I am going to go through the drawers and Dad's pockets to see if I can find any names or addresses. In the mess last night, did you see any papers?"

"No, I didn't," Danny sighed wearily. "I just want to sleep."

"After your nap, we need to make certain we don't have any homework and take our baths." Sissy said importantly. "And if we have any homework, we need to do it."

Danny considered, "I don't. But I don't want to wash my hair!"

Sissy, evaluating his hair, offered, "You wash it tonight, and maybe next Saturday we can go get you a haircut. I think it would be easier to take care of if it were shorter."

Danny's heavy mop of dark brown hair was a significant asset to his appearance, and he knew it.

"Yeah, it would be easier but also colder," he said justifying the longer locks.

Sissy, unaware of his vanity, remarked, "Well, if I were a guy I'd sure want mine short!" She then assiduously started going through all the pockets of both shirts, jeans, and the coats that belonged to her father. Danny dutifully marched into the bathroom and started his shower, singing "America the Beautiful" at the top of his lungs and forgetting altogether about his nap.

"Hey, where are those towels?" he bellowed.

"Hey, hey!" Sissy warned. "You'll be bothering the neighbors! Here are your underclothes and a towel," she continued, opening the bathroom door a crack and throwing both the items within Danny's reach.

"Do your hair well and when you're finished, I'll comb it before it gets tangled."

Danny finished his shower and put on the pajamas and the clothes he had been wearing over them. "I don't need help with my hair, but do you think we can get the new underwear next Saturday?" he asked.

"I found addresses and names!" Sissy shrieked as she jumped up and down moving out of the bedroom into the living room.

"Now who's noisy?" Danny asked accusingly but grinned neverthe-less. "Show me, show me! What did you find?"

"I have two unopened letters; one from each set of grandparents in this jacket pocket!"

"How old are they?" Danny asked. "Sometimes you can read the date on the postmark. Do you think we should open them and read them? Where are they from?"

"One question at a time," Sissy giggled, spirits high. "Ooooo, this one's not new; it is from January two years ago and was sent to St. Louis. It was mailed in Chicago and the return address is Dr. and Mrs. Jonathan Taylor, 2342 North Edington Chicago, Illinois."

Holding up the other envelope, which was red, she continued, "This one's probably a Christmas card. Yes, it's from the December before that January, and it was sent to the same address in St. Louis. So it's even older than the first letter. The return address is Dr. and Mrs. Henry Denton 307 Magnolia Lane Longview, TX."

"What do you think about reading them? I think it would be OK," Danny asked. "They're addressed to 'Mom and Dad and family' and that's us, sooo it's not as if we'd be reading someone else's mail," he persisted.

"Sure!" Sissy agreed. "We could learn something that could help us." She tore the edge of the red envelope and pulled out a sparkling Christmas card with a manger scene featuring small chubby children on the front. Inside the written note said:

Dear Zack, Elaine, and youngsters,

We do hope you're having a good Christmas. We miss seeing you or hearing from you so very much. We pray for you every day! Never hesitate to call us if you need anything; we're wishing you would come for a visit.

With Christ's love
Mom and Dad

"Wow! They sure do sound religious!" Danny commented. "I think they must believe in God, but God's not been doing much for their prayers."

"They sound like they care about us," Sissy said, "but there's no mention of Christmas gifts."

"Yes, that's odd," Danny agreed. "Well, what's the other letter say?"

Sissy carefully tore the edge of the other envelope, opening the one-page typed letter reading:

Dear Zack and Elaine,

We were heartbroken we didn't hear from you at Christmas. As per your stated wishes, we did not come to visit or send gifts, but we felt bereft not seeing the children! We hope all of you are well and do want you to call or come see us at any time. In the next few months we'll be moving to Ft. Walton Beach, Florida, which you know is in western Florida. It's unfortunate that the distance will make us even farther apart. We don't know the phone number or the address, but we will let you know both as soon as we arrive and are settled. Your mom's new cell phone is 308-422-1968, and you should be able to contact us that way if you ever need us for anything. Give both of the children hugs for us; we think of them as just little tykes chugging around the house, but we know they both must be growing so fast. We hope they're doing well in school. Please call or visit at any time. I talked to your brother, Evan, yesterday. He's still in Belize and still single with no particular interest in any girl, but he seems to stay in good spirits. The job he's on will last for months, but he promises to come back to the states from time to time to see us.

Again, we send lots of love and more hugs for the kids!
Here are two for you both as well,

Love, Mom & Dad

"Well, they certainly seem friendly enough," Danny commented, "maybe not so religious, and we even have a phone number."

"Yes, they both seem really nice," Sissy agreed. "And those letters are going to make it a lot easier to contact them. I think we could be with them much sooner, and our money may not have to last so long."

"Yes," Danny agreed. "Now maybe we ought to try to find Dad too."

"How?" Sissy questioned with a frown.

"The thing I thought of was the license plate on the SUV," replied Danny.

"Yes, but we never even thought of that when we saw it. We were both too scared."

"I know," Danny said thoughtfully, "but maybe if we'd go back to McDonald's at the same time of day as before, those guys might come back in and get supper, and we could get the license plate number."

"I doubt they'd go to the same place two nights in a row; I think you're just angling to get another cheeseburger," Sissy said accusingly but in good humor.

Danny grinned, "That would be a side benefit. I don't know anyone other than the police that can trace a license plate number, but it sure wouldn't hurt to have it."

"Well," Sissy said thoughtfully, "we were there about 5:30 last night, and its 4:00 now. If we take a nap and leave at 5:00 or so, we'd have time to get there and watch for them. We'll look suspicious if we stay there too long."

"We could buy a newspaper to read while we wait," Danny suggested. "I haven't seen the funnies for ages."

"Last week when you were at the library," Sissy remarked, rolling her eyes.

"Well, that was ages!" Danny held his ground.

So the children napped before venturing out into the cold blustery afternoon. They slept until 6:30 and on awakening were dismayed to see the time.

"Shoot! Let's just go anyway," Danny said, frustrated. "I'm hungry!"

"Me too!" agreed Sissy as they prepared to go out into the cold, where the temperature was even lower than in the morning.

Again the ice crunched under their feet, the traffic roared, and they hunkered down while they walked trying to protect themselves from the cold sharp wind. They picked up a paper from the newsstand and carried it into their same seat at McDonald's. They ordered the same burgers, and Danny read the comics as Sissy watched the parking lot cars. They'd been there no more than ten minutes when the back SUV did arrive.

"I can't see the license," Sissy whispered, jumping out of her seat and hurrying outside.

Danny looked up furtively and watched the same two men order the same food they'd ordered the night before. Flushed, Sissy returned and jotted down the number.

"It's a Kansas plate," she said, whispering. "They probably don't live here."

"We're in St. Joseph, so Kansas isn't too far," Danny declared, showing he knew his geography.

The men left, and the children quietly finished their food.

"Which grandparents do you think we should contact first?" Sissy asked.

"Well, the Taylors will be easier because we have that number. I bet they'll probably have the Dentons' number, and as soon as they know where we are they'll come and get us—at least one set of them will. Do you think we should try to call them tonight?" Danny continued.

"I really don't know how to use a long distance phone," Sissy said. "I think we should plan a few days and think about it. I really want to go see them. Maybe we should ask Mrs. Jonas to help."

"But that's clear next Saturday!" Danny complained. "What if people notice that we are alone?"

"Well, if Child Protective were to get involved, we now have addresses and a phone number. I don't think they would not let us see or be with the grandparents."

"OK," Danny said, "but I'm ready to go back to bed. School's in the morning, and we can't oversleep. Hey, wouldn't it be fun living somewhere warmer than here?"

"Yes," agreed Sissy, "but it gets awfully hot down there in Texas and Florida in the summer."

"Maybe they live on the beach," Danny said thoughtfully.

Conversation ended as the children headed back out into the night. The noise of the wind and the traffic made the effort of speaking an obvious challenge.

"Race you this block," Danny shouted, getting a head start on his sister, but she soon overtook him and was several steps ahead of him at the end of the block.

"Beat you!" she jeered.

"Race you again next block," Danny said, crossing the street. This time he arrived first because Sissy had slowed.

"Side ache," she yelled and they hurriedly moved on together, unlocking the apartment door and once again headed off to bed.

CHAPTER II

Late Saturday March 1

Two and a half miles away as the children were going to sleep, Zachary Taylor awoke groaning. In his first conscious thought, he wondered who was groaning, but then recognized it was his own voice.

Man, I hurt all over, he thought and began to inventory his aches and pains. Mostly his head ached, but he was also very thirsty, and his left shoulder hurt. The pain continued to his lower back and down into his legs. He desperately needed to use the restroom. He sniffed, and the odor of dried blood and stale sweat assailed his nostrils. The events of the past couple of days began to slowly come back to him.

There was a foggy memory of a card game at the bar when he was nearly drunk but winning one hand of cards after another. The sharp words he'd had with the other players when he'd picked up his winnings, the terrible hangover he'd had on Saturday morning sitting at the kitchen counter and noticing the black SUV and the men with the ski masks approaching the apartment complex. Slowly, the memories began to emerge. Intuitively he'd known they were coming after the money, so he'd hastily written a note to the children on the back of their grocery list and stuffed it with the money into the cereal box. He'd then checked the door locks and put on his coat and slipped on his shoes. He'd been surprised that it had taken the men so long, but soon realized the reason when he saw they'd found and conscripted the sleepy elderly apartment manager who had unlocked the door. With the speed of rapid fire a chain cutter destroyed the chain lock, and the men walked in. Two one hundred dollar bills were handed to the apartment manager and the leader said, "If we even think you called the police about this, we'll know where to find you. Now, give us that key and get!" The old man did as he was told and tottered off.

"Now, where's the money?" the spokesman had asked.

Visibly shaken, Zach had replied, "What money?"

"The twenty grand!"

"What twenty grand?"

"Don't go stupid on us," the spokesman had said, lifting his gun. "We'll leave here now and make you talk; we can come back for the money later."

Zach had been roughly pushed from the apartment and, with two obvious guns pointed at him, had walked along quietly. He remembered his throbbing head and that he'd had no idea how to get out of his situation. Because he'd been broke and needed the rightfully won money, he'd been stubborn enough not to retreat easily. He'd felt hot-headed and angry and hadn't considered the extent of the danger the situation represented to not only himself but also the children. As he'd walked out into the cold air, he'd wished for some alcohol—anything to relieve his throbbing headache. The men had shoved him into the middle of the rear seat. Zach thought perhaps he'd seen a glimpse of his children coming up the walk but was uncertain and didn't want to draw any attention to them.

He was blindfolded shortly after the ten to fifteen-minute drive began and he'd ridden in dark silence. The trip ended in large building. He'd heard large metal doors open and close, scraping and echoing in the big space. Being shoved summarily out of the vehicle, he'd been pushed into a room. Both hands and feet were shackled to a hard chair.

"Okay, now's the time to talk," he was told. "Where's our money?"

Zach had been silent

Slap. He'd felt the painful sting of a leather glove against his face.

Slap, slap, thunk. More blows were given; the last with a club to the head.

Sill he'd been silent. There were three successive blows to the back of the head, and Zach's thought processes had blanked out.

Now on awakening, Zach considered that the questioners had certainly obtained very little information. He wondered if he'd talked more subsequently and if they knew more than he remembered saying. He recalled that they'd mentioned they were going back to the apartment and worried that they'd find Sissy and Danny. He desperately wished for some beer or liquor but soon passed out again.

Later Zach woke in the dark. His aches and pains were all still there; his head throbbed, and he was desperately thirsty. He no longer felt the need to relieve himself and realized he was lying in a puddle of his own urine. Reaching around in the dark, he found his hands were manacled to a rope as were his feet. He was no longer tied to the hard chair but was lying on a rubber mat. It was pitch-black but warm, and the roar of a furnace could be heard nearby. His own clothes were missing, and his only covering was a flimsy hospital gown. He smelled of urine, sweat, and dried blood. Reaching out his arm, he discovered several bottles. Beer, he hoped, but as he unscrewed the lid he recognized it was water which was perhaps as well. He drank one of the bottles, then lay back down and moved on to a troubled land of nightmares, hallucinations, and fright that lasted for the next three days.

This time on awakening, he recalled he'd been surrounded by unbelievably horrid apparitions that had seemed extremely real—undulating waves of cockroaches crawling on the furnace, angry men with bazookas following him in packs and hunting him down, man-sized spiders slithering down from the walls to attack him, and last but not least, quicksand all around him sucking him down. It had been up to his shoulders; his arms were held high above his head as he struggled to free himself before suffocating in the sand. He also remembered men in the dim light giving him water in bottles to drink and urging him to eat hamburgers and fries. He remembered vomiting and diarrhea and being forcibly dragged to the shower, but mostly he remembered the fear and shaking and the yelling. Always the yelling. Again he passed out.

The following day he awoke, nearly lucid. He felt tremulous inside, but he knew who he was and where he was. He lay on his mat groggily amazed as he again recalled the terribly unsettling events that had occurred in his mind over the past few days. He now attempted to move but found that his wrist and ankle shackles were still in place and that all four restraints covered circular open sores where he'd been yanked and jerked. A wave of dismay washed over him; he wondered how long he'd been there and what had happened to him. He reached out grimaced with pain, and found the bottled water. He drank sitting and hugging his knees. He smelled sweaty, but the blood and urine were gone. He wondered if all the frightening dreams were caused by the blows to his head on the first day.

Voices interrupted his reverie.

"Hey peons, how's your patient today?" an unfamiliar voice inquired roughly following the question with curses.

"He's been quieter this past night, boss," was the reply. "He hasn't yelled now for the past eight hours, and it was yesterday afternoon that he last had diarrhea. He was still awfully weak and shaky yesterday when we cleaned him up."

"Do you think it is still gonna take two of you jerks to handle this guy?" the boss said.

"Probably not unless he changes again to the way he was. He's a big bastard, but we never thought he'd be this hard to manage. He's been a bear. What's wrong with him?"

"I talked with my wife's brother-in-law who's a nurse. He thinks the guy's going through DTs. If that's so, he'll be coming around pretty soon. Apparently, people can act pretty sorry when they're withdrawing."

"Oh, DTs—he's a drunk, huh? I should have thought of that; my old man was a drunk, and he did that several times when he couldn't get his liquor. We called it 'snakes in the boots.' He had horrible nightmares. This guy did act the same way. I guess I just figured it was the hard thump on his head. What are we going to do with him?" he continued.

"I haven't decided yet, but I'm not planning to turn him loose anytime soon. He'd just rat on me! I'll probably move him south."

"Are you pretty sure he's your card shark?"

"Well, that's a question I can't be certain about, but I have little doubt. I followed him that night when he left the bar with most of my money. He went into the apartment building where we found him. There were some mud smudges by his door when I went down his hallway, and I'm pretty sure he's the same guy; he has the same build, but it wasn't very bright in the bar. Let's have a look at him."

Zach quickly lay back and feigned sleep. Behind closed eyes, he could see the brighter light from the opened door, but he lay appearing to rest quietly.

"Hey, bastard, can you wake up?" the boss queried, giving Zach a rough jerk and kicking him in the side.

Zach opened his eyes and acted startled. "Where am I?" he asked, looking about with a dazed expression on his face.

"That's for me to know and you to find out," the boss answered. "You've sure been a mess the past several days. I was about to put you in a bag and throw you in the river."

Zach was silent.

"So scum, where's my money?"

"Money?" Zach asked, continuing to look perplexed.

"Yeah, money, you filthy maggot. Stand up," he said with another kick of his foot into Zach's side.

Zach stood tottering, and when the boss jerked the wrist restraints he gasped, catching his breath due to the pain.

"First time he's been up on his own, boss," said the thug who had been one of his caretakers.

"Well if he eats and keeps making improvement, get him into some decent clothes. This gown makes him look like some silly sissy. Are you a sissy, bastard?" the boss asked, looking directly at Zach.

Zach looked at him with a flat expression, saying, "I think you've got the wrong guy. Why would I have your money?"

"You stole it from me in a card game."

"Can't be me … I'm not a good card player."

"You're a low-down bloodsucking liar," the boss said, aiming his pointed boot tip at Zach's sore ankle and hitting the sore straight on.

Zach stumbled and nearly fell but grabbed one of the ropes to which he was shackled and regained his balance. The boss left, and the caretakers let out a low whistle.

"You sure made him mad! He talked about putting you in a bag and dumping you in the river."

"What is going to happen to me?" Zach asked.

"Who's to know? We do as we're told," the caretaker said. "He also said something about sending you south."

"Where's south?"

The caretaker shrugged, "Most of us know very little about what goes on in the other parts of the outfit, but I think he probably means to South America or Central America; they have things going on down there. Are you hungry?"

"Yes," Zach said, "but how about some eggs and sausage or an omelet?"

"Hoity-toity," the caretaker mumbled. "How about an Egg McMuffin or two?"

"Great," Zach responded positively, "but I'd like some milk too."

"Hey!" the caretaker replied, "I'm glad you want to eat. It's just the choices are pretty slim. I'll go get something and will be back in an hour or so." He left mumbling about waiting on drunks.

Zach kept his mouth shut despite the hunger pangs and sat down carefully to wait. He realized he could slide his mat over to the cement block wall but moved cautiously to avoid rubbing his sore wrists and ankles. He sat thinking how he never wanted to experience the last three days again. He never had considered how miserable alcohol withdrawal could be. He knew even now he wanted a beer but knew also that the next beer would have to look terribly good for him to take the risk of going through the experiences of the past several days again. He wondered how many times during the ordeal he'd thought he was dying. He recalled his father-in-law saying, "Once an alcoholic, always an alcoholic, and the only way to stay sober is to never drink." He thought about Sissy and Danny, hoping they'd found the money he'd left. He worried that his captors may have returned for it but realized they'd likely not been successful or they wouldn't be asking him about it now. He knew his children were quick, but he feared for their welfare. Guilt overwhelmed him as he thought about their plight, his lack of care for them, and the situation with Elaine. Self-pity also rose as he thought about her drug use, his anger, and life without her. *Things couldn't be much worse*, he pondered, *but I could be dead, and who knows how soon that may be!*

Zach thought of escape but realized it seemed unlikely given his current confinement situation. The leather restraints on his wrists and legs each had a small padlock holding them in place, and the ropes for his wrists were tied to the ceiling, while the ones for his ankles were tied to the wall at a distance he could not reach. He slowly scratched his back against the rough wall and tried to think how he could cope with the situation.

First, he thought, *I'm alive and basically well. If I hold still, I'm not miserable. Secondly, I don't have any permanent injuries. Third, they're giving me food and water, so survival is tracking a course and holding on.* Zach stood to his feet. *I need to keep moving*, he thought, raising his arms as high as he could holding onto the ropes. He tensed the muscles in his arms and shoulders and realized that he could do some pull-ups if he were careful not to rub his wrists or ankles, so he set about counting. Pitifully weak, he wanted to quit after the tenth count, but he soldiered on to twenty-five. He drank another bottle of water while he sat exhausted on the mat and then lay down only to doze off.

"Hey, big boy. Here's your food and some togs," the caretaker said, noisily banging open the door. "Eat, and then I'll get you dressed."

The open door let the frigid outside air in, and Zach asked carefully, "Is it OK to close the door?"

The man looked at Zach testily and slammed the door shut. Zach took the McDonald's bag and quickly consumed the two Egg McMuffins and the container of milk. "Thanks," he said. "Now, how do I get the clothes on?"

"One cuff at a time," the caretaker said, handing Zach a heavy short-sleeved shirt of a blue-gray color. He examined the wounds on both of Zach's wrists. "Put your arm in this and I'll go get some ointment and tape," he said, leaving Zach with nothing on but one arm draped through the shirt.

Zach tried to flip the shirt over his back to the other shoulder but was unsuccessful.

"This stuff works pretty good," the caretaker said, smearing the ointment on the wounds liberally and covering them with gauze and then adding adhesive tape. "We'll change these each time you take a bath, and you'll be surprised at how soon you heal." The wrist was then reshackled, and the same routine was completed on the other three limbs.

The pants were heavy denim shorts, and Zach complained, "Why shorts? It's the middle of winter. I'll be cold."

"Not in here you won't," the man laughed. "This here place is a regular oven most of the time. None of us want to stay in here very long because it's hot, and you've been sweating and making it stink so bad. We've had to wash the floors down eight times in the past three days, so we're glad to see you making more sense and stopping all your yelling."

"How long have I been here, and how long do they plan on keeping me?"

"It's been four days and a night, and I have no idea how long you'll be here. Most of the time there's nobody here, but when people are here it's usually only for a day or two."

"Where do they go?"

"Well, if they die we put them in a body bag. If they don't die, who cares."

"What kind of operation is this?" Zach asked.

"I don't know, and I wouldn't ask questions if I were you. The less you know, the better off you be. Now, this big can here is to use if you need to relieve yourself. I'll be back in several hours."

"Do I get my things back? My phone, billfold, or keys?"

"You don't get nuthin' back. Nobody does. Be glad you're alive!" With that, he closed the door behind him, and Zach was left by himself.

"Without anything to do here, I'll go crazy," he said to himself. "I've got to have a plan. What I'll do first is to keep track of the date by counting the cinderblocks away from the door and making a calendar in my mind. This must be Thursday if I've been here four days. I think this must be morning since there's a little light coming in from the window above the door. I'm guessing it's after 8:00 a.m. and sometime before 11:00. Right now sleeping and exercising are all I've got. Now that I've got dressings on these sores, I can be more active with less pain." So, Zach got up, jogged in place, did a few more pull-ups and whiled away an hour or so before laying down again on the mat with his head on his arm and once again fell asleep.

He awoke a couple of hours later as he heard the door slam. Beside him was a bag with a Big Mac, large fries, and a Coke. He surprised himself by being so hungry but suspected that the last several days had offered him less than his normal amount of food. The meal was soon gone, and he put himself through his exercise routine once again. He recognized that already he was regaining some of his strength.

Sitting down, he thought of his years growing up in a Chicago suburb with his brother, one year younger, and the good times they'd had. Unlike many brothers who fought more than they agreed, the two had always been pals and had remained so until Zach had gone off to college in Normal, Illinois. It was there he'd met Elaine, dropped out of college, and found a job at a packing plant in Omaha, NE. He and Elaine both worked at the plant, living together and enjoying the time they shared with minimal responsibilities even when there hadn't been much money. Both sets of parents were dismayed at their choices but attempted to keep the lines of communication open. Zach's brother, Evan, had come to visit and confronted him with the danger of no further education and the embarrassment to the family of his shacking up with Elaine unmarried. Zach had blown up at Evan, telling him to mind his own business and leave. The couple continued to live in a small apartment in south Omaha, finally deciding to get married when Elaine became pregnant.

For the next three years, the situation stabilized with several visits of the couple to Chicago to see Zack's parents. There was also a visit down to Texas to see Elaine's folks, but with sorely restricted finances caused by Danny's arrival one year after Sissy's birth, travel was minimal. With the long hours on her job, all the housework, and the total care of the children, Elaine became depressed. She'd leave work late, pick up the children from daycare, and head home, struggling to have enough energy to handle all the tasks at the house and still meet the needs of the children. Zach would stop after work at one of the local bars, have drinks with his friends, play pool, and come home late. Despite Elaine's persistent requests, he'd refused to shoulder his share of the childcare feeling that she was simply being quarrelsome all of the time. Elaine had initially been the one to break relationships with both sets of parents, feeling they were apt to be condemning her and somehow blaming her for their limited financial circumstances.

Sissy had been a first grader when Zach had first noticed erratic behavior in his wife. At times, Elaine had seemed inordinately cheerful followed by frightening spells of heart-rending sobs for no apparent reason. Not long after that, she became slovenly in her appearance. Zach arrived home one_evening to find the children in front of the TV and Elaine asleep in bed. He'd already been suspicious, so he began quietly going through the bedroom drawers where she kept her belongings. He'd found drug paraphernalia and demanded that she get help. She'd gone willingly, but as soon as the program ended, she was right back to using the drugs.

He'd obtained a different job at a warehouse in St. Louis and moved the family there, hoping a change in environment would be less tempting. Elaine eventually moved through her third drug rehabilitation program but returned home only to pick up her old habits.

After Zach had told her he couldn't live with a drug addict, she had willingly gone her way leaving him, the children, and her responsibilities with little disagreement. The task of raising the children then lay squarely on his shoulders. He first moved to Kansas City and then on to St. Joseph, making no effort to contact her. He was angry at her, but he also knew that he missed her. He felt guilty about telling her to leave but felt he was doing the right thing. He'd known his life was a mess but had refused to talk to his parents about it and had gradually begun to drink more alcohol as the months went by.

Now that he found himself a prisoner, in a state of forced sobriety and with minimal distractions to prevent him from thinking, Zach suddenly saw his life from a new perspective. He saw that the early freedom he'd gained by not pursuing college was freedom wasted. He saw that his own addiction to alcohol was as damaging to him as Elaine's drug addiction had been to her. He realized that both addictions had equally harmed the children, and that those same children who had seemed only days ago to be a chain around his neck were actually the only bright spots in his terribly bleak world. He missed Elaine, but told himself that was past. He began to agonize about the present, especially the plight of the children. "How will they handle the money?" he wondered. "Would they be picked up by the state? Were they frightened? How could I get word to them as to where I am and that I am alive? Would they be able to figure out how to contact their grandparents? How could I have left them in such a state?" Freezing fear gripped him as he considered their situation in the heart of winter. He thought of the cold apartment and the lack of food. He thought of their pitiful lack of clothes; he'd known they needed warmer clothes. "What an idiot I had been! How could I have let alcohol have that much of a grip on my judgment?" Zach stood and doggedly started his exercise routine. *About the only thing I can do for the present is to stay fit and healthy*, he thought.

A couple hours later, the caretaker reappeared grinning in the dim light, seeing Zach moving.

"I guess I can stop worrying about you," he said. "I'll get a bucket of water, some soap and a towel, and you can clean yourself up. You'll be a lot less work for me if you do it yourself."

"What's your name?" Zach asked pleasantly.

"We don't use names," was the reply. "While you're here you don't ask anyone's name or give yours; it's one of the rules."

"May I have a pencil and writing tablet or a book or magazine?"

"No, only clothes, food, water, and cleaning things," he said, pointing to the soap, washcloth, and towel. "I'll be back in two hours with food. If you gotta go, you can use the bathroom there," he continued, now pointing at the large can.

"Is it OK to not have McDonalds?" Zach asked.

"Yeah, sometimes."

"How about a Subway sandwich? And I'd really like some milk."

"I'll see," he said noncommittally, walking out the door mumbling again about feeding stuck-up, messed-up drunks.

What a nasty outfit! Zach thought, looking at the closed door. *It'd be intriguing if not so frightening,* he thought as he sat. Soon he was napping again, awakening later to painstakingly work at cleaning himself standing with his bucket of cold water and washcloth. He partially undressed himself as much as possible with the shackles, attempted a primitive wash; he then put the clothes back on. Washing his hair was one of the biggest challenges, and even though he strained to lean over the bucket while he washed, he left a rather large puddle of water on the floor.

After cleaning, he began his exercise routine until the caretaker appeared as promised with a foot-long Sub and a two-quart plastic bottle of milk.

"Thanks," Zach offered.

"Eat it," the man replied "and get your rest. There's been a shake-up, so you're probably gonna be moving any time."

"Can I get all my own clothes? I know it's probably really cold outside."

"Oh, your duds are long gone, buster. They'll find some other stuff for you. They don't want people sick, so they keep them warm and fed."

Zach savored his sandwich and drank half of the milk, then proceeded with another stint of exercising before he turned in for the night.

Despite several naps and possibly because of his vigorous exercises, Zack fell asleep immediately on the warm mat with the furnace droning on. Suddenly, in the wee hours of the night, he was awakened by voices yelling loudly outside of his door. He scrambled to his feet in the pitch blackness but was unprepared for the burst of light, activity, and noise when the door was opened. Two men with guns rushed into the room.

"Hey, scum, we're leaving in a few minutes," one of them swore and shouted, "just as soon as this bum gets you unlocked. Get in these clothes and put on these boots. These guns are aching to pop if you try any shenanigans!"

The caretaker fumbled with the locks as he hurried, and Zach obediently put on the blue denim coveralls that had been thrown at him. He put his feet into the boots and followed with the galoshes, coat, and cap that had been part of the pile. The boots were a bit large and the coat tight across the shoulders, but both were adequate.

"Hop, hop!" said the speaker, and Zach moved into the next room and was summarily scooted into the rear of a van with the windowless doors securely locked behind him. A cage barrier separated the front seat from the rest of the vehicle, and two other men dressed just like Zach were sitting on a side bench in the back section of the van.

Zach nodded to the two men and moved to a bench near the doors at the back of the van.

"You don't want to stay there. It's warmer up here closer to the front," the larger of the two men said. "Cold drafts come in the back."

"Thanks," Zach replied pleasantly and moved to the front, sitting on the bench across from the other two. "Any idea what's up?" he asked.

"All we know is that we don't want to be here."

Zach remembered his instructions and decided not to ask any further questions. Soon the driver took his seat, and a man with a pistol rode shotgun.

The gunman turned to the rear and began to wave his weapon, pointing at each of them in turn. "For security," he said. "My security, not yours," he said, laughing rowdily.

The van moved out of the warehouse, and Zach could see that they'd been in an industrial part of the city. He suspected it was near the river. Mr. Gunman turned and struggled to release the ties on a canvas drape that fell in place over the cage, blocking their view.

"Hey, have you guys been with these people long?" Zach asked his fellow travelers.

"Too long," the shorter man said as he stared at Zach blankly.

The van creaked and rattled even though it seemed in good condition, and within twenty minutes Zach could tell that it was picking up speed on an open highway. After an hour of sitting and dozing, Zach attempted conversation again.

"I'd like to lie down a while, but there are only two benches. Do you fellows want to rotate, two down and one up?"

"Heck no," Tall Man said. "We've been in bed for two days. Sleep if you want."

Zach lay on his side, curled up, and was glad to be able to sleep without his restraints on as they traveled through the night.

Sitting up and being drowsy was one thing, but lying down on a fiberglass bench and attempting to be comfortable enough to sleep was another issue entirely. Zach's head vibrated as he attempted to rest it on his arm. He took off the coat and bunched it up under head but soon became chilly. He attempted lying on first one side then the other. Finally, he tried lying on his back but sleep wouldn't come, and his travel mates sat on the opposite bench staring at him saying nothing. He finally settled for lying on his back with his coat on and his hands clasped behind his head carefully avoiding pressure on any of the wounds that were on his wrists.

Every mile is a mile further from the children, he thought. What possibly were his captors going to do with him? Could they keep him a prisoner indefinitely? Was he going into some type of forced labor? It seemed improbable that this could be happening in the United States.

Hour after hour they travelled. Zach could see the sun was rising due to the light in the crevices at the edge of the canvas curtain. Once again, he attempted conversation with his fellow passengers.

"Sure wish we could have a restroom break," he said in a comradely fashion.

There was no response.

"Are you fellows hungry?" Zach tried again.

"Shut up," Short Man said as they both stared at him stoically.

Zach sat up, and they rode on. Finally, he could tell that the van was leaving the interstate and pulling off onto a side road. From there they moved on a short distance and turned onto a gravel road with the van coming to a sudden stop.

"Bathroom break," yelled Shotgun. "One at a time, you bastards, and no monkey stuff; my guns are loaded and ready."

Zach let the other men move first. Not a word was said among them as one of the double rear doors opened. The outdoor light seemed bright; the day was sunny, and it seemed warmer than it had when they entered the van. There were no buildings visible, and when Zach's turn came, he saw an open pasture at a distance but woods nearby.

"See that bush?" Shotgun pointed with his weapon to a bush about ten yards away. "That far and no farther. Now, get a move on. We'll stop for food in a half hour or so."

One by one each of the men took care of their business, Zach being the last. When he hurried to climb back into the van, he was surprised to see both men stretched out on the two benches. He was feeling no inclination to complain, so he took a seat on the floor in the middle with his back against the barricade cage. He was startled to realize that he could now hear the conversation between the driver and Shotgun even though they kept their voices low.

"Twenty minutes to Joplin," the driver said. "And then on to Houston. We can make good time after Joplin since we're not going down through the Ozarks."

Zach could tell when they left the main highway and could hear the driver order Egg McMuffins and coffee, but then the van took off again. His stomach growled with hunger as they traveled for another fifteen or twenty minutes before the vehicle stopped. The backdoors opened, and the ever-present gunman stood alert as the driver began to hand out the Egg McMuffins, coffee, and bottled water.

"Don't drink much," Shotgun said. "We don't stop often." The doors were slammed shut, and they were on their way again.

Do they always eat McDonald's? Zach wondered as he sat back savoring his sandwich and the coffee, which he wished had milk. After the meal, he stood for a while bending over in the van and stretching his legs.

"Sit, down! You're making me nervous," the short man complained.

Zach grinned. "Standing helps my legs, but I'll admit it's not doing much for my back. I heard them say up front that we're heading for Houston," he informed them in a whispered voice. The men looked at him blankly but offered no response.

Zach tried again. "Are you guys together?"

"What's it look like?" the taller one responded. "Now, shut up if you don't want a pounding."

So Zach shut up, whiling the time away by making up life histories for the rough men. Eventually they both stretched out again on the benches, Zach stretched out on the floor, and all three nodded off to sleep.

CHAPTER III

FRIDAY MARCH 6

Friday afternoon found Sissy and Danny excited. The week had been uneventful at school. The suppers they had purchased had been adequate, and their classmates had been less disdainful of their new clothes than the previous misfit garments. They had planned their time and recleaned the apartment on Wednesday, finished the laundry on Thursday, and made a shopping list and intended the grocery store run for this Friday. After the last bell had rung they hurried from their classroom, still buttoning and zipping their coats, and arrived on the front sidewalk of the school anxious to begin the implementation of their plans.

"We'll see Mrs. Jonas at 8:30 at the library tomorrow morning and see if we can make the call. We'll ask her of a good place to buy underwear, too," Sissy said, laying out their plans. "We'll probably have to take the bus to get the clothes. After we do that, we can bring them back to the apartment. Then we can go get your hair cut at the shop by the corner."

"How much will that all cost?" Danny worried.

"The bus fare isn't too much; maybe fifty cents or a dollar," Sissy guessed, "but we'll need to get some change from the grocery store tonight."

"Do you think we might go to McDonald's again?" Danny suggested. "We might see the SUV again, too."

"Yes, but we should probably go there first, so we won't have the full cart of groceries with us."

"How about putting some cookies on our list?" Danny cajoled.

Sissy squinched her mouth. "Naw, let's do fruit instead. We can do without cookies."

"Naw," Danny mimicked, "we can do without fruit. Let's do cookies instead."

They both laughed in good spirits and continued rushing along to the apartment for their shopping cart and shopping list and heading on out to McDonald's.

"Hey! How about a Happy Meal?" Danny considered. "Wait, it's $4.67, and that would be over $9.00 for both of us. We better stick with the two cheeseburgers and get some fries!"

They ordered their food, sat down, and gazed out the windows but saw no black SUV.

"We haven't been here very long," Sissy commented. "We can't say anything's changed just because we didn't see them."

"No, all we can say is that we didn't see them," Danny agreed as they pushed their cart out onto the walk and headed for the grocery.

After making their selections, they headed for the checkout hoping to avoid the chatty cashier, but she saw them anyhow and hurried to their alternate line to speak to them.

"Well, how're the little shoppers this evening?" she greeted kindly. "My, you do look nice in your coats. Aren't they a lot warmer? And they look nearly new, too!" she said approvingly. "Isn't your daddy feeling any better? I haven't seen him. Is he up and about?"

"He wasn't able to come with us," Sissy replied primly.

"The coats are warmer," Danny inserted, trying to steer the conversation away from his dad.

The lady hurried back to her post, and the children moved on out the door. The evening air was warmer than the previous week but not warm, and there was a hint of moisture in the air.

"My teacher said it might snow tonight," Danny said excitedly. "Wouldn't it be fun to be snowed in next week?"

"No, I think it would be boring. You know, we need to find a used bookstore like the used clothes store," Sissy responded.

"Let's go back in and ask the cashier lady if there's one nearby," Danny said, agreeing with the idea.

They turned and hurried back into the grocery store, and as they walked up near the cashier, she caught sight of the two children.

"Forgot something, dearies?"

"No, we just wondered if you know of a used bookstore anywhere close around here."

"Why, sure enough," she replied cheerfully. "There's one a block and a half up the street and on the other side. You'll need to hurry, though; they close at 6:30 p.m."

"Thank you, thank you!" Danny exclaimed, jumping up and down in his excitement, and the children hurried out the door and on up the street.

"Some things to read!" the excited boy continued. "I wonder how much they'll cost."

"It will probably depend on their condition. Paperbacks will likely be cheap, but you can't learn very much from them. Let's each spend five dollars on what we want."

"Great, I'm going to see if they have any magazines like *Popular Mechanics* or *Boy's Life*."

Arriving at the store, they parked their home cart just inside the door and asked the clerk politely if they could leave it there while they shopped. He gave them a puzzled look but nodded. The store was very crowded and the shelves were tall, separated by narrow aisles. They walked about a few minutes and returned to the proprietor.

"Do you have any magazines or action stories?" Danny asked. The proprietor pointed in the direction that Danny should look.

The half hour they spent in the store passed so quickly that the children nearly panicked attempting to make their final selections. However, when closing time came and the clerk rolled the shade down on the door window and flipped the sign to "Closed," they'd brought their choices to the counter.

"Find some things?" he asked pleasantly.

"Yes, sir!" Danny said cheerfully, showing two old copies of *Popular Mechanics*, a book on Civil War battles, and one on mountaineering in the Canadian Rockies.

"We don't have a TV," Sissy commented, "so reading's what we do."

"Good for you," the man said, ringing up the total. "Well, you kids be careful going home; it's beginning to get dark."

"I can't wait to get home," Sissy said as they walked out the door and along the sidewalk. "I got four books for a dollar each, and they are all hardbacks."

"Yes, we should make some hot chocolate and read," Danny suggested. "Is there any cocoa mix left? We could warm the milk."

"We'll look," Sissy replied. "It was up by the coffee on the top shelf. I haven't looked up there lately."

Arriving home, they hung their coats up, put the groceries away, and found the cocoa mix. They made their hot chocolate and put their cups on the coffee table. Wrapping themselves in blankets, they read companionably until bedtime. They set the alarm for 7:00 a.m. to be certain not to oversleep. They didn't want to miss Mrs. Jonas at the library.

The following morning, the children left the apartment and walked into a wonderland of new-fallen snow. It was cold, but the busy noises of the city were muted by the fluffy snow. People were out shoveling driveways and sidewalks, and the children marched happily along, arriving at the library only to find a large sign that said, "The Library is closed indefinitely due to fire damage. Repairs are in progress. Your city tax dollars at work."

"Great!" Danny groaned. "How will we make the call? There used to be phone booths out here, but they took the only close one out."

"Let's wait a while; it not 8 30 yet," Sissy reasoned. "Let's walk up and down the sidewalk here and see if she shows up; she seems like a really nice person who sticks to doing what she says."

The children moved up and down the walk in front of the library entrance avoiding going too far for fear of missing Belle. Suddenly a cab stopped, and she stepped out. The children ran to her, telling her they'd found phone numbers for the grandparents and that the library was closed.

Reading the sign, she said, "Well! If it's not one thing, it's another. Where do you suppose we should go?" She quickly turned and motioned for the cab to return to where they were standing. "Please take us to the Sheraton up on 6th," she directed the cab driver. The driver nodded his assent, and the three of them climbed into the backseat of the cab.

"We probably can't pay for a room there," Danny said worriedly.

"Oh, don't be concerned. We won't," Belle responded, "we're just going into the lobby, and I'm going to teach both of you how to use pay phones. Most big hotels still have them even though many of the outdoor phone booths are either broken or have been taken out. The hotel lobbies are quieter than the streets and warmer. First, we'll need to get some coins," she continued, "dimes and quarters, chiefly. Do you know how to get those?"

"How many will we need?" Sissy asked.

"Well, I'd start with five dollars' worth, and you can generally get that from the front desk; just tell them you need to use the pay phone and they will usually help you. If not, you can go into the gift shop in the hotel and get change."

"Oh, I'd intended already to have done that; I forgot!" Sissy exclaimed.

"Your stop, ma'am," the cab driver said. The three of them stepped out, and Mrs. Jonas turned to pay the driver.

"How much did that cost?" Danny inquired.

"You shouldn't ask questions like that," whispered Sissy.

"That's all right," Mrs. Jonas said. "It was seven dollars. Why do you ask?"

"I just wanted to know in case some time we would need to get a ride."

"It would always be OK to ask the driver how much he would estimate the cost to be before you go," Belle said. "The cost depends on both the distance and the time it takes to get there."

The three of them walked on into the hotel lobby and looked for the payphone booths.

"Over there," Sissy pointed, "See the little phone sign? Mrs. Jonas, do you want to sit here while we go get the money?"

"Sure," she said, sitting in an overstuffed chair pleased at her prodigies who were soon back with their coins, and the three headed to bank of phone booths.

"I could be using my cell phone, but you children don't have one, so we'll use the payphones instead. You need to have your coins and telephone numbers ready. Not all payphones are the same, so you always need to plan to read the instructions before you start.

The instructions read:

(1) Pick up the phone

(2) Insert quarter and listen for the dial tone.

(3) Dial your number. If it is a long-distance number, dial 1 followed by the area code and then the telephone number.

"Which one of you wants to try it?"

"I'll do it, I'll do it!" Danny offered happily.

"OK, but I probably need to talk," Sissy countered.

"OK, I'll dial; then you can talk, and then I'll talk," Danny cheerfully assented.

"I'll just sit over on the chair so you children can have some privacy," Mrs. Jonas offered graciously. "One of you can come over and get me if you need any help."

Danny picked up the receiver, put in his quarter, listened for the dial tone, and then dutifully dialed the numbers as Sissy read them off to him. He was startled when a lady's voice asked him to put six more quarters into the slot. He scrambled to get them and put them carefully in one at a time. Soon he heard the phone ringing.

"It's ringing!" he whispered loudly.

"Hello, Taylor's cell phone," a deep voice said.

Suddenly Danny froze then squeaked, "It's me, Grandpa!"

"It's who?"

"It's Danny! Here… you talk to Sissy," he said, handing the phone to his sister.

"Hello, this is Sissy Taylor," she said. "Is this Grandpa Taylor?"

"Well, sure enough! How are you kids doing? Hey, Thelma, it's Danny and Sissy calling!" Again he asked, "How are you guys? Is everything OK?"

"No," Sissy replied, "that's why we're calling. We're in trouble, and we need help. Momma's gone, and Dad was taken away by men with guns and black ski masks."

"What? Did you call the police?"

"No, we were afraid that Child Protective would come and take us away."

"When did this happen?"

"It'll be a week tomorrow."

"And you haven't heard from him since?"

"No."

"Sweetie, how come you didn't call sooner? How have you managed?"

"We have some money, but we didn't know your number. We looked around and finally found an old letter. It had your address, and a nice lady we met at the library helped us make this phone call."

"Thelma, do you want to talk to Sissy?"

"Hi! Little Sissy!" Thelma took the phone and looked questioningly at her husband. "We're so glad you called, precious. Where are you? Who's with you? Where are your parents? How are they? Do you know your address? I know we'll want to come see you just as soon as we can."

Sissy couldn't get a word in to answer one question before her grandmother asked another.

"I just told Grandpa they're not here. Momma's been gone for months, and Dad was taken away last week."

"Oh, dear! By the police?"

"No, no, by men with guns and ski masks."

"Guns and ski masks? Where'd your mother go? What's this all about?"

"We don't know where Momma went. She was using drugs, and Dad told her to leave and so one night she just left and never came back." Sissy began to cry, realizing that she could tell all of this to her grandparents and that they would be sympathetic to their plight. They would help her and Danny. She didn't have to be the responsible one anymore. She scrubbed the tears from her eyes and handed the phone back to Danny.

"Hi, Grandma," he said. "This is Danny. Sissy is crying, but we really are OK. We have food and some warm clothes, and we are going to school every day."

Both grandparents were surprised at how mature the children sounded and how well they were handling the situation.

"Oh, you poor little sweethearts!" Thelma exclaimed. "We'll come up there as soon as we can get there. We'll pack and leave today and be there sometime tomorrow. Can you tell us your address?"

Danny gave the name and address of the apartments and then told his grandparents the apartment number. Grandpa Taylor took the receiver back, and Thelma leaned in so she could still listen.

"Danny, you certainly sound grown up," he bragged. "Do you think you are safe in the apartment?"

"After the men took Dad, someone came back up and messed everything up."

The conversation was interrupted and a voice requested that an additional six quarters be inserted. Again, Danny scrambled for the money.

"What's that?" Mr. Taylor questioned.

"We're at a payphone. I had to put in more money," Danny explained.

"Oh, I was afraid I had lost you. Well, son, when the people came back did they steal anything?"

"We don't think so. We think they were looking for the money that Dad left. He hid it in a cereal box."

"Money? Where did the money come from?"

"We don't know, but Dad left it in the box with a note telling us to be careful with it, and we're being real careful!"

"What a little man you are!" Mr. Taylor said encouragingly. "May I talk a little more with Sissy?"

"Sure," and with that Danny handed the phone back to his sister. "Here," he said, "Grandpa wants to talk to you again."

"Sissy? You don't know how glad we are you both have called. Have you talked with your other grandparents?"

"No, we only had your number."

"Well, sweetheart, we'll give them a call. We're going to hurry and pack and be right on our way. We'll be there by tomorrow evening so you two hang tight. Does the lady that's with you know that both of your parents are missing?"

"No, sir, we told her Mom was gone and that Dad was sick," Sissy admitted. "But that really is the truth because before Dad left, he was drunk all the time and that's the same as being sick."

"Sissy, be sure and thank the lady for helping you. Is there anything else we need to know before we get started? Your grandma is already putting things into the suitcase, so we'll want to be out of here just absolutely as soon as possible. We love you guys so much and have wished we could see more of you. We'll probably stay there a few days and get things settled before coming back. We're proud of both you, children. Be sure to lock your doors and call us again at this number if you need us. It's a mobile number. Do you have a telephone at all?"

"No," Sissy said. "There's not one at the apartment, and Dad's cell phone was probably with him."

"We'll get the police involved when we arrive," Mr. Taylor said. "We're in a hurry to get started, so I'm saying good-bye, sweetheart."

"Bye-bye Grandpa," Sissy said in a clear voice, and then she heard the line go dead. Once again, tears began to form in her eyes.

"Don't cry, please don't cry!" Danny said.

"Oh, I'm crying because it's good!" Sissy exclaimed.

Whereupon Danny started hopping over to Mrs. Jonas crying out with great glee, "They're coming, they're coming, they're coming!"

Belle smiled widely holding her index finger over her lips, "That's great, but we mustn't disturb the other people here. When will they be here, and do you think your dad will be OK with this?"

"They think they'll be here tomorrow, and it will be so good!"

"Now that we've made that call, we need to celebrate a little, don't you children think? How about some ice cream sundaes in the hotel restaurant?"

"Wow, do they have ice cream here?" Danny asked, amazed.

"Sure, let's do it," Belle said, rising and leading the way to the restaurant entry.

"You have been very, very nice to us," Sissy commented. "Why have you been so nice when you didn't even know us?"

"Well, I have a Bible verse that I like to act on. It says: 'For whatever you did for one of the least of these ... you did for me.' It means that if we do things for others, it's like doing it for God."

"Wow!" Danny responded, "We were wondering the other day if God even cared about us."

Belle blinked back the tears as they were seated in a booth. "You kids are really special, and I have a little surprise for you before we order." She reached into her purse pulling out two small billfolds—one pink and the other brown. "Here are some billfolds for you, and I have a card with my name, address, and phone number on it for you to carry. Keep the cards in your billfolds, and you can contact me if you need me again. Of course, you can carry small pictures and money in the wallets also."

"Thank you so much!" Sissy exclaimed. "You just keep doing and doing." The children sat examining their gifts and fitting Belle's cards in the various pouches until the sundaes arrived.

"We needed to ask you a couple more questions," Sissy remembered as she savored her dessert. "We need to know a cheap place to buy underwear and how to ride the bus, but I guess the bus may not be so important if our grandparents are coming tomorrow."

"Is your dad unable to drive?" Belle asked.

"We don't have a car anymore," Sissy said, fielding the question. "We think Dad was drinking too much and got into trouble because of it. We don't ask him any questions about it. We just need a way to get new underwear."

"You know there's a Macy's a few blocks over, and we could walk there. Macy's a big store and on the main floors they have standard prices, but this store has a bargain basement and you can often purchase quality items at a good price."

"Great," said Danny. "I wanted some long johns, but we may not need them if we move to Florida."

"Grandma and Grandpa didn't say anything about us moving," Sissy objected.

"Well, still I'll only get two pair, just in case," Danny qualified.

The three soon finished their treats, heading to Macy's and making their purchases. Belle was impressed with the insightfulness of the children as they searched for socks and underwear in their own sizes. Soon, they were ready to go back out to the street whereupon Belle helped them read the bus schedules.

"If you don't understand the schedule, you can generally ask a waiting passenger what number of bus will take you to your area, and then when you get on the bus, ask the driver if he's going there," Belle informed the children. "It looks like you're to ride number 18, so I'll wait here with you and we'll ask." Belle squatted down to the children's level as they stood on the sidewalk. "Each of you give me a hug before we say good-bye. Do call me, even if you're not in trouble. Remember that I will be praying for you, and I want you to know that God does care about you." Both of the children gave Belle a big hearty hug just as bus number 18 came to a stop before them.

"Does this bus go by the Riverview Apartments?" Danny called out loudly to the driver.

"Sure thing, bud," the driver replied pleasantly. "Do you have a token?"

"No, sir, but we have money," Sissy said.

"Well, put in two quarters apiece for each of you," instructed the driver, pointing to the fare slot.

"Thanks, man!" Danny said with shining eyes.

The children waved sincere good-byes to Belle and rode away on the bus. Since the loss of the family car had been recent, they'd not been on a bus for several months, and never had they ridden one on their own. This was quite an adventure, and the trip seemed like it was over before it had barely begun.

"Here you are, kiddos," the bus driver said, pointing. "Your apartment is that direction—two blocks. Do you know where you are?"

"Yep," Danny said.

"Thank you," Sissy offered as she gathered up their bundles.

Down on the sidewalk, Sissy asked, "Should we go back to the apartment first or stop by the barbershop?"

"Let's go to the barber first and get it over with," Danny said, frowning reluctantly.

"You'll look more respectable," Sissy reassured. "Your hair's really long and in your eyes. I'm surprised your teacher hasn't complained."

"She has," Danny grinned. "She wanted to put rubber bands in it to keep it out of my eyes." They both laughed as they thought of how that would look and walked on headed to the barbershop.

The shop had several customers waiting when they arrived, so the children sat reading from the stack of tattered magazines.

"What can I do for you, urchins?" asked the barber when their turn arrived.

"He needs a haircut," Sissy directed. "Take as much off as he'll let you."

The barber looked at Danny and raised his brows, "So, how short is it going to be?"

"This long," Danny instructed, holding his thumb and index finger apart about three inches.

"All over?"

"No, just on top and in the front. You can cut the back shorter."

"Do you children have the twelve dollars to pay for it?"

"Yes," Sissy answered. "Would you charge the same amount to trim the back of my hair and cut bangs for me?"

The barber looked at her, considering, "Sure."

"Can you break a hundred dollar bill?" Sissy questioned.

"No problem," the barber said. "Where'd you get a hundred dollar bill?"

"Dad gave it to us," Sissy said, trying to avoid the direct questioning. She watched her brother squint his face as the hair tickled his nose, but then started making faces at her to make her smile.

"Hey, son," the barber chuckled, "hold still. Is this pretty gal your girlfriend?'

"Naw, she's my sister, but we are friends?"

"Good boy! A sister that has your back—that's a good thing."

The barber clipped away quietly, first on Danny and then on Sissy. He made change for the one-hundred-dollar bill, and they moved quietly back onto the street with their bundles, heading on to the apartment.

"One more thing done," Sissy remarked. "Now all we have to do is wait for Grandma and Grandpa."

"I wish they were here already," Danny thought out loud.

"Yeah!—Yes," Sissy responded. "I wish we had something to do other than just go home and read. Almost everything we need to do has been done."

"Reading's all I want to do," Danny asserted.

"Yes, but tomorrow's Sunday, and we have all day to do that until Grandma and Grandpa come."

"Well, what else is there to do?"

"We could go to church," Sissy offered.

"Where?"

"We could ask Mrs. Jonas; she'd probably like us to go with her."

"How about the church over by the library?" Danny asked.

"We don't know anybody there," Sissy commented.

"Yes," Danny replied, "but we don't know anybody anywhere else either."

"That's why I thought we could go with Mrs. Jonas."

"Don't you think we've used up too much of her time already?" Danny asked thoughtfully.

"Well, yes," Sissy said, "I guess we don't need to know anybody just to go to church. When I was little, I went to a church often. It's when we lived in St. Louis. I rode on a Sunday school bus by myself. Momma and Dad didn't go. I was six, I think."

"I don't think I remember going," Danny said, trying to think back when he was little.

"You didn't. You stayed home."

"What do you do when you go to church?"

"They sing and pray and read lessons from the Bible."

"They sing?" Danny said, his interest being peaked. "What do they sing?"

"Hymns—songs about God. They often have a piano or organ to play music."

"Well, that does sound interesting. Let's go to church by the library. We need to know what time it starts and what time we need to get there."

"There's a sign in front that gives the time," Sissy reminded him.

The children entered the apartment building and moved onto their own unit. When they opened the door, everything was just as they had left it.

"What do you think Grandma and Grandpa will think of the way we've cleaned the apartment?" Danny asked eyeing the clear counters, table, and clean floor.

Sissy, looking around, considered the appearance of her surroundings. "Well, there's no clutter, and the things are clean, but the carpet's so bad and the walls are so bare I think they'll not be very impressed. They'll probably notice we've been cleaning things, though."

"I don't want to wait until they come. Are they good at answering questions?" Danny asked.

"Yes, they should be pretty good. They were both teachers, you know. What are you thinking about asking?"

"I've been wondering if they know why we've had more problems with our family than other kids our age."

"Lots of kids our age have divorced parents, and some of the parents use drugs and alcohol, but I don't know anyone whose dad was taken away by gunmen."

"See," Danny said, "that's what I mean, maybe Grandpa or Grandma know why this is happening."

"Let's get our blankets and read a while before supper," Sissy said.

"What should we eat?" Danny asked. "I bet we'll have more special food when Grandma gets here," Danny enthused. "Cereal, bananas, beans, and tomatoes may be good for us, but they sure are boring. Weren't those sundaes good? I think we should eat one every day."

"That probably wouldn't be good for us," Sissy said," but it sure would be nice."

The children settled in again on the couch with their books and blankets, and eventually both nodded off, not reawakening until after dark. They made their supper, but still feeling groggy, they went off to bed early.

Sunday morning arrived bright and somewhat warmer with a soft south breeze melting the snow and making even the formerly dry sidewalks damp. Both children awoke with the light of a new day and lay quietly in their beds.

"Sissy?" Danny whispered, "Are you awake?"

"Yes," she replied quietly.

"This may be the last morning we have to be alone."

"Yes," she said slowly. "We've done pretty well, but I won't mind having someone to help us get things done!"

"Do you think Grandma and Grandpa will seem as nice when they get here as they seemed on the phone?"

"They were nice when I was little, but that was years ago. It's possible they might like very small children but not older ones. It probably depends on how we act."

"Do you think we act badly?"

"No, we do pretty well. I think children a lot of times do what they have to, and if they can get by without needing to do much, they do."

"What do you mean not needing to do much?"

"Well," Sissy considered, "it's like if your mom makes breakfast for you, you don't have to make it for yourself."

"Oh, and if somebody else cleans the floors or counters, then you don't have to," Danny agreed. "You know my neck itches," Danny continued. "I probably should have taken a bath last night and washed my hair. And … we didn't check on the time on the church sign."

"Ah!" Sissy said. "Maybe we could look in that old phone book, but I guess they could have changed the time; the book isn't new."

"If we really want to go, we could walk down and read the time and then go back when it starts."

"That seems like a lot of trouble," Sissy said thoughtfully.

"Yes, but it's still really early, and I don't want to sit around here. I don't want to just sit and wait for Grandma and Grandpa to come. I want to stay busy," Danny said, pursuing his point.

"Do you have any homework?" Sissy asked.

"Only a little. How about you?"

"We can do it this afternoon," Sissy brightened. "Let's get going."

The two children hurried through breakfast and donned their coats after cleaning up the dishes. They rushed down the apartment hall and out the doors only to be surprised at the warmth of the day.

"Wow!" Danny said. "We hardly even need our coats; it almost seems like spring."

They rushed the several blocks to the church, noting that Sunday school started at 9:45 a.m. and church at 11:00.

"Sunday school's more fun," Sissy said, considering the time. "But that's pretty soon. Let's just do church. It'll give us more time to get ready. I'll race you back," and she started off, leaving Danny behind.

Danny, remembering their race last week, did not give up hope at her head start but persistently ran even though her lead initially widened.

Soon, however, he recognized that he was catching up as Sissy slowed down holding her side.

"I win!" he gloated passing her.

"Hey, OK, you win," she agreed. "Let's walk."

Danny turned around walking backwards. "Why do you think it feels good to win?" he asked.

Sissy looked up perplexed and attempted an answer. "I think we want to prove we're better than someone else."

"Why do we want to do that?"

"To make us feel good."

"That's what the question was in the first place," he exclaimed.

"It's another question for Grandma and Grandpa."

"How far do you think they've come?" Danny pondered. "When they leave Florida how do they go to get to St. Joseph?"

"Well, mostly north. I'd need a map to see, but it's some west too, I think. You know, I saw a map in the phone book."

"Do you really think they can get here by tonight?"

"They acted like it," Sissy said.

By that time they were back at the apartment and proceeded to get their baths and change clothes.

"Now I wish I had different shoes and a dress that fits," Sissy declared.

"I don't think it matters," Danny said, trying to reassure his sister.

"Yes, but you're a boy; boys wear the same things all the time. Girls need to wear clothes that fit in."

"We'll just sit in the back. I think that if we're quiet, no one will care. They might not even notice us."

"I'll care. But you're probably right. We might want to keep our coats on, too. I've also been thinking I might want to change my name."

"Why?"

"This would be a good time. We're probably going to move, and it will be easier for Grandma and Grandpa to get used to a new name rather than later. Besides, I'm tired of being called Sissy!"

"I like Sissy, and that's how I know you."

"You'd get used to it."

"Get used to what?"

"Brenda Elaine."

"All of that?"

"No, just Brenda."

"Why just Brenda?"

"It's shorter."

"Maybe I should shorten my name to Dan."

"Because?"

"If you can, I can. Are we going to tell them at school?"

"No, but we'll start at church this morning. It'll be Brenda and Dan—the Taylor kids."

"Well, we'd better get started," Danny said, a little worried about these new changes.

"OK, but our hair's still wet. I guess it will dry if it's not too cold. I wish I had a blow dryer."

"Grandma will probably have one."

"Yes, but that doesn't help now."

The children started out again for the church and hesitantly walked until they arrived at he steps that led to the front of the church.

"Shh, don't talk," Sissy warned.

"Yes, Sissy," Danny answered in a high trembling voice, responding to her bossiness.

"And remember I'm Brenda."

"Yes, Brenda," he continued in that same high register.

They started up the steps and opened the door. An elderly couple greeted them and handed them a bulletin looking at them quizzically.

"Are your folks coming in?" the lady asked.

"No, it's just us," Brenda replied. "We want to sit back a ways, and we'll be quiet."

"Tell the ushers," the lady said, "they'll be glad to help you. We're glad that you are here."

The children entered the sanctuary and looked about at the high ceiling and the beautiful windows. Almost immediately the organ began to play, and the children were seated near the back by an elderly usher. They were amazed at the beautiful music. They read along in the bulletin, attempting to follow the sitting and standing instructions during the worship service and then sat quietly during the prayers and sermon. At the end, they attempted to slip out quietly, but who to their wonder should appear in the aisle beside them but Belle Jonas.

"Well, if it isn't my friends—Sissy and Danny Taylor," she exclaimed. "I should have invited you."

"We didn't know you would be here," Danny exclaimed. "We thought about asking to come with you."

"What a coincidence that I would…," Belle enthused, "that I would be here!"

"We want to be like you are. We want to be helpful to others."

"You children are too much. Have you heard anymore from your grandparents?"

"Not since yesterday," they both answered. "They said they would be here by tonight."

"I suspect you can't wait to see them."

"We're trying to stay busy and not think about it," Danny explained.

"What does your dad think?"

"He … doesn't know … yet," Danny hedged.

"I think he'll be glad they're here," Sissy quickly inserted. "How long do you think it will take for them to get here?"

"Well, where in Florida are they coming from?" Belle asked.

"Ft. Walton Beach," Danny replied. "We had a map in the phone book, but it didn't have Ft. Walton Beach on it … just the big cities."

Belle grinned and laughed as she said, "I believe it's close to Pensacola clear at the west end of the panhandle, so that makes the trip much shorter than if they lived down in Miami or Tampa, but it's still a long way. I'm guessing twenty hours of driving or so. Did they say anything about flying?"

"No," Sissy said, "but they did say we could call them if we have a problem, but we don't have a problem."

"I have my cell phone," Belle offered. "Why don't we step around to a quieter room here in the church and give them a buzz. We can see how they're doing. Then you'll know about when to expect them."

On following Belle to the room, Danny dutifully got his billfold out of his pocket and pulled out the slip of paper with the number on it and handed it to Belle while Sissy stood close by. Belle dialed the number and waited.

"Hello, Thelma Taylor speaking."

"Hello, Mrs. Taylor. This is Belle Jonas. I have your grandchildren here at church with me. They are fine but wanting to talk with you about when you may be arriving. They are very sweet children and are not having any problems. Is it possible for you to speak with them?"

"Oh, certainly, but before you put Sissy on the line let me thank you for helping them make the calls. We really, really appreciate being in contact with them, especially when they're needing us. Thank you again. Thank you ever so much!"

"Well, like I said they are both delights, and I'm so glad I could help. Here's Sissy now."

"Hello," Sissy said tentatively.

"Hello, Sissy," Mrs. Taylor said warmly. "I hear you want to know when we'll be there. We've made good time and are just leaving St. Louis, so barring any difficulty, we hope to be there around five or six this evening. Don't eat supper. We'll plan to go get something as soon as we arrive. So you went to church with Mrs. Jonas?"

"Well, not exactly," Sissy explained. "We came to church, and she found us here."

"Did you go to Sunday school, too?"

"No, just church. It was out first visit."

"My, my, we can't wait to see you, but it won't be long now. Remember, we love you!"

"Oh, Grandma, we're so glad you're coming," Sissy replied as tears again filled her eyes, and she handed the phone to Danny.

"Hello, Grandma?" Danny enthused. "Are you driving or flying?"

"Oh, we're driving, sweetheart, but we're coming as quickly as we can. How's my Danny boy doing?"

"Well, we've changed our names today," he informed his grandmother. "I'm now Dan and Sissy is Brenda. We decided it seemed more grownup."

"So you don't want to be my Danny boy?" Thelma asked.

"I can be your Dan Boy, though," he negotiated. "Is Grandpa driving?"

"Yes, do you wish to talk with him?"

"Oh, yes, please, but good-bye Grandma. We think you can sleep in Dad's bed. We washed the sheets and made the bed up."

Mr. Taylor got on the phone and said, "Hi, Dan! Your grandma says you're Dan, not Danny now."

"Did she? That quickly? Well, Grandpa, how are you doing driving so far and so fast? What are you driving in? Is Grandma driving too? Are the roads OK?"

"Hey, wait a minute," Grandpa said, laughing. "One question at a time. Yes, we're doing just fine with the roads; we're in a white Dodge Durango, and your grandmother's a good driver and has driven about a third of the time when she's not sleeping. Did I answer all your questions?"

"Yes, I guess. When will you get here?"

"Well, without any unforeseen mishaps, we think it will be around five or more hours. It depends on how well we can get around Kansas City. I don't know how long that will take."

"Have you decided how long you will stay here? Can we move back to Florida with you? I think it would be fun to live on the beach."

"We'll talk about that when we get there. We've talked with your other grandparents in Texas, and we might go down to see them when we leave St. Joseph. Have you heard anything by any chance from your dad?"

"No."

"Well, we'll deal with that when we arrive. We sure are looking forward to seeing you. May I speak with your sister?"

"Sure," Danny said, magnanimously handing the phone over to Sissy. "He called me Dan!" he whispered excitedly to Belle.

Sissy made a few more comments, closed the phone, and handed it back to Belle.

"Children," Belle asked, "how can they sleep in your dad's bed if your dad's there?"

Danny and Sissy looked at each other and Sissy said, "Our dad's been missing since after the first time we saw you. We've been afraid to tell anyone because of Child Protection Services; we were afraid they'll take us away."

Belle looked aghast. "So you've been alone the whole past week? What have you been eating? Have you been in school?"

"There was some money at the house," Danny answered. "We bought food and used clothes and went to school every day," he continued, catching his sister's eye to get her response from his comment.

"Oooofff," breathed Belle. "Knowing this, I don't think I should leave you by yourselves this afternoon until your grandparents arrive. How about coming over to my house and having lunch with my daughter and me, and we'll all go back over to the apartment together in time for your grandparents to get here; we'll be waiting for them."

"We don't want to be a bother to you," Sissy said. "You've already been very helpful."

"But Sissy!" Danny exclaimed, "the food will be much better than ours, and the time is going to drag by horribly waiting for them to come!"

"Just so," Belle agreed. "Sissy, you'll very much enjoy meeting my daughter; she always has such a splendid time when there are youngsters in the house."

"How old is she?" Sissy asked

"Twenty-nine." Belle replied. "She's a nurse and had to work last night, so she wasn't at church with me. She's likely awake now and might even have lunch ready for us. Is it a plan?" she asked, making certain Sissy agreed.

"Well, thank you." Sissy said primly. "If it's not too much trouble."

CHAPTER IV

SATURDAY MARCH 7

Zach was never so glad to see the end of a trip as when he'd arrived in Houston. The tenseness of having two almost totally noncommunicative fellow travelers had been as wearing as the uncomfortable benches. As much as he'd feared what might lie ahead at trip's end, he was grateful to be hearing city traffic sounds. At one rest stop somewhere in east Texas, he'd ventured to ask the guarding gunman if he knew what he would be doing at the end of the journey. "When people start asking me questions," the man had replied, "my fingers start getting itchy!" He'd then rapidly waved his revolver back and forth toward Zach and shot a post not twenty feet away.

Upon moving off a main highway in the city, the van stayed on a rough road for twenty minutes before stopping. Zach could hear large motors whining, machinery creaking, and the swish of waves. He wondered if they could be in Galveston but suspected not enough time had elapsed after the Houston traffic. The driver and gunman left, slamming their doors behind them, and the passengers sat immobile, listening to the sounds. Zach lay down again on his bench and dozed for a couple of hours before being roughly shoved by the larger man who muttered. "Time's up! I want to sleep there!"

Zach dutifully moved to the floor and quietly started doing push-ups and stretching exercises.

"Sit down and be quiet, or you'll wish you had," he was briskly informed. Although Zach was younger and likely stronger than either of the two, he didn't think a fight would be in his best interest especially with two against one. He quietly held his peace, sitting again with his back to the barrier and attempting to come up with some sensible plan of escape. He believed it would be unwise to include the others in any plans, but on his own he could think of no viable scenario.

After dark the driver and gunman returned, opening the rear door and handed each man water and sandwiches.

"Eat this grub quickly," they were told. "We'll be moving in about ten minutes." The passengers hurriedly ate and drank, and the now armed driver and the gunman motioned with their guns for the three to move out of the van.

"Step sharp," they were told. "One misstep and we'll have smokin' guns!" Quietly they were directed to what looked like a small fishing boat. There were nets, rope, and fish lines on the deck, but as soon as they went down the stairs to the cabin, Zach saw at once that they were simply moving from one traveling cage to another.

"Relieve yourselves there," said their captor pointing to a pot. "Any noise from you is a certain bullet between the eyes."

Three army cots filled most of the space; the three men each sat on one and soon lay down, listening to the lapping of the waves after the iron mesh gate clanged shut and the lock was snapped into place.

Great! thought Zack. *So what will we do should this thing sink while we're on here and all locked up?* However, lying on the more comfortable cot with his coat bunched up under his head, he was soon asleep again.

Several hours later he was awakened by the sound of the boat engine being started, and after twenty minutes they moved away from the dock. Through the open staircase doors above him, he continued to see flashing lights and at first thought they were moving along a shoreline, but at length with the flashing continuing, he realized it was more likely they were moving down the Houston shipping canal.

Where to from here? he wondered.

He realized they were out on the open gulf after a time with the swell of the waves increasing. Zach lay on the cot listening to the drone of the motor nearly covering the snuffling snores of the other men. Later he could tell the waves were becoming rougher; suddenly, the smaller man awoke and rushed to the pot vomiting. No sooner had he finished than his partner did the same. Although the odor of their mishap was unpleasant, Zach was surprised he didn't feel the least bit nauseated. Both men knelt moaning in the near darkness beside the pot only inches away from where Zach lay resting.

"Help!" the larger man moaned louder.

Zach arose and unsteadily stepped to the cage door pounding on it.

"Shut up down there," the gunman said, appearing at the top of the stair.

"These fellows are seasick and vomiting. Are you able to help them?" Zach asked.

"Poor slime balls need to buck up; they won't die. I'll bring down some water down later."

Zach resumed his place on his cot, and the men continued to moan, retching at intervals.

The rough seas increased in intensity, and Zach could hear the wind whistling overhead. He felt helpless and trapped as the hours dragged on. Finally morning dawned and the wind decreased, but the waves rocked on and on. Zach could see both men lying on the floor with their hands on the pot, and he tried not to think about the smell. Finally, he went back to sleep.

Well into the morning the captors brought water and cold Egg McMuffins to their prisoners. The stinking pot was handed off, and the sickly travelers were raunchily cursed despite their misery. Zach silently ate his food and drank his water enduring the abuse. *What other recourse do I have?* he considered. So began two days of endless waves and rocking.

Although Zach never became ill, his fellow travelers never fully recovered. They drank their water and nibbled their food and at intervals moaned with nausea. On the third day the boat stopped, and Zach was quite certain they came near another vessel, although he never saw it. His two roommates were directed out of the cage and up the stairs never to be seen again, leaving Zach alone in his confinement. With this solitude, he felt much more comfortable carrying out his exercises in an attempt to maintain his strength. His meals had become preprepared sandwiches, apples, water, and bananas. On the fourth day they pulled into a port, stayed for a couple hours, and were back on the sea for another day and a half before entering another port about midday.

When the gunman came to move Zach out that night after dark no questions were asked, and he had no idea where they were. However, he did see a sign in English that read "Port of Belize City" and immediately was cheered by the thought that he was at least in an English-speaking country.

I wonder if Evan's still down here? he thought. *How on earth could I contact him if he is?*

He was led to a van similar to his US transport and taken to a large building near the docks. He was directed through a large metal door centered in a huge blank wall, and the door was firmly locked behind him. He looked about, attempting to determine the nature of his surroundings. He was in a room with high ceilings of uncovered girders with a dim bulb near the top. There were three cots against the wall near the door and only one sleeping occupant. Opposite the door was a wall with two machines that appeared to be an industrial dishwasher and a metal press. Additionally, a conveyor apparatus, now still and silent, stretched across the corner from one wall and into another. There were also two standard pallets that held large vats made of a black fiberglass material. The place reeked of coffee, and Zach walked over to peer into the vats. One did hold coffee, and the other was filled with plastic bags of white powder.

Drugs, Zach thought. *This is drug cartel business! How much chance is there to even get out of here alive?* He felt immensely discouraged but moved to one of the vacant cots and lay down, contemplating the situation. Eventually he fell into a fitful sleep.

Zach was awakened by a loud factory buzzer.

"Buenos dias! It's 6:00 a.m.," his fellow cot partner said with a Spanish accent. "I'm Herman, and I've been instructed to show you the ropes. If you'll notice the three cameras above us in the room, you'll see that we're carefully observed around the clock. That's why the lights never go completely out. We're only to talk with each other about work," he went on but winked. "We work in a factory that appears to can coffee. Our job is to dump the cans of coffee that come in on the conveyor into the coffee vat, put a bag of the white powder into the can, and seal the can lid into place with this metal press. The can then runs through this high-pressure washer to remove any external powder from the can and immediately moves out of this room on this conveyor into the next room. In the next room we put the coffee label on the can and are never in actual contact with the can, observing it through glass and using rubber gloves through openings in the glass so as not to contaminate it before it leaves that room on the continuation of the conveyor. To other workers in this building, I believe it appears to them that what we do is all automatic, and they have no idea we're working here."

"I understand that washing the cans and then labeling them in the same room would contaminate them," Zach said.

"Right you are," Herman grinned. "So the labeling is done in the next room. After the cans leave our room, the conveyor takes them to another room where an expiration date is stamped into the cans, and then they're returned to the room next door where we run the labeling machine, but we never handle the labels or cans again. We can handle them only with these sealed rubber gloves, seeing them through a window. Surprisingly, however, wrinkled or damaged labels are pressed back into a slot that comes into that room."

"Have you been doing all of this by yourself?" Zach asked.

"No, I had another fellow in here until two days ago. He suddenly became ill with belly pain and kept vomiting. He couldn't eat anything, so they came and got him, carried him out on a stretcher, and the conveyor's been silent ever since. Yesterday, I was told you'd be coming and that we'd start as usual at eight o'clock. They bring breakfast at 7:00 a.m., and if you come through the door, I'll show you the restroom."

Zach wondered why he didn't just tell him where the facility was but followed Herman through the door.

"This is the gloved access to the labeling device," Herman pointed out. They both peered through the window into the dim recess on the other side.

"The lights come on over there with the conveyor belts," Herman explained. "And the restroom's over here with a shower. They bring clean clothes and towels a couple of times a week." He stepped into the small space with Zach behind him and flipped on the light switch. He silently pointed to a strip of paper folded on the floor that said **READ** printed in bold letters, and he winked at Zach again.

"You can go ahead and use this room now should you need to," Herman said, stepping out of the small cramped room and Zach stepped in shutting the door behind him. Zach picked up the small folded paper and, unfolding it, realized that it was a strip of coffee can label with irregular cuts along the top—a discarded label with a message.

"You are in the only unmonitored part of our living and working quarters," he read. "Under the clothes hamper there are several pens, and I use these discarded labels to communicate with fellow workers. To talk about anything other than work is a certain way to get hauled out and beaten. After several infractions you're gone for good and, I suspect, killed. Do not feel required to communicate this way with me. If you decide at any time to leave me a message, leave it folded in the trash can. I tear the messages up into tiny pieces and flush them. Please do this now to this note. I believe God will get us through this!"

Zach read the message twice, tore it up into small shreds, and flushed the commode. He moved the heavy hamper and wrote on a new slip of paper, "Thanks, I need to think about this!" He put his folded note in the trashcan as instructed, wondering what good God could do in this situation. It was comforting to know his imprisoned partner, however, did appear to be a friend and not of the same ilk as his former inmates. He stayed in the restroom and decided to shower and shave as clean clothes and a safety razor were on high shelves. He considered growing a beard but decided he wanted to maintain himself as best as possible, hoping in doing so he could keep his spirits up. There was underwear on the shelf along with blue overalls. The underwear fit too tightly, but the overalls were large enough. After cleaning up he left the restroom, passed through the labeling room, and reentered the larger room where he'd slept and where the vats were. Herman was waiting there and said gruffly, "Breakfast's at seven, and I'm going to get cleaned up, too. Don't talk to me about anything except work. I think you should probably work in this room today as I've had more experience with the stamping and labeling room. The person who watches our camera monitors does check to see how we're doing and will slow the conveyor belts if we push this red button. He pointed to a large plastic red button near the conveyor belt. Too much stopping causes us to miss meals. There's a ten-minute break every two hours and thirty minutes off at lunch. We start at eight o'clock and run until five thirty. I believe the hours are national standards and are dictated for the factory for the other workers." With that, he left.

Zach decided to use the time before breakfast to exercise, so he jogged in place for fifteen minutes and did pushups and sit-ups for another fifteen minutes before Herman came back. Herman didn't smile but winked at him and said nothing. Zack wondered what the wink meant but on thinking decided it may well mean there was a new message in the trash. Suddenly the door slammed open, and two men entered. One had a gun, and the other had breakfast, which consisted of egg-burritos, coffee, milk, bananas, and a pill. "What's the pill?" Zack asked.

"Vitamins," Herman replied tersely. "Don't talk."

The breakfast was good, but the burrito was not warm. Zack was so hungry he hardly cared; he was fearful that the portions would be too small in the future for him to ever get enough to eat. The two men bringing in the food stood silently watching them eat. "He's a big bruiser," one commented, then threatened. "We'll be real willing to use the gun if you act up."

After breakfast, Herman threw the plastic food containers into the trash and, without saying anything, began to walk. Zack sat and watched him for a time but decided to follow him for the additional exercise; time was weighing heavily. He almost wished he were already working since he could not read, talk, or listen to the radio. At seven forty-five, he went to the restroom and retrieved a new note from the trash. It said, "I know not talking is hard; what I do is pray for my family to get out of here. It keeps me sane. There is nothing to read at all."

Great! Zack thought, *A holy Christian to deal with! I wonder if he was like this before he got here?*

He responded writing, "I'll do my best to keep quiet. Thanks for the warning. I don't pray much. I've lived a pretty selfish life ruined even more with alcohol. I do worry about my wife and kids who aren't together." He flushed Herman's note after tearing it into tiny pieces, put his note in the trash, and went out to face the day.

His task of dumping out the coffee from the cans and replacing them with the bags of dope was not difficult but was extremely monotonous. He hummed as he worked, hoping the noise from the machines would cover the sound. The breaks came slowly but passed quickly, and at the end of the day he was exhausted not with the work but with boredom. On his last afternoon break he left a note for Herman, asking him how he endured the tedious boredom of the work, especially being unable to talk.

Both lunch and supper were delivered by armed gunmen. The only break in the day had been the exchange of the vats with a new vat of bagged dope replacing the old one and an empty vat for coffee replacing the one he'd filled. After supper Zack went to the restroom and wrote a long note to Herman asking how long he'd been there, had he ever been beaten, where had he come from, how he'd gotten there, did the organization even change working locations, and again how he endured the silence. Zack then whiled away another hour running in place and doing his other exercises making himself short of breath. Herman reentered the main room after having spent a lengthy time in the restroom. After restarting his walking routine, he winked at Zack as he passed him.

Zack sat catching his breath for ten minutes watching Herman walk, then ambled unobtrusively back to the restroom. Herman's note was long. "I've been here about a year. I was beaten before I came because I'd tried to escape these captors. I was a coffee farmer in the southern part of Belize living on the same farm that my parents and grandparents had. I had an older brother working with me, and the drug lords came to our place demanding that we sell them our coffee. We felt bad about it but were afraid not to sell to them, and the first year they paid us the standard price. However, the second year they paid us only half price, so my brother confronted them about it. They responded several days later during the night by sending a half dozen armed men to the cottage at the front of the farm where he lived alone. My brother had expected their coming and, planning to protect himself, had several loaded guns in the house. When they arrived, he was awakened by gunshots and went to the window with his ammunition. I think he may have gotten off a couple rounds, but we found him the next morning with gunshot wounds in his head and chest, and the whole front and side of the cottage were riddled with bullet holes. I went to the police, who started an investigation, but three days later after having left the farm in my pickup to run an errand, another set of gunmen forced me off the road, jerked me out of the pickup, started beating me and telling me it was because the police were involved. They kept me in a locked room for nine days while my wounds healed and brought me here. I have a wife and two children who likely have no idea where I am or if I'm alive. My father still can run the farm if they've left him alone, which may be doubtful. My children are a girl thirteen and a boy fourteen; they're very sweet and kind; I miss them and my wife horribly. There have been four other fellows with me here since I've come. The first one swore horribly and would not follow the no-talking rules. He had several beatings before they came and took him out the door. I think they shot him immediately because there were two gunshots shortly after he was taken out. The second fellow was here for a couple months; I never knew what happened to him. He'd unintentionally talked a couple times and gotten beaten, coming back all bruised and bloody. Then one day they just came and got him and brought the last fellow who was a prince of a guy. He was quiet but set up this writing system that, so far, has worked without a hitch. He wrote many notes to me. I'd been very angry and depressed, but he helped me start trusting in God, praying for my family and relying on God in general despite this hellhole and the violent ways we are treated. I don't know how tell you to tolerate the boredom and lack of reading material. Partly it is getting used to it, and partly, for me anyway, it's now committing it to God for him to make me grow because of it. The last fellow—his name was Hosea—said we should pray for deliverance. My hope is that they got him some medical care, but I again fear they may have just killed him. Even so if he was killed, he's in heaven! You seem like a decent fellow and I'm sorry you're here, but if we can work together there may be better days ahead."

Zack read the note three times before he tore it up and flushed it. He didn't want to forget any of it because he knew he couldn't go back and read it. He thought about writing again telling Herman some of his story but decided against it, not wishing to stay in the restroom too long. So he wrote, "Thanks for the long note. I'll tell you more about myself later. I think I've been here in the restroom long enough."

CHAPTER V

SUNDAY, MARCH 8

Belle and the children drove in Belle's car to her home and entered to find the house warm and with the inviting odors of cooking food.

"Helloooo!" Belle called out. "I'm home and we have company." Seeing her daughter as she stepped into the kitchen doorway, Belle continued, "This is Danny and Sissy, the children at the library I mentioned to you last week. Danny and Sissy, this is my daughter Esther; she's the nurse who worked all night. Lunch really smells great!"

"You're right!" Danny agreed. "What is it?"

Sissy cleared her throat meaningfully saying, "It does smell delicious, but I apologize for him asking what it is."

"That's OK," Esther responded, "I'm glad to see some extra consumers; I fixed a new recipe called chicken picatta, and it says it is enough to feed six. I don't think Mom and I would have been able to clean that up at all. We'll set on a couple more plates so there will be five of us."

"Five?" Belle queried.

"Yes, five," Esther answered. "Uncle Mike called saying he was coming through town this noon on his way to a meeting in Omaha and wanted to have lunch with us."

"Well, I never!" Belle exclaimed. "He couldn't be showing up at a better time! With his work, he's the one we need to be talking to. I've learned just a bit ago that the children's father has been abducted, and that's the reason I brought them home for lunch."

"Abducted?" Esther asked, walking back into the kitchen and starting to get more plates and silverware from the cabinet.

"Yes, with a gun by masked men a week ago yesterday," Danny supplied importantly. "Why do we want to tell your uncle about it?"

"Because he's a chief police officer in a suburb of Kansas City; he'll know best how to handle these things."

"Where are the children's grandparents or other family—aunts and uncles?" Esther asked.

"One set of grandparents is coming in tonight from Florida," Belle replied, rearranging the chairs around the dining room table, "around five we think. Oh! There's the doorbell; it's likely Mike," she said, rushing back to the front door.

"Oh, brother-in-law, you don't know how glad we are to see you," Belle greeted. "You couldn't be showing up at a better time."

"Well, glad to see you, too," Mike replied, laughing. "I'm thinking my timing was pretty good also, judging by the way it smells in here. Who's the cook, and who are these youngsters?"

"These are Sissy and Danny," Belle introduced. "And Esther cooked the meal."

"Hi," Danny greeted, grinning, "and it's chicken piccata, a new recipe for her," he informed sagely.

"Well, hi yourself," Mike replied. "Are you children from around here? Do you do all the talking for your sister?"

"No, I speak for myself," Sissy responded. "We live in an apartment near Belle's church, and she brought us here from there.

"Did you go to church this morning?" Danny asked, looking at Mike.

"'Fraid not," Mike replied. "I worked yesterday and need to be at a meeting tomorrow in Omaha so couldn't get to church today."

"We must sit down and eat before the food gets cold," Esther inserted.

"I was in church for the first time ever, I think, this morning," Danny said, looking at his sister for confirmation.

"I believe it was the first time you could remember it. We went with our grandparents when you were very small."

"Let's return thanks," Belle directed. "Mike, would you?"

Grace was said, and Danny immediately asked, "Why do you say return thanks when no one was thanking you in the first place?"

"Danny!" Sissy cautioned.

Belle smiled saying, "I believe it means God's given us the food and that we're thanking Him in return."

Danny pondered her answer and responded with, "That makes sense." He was quiet as he passed the food and secured himself a piece of chicken.

"Mike, the reason I was so glad to see you was because the children's father was abducted last week. I just found out about it this morning after church. We've been in contact with their grandparents, so we'll go to the apartment to turn the children over to them at five today. They're coming up from Florida. The children say they saw some armed masked men take away their dad from the apartment. They've not contacted the police fearing they'd be taken into the custody of child welfare. What do you think?"

"I think the longer you go without finding him, the harder it will be to find him. The police will need a description of him and the last clothes he was wearing. Was there anyone you knew of that was mad at your dad?" Mike asked, directing his question to the children.

"We don't know of anyone," Sissy replied.

"Can you think of any reason that someone would want to hurt your dad?" Mike asked.

"Well," Danny said, again looking at Sissy, "we think he might have stolen some money. He left some money in our cereal box telling us not to waste it because it was all he had. It was a lot, and we didn't think he had any money before that, at least not that we knew of. We've not heard of him ever stealing before."

"Do you think he could have been using or selling drugs?" Mike asked.

"I'm pretty sure he wouldn't have anything to do with drugs; he was very, very much against drugs ever since Mother used drugs and he told her to leave. He did drink a lot of beer, though," Sissy informed. "Nearly every day he came home from work drunk for the past several months, but then he went to work every weekday. He was drunk so much at home we were afraid something bad would happen, so we went to the library to find our grandparents and Miss Belle helped us there."

"Do you know anything about the people who took your dad?" Mike questioned.

"We know they drive a black Tahoe SUV with two tall aerials and have a Kansas license plate; we have the number. They also buy a lot of food at a time at McDonalds," Danny intoned.

Mike glanced at Belle with a grin and asked, "So how do you know all that?"

"They came to the McDonalds where we were eating; we recognized the car, and the second time we saw it we got the license number," Sissy informed. "They ordered a lot of food when they were there."

"So what did they look like?" Mike asked.

"There were four of them when we saw them the first time with Dad," Sissy answered. "But when we saw them at McDonalds, there were only two. They were dark-complected, muscular, and wore only black clothes—leather jackets. I'm guessing they were between thirty and forty years old, maybe a little older."

"I think they were younger than thirty," Danny corrected after swallowing his mouthful. "One of the two at McDonalds had a beard. Grandpa said we'd talk with the police when they got here. So I thought that would be tomorrow."

"Well, that may well be soon enough," Mike considered. "Not much would likely get done on a Sunday evening on a one-week-old missing person case that won't be handled as well tomorrow, and in fact, Child Protective will not need to be involved if the grandparents are on site. Belle, you should be with the children tonight until they arrive."

"Yes, that's what I was planning," she agreed.

"What happened with the money?" Mike asked, returning to the past situation.

"It was in the cereal box when we got home, and we've kept it in our pockets since then, which was fortunate because someone (we think it was the bad men) came and messed up the apartment while we were gone shopping for clothes," Sissy responded.

"Oh, really?" Mike asked astonished. "Weren't you terribly scared?"

"Boy, were we ever!" Danny said excitedly. "We pushed the furniture in front of the door to keep them out. Even if Dad stole the money, they shouldn't be taking him away with guns! But they haven't come back."

Mike smiled at Danny's enthusiasm and deductions, "Yes, so we still must consider them dangerous. Your grandparents will likely need to talk with the apartment managers about changing the lock."

Danny and Sissy caught each others' eyes.

"The chain lock's broken," Sissy said.

"Was the door torn up?" Mike asked.

"No," Danny replied.

"Well then, they likely had a key," Mike pondered. "I doubt your dad would let them in if he had any idea why they were there. He had to know there was trouble if he put the money in a cereal box. He might have answered the door leaving the chain lock in place, and then they cut the chain lock. In that case, they wouldn't have had a key."

"Yes, but when they came back we're pretty sure the door was locked, and they got in without damaging the door," Sissy deducted. "I think they have a key."

"You're probably right," Mike agreed.

"I'm so thankful you children are still OK!" Belle exclaimed fervently.

"Absolutely," Esther agreed. "God's been watching over you two!"

"It didn't feel much like it," Danny frowned. "It seemed to us that things were pretty bad, but the money helped because we were able to get warm clothes and food. I think God's sort of been falling down on the job of taking care of us."

"It may seem so, but you're all right now," Belle said. "Let's just look at the bright side for now and see how things turn out. I'm so thankful that your grandparents are on their way!"

"Me too!" Sissy contributed. "It is going to be so good to see them; we haven't been with them for years and years. We think Mom and Dad didn't want to see them."

Mike, Belle, and Esther exchanged glances getting a new understanding of the family situation. The conversation moved on to other topics, and soon Mike declared that he needed to get on the road. "Keep in touch with me, Belle," he said. "You're a sweetheart and a lifesaver for these youngsters."

"And the chicken piccata should bring your price up considerably on the marriage market," he grinned, winking at Esther.

Esther's cheeks turned pink, and she replied brashly, "I'm afraid Mom would pay to have someone take me off her hands not be expecting to be paid herself!"

"I didn't think paying for brides was done anymore," commented Danny questioningly.

"They don't," Sissy explained. "They're joking."

Danny frowned then grinned. "We need to help you find a wife!"

Everyone laughed and said their goodbyes to Mike as he excused himself and left, giving both ladies a big hug.

"That guy is such a hero," Esther commented as she watched through the front window as her uncle backed out of the driveway. "He's like a second dad to me; we're fortunate to have him."

"You couldn't be more right," Belle replied. He and your dad were great buddies growing up. I think he almost misses John as much as I do. Say, since I'm planning to go with the children over to their apartment and stay with them until their grandparents arrive, I'll walk so you can have our car to drive to work.

"Was John your husband?" Sissy asked quietly.

"Yes," Belle answered, sighing heavily. "Let's get these dishes cleaned up. Esther, you made this delicious meal, so you need to go take a good nap before going back to work. Thanks so much for the meal."

"Thank you so much!" the children said in chorus, recognizing their manners would be remiss by not responding.

"I think chicken piccata's now my favorite food, but I don't think you should wait for me to grow up to marry me; you'd be too old," Danny commented.

"It probably isn't nice to tell a lady she's too old," Sissy corrected.

"But in any case he's actually right," Esther agreed. "I'm delighted that you enjoyed the food, and I am going to take the nap. Have fun with your grandparents, and I'll be praying for both your mom and your dad."

"I doubt that'll do much good," Danny contradicted. "They haven't acted like very good parents, so God may not listen."

"I believe God cares about them no matter how they've behaved," Esther replied. "His bringing them back to you may be God's response to my prayers or because of His grace and forgiveness."

"So what's grace?" Danny asked.

"It's doing nice things for you that you don't deserve."

"Why?"

"Because that's the way God is; he does good things for bad people all the time."

"That doesn't make any sense. Why be good if God's going to be good to you even if you're bad?"

"If you're good and honor Him, He has even better things for you than otherwise," Esther said, smiling and giving him a hug and walking off to her room shutting the door.

"Are you children up to helping me in the kitchen?" Belle asked.

"Sure," Sissy replied. "We do it all at home; do you want me to bring things from the table?"

"Yes, bring them in and I'll show you where to set them. Danny, you can stand here in front of the sink where I'll hand the dishes to you and you can rinse them off before I put them in the dishwasher. The more we stay busy, the faster the time will go before your grandparents arrive."

"I like the yellow on the walls in here," Danny said as he glanced about the room, diligently working at his task. "It looks warm and happy."

"Thanks," smiled Belle, "I feel the same way. When I first painted it, I was afraid I'd gotten carried away making the yellow too deep a color, but now I'd feel something was missing if it were different."

"Well, I like all those teacups on the ledge up there," complimented Sissy, pointing to the high ledge above the cupboards. "Do you collect them?"

"Yes, well, I did and do," Belle responded. "John used to travel a good deal and he'd bring them back for me on his trips, and I'd buy them on our vacations to commemorate the event. See this thin one with the green shamrocks? I bought it when he surprised me and took me to Ireland for an anniversary," she said, pausing. "He was killed in a motor vehicle accident five years ago, and I've not added many since."

Conversation drifted on and the pleasant group finished their task, soon slipping into their coats and heading in the cold crisp afternoon for the apartment several blocks away. A light breeze caught Danny's hair as he danced along the sidewalk backwards while maintaining a conversation with his two companions. "The grands are coming! The grands are coming!" he exclaimed in glee.

"Be careful where you're going," his sister warned, smiling.

"Where do you think they are now?" Danny asked, addressing Belle.

Belle looked at her watch. "I suspect they're probably going through Kansas City by now. It's only a couple more hours now or less until they arrive. Do you think there's anything we need to do before they get here—preparation for their coming?"

"The apartment's pretty straight; it's as clean as we can get it, anyhow," Sissy considered.

"We have a little food; we're not very good cooks, so we're just eating the basics. It will be so fun to cook with Grandma again; when I was very small, she used to allow me to sit on the counter with her while she was fixing food. Before Mom left, she hardly cooked at all; we ate food out of packages that she warmed up, and Dad complained that food like that cost too much. She said she was too tired to fix other food. They seemed to complain about everything each other did. Why do you suppose they were so unhappy?"

"Part of being happy in life," Belle said, "is intending to be happy in spite of the way things are. Most of us can find things about which we can be unhappy, but if we focus on the good things, our brains do better staying happy. In fact, I think that's what joy means. It means intending to be happy in spite of the circumstances."

"It's hard to be happy when you're cold and hungry," Danny contributed.

"Yes, you're right. But I have some friends who live in a small house over close to the river. They have very little money, and to be frugal they leave their house cool in the wintertime and barely have enough to eat, but they're some of the happiest people I know. They like to sing; she plays the piano, and they wear their coats in the house much of the winter. Their house is clean even though plain, and she makes quilts to sell while he can hardly do anything because of a stroke. I wonder how they survive, but they're certainly happy."

"I don't think I can be that way," Danny declared. "When I'm cold I'm grumpy, and I'm grumpy when I'm hungry, too."

"Part of it is growing up, I suppose," responded Belle. "Part of it, though, for me is to intend to be happy and to consider all the good things there are in life. Also, trusting God for the future helps."

"How can you trust God for the future if He's not helping you now?" Danny queried.

"Well, most of the time like now if I'm honest, I have to admit that He is helping me. You know this is a pretty serious conversation we're having."

"Yeah—yes," Danny corrected himself, grinning, "that's the best kind because you get things accomplished in your brain."

"You!" Sissy said with a somewhat proud motherly smile on her face, "take the cake!"

"We live on the third floor," she explained as they entered the apartment building and started up the stairs.

Belle was taken aback as she entered the rooms after the children had unlocked the door. The place was dingy, the walls bare, the carpets grimy, and the furniture scarred. However, she recognized that there was no clutter either on the floor or on the counters, and that there were no dirty dishes in the sink.

"You need to see the new books we bought at the used bookstore," Danny offered as soon as they arrived. He moved to the coffee table and displayed his trove. "We can't check books out at the library, so we got these to read here. Do you like to read about the civil war?"

"I'm not very knowledgeable about it, but I find it interesting," Belle replied.

"Well, come let me show you some of the pictures. Have you ever been to Vicksburg or to Gettysburg?"

"I've been to Vicksburg and gone through the Civil War cemetery there with John. We got to see many monuments in honor of the men of the various fighting units that lost lives. There's also a place by the interstate where you can climb up a hill overlooking the river where cannons were placed to control the river traffic. They still have some cannons there now."

"Oh, really? Neato!"

"I thought it was sad, considering all the people that died on those hills in the cemetery."

"Dad said his great, great uncle was killed in the war, but I don't know where that was. He also said that Mom had relatives that were from the South and that they might even have been shooting at one another. I think that's a scary thought!"

The time passed, and Belle kept the children engaged reading and discussing their homework assignments. The children, at intervals, would look out the kitchen window, which had a good view of the street, particularly if they heard the slam of a car door. Belle was reading aloud to them when a knock did come.

"They're here, they're here!" Danny crowed as he rushed to open the door, but as the door opened, he became suddenly shy, saying, "Come in please," in a quiet formal manner.

The Taylors had heard the noisy excited announcement through the door but hesitated at the sudden formality. "Good evening, young man," Thelma greeted pleasantly. "Are you perhaps related to us?"

"Oh, yes!" Danny exclaimed. "We're so glad you came; we've been waiting and waiting!"

Thelma knelt, saying, "Well then, give me a hug!"

Danny hugged, bursting into sobs, "I'd almost forgotten what you were like." He didn't turn loose.

Jonathan, realizing the swell of emotion, stepped in, "Hello, ladies, we're glad we're here too!"

Sissy who had been moving toward the door from her seat on the couch rushed to him, saying in a tearful breaking voice. "Oh, Grandpa!" She leapt into his arms, put her arms around his neck, and wept as well.

Both Thelma and Jonathan struggled to maintain their composure, steadily holding the children they'd missed so much now being grateful they were finding them unharmed. When Sissy slid down from his arms, Jonathan kept his hand on her shoulder and continued his greeting. "You must be Mrs. Jonas; we are terribly grateful about your help with the children! I'm certain you can understand our concern for them."

Belle replied with a gracious grin, "I do, I do. To know them is to love them. In a way, they've grown up too young, but they're doing well. I know you must be worried sick about their dad. I didn't realize until today that their dad was missing; even yesterday when they called you, I didn't know. It was fortunate that they showed up at church this morning, and I felt then that I ought to stay with them until you arrived. This afternoon we discussed their dad's situation with my brother-in-law who's a police chief. He thinks we need to get in touch with the authorities as soon as possible to report a missing person. The children were fearful of notifying the police because of Child Protective Services involvement. Now that you're here every day's important, but my brother-in-law thought tomorrow would be OK."

Thelma, still hugging, looked up, "Do we have any idea who would take him at gunpoint? I'm sorry, I should introduce myself. I'm Thelma. Where do we think he got the money?"

"I don't think he was selling drugs," Danny stated loyally. "He hated drugs!"

"What makes you say that?" Jonathan asked cautiously.

Danny glanced at his sister but forged ahead, "He was very mad at Mom for her using drugs. We heard him say so many, many times. Finally when she wouldn't quit he told her to leave, and he told her then too that he hated drugs. I just don't understand why he could have been so against drugs but then would drink so much."

Thelma and Jonathan exchanged glances; Danny's comments were revealing much of what they'd not known but feared. Indirectly they'd known of Elaine's drug use but not of her leaving nor of Zack's drinking. "I'd hate to think he stole the money," Jonathan said. "In spite of everything, he always did seem to have a good sense of honesty and justice."

"If it were stolen, you'd expect the police to be picking him up, not armed men," Thelma observed. "Unfortunately, it does sound like some criminal element is involved. Children, did you ever hear of anything that sounded like he knew anyone in the mafia or organized crime?"

The children looked at each other and Sissy said slowly, "No, I don't think we ever even talked about it."

"Oh, I did once," Danny corrected. "I was telling Dad about a book I read about the mafia. He said he knew there were some in Chicago where he grew up, but he didn't think there were any here in St. Joseph."

"At this point, we need to make it a matter of prayer," Belle commented. "I need to be on my way, and I know these children are getting hungry. It has been such a wonderful thing to be with them that I don't want to lose touch. They do have my phone numbers. We can all be praying for your dad, children. Please let me know how things go with the police investigation. My daughter and I are here, and as you're planning on going to Texas, if you need someone to do something here please let me know."

"You can't imagine how grateful we are for your help!" Jonathan exclaimed. "Thank you so much again," he continued as Thelma moved over to Belle, giving her a hug.

"You've been a dear; you've been a friend when we needed you and didn't initially know we needed you. We will call. Thank you again!"

As Belle departed, Jonathan asked, "Well, what will it be for supper? How about some IHOP?"

"Are you certain that won't cost too much?" Danny queried.

"I believe we can work it into the budget," his grandpa answered. "We need to call your uncle Evan and tell him that we're with you."

"How old is he, and what does he do?" Danny asked. "We met a nice nurse, Belle's daughter, this afternoon, and she needs a husband."

"He's thirty; he lives in Belize working on an engineering project, but he's engaged to a teacher down there."

"Oh, wow, so he's an engineer then? What are they building? Isn't Belize one of the little tiny countries in Central America?"

"Hey, right you are. They're revising the sanitation system in the city. He's been there a couple years but likely will come back to the states fairly soon. You children put on your coats so we can get going."

"So, when are they getting married?" Sissy asked, twirling into her coat.

"I don't believe the date's been set yet, nor do they know where the wedding will be. It is a problem for them because they have friends in so many places," Thelma said. "We'll just have to wait and see; we will all want to go to it!"

"I think weddings are so sweet," Sissy said dreamily.

"I think they're really serious," Danny corrected.

"I think you're both right," Jonathan agreed, chuckling as they walked out the door and down the hall.

CHAPTER VI

WEDNESDAY MARCH 11

Zack slept fitfully and awoke the next morning feeling bleary-eyed and out of sorts. When he read his note from Herman, all it said was "There's plenty of time to tell me about yourself. I think you're doing great; keep it up. I'm here to be your backup and to keep you out of trouble as much as I can. I find this daily grind very frustrating, and I daily have to remind myself to trust in God!"

More God, Zack thought negatively. *I wonder if a person runs into this everywhere.* He cleaned up, did his exercise and, as the bell rang, patiently resumed with the same job as the previous day. His mind wandered as he moved through the day. When the lunch hour arrived, he was more than ready for the break. When the food was brought in, four men accompanied it. The man with the food set it on a chair and pulled a gun out of his pocket, pointing it at Zack. "Take offa your shirt an get downa on your knees," he commanded in a strong accent.

Zack looked at Herman, who nodded surreptitiously and complied with the command.

"Head on da floor," the gunman demanded. "Whip ya some sense into dis rat," he continued addressing his cohorts.

Zack heard leather belts being pulled from jeans and then felt stinging lashes as both men used their belts on his back. He did his best not to cry out, but the pain was intense. After thirty to forty lashes (Zack didn't keep track), the gunman said, "Dat oughtta assist his thinkin'. Youa fellows have a nicea lunch; you be certain donna get started late."

Zack was angry, hurting, and embarrassed. He looked at Herman who looked him back in the eye and slowly shook his head. Zack was silent as he slowly put his shirt back on. The welts burned as the cloth lay on his skin. *What did I do to cause that?* he wondered. He ate slowly and turned to his afternoon's work.

When he checked the wastebasket for messages that evening, Herman had written. "Most times there's a recognized reason for the beatings, but sometimes there isn't. I probably should have warned you. These men are mean and dangerous, as you can see. Every day is a definite challenge not to irritate them in any way. They may have had instructions to beat you when you arrived. Keep your chin up; remember that we have food, something to drink, and each other."

Zack wrote another note thanking Herman and outlining some of his own history including the circumstances of his abduction. "It's really like we're slaves here, isn't it," he wrote in his last sentence. "Do you think God is punishing me for my behavior?"

Later that evening, after more exercise, he read another note from Herman. "It is slavery! Precisely! Who's to know what the punishment of God is. I think often the bad things that happen to us are the results of wrong decisions in our lives rather than God delivering punishment. Had you not decided to go gambling, this never would have happened to you. These evil people wouldn't have had any contact with you. What we must do now is focus on survival from day to day and pray for this to end! Are you a person who trusts in God?"

Zack's written response was, "I haven't really even considered God. I know I've been pretty stupid about the way I've run my life, and I've always felt that God didn't exist, and even if he did exist, that he'd likely not do much either way no matter what I did. This may have been just more of my stupid thinking. If God can get us out of this situation, I'll have a hard time not believing. It seems awfully grim! I'm willing to pray if you think that'll help. We've got very little to lose. When I was young and home with my family, we went to church regularly; I resented it, and as soon as I went to college, there was no more church for me. My brother, however, stayed in church, stayed in school, and is somewhere here in Belize for his job. I guess I should pray that I can find him or that he could find me."

Zack went on to bed but again had a difficult time sleeping. He not only continued to feel ill at ease about his circumstances, but also every time he'd move he'd reawaken with the pain of the welts on his back.

The next morning he awoke feeling as bad as he'd felt the day before. *Another bum day*, he thought. *I wonder if I'll get another whipping today.* Again he got up, did his exercise routine, ate breakfast, and started his tasks when the bell rang. He grinned at Herman, who only frowned back gesturing with his head and eyes toward the camera. *Boy*, he thought, *not interacting with someone else at all is extremely hard.*

The day progressed as before with lunch at noon as well as the exchange of the vats of drugs and coffee. However, early afternoon the cans on the conveyor belt stopped, and later that afternoon they heard gunshots outside the door. No one brought supper. The lights remained on, and the two men attempted to maintain their usual routine of exercise. Herman's note that evening read, "This has never happened before. There's always been food. Sometimes the belts have stopped early, and a couple times we've heard gunshots. We need to have a plan of getting out of here; I doubt that all the other workers in this place know we're in here. I think they see the cans come in here on a conveyor and see them come out with lids and labels and assume that the two activities are mechanically automated. I suspect only the owner/operators and the security men with the cameras know our existence and function. Tomorrow if there's no food, I think we should risk trying to get a response from the camera men. Do you have any suggestions for an exit plan?"

After reading Herman's note, Zack looked around. The rooms had almost no articles that seemed of any use to break out of the metal walls and the metal doors. The beds were regular canvas army cots that could be disassembled, leaving canvas and wooden braces. The chairs were one-piece plastic lawn chairs. The can washer, however, was heavy and on locked wheels. He returned to the restroom and wrote, "I think we could unhook the washer, unlock the wheels, and ram it into the door. It would make a huge amount of racket. You're right, we can't last long without food, and we don't want to allow ourselves to get weak before we make a move. We also have no desire to have someone come shoot us. What can we do to take care of ourselves once we're out? My hair's pretty ragged, and our clothes are their standard issue, so they'd be able to recognize us. We have no money." He left the note and winked at Herman as soon as he'd left the lavatory.

Herman let no grass grow under his feet before he was back reading the note and writing. "Good idea! I wish I'd thought of it. I think we can take the coffee and sell it by the can in the market. We could use unlabeled cans, promote it as second rate so as to sell it at a very low price to get it to move. That way we wouldn't be misrepresenting it. There are probably forty or fifty unlabeled cans we could fill and lid; we'd have a tough time hauling more than that anyhow, and I'd certainly like not have to come back here. Let's think about it, pray over it, and sleep on it Let's see how things are going in the morning."

The men continued their evening routine, but again in the early part of the night Zack slept poorly. The next morning he awakened later than usual with no warning signal having rung. Fortunately the lights were still on, so the men cleaned themselves and prepared for the day. Two hours after breakfast would normally have appeared, Herman stood up waving his hands wildly directly under the camera. "Is anyone there?" he asked first in a normal tone. With no response, he yelled the same question. There was still no response. "I think we need to start placing lids on the coffee," he said. If they should still come and question our activity, we can let them know we're attempting to stay busy. Let's stack them in piles here in this room."

"What a relief to be able to talk!" Zack exclaimed.

"For the time being in case there's still monitoring, let's keep our comments to a minimum," Herman cautioned.

The two set about running full cans of coffee through the lid machine and setting them on the floor in stacks.

"I'm terribly hungry," complained Zack. "Do you think we should wait until night?"

"Probably," Herman said slowly. "It's risky no matter when we do it, but it might be a little safer at night."

"How long do you think we could go without food before we start to weaken?" Zack asked.

"Longer than until tonight," Herman answered. "Let's be certain to not get dehydrated, but we'll likely be able to move better without full stomachs. Do you think we can make these cots into carrying racks?"

The men set about trying various ways of folding the canvas in the cots after disassembling them attempting to fix backpacks for the cans of coffee. They then unhooked and pulled out the large washing machine; the wheels screeched loudly as they started to move it and startled them. They laughed in relief at themselves, recognizing how anxious they felt with the possible danger of their activities.

"Night's still a long way off," Herman said, chuckling. "Let's put the cots back together and try to nap while we wait."

Contrary to Zack's expectation, they were both sleeping soundly in a few minutes. He awakened several hours later in total darkness. Not only were the lights off in the building, but the fans had stopped as well. The quietness seemed deafening. He lay listening to crickets inside the building and was surprised he'd not been able to hear them earlier with the noise of the fans.

"Hey, Herman," he whispered loudly. "The electricity's off, and it's totally dark."

"I hope its dark outside, too," Herman responded groggily. "Man, we can't see anything! How long do you think we've slept? There are no windows in these rooms, but there's a small crack on one side of the door; I don't see any light coming in there, so it must be dark outside as well.

This area was hit by a hurricane several years ago and has never recovered well, so there are a lot of empty spaces and very little shelter once we get outside. Do you think we can get these cots apart and loaded with coffee in the dark?"

"Maybe we should smash the door open first and gather up the coffee later," Zack considered fumbling about in the dark.

"Well, let's at least try. We may need to leave in a hurry after making all our noise," Herman surmised. But a bit later he said, "This is going no place; let's give our battering ram a try."

Both men got behind the washing machine, feeling unstable in their movements in the blackness. "Stop," Herman commanded, "let's pray first. We will need God's help now if we ever will." He forged on ahead, "God, please help us knock this door open in the name of Jesus Christ!"

"Amen!" agreed Zack. "One, two, three, push!"

The wheels screeched again, and the machine crashed resoundingly against the door without breaking through. However, a crack had appeared in the doorframe, and the men could see some distant lights of the city. Again and again they crashed until the door suddenly twisted, leaving a passable opening.

"Thank you, Jesus!" Herman exclaimed.

The men then stood together quietly listening for any response to their actions. No sound was forthcoming and they moved, feeling around in the dark to gather their canvases and coffee cans. They then set out with their loads, staying on the darkened streets. The electricity was off in the whole area, but there were lights ahead, toward which they made their way.

"How much danger do you think we're in at this point?" Zack asked.

"There's some anywhere in the city just because of the gangs and poor police coverage, especially at night," Herman replied. "By the fact that you're a big bruiser and that we have these wooden cot braces in our hands, we probably don't look too vulnerable, but then sometimes the gangs will confront any sign of strength just to assert their power."

"Are you pretty well acquainted with the city?"

"Yes, quite a bit. Even though they moved the capital to Belmopan back in the seventies after hurricane Hattie, it's still the largest city in the country, so most of the business still goes on here. There's been a good deal of tourism, but even that is getting damaged with the rise of the gangs and drug trade."

"Do you think we should be going to the police?"

"No, there's a big risk of the police recognizing our clothes as our involvement with one of the drug operations. We could in the worst case be put in jail, and then turned back over to our captors out of fear by the police of reprisal should it be learned that we were assisted. I think our best bet is to lay low until we can get cleaned up with different clothes."

"Do you think there's a Salvation Army or YMCA that could help us? How about me finding the American embassy? Perhaps there's a public phone booth where we could find the addresses for those. If Belize City's the largest town, I'm still hoping my brother might be here."

"Yes?" Herman questioned, "What does he do?"

"I'm not certain. I believe it has to do with a US-funded reconstruction project or something like that. I don't think its military, but I'm not sure. He'd have no idea that I'm in the country, and to show up without calling him would really knock his socks off."

"What's knock off your socks mean?"

"It means a big surprise."

There were two utility trucks driving down the street toward them with flashing lights that stopped a quarter block away. Zack and Herman slowed their pace watching men get out and move the trucks in position for repair of the high lines.

"That explains the power outage," Zack commented. "Don't you think it would be OK to ask them if a YMCA or Salvation Army center exist?"

"Sure, let's walk closer, and you stay with our stuff on the other side of the street while I go over by myself and ask. We don't want to appear intimidating at all. Sometimes these night utility crews have trigger-happy security people with them."

Herman walked over, conversing with the workers for some time and returned to say, "Both organizations are here. They didn't think the Y had any bedrooms; they thought it was an exercise place, but they gave me the address of the Salvation Army. It's 41 Regent Street; we go back to Caesar Ridge Road, follow it to Yarborough Road, and then that turns and becomes Regent Street. It's in some of the oldest part of the city. They said it was past the Coningsby Inn, and I know where that is. We'll need to walk at least a couple miles. Even if they can't bed us down, they'll likely have clothes and let us use a phone. Fortunately we've had a good nap."

"Yeah, I'm not tired, but I'm extremely hungry," Zack responded, "but I'm so glad to get out of that prison some hunger's a small price to pay. Did you by any chance ask anything about the shooting we heard? Did they know why the electricity was out?"

"They said it looked like the lines had been vandalized, so I'm expecting the two may be related, and the sooner we get away from this area the better it'll be," Herman replied.

The two men trudged in silence, carrying their loads and walking along the side of the street. There was minimal traffic, and the area appeared commercial and run-down with a number of vacant buildings. They met a pedestrian who briefly nodded showing no interest in them. They moved steadily from one patch of light to another along the dimly lit road. A police cruiser moved up the street slowly behind them, slowing even more as it passed them. Zack looked at the officer and nodded; the fellow nodded back. Zack felt relieved, saying, "He likely thinks we're a couple bums."

"Belize City is filled with all kinds of people, so he can hardly tell what types he's dealing with. Probably as long as we look quiet and not threatening we're OK. This area of town used to be quite nice when I was a kid. Since the British are mostly gone and with the rise of the drug cartels and lack of safety, almost everything is doing worse than it was. I don't know how it can be fixed. With as much money as the US has, and they still have problems, our country seems hopeless to me. I know we need to keep trying, but it's no wonder so many of the younger ones are constantly seeking ways to emigrate to the US or thinking about it. I've always considered myself a pretty loyal citizen, and see what's happened to me? I must get back in touch with my family, but I don't want to endanger them by doing so. I'll need to be cautious."

"I wonder if you might not qualify for asylum in the US," Zack offered. "I could talk with the consulate at the embassy, if you wish, when I go there. Do you think the embassy is here?"

"Talking wouldn't hurt; I have no idea what I'll be able to do since I've no idea how things stand at home. I know the US embassy used to be here, but I think I heard it was being moved or had been moved to Belmopan."

"Hey, here's Yarborough Road," Zack said, pointing up to a dilapidated street sign, "What time do you think it is?"

"The utility men said it was nine o'clock when we were there. They didn't know how late the Salvation Army stayed open. I'm hoping until ten. I've understood that a lot of mission type places have a religious service most evenings that people must attend before they can get a bed."

"We can do that."

"Yes, but it may already be over before we arrive. Fortunately, it's neither too hot nor too cold; we could sleep outdoors if necessary."

"How safe would that be? I guess we could take watch shifts if we needed to. We'll hurry and then see."

The two men walked along in silence, each contemplating the reordering of their lives and hoping steps could be made to better their situations. Zack thought about the children and feared for their safety. He considered the best way to contact his brother. Should he try to contact his folks first? He knew their old Chicago phone number but had heard from a mutual acquaintance that they were moving down to Florida. He remembered the unopened Christmas card and kicked himself for being such a self-centered, self-indulging idiot. His face burned with anger at himself; his emotion then turned to embarrassment and concern as he thought about his wife. *God*, he prayed to himself. *Let me have a chance to make this right for them. Help me get back!*

Herman thought about his dead brother and how he'd died protecting the family. He wondered if the family was still on the farm or if it had been seized by the drug cartel. He considered the safest way to contact them and decided to call a cousin first rather than make direct contact with his immediate family. "Here's the beginning of Reagent Street," he said as the road curved to their left, "the ocean's only a block over there." He pointed to his right.

"Not much wind or waves," Zack commented, "I can smell it but I can't hear it over the traffic noise. We must be closer to where the action is. I think that's the inn sign ahead, isn't it?"

Arriving at the address, they recognized the Salvation Army sign. "It looks like there's a school here but no people," Zack observed.

"Maybe we can walk around back," Herman suggested. The two men followed a sidewalk near the first building and approached a lighted residence in the rear. Zack knocked; he waited and knocked again. Finally he heard footsteps, and a lady's voice called out through the door, "Who's there?"

"Two men needing assistance," Zack answered.

"I'll get my husband; he'll be here in a bit," she replied.

Soon there were more footsteps and the rattling of keys in the lock before the inside door opened, leaving the screen door shut. "I'm Officer Smith. How can I help you, fellows?" a pleasant middle-aged man greeted them.

"We've just escaped from imprisonment by a drug cartel and are needing shelter and food and to contact out families," Zack replied. "Are you able to help us?"

"Wow, how'd that all happen? You'd better come in and tell me about it," the man said as he unlocked and opened the screen door. "This is my wife Linda. Sweetheart, please go fix each of these fellows a couple sandwiches," he directed as he motioned the men into chairs at a rough table. "So where are you from?" he asked.

"We met at the drug cartel coffee/drug packaging factory where we were imprisoned," Zack began.

"I'm Zack Taylor from St. Joseph, Missouri, and my buddy here's from Belize; he had a farm near Punta Gorda that the cartel took over after killing his brother in the process. He doesn't know if his family's alive or not, and he's fearful of contacting them directly. I was taken prisoner by the drug lords because I would not return money to them I'd won gambling in a card game. I'd been drinking. After they took me in, I went into DTs because they weren't giving me alcohol. I realized at the time what a fool I'd been, but by then I was on my way down here. Herman's encouraged me to trust in God, so that's sort of why we're here. I have a younger brother who is in Belize working as an engineer. I'm hoping I can contact him and perhaps he can help Herman and his family escape to the US. Do you have suggestions as to how we can reach him, Officer?"

"Call me Jim," he replied. "So what's your brother's name? Do you think he lives in Belize City?"

"All I know is that he was in Belize and that was a couple years ago, but the project he'd been assigned to was pretty large. His name is Evan Taylor."

"Evan Taylor? I thought you looked familiar; you're built just like the Evan Taylor I know!" Jim exclaimed.

"You think you know him?" Zack asked, nonplussed.

Herman who had been quietly listening to the interchange, whispered, "Well, praise to God!"

"I'll be surprised if he's not the one," Jim said. "He's been here a couple years; he's an engineer working on the revamping of the city sanitation system, and we know him well because he's engaged to one of the teachers in our school. I don't have his number but I have hers. He lives on the other side of town."

Zack was nearly overcome with emotion and relief. "Thank you, thank you!" he exclaimed. "He'll have a difficult time believing I'm here because I've had no contact with him for years and years. How soon can we call?"

"I'll call Alice Seymour, his fiancée, now, and you fellows eat this food," Jim instructed as his wife entered with a plate of sandwiches. "I'll bet that neither hell nor high water could keep your brother from helping you out."

"How exciting!" Linda squealed. "I heard from the kitchen. Evan is going to be so tickled! Eat now."

The two men bowed their heads, and Herman prayed, "Lord, thank you for this food and for this miracle." They ate, both attempting not to wolf the food down impolitely.

"Hey Alice," Jim said after dialing, "can you believe that one of your future relatives came knocking on our door this evening? Its Evan's brother, Zack. I need Evan's phone number. Yes, he seems OK. Oh, so he's been worried about him and praying for him? Well, he's going to be a happy guy. Sure, you can come over if you wish; I'm certain Evan will want you to know. We'll see you in a bit. Yeah, I have pencil and paper in hand," he said, jotting down the number. "Bye."

"Do you want to call him or do you want me to?" Jim asked.

"You'd better," Zack replied, "I think he'll handle it better initially from you."

The number was dialed and a voice responded. "Hi, Evan, it's Jim. Are you doing OK tonight? Well, you probably better sit down; I've got some big news for you. Are you sitting? Your brother Zack is here at our place needing your help. He's fine; he's just finished eating a couple sandwiches. He's with a friend who may also need your help. Yes, he looks fine, maybe a little rough with long hair and all, but considering what he's been through with a drug cartel, he looks great. Sure, come on now. I had to call Alice to get your number, and she's on her way over as well. Don't drive crazy. Be safe. Bye!"

After hanging up, Jim asked, "How was it you fellows got free?"

"We don't actually know," Herman replied. "We'd heard gunshots yesterday, and then they stopped bringing us food. Then the plant stopped running. We were locked in, so we had to bash the door down to get out. We don't know whether there are any of our captors around yet, so we need to be very cautious about who sees us, especially in these clothes, which are apparently like a uniform for their prisoners. I sort of blend in with the native population, but Zack's too big to miss. Even if he trims his hair and grows a beard, he's probably recognizable."

"If I were to shorten and bleach my hair and then hang around with Evan, we'd look like obvious brothers. That might work," Zack suggested. "We do look a lot alike except my hair's always been much darker. When we were high schoolers, people would get us confused even with the hair color difference."

"The drug traffic men are a horrible, increasing problem," Jim explained, "Belize City's not big, only about sixty thousand or so, but we're regularly hearing of deaths related to the problem. These men are out there, and who's to know who they are. Our school hasn't been involved, but attendees at our church have been. You're sensible to lay low until you're pretty certain of your disguise. Honestly, I do think you'll be better off with your brother who's a known foreigner than here with us; I have to think of the safety of the school children."

"Well, thank you for your help; that makes sense. We certainly don't wish to bring you harm," Zack responded. "How long do you think it'll be until Evan gets here?"

"Oh, it takes only fifteen minutes or so to drive across town. It's not late, so traffic blocks won't be up yet generally. We remain suspicious of the police with the amount of drug trafficking. We keep hearing rumors of corruption, but the paper doesn't report it. We do have a room over at the school full of used clothes sent by American churches and can go over there and at least get different togs for you. We'll go now," Jim replied.

With that, the men headed off to look at the available options. Jim led, locking the door behind him and unlocking the rear entrance of the school building. "It's ironic, but we'll have less difficulty outfitting Zack than Herman. Since most men in this area are not large, we have all these clothes from American men who are big."

Clothes were chosen, and the men were directed to the restrooms to change. "We'll burn the clothes tomorrow," Jim said. "If they might be dangerous for you, they might be dangerous for anyone else too. Hey, a car's pulled up in front. That's probably Evan. I'll bring him back; you stay here."

"Hi, Evan," he called, "we're out here. Come on around."

Zack watched his brother walk around the schoolhouse in the dim moonlight wondering how much his years of rejection would affect things. Evan simply walked up to him, giving no opportunity for a hand-shake, reached out, hugged him silently, holding his arms at his sides. Zack could see the glisten of tears on Evan's face as he stepped back.

"The folks called and told me Sissy and Danny had called them and that you were taken at gunpoint," he said. "We were afraid we'd lost you, man! What's gone on? Why are you here?"

"I want to tell you, but first what do you know about the kids? Has anyone heard from Elaine by any chance?"

"No word on Elaine; the children found an old Christmas card with the folk's address and phone number and contacted them in Florida, and they've gone up to St. Joe to pick them up. Apparently, they're taking them down to Texas to be with Elaine's parents."

"Do you know if they're OK? I was such a fool taking care of them. I'd left them some money, but I should have given it back considering what's happened."

Evan regarded Zack seriously, "As miserable as you may have been, you're a different guy than the brother who told me to leave and never return. What did happen?"

Zack reviewed his gambling, the capture, the DTs, his recognition of his own selfish behavior, the journey, and the factory work, and the influence of Herman's faith briefly as the four men moved inside to sit around the table. Soon there was a knock at the door, and Alice made her entrance.

"Hi, sweetie," Evan said, standing and giving Alice a peck on the fore-head. "Here's my big brother and his friend, Herman. Fellows, meet my wife-to-be, Alice Seymour!"

As Alice approached Zack, shyly extending her hand, she said graciously, "What a surprise to see you! Evan's nearly lost his appetite recently worrying about you. We simply had no idea you were anywhere near us. You fellows certainly look like brothers; you could almost be twins!" She then greeted Herman, "Thank you for being his friend; how did you meet?"

Zack again recounted his mishaps and adventures finishing with Herman's plight and then asked, "Where do we all go from here?"

"To my place for tonight. I have a guest bedroom at my apartment where Herman can sleep. Zack can bunk in with me, so I can suffocate him if he snores," Evan answered, grinning, "We can sort things out tomorrow with the US embassy and all."

"You may be bigger and stronger than in the past," Zack said, "but you're still my little brother. You may attempt to suffocate me, but the chances of it happening are slim to nothing." Turning to Alice he continued, "Tell him he's the host, and it wouldn't be polite to suffocate a guest."

"I will let his conscience guide him!" she said archly with a smile. "I am not privy to the accounts of the past that need to be settled, so I'll refrain from interfering.

"Don't expect any support from her against him," Linda offered.

"Yeah, you need to remember they're in that early phase of love wherein the other has no faults," Jim explained.

"But really, he doesn't have any faults!" Alice defended seriously as the others looked at each other, laughing.

"Hey, I love you!" Evan declared. "You're my champ. Keep it up! We need to get going so these folk can get on to bed; there's school tomorrow. Alice, thank you for coming; let me walk you out to your car," he said, taking her hand and leading her to the door.

"See how nice he is?" Alice supported her position, looking back over her shoulder.

"Thank you! Thank you again," Zack said to Jim and Linda following Herman to the door. "It was amazing how you were able to help us."

"You need to remember God had a hand in this," Jim responded. "Yes I helped, but the circumstances were arranged by God."

"I want to give a hearty amen to that," Herman added, "but I do want to thank you for your willingness to be His hands here in this city. Also, thank you for the food and clothes. God bless you," he concluded, shaking Jim and Linda's hands.

Zack and Herman walked around to the front of the building where Evan was completing his goodbyes to Alice. "We'll follow you home and then go on out to my place," Evan instructed as she drove off, rolling up her window. "Hop in, guys; it's unlocked," he said, turning to the two men. "We're having to be increasingly security-conscious," he explained. "Roadblocks are increasingly common, and you never know what some policeman may require unexpectedly. Your driver's license and car registration are all that is required by law, but sometimes they'll want your passport and other items if they think you're a foreigner and don't know the laws. They'll mention a large fine and then a discounted amount if you'll pay right then in cash."

Evan had hardly finished his explanation when uniformed officers with red flashlights halted Alice ahead of them. They sat in line quietly behind her and moved up as the police motioned them forward.

"Where are you gentlemen heading tonight?" the portly officer questioned.

"I'm following my fiancée, the lady just ahead of us to see she gets home safely," Evan replied.

"Who are the gents with you?"

"My brother and a friend. Do you need my license?" Evan answered, handing him the required documents.

"Thanks," the officer said, looking summarily at the papers, handing them back, and motioning them on.

"That could have been much worse!" Zack sighed with relief as they drove on following Alice, who'd slowed ahead of them waiting for them. "Like as not they could have asked for your papers, too, which of course you don't have. The sooner I get you to the embassy, the better. We'll probably try to drive over to Belmopan tomorrow. Herman, how do you plan to contact your family? Maybe we should ask at the embassy the safest way to accomplish that contact."

"I have a cousin in Punta Gorda who probably knows what's going on," Herman offered. "In case his home is wiretapped, I could call him with a cryptic message that only he would understand but would know it's from me, and he could call me back on a payphone. I feel so fearful about the situation that I feel nearly paralyzed about approaching it, but I know I must as soon as safely possible."

"I have several days of vacation I can take to work on these things; I've been saving them up for a honeymoon, but some can be used now," Evan offered.

"So, when is the wedding date?" Zack asked. "We obviously don't want to cut you out of that."

"The date's not been finalized; we've only been engaged a few weeks. We're still trying to work it out with my folks and hers. We thought about having it here, but then our friends from the States would have to come here, and that'd be expensive for them. She's from San Antonio, so wherever we have it some friends must go a distance. You'll probably be in Longview at least initially. Our folks are in a retirement community in Florida that doesn't allow children in residence, so the children will be with Elaine's parents until you get there. You may wish to stay there for a while until you get your feet under you. When I talked with Mom and Dad, they didn't know where you were, of course, and were already planning to move to Texas so they could help with the kids as soon as their yearly lease was up in Florida. Elaine's parents are capable but getting pretty old to care for a couple youngsters."

"You are all rearranging your lives to help; I've really been a stupid fool," Zack sighed.

"You don't know how glad they're all going to be to have you back, and for me it is as if the biggest loss in my life has been returned to me!" Evan exclaimed.

"I don't deserve you," Zack responded slowly, and silence filled the car until Alice pulled into her drive, hopped out of her vehicle, waved blowing a kiss, and disappeared into her side door.

"My place is only a few minutes from here. Are you guys still hungry? I don't have much prepared food in the house," Evan offered. "We could stop and get something if you want."

"We were terribly hungry when Linda fed us the big sandwiches," Herman said. "I'm fine now, though."

"I'm not hungry at all," Zack agreed. "My stomach is tied in knots with all that's gone on. I'm so glad the kids are OK, but I feel so guilty about Elaine."

"Why did she leave you?" Evan asked. "It seems so unlike the Elaine that I knew."

"She left because I told her to," Zack admitted. "She was using drugs and had gone through rehab programs three times and was right back using. She didn't argue; she just left. She knew she didn't want the kids exposed to drugs, I think. I've felt guilty about it ever since."

"You can't make someone else behave," Herman commented.

"You're right," Zack exhaled. "The problem was that had I helped her more with the children and dealt with her depression, it probably wouldn't have started."

"You know, accepting responsibility is a good thing," Evan offered, "but that's the past. Of course, you're probably going to want to see if Elaine can be helped down the road, but we've got to get you out of here first. Let's get you back in the US, see if we can help Herman and his family as well, and deal with all of that later. We're still young. Here's my place. Come on in and act like you're at home."

"I feel old and stupid," Zack grumbled as he got out of the car.

"I'm going to try to knock that out of you!" Evan said, punching him on the shoulder. "A little brother has to have some necessary function! Don't expect to be impressed with my digs; I am a bachelor," he added after opening the front door.

"This is sure better than our last residence," Herman laughed and followed them in. "I'm not going to miss that cot in the factory a bit. Even though we had a long nap this afternoon, I'm tired. There's been a lot of emotional water gone under the bridge since then."

"The restroom and shower are down the hall on the right. Herman, your room's the first one on the left. I'll get you some clean underclothes, which will be large but wearable, and some towels. I am so glad to have this bratty big brother back that I don't want to hear any thank-yous. It's eleven thirty, and I'm tuckered out. If you fellows want to shower and clean up, fine. I'm going on to bed," Evan said as he walked to his room, bringing back the towels and clothing.

Herman winked at Zack. "Thank you so much," he said dutifully.

"Thank you so much," Zack mimicked. "We'll be quiet."

Evan went right on to bed but Zack and Herman opted for showers. Herman showered first and Zack waited, sitting on a kitchen chair letting the events of the day wash over him. When he thought of Elaine he felt despair, but when he remembered the children, all he could think was, *Thank you, thank you, thank you, God.* After his shower, he sank quietly into bed beside his sleeping brother and stared at the ceiling. He couldn't sleep; thoughts of the despair he'd felt during the imprisonment kept replaying in his mind. Concern for his wife and children followed. Gratitude to Jim and Linda, his parents, and Elaine's parents gripped him. He wondered how they all felt about him; then he considered how they were all there when he needed them. It was as if there was no animosity at all in spite of what he'd done. Evan turned restlessly in the bed beside him.

"Are you awake?" Zack asked.

"Yeah, I was asleep until you came in, but then I woke up and can't get back to sleep."

"You're not used to someone else in your bed. I could go sleep on the couch."

"No, it's not very comfortable. Besides if I get married, I'll need to get used to sleeping with someone," Evan chuckled. "I was remembering the last time we slept together was in the state park in a tent before you ran off with Elaine. Those were good times."

"You know I've spent the last several years feeling so miserable I've not thought of all that. I think my involvement with the alcohol and wanting a drink all the time just absolutely blocked my thinking. I need to tell you how sorry I am for the way I treated you the time you came out and tried to encourage me to get back on track with my schooling, but I'd looked at our folks and decided they'd had to work too much of their lives for the rewards they'd gotten and that there was an easier way. Looking back, it was stupid thinking."

"I'll forgive you willingly," Evan said slowly. "I can't forgive you for the pain and sadness you brought to both sets of parents, but knowing them all well, I think you can count on their forgiveness, too. I agree that was stupid thinking, but I was tempted to take the same path you were and even envied you for several years seeing your freedom from school. Later as I became employed and enjoyed my work, and then for the past year having now come to know Alice, I've been so thankful I stayed on the right path. I was pretty much into working and making money until I met her, but becoming acquainted with Jim and Linda and realizing the value of helping others has opened my eyes."

"They were a Godsend to us for sure!" Zack exclaimed quietly, and the two silently drifted off to sleep.

CHAPTER VII

FRIDAY MARCH 13

The following morning the three men had breakfast, Evan notified his work of his need for at least two days off, and they sat around the kitchen table as Zack dialed the number of the American embassy on Evan's phone, inquiring as to how they could get assistance. He explained his lack of a passport and was told he needed to appear at the embassy for processing. When he additionally mentioned Herman and his need for asylum, he was told to bring him along, that a separate area of the embassy handled US citizen and native citizen requests and that even if Herman and his family needed asylum, it would be easier if they had US citizens who could be their sponsors.

"Let's clean up and get going," Zack said. "Do you think I could call the kids on our way over there?" he asked Evan.

"Sure, but you do really need a haircut," Evan considered critically.

"Yeah, I know," Zack agreed. "I thought about bleaching my hair to look like yours to look less recognizable, but if we're going to hurry right on over to Belmopan, we don't have any hair bleach, and even if we did, I wouldn't know how to use it."

"Some peroxide might work," Herman suggested.

"I don't have any of that either," Evan countered. "How about just shaving while I go get some of my stuff out of the car so we can get going. I'll get you both a couple razors," he added.

They each proceeded with their tasks, but Evan returned immediately after going outside. "Bad news, fellows," he informed. "I don't think disguise is going to be very helpful. Someone's slashed two of my tires. We're going nowhere fast. I'm calling the embassy right back to see if they can by chance send someone here with security to get you."

"But they'll likely call the police!" Herman exclaimed.

"Better they call them than us." Zack said.

"Maybe they could send the car and call the police shortly before they arrive here," Evan considered. "Maybe they wouldn't have to call the police. I'll call again to the embassy."

"Do you have a gun?" Zack asked his brother.

"No, not here, obviously. I probably should have," Evan replied as he started dialing his phone. "I only have a hunting rifle back in storage in Chicago."

The two guests returned to completing their shaving, one in the kitchen and one in the bathroom, while Evan talked with the embassy. Evan was on the phone a lengthy time, mostly at first on hold and then listening. He finished by getting a piece of paper and jotting down a couple names and numbers. "Here's the scoop," he said. "When I explained the situation, they got the consulate to come talk to me. He said he couldn't send someone to pick us up. He understood our concern with the police but felt if we had immediate difficulty, we needed to head straight to the nearest police station. If the police called, he could come get you at their request. He thinks we should still try to come there on our own if that is possible." They were all quiet as he held up his hand for a few seconds and then continued. "I have an idea. I've a good buddy at work that's sort of a car buff. He's got an old army Humvee with a souped-up motor in it. He also is a marksman and has several pistols and rifles; I bet if I called him explaining our predicament, he'd be right over! Do you fellows feel comfortable with that? He's probably at work, but he doesn't live too far away."

With the agreement of his guests, Evan called his friend Josh Ash, who was more than enthusiastic to help. Closing the call, Evan reported on Josh's response, "He says it's for situations just like this that he's prepared. When he was in the service he was a military police, so he feels pretty confident about his role, as you'll see when you meet him; he's a card to deal with, but he's got a heart of gold."

"How soon do you think he can get here?" Herman asked.

"He thought half an hour," Evan said.

"I somewhat hate to call the kids and folks if there's still danger, but they need to know where I am," Zack said.

"Yeah, they do need to know," Evan agreed. "You can keep it short, telling them we're in a rush. That way you can control the extent of the information you give," he continued, pulling up the number on his phone and handing it to Zack. "This is Dad you're calling."

Zack waited as the dialing sounded and the ringing started in his ear, but stood suddenly, walking back to the bedroom for privacy, "Hi, Dad, this is Zack," he stated quietly." There was no response on the line. "Dad, can you hear me?" he asked. "Can you hear me?"

"How are you calling from Evan's phone?" Jonathan queried. "This isn't a bad joke, is it, Evan?"

"No, Dad this is really me, Zack, calling on Evan's phone down in Belize. I was brought down here by a drug cartel because I wouldn't return money to them I'd won in a card game; I've essentially been their prisoner until late yesterday. We got out and found Evan, who is helping us get to the American embassy this morning. Are the children with you now?"

"I'm having a hard time believing it's actually you. No, the children are with your mother out getting groceries. Are you OK?"

"Well…, to be honest things are still tense, but I do believe God is helping me. I have a lot of explaining to do and a bunch of humble pie that needs to be eaten. I've made such a mess of things! I do need to ask you and Mom for forgiveness as well as the children. How are they?"

"Your children are more than fine, Son. Of course, we'll forgive. I'm afraid you'll have some backtracking to do when you see them because they're saying some pretty negative things about you."

"Dad, it's all true. I didn't take care of them properly, especially toward the end. Just tell them I love them and that I'll be a different dad when we get back together. Are you still in St. Joe?"

"Yes, but we're planning to head for Texas the day after tomorrow to be with the Dentons."

"Oh, yes," Zack said, "Evan told me, and I'll be happy to never see St. Joe again. When I get back, I'll come to Longview. How long do you plan to be there?"

"We don't know; we'll need to see how much help your in-laws need before we go back to Florida. We'll stay there until you come. Do you have any money to get a plane ticket?"

"I have nothing here, but there is the money I left the children. Do they still have it?"

"Yes, the little packrats were keeping it all in their pockets so it couldn't be stolen. After you were taken, someone came back to the apartment while they were out and tore it up they said. Where did the money come from?"

"I won it gambling in a card game, and the losers were the drug cartel men who came after me to get it back. I wish I had given it back. The drug men have the apartment manager's key. They took it from him at gunpoint and paid him not to report. Dad, I've really been dumb, and I'm embarrassed and sorry about it!"

"If you change your ways, bud, this may all be worth it. We've placed a missing person's bulletin with the local police, so I'll notify them you've been found. You may have to come back here eventually to give them any information you have on these criminals. There's a lady by the name of Belle Jonas who befriended the children and helped them to contact us. You'll need to thank her."

"Dad, I want to talk longer but I shouldn't. We've got to hurry and, like I said, things are tense. Should anything bad happen, know that I love you and Mom and the kids. Tell them that. Pray for us, and I mean it!"

"We will, we will, Son, and depend on Evan; he's pretty level-headed."

"Yeah, Dad, he's a champ, but only God can have made this happen as well as it has. Good-bye, I've got to go!" and with that he hung up, not hearing his dad say his final good-bye.

Zack headed back to the living room where Evan was furtively peering out between the window blinds at the neighborhood. "Do you see anything?" he asked.

"There's a black Mercedes down the street I don't recall having seen before. It's too far away to see if it has occupants. Josh should be here any time. I got you a jacket; the Humvee always seems cold to me, probably because he always leaves the windows down and the back open. Hey, here he comes now. Boy, has he made it in record time. Let's let him come on in and give us some idea of his plan." Evan moved to open the front door and wave his friend on in.

"What's up, bro?" Josh asked, shaking Evan's hand.

"I've noticed an unfamiliar car down the street," Evan replied.

"Yeah, I saw it too. It's a little too ritzy for even this neighborhood. There's no doubt who's your brother," he smiled, walking over to Zack and shaking his hand.

"Yeah, that's Zack, and this is Herman," Evan said. "He's the farmer from Punta Gorda imprisoned by the drug traffickers."

"If that's a surveillance car, we need to get moving and fast," Josh instructed. "As soon as they've seen my vehicle, they'll be calling in reinforcements. This is what I think we need to do: in about one minute, we all need to rush out to climb into the Humvee. It's unlocked. Who can shoot a gun?"

The brothers exchanged glances, "We both did target practice when we were high schoolers," Zack answered.

"OK, then we'll have Herman drive. Can you handle a stick shift?" he asked, then answered himself, saying, "Sure you can, you're a farmer. You drive, and, Evan, you take shotgun so you can help navigate; Zack and I will ride in back." He stripped off his shirt and a bulletproof vest, handing the vest to Herman. "Put this on quickly. I've several more in the back of the vehicle for the rest of us. Now when we start out, Herman, drive to lose them if possible. Don't do anything stupid, but make some serious tracks," he continued, redonning his shirt. "Questions? OK, let's go. Evan, lock the door."

The men quickly moved to the Humvee and were out the drive in less than fifteen seconds. Josh handed out the vests, watching out the rear window. "Yes, they're following us!" he exclaimed as he opened a case on the floor of the vehicle and started distributing the guns, handing a Colt forty-five to each of the brothers. "They're already loaded. All you need to do is release the safety to shoot. Do you need me to show you?"

"We've got it," Zack replied.

"Try to lose them; make some extra corners," Josh directed his instructions to Evan, knowing he was more likely to know the neighborhood.

After several rapid sharp corners, Josh reported, "They're not behind us, but we can't let our guard down. They've probably figured out that we'll be heading to the embassy and may try to stop us on the way."

Herman drove back on through the city to West Road leading to the capital. As they were speeding up passing a filling station on the edge of town, three bullets rattled off the right side of the Humvee, and the black car spun gravel as it entered the highway behind them. Josh rested his rifle on the back of the rear seat and attempted to focus in on the car, which was rapidly closing in. "Lower the back window, Evan," he said. "I'm going to try to take a shot at their radiator."

Zack could make out two men in the front seat of the car behind them. He jumped as Josh delivered three shots from the semiautomatic.

Josh yelled, "Get the window back up! I do believe I did it!"

The Mercedes initially came closer but then rapidly slowed, pulling off the road into the ditch. "We still can't relax," Josh informed, "because they may well have cohorts in Belmopan who'll attempt to ambush us as we get into town. We need to call in to the embassy, letting them know that we're on our way so they can be expecting us and have some firepower out by the gate as we arrive. When you call, ask for Gregg Altman. He's one of the older guards, and I think has the clout to help us out. He's a hunting buddy of mine," he finished, winking at Zack. "Tell him its Josh Ash calling; he'll answer unless he's not working. I'll talk to him."

Herman pushed the Humvee along at eighty mph; Evan got the embassy back on the line, asked for Gregg, and handed the phone to Josh, who sat nervously scanning the rear view while on hold. "Hey, man," he greeted, "I'm coming from Belize City with some legit fellows who have escaped from some drug traffickers. We're about thirty miles out; my Humvee was fired on from a black Mercedes as we left Belize City, and then it followed us but it was never close enough for me to get the license. We're headed your way and sure would like for you to arrange some fire cover as we approach the compound. OK, OK, well, call me back for further instructions."

"He didn't think there'd be a problem," Josh reported. "Herman, don't be surprised if someone attempts to pull right out in front of you, especially as we get closer to Belmopan. I think your traffickers are well-heeled and organized. If you need to graze the front of their vehicle, we can handle it. If you need to leave the road a little, we're OK with that, too, as long as we don't tip over and get stopped, and if the police start following us, head right on to the embassy. Evan, do you know the best route there? If you don't, use the GPS."

"Aye, aye, sir," laughed Evan. "I'm certainly glad I thought about your firepower for this venture!"

"Yeah, I hate think how we'd be faring without you," Zack agreed. "Have you been here in Belize long?"

"Eight years. I married a girl from here while I was in college after I got out of the service. Her family's here and I didn't have one, so I decided to stay here. Evan and I rub shoulders nearly every day at work."

"What does your wife think about all these guns and the Humvee?"

"Well, I think she thinks they're just part of the package she signed on with when she married me. She likes hunting and riding in this thing as much as I do. She'd be here with us today if she weren't eight months pregnant."

"Hunting's a bit different than being shot at, though," Zack persisted.

"Do you want me to leave?"

"No, no, oh no!" Herman inserted from the front seat.

"Ditto no," Zack grinned. "I'm just trying to figure you out."

"You can give that up," his brother laughed. "That's what I try to do every day."

The four men bantered on as they moved swiftly down the highway covering the tension they were feeling with talk. As they approached the city Herman slowed, swiftly turning left onto a gravel road.

"Hey, where are we going?" Josh asked.

"This road's a shortcut to George Price Boulevard," Herman replied. "I figure as much as we can stay off the main approach to the embassy. Stay on residential streets; we'll be less likely to pick up firepower."

"Great," Josh agreed, "there are only two good direct roads into town, and they're very likely to be covered. Don't worry about the city speed limits. If we pick up police following us, they'll be at the scene going in the gate. Evan, call Gregg back again and tell him we're close. Make certain he's ready."

Herman careened around corners while Evan made his call. "Gregg says come right on through the gate and they'll close it behind us. Don't hesitate even if it looks like there's no one around. They do see a couple suspicious vehicles in the immediate area," Evan reported.

"God be with us!" Herman prayed, racing down the residential streets, squealing his tires on each turn.

"We've got company!" Josh yelled. "Be ready to shoot as you leave the vehicle. Although these are bulletproof windows, who's to know what ammunition they may have."

As the Humvee moved into the last block before the embassy, a black SUV drove into the street blocking the way, but Herman jumped the curb into a grassy patch and curved back onto the street. "Thank you, Jesus!" he breathed, driving on.

Gunshots rang out from behind and in front as the men's vehicle skidded into the drive of the embassy, and the large metal gate slowly closed behind them. Two more bullets clattered off the Humvee, and suddenly the air was filled with the sound of multiple sirens as six police cars screeched to a stop blocking the black SUV and two more late-model black cars from which the shooting had come.

"Great, we've got cover!" Zack exclaimed.

"Yeah, but we're not inside yet," Josh worried. "Herman, drive us as close to that open door as you can. Guys, safeties off on your guns, and let's exit on the right. That goes for you too, Herman, even if you must climb over. Go!"

All four men scrambled into the building being met by a smiling Gregg, who slammed the door shut behind them. "You're nothing but trouble," he grinned, giving Josh a cuff on the shoulder, "but you certainly bring interest to the day! The consul knows you're here and will want to meet you, but first with the paperwork. So, you fellows are brothers?" he continued, greeting Zack and Evan. "Who's your driver? We may need him to teach the police stunt driving."

"He's Herman Hernandez," Zack answered. "He and I were the drug trafficker's prisoners in Belize City before we escaped yesterday. I'll not only want to talk with the consul about my getting home, but also about getting him asylum in the US. Yes, this is my little brother Evan Taylor, and I'm Zack," he continued, smirking a little as he winked at Evan.

"OK, both of you little fellows and Herman and Josh follow me to my office, so we can get all the forms filled out," Gregg responded with a grin. "Josh, I know you've been a lifesaver for them, but as you know, no good deed goes unpunished, so we'll need you too."

"We'd much rather be filling out forms than serving as bullet targets," Evan responded cheerfully, ignoring Zack's slight on his manhood.

CHAPTER VIII

SATURDAY MARCH 14

"Hello, Dad, this is Zack again."

"Well, hello, Son, how's it going? I think your last conversation was so short that I was almost more worried about what was going on than before you'd called."

"Yeah, I figured that, so that's why I'm calling back as soon as I am. I believe we're both safe now in the US embassy here in the new capital, Belmopan, but we had quite a ride getting here with the drug cartel fellows shooting at us. Fortunately we were in an Army Humvee with bulletproof glass, and we were armed. The Humvee owner shot the radiator of our pursuers, but we didn't pick up more assailants until we arrived nearly at the embassy gate. Several police cars showed up as well just as we came in and were able to arraign those new gunmen who were after us. Even though they'd delivered fifteen or twenty shots at us, the Humvee took them all. Needless to say, it was a bit frightening! One Belize policeman was shot in the leg, and they took him to the hospital."

"Wow! So, you're at the embassy! When can you come home?"

"I'm not certain, but I think soon. We've spent several hours filling out forms and then giving our stories to the officials. We did learn there'd been a police sweep of the factory where we were prisoners and that's why it had stopped running before we broke out, but as we'd suspected, hardly anyone knew we were there, so they'd not looked for us. It may have been in our favor because the police may not have known we were prisoners. The consular here thinks that Evan should come home with me since we look so much alike. Although they've picked up several of the actors in this cartel with the factory raid and today's event, they suspect there may well be more, and I'd certainly be a target and Evan now, too."

"What's Evan think of that?"

"He'd be OK with coming home if it weren't for Alice. He says he's in the process of wrapping this job up to completion and that they can finish it without him. He thinks his company will want him out now that this has happened anyhow. He doesn't want to leave without Alice, and she has another two months in this school term. He's talking with her and the head of the school to see if there's any possible replacement for her. I feel like I've put them all at risk. So, that's where we are. How are things coming along there? May I talk to Sissy and Danny?"

"They're not here again. Thelma's got them out getting some items for our trip. Since your previous call, we've continued planning to go on down to Texas tomorrow. I've talked to the police to report your whereabouts, and they are interested in debriefing you. One investigator told me there'd been an attempted raid on a suspected drug outfit here in the city several weeks ago, but that it had been entirely unsuccessful because the perpetrators had been informed and disappeared. They found a small stash of drugs but nothing else in an old warehouse down by the railroad tracks. Because we're now planning to leave tomorrow, I've talked to the apartment manager and the electric company about your bills; I've told them to forward the bills to Texas until you can get back. The children don't know where you've worked, so if you could give me that phone number, I'll call them and let them know what's going on."

"Dad, I don't remember the number. It was in the cell phone they stole from me. The name of the place was S and T Welding and Repair, and you can find it in the phone directory. They deposited my checks directly into my bank account. You probably need to call Sprint, too, and tell them my phone was lost and for them to close that account. They may need to call me here for verification; they can call on Evan's phone. You have his number, don't you?"

"Yes, I do. Will it be OK for me to have the children call you when they get back? Also, what do you want us to bring from here for you?"

"Well, only some of my clothes. I know I'll need to come back for the rest of the stuff, but I'm not certain how I'm going to arrange that. I hate to tell you this, but I had a DWI and lost my driver's license. Maybe I can get up there on the bus or a train. Almost all the furniture's nearly worthless."

"Perhaps we can come back on up together. Remember I'm retired now and my time's my own. You need to attempt to focus on the future now, despite the past. I understand you wanting to beat yourself up, but that only worsens problems. You've heard me say before that every day's the first day of the rest of your life; I believe that, and we're all here to help."

"Thanks, Dad," Zack replied with a catch in his voice, "I do know I don't deserve it, but thanks so very much! I'd probably better hang up now before I start blubbering, but do have the kids call me as soon as you can."

"Love you, Son."

"Thanks, Dad, love you, too," and with that the conversation ended. Zack sat on the chair in the small, dim briefing room with elbows on his knees, thinking about the interchange fighting tears of remorse. As the wave of emotion passed over him he sat up, squared his shoulders, and walked out the door and down the hall to talk to his brother.

Danny and Sissy skipped along beside their grandmother as they walked through Target. Thelma was checking her shopping list as she purposely moved forward. "Do you like nuts?" she asked, "I think we'll want some snacks while we travel."

"Yes!" they chorused.

"But, they're expensive," Danny opined.

"They are somewhat costly, you're right," Thelma agreed, "but they're good for us; they make a good snack, and are within our means."

"Well, what are our means?" Danny pursued.

"Danny," Sissy cautioned, "you shouldn't ask that."

"We can't be extravagant, but there's adequate income for us to be comfortable," Thelma explained.

"You need to leave the worrying about expenses to me. You children did a great job of being resourceful with the money while you were alone, and we'll not be spending any of that now. I'm glad to have you help me, though, pay attention to the prices while we shop. Being careful about costs is a good habit for all of us—everybody."

"Dad wouldn't let us spend money on anything!" Sissy commented. "But he always had money to spend on beer."

"I'm sorry things were so rough," Thelma sighed. "However, I do think they'll be better when he returns. Your grandpa said your daddy is very sorry for his drinking and the way he poorly cared for you. As much as you can I think you'll need to forgive him, and I trust you'll find him a different fellow when he returns. There is one thing in his favor: as far as we can tell, he does not have a lot of debt."

"I think you're right," Danny said. "He wouldn't let Mommy spend much money, and they argued about it."

"He also told us later that when we grow up we shouldn't borrow money. He used to be a lot of fun when he was home during the weekends. He'd laugh and tickle us, we'd ride him piggyback on the floor, and he'd read with us. After Mommy left, he just got grouchier and grouchier and hardly talked, staying out late nearly every night."

"Let's get some car games," Thelma suggested, changing the subject. "Have either of you played Scrabble?"

The children looked skeptical. "What's it about?" Sissy ventured.

"Well, you have letters, and you make words with them," Thelma explained.

"Oh, cool!" Danny exclaimed. "We get to make up new words?"

"No, you use real words, but it's a lot of fun," Thelma corrected. "Both of you enjoy reading, so I think both of you will find it interesting. I like playing it, and so does your granddad."

"So, can he play while he drives?" Sissy worried.

"No, but I'll be driving some, and he can play with you then."

"How long will it take us to get there?" Danny questioned.

"Let's see," Thelma said, thinking out loud. "Its two and a half hours to Kansas City, and it'll take us about an hour to get through the city, and then it's about eleven hours of straight driving to get down to Longview. We'll need to stop two or three times to get gas and eat, so that'll add another hour and a half as well so that would add up to seventeen hours."

"We'll need bathroom breaks, too," Danny inserted.

"I allowed for that in the eating and gasoline breaks," Thelma smiled.

"I liked the way you added all that in your head," Sissy commented. "You must be pretty good at math."

"Yes, well I taught math for years and years. I've had a lot of practice."

"I like arithmetic," Danny contributed. "I especially like getting one hundreds on my papers!"

"Yes, he was the best in his class," Sissy bragged. "I like math, too; it makes so much sense. Things are either right or wrong. When the answer is right, it is right, and you can't argue with it. When questions on tests are asked about stories, there often is more than one right answer, and then there's the problem of deciding which answer the teacher really wants."

"Great observation!" Thelma responded. "You children are a hoot! Let's go check out. Perhaps your dad's called again, and we can find out more of where he is and when he'll get home. He said things were tense and to me that sounds dangerous. I'd hate for us to miss his call because I know he wants to talk with us. Your granddad said so."

They finished their shopping and on the way back to the apartment, Danny asked, "If it takes seventeen hours, can we do that in one day?"

"Sure we can," Thelma replied. "We'll get everything packed today, so we're all ready to start early in the morning at about five thirty. We'll have a late breakfast on the road maybe around ten or so, and if you're hungry before then, we'll have the snacks. By noon, we'll have been on the road six and a half hours with ten and a half hours left. That should allow us to get to Longview by about ten thirty. We may make better time than that because some of the speed limits have recently been raised."

"Why did they do that?" Danny asked.

"So we could get places faster," Thelma replied. "Twenty-five years or so ago they lowered all the speed limits to cause people to use less gasoline; now they're changing them back."

"Who's they?" Sissy asked.

"Who are they?" Danny corrected.

"Who's they sounds better, don't you think, Grandma?" Sissy defended.

"Yes, I'm a little uncertain on that one myself. Let's ask your granddad about it; he's our local expert on grammar. I can see how Danny'd be right, though, because the 'they' is a plural. Anyhow, the 'they' means the politicians, I guess. Danny, how come you're so concerned about correct grammar? It seems pretty unusual."

"My teacher said people listen to you better if your grammar's good, and she asked, 'Why say it wrong if there's a right way to say it?' Sissy and I both try to help each other say things right. You know, Dad really didn't make many mistakes, so we are used to hearing things right."

"Momma spoke good English, too," Sissy said wistfully.

"She did, indeed," Thelma agreed. "She was an English major in college when I first met her thirteen years ago. She was very pretty and a lot of fun."

"I really miss her," Sissy said, tearing up.

"Yeah, I do, too," Danny agreed.

Thelma stopped the vehicle on the side of the street, got out, and quickly opened the passenger doors away from the traffic, knelt on the snowy grass, and opened her arms. The children read her actions, rapidly extracting themselves from their seatbelt and flew into her arms.

"Know this," Thelma said, "we miss your mother, too, and we'll do our best to find her, but even if she won't come or if we can't find her, we'll always be here for you. We love you and are so glad we have you back. It's OK to be sad about your mom; we're sad too. We'll be sad about this together until we can find her."

"Sissy and I are never, never, never going to use drugs or alcohol!"

Danny declared emphatically. "We've promised each other. They make bad things happen!"

The children settled into the hug for a good five minutes, with both weeping and sniveling into Thelma's brown quilted coat. Finally, the three of them quietly got back into the SUV and finished the ride home. Upon arriving at the apartment and entering, Jonathan greeted them warmly, telling in detail as much as he could about Zack and Evan's situation mentioning that Zack wanted them to call him back. Thelma turned pale at the mention of gunfire on both of her boys, and Sissy was nearly in tears again, fearing the danger, but Danny was only excited.

"You mean they were shot at but never got hit or hurt?" he asked. "I've seen Humvees in TV clips from Iraq. I knew they tried to make them bulletproof. When is Dad coming home? What kind of guns did they have? How is he safe in the embassy? How will he get out of there and to the airport to come home?"

Danny's questions broke the emotional tide of the moment.

"Well, one question at a time, please sir," Jonathan grinned. "Yes, they're all four fine without injuries. One of the Belize police was shot in the leg and taken to the hospital. There are armed guards at the embassy, and they'll have a plan for safety as they go to an airport. Your dad doesn't know when he'll be able to get back but thought it would be soon. Evan'll probably be coming back too and maybe even his fiancée, Alice."

"May we call them right now?" Sissy asked excitedly.

"Sure," her grandfather agreed, "I see no reason why it should be delayed. Who should talk first?"

"I will," Danny offered quickly.

"Maybe his mother should be first," Sissy corrected, raising her brows.

Thelma opened her mouth, closed it, and spoke, "How very gracious of you children! That is very, very kind of you to offer. You don't know how many times over the past several years I've wished to hear your dad's voice on the phone!"

Jonathan dialed, and Thelma waited for an answer.

"Hello, Evan Taylor, here."

Thelma was a bit disconcerted hearing the wrong son answer but replied, "Hello, Evan, this is your mother, and I'm hoping to speak to Zack."

"I bet!" Evan exclaimed. "You want to talk to that ratty old brother of mine; I always suspected you might love him more than you love me."

"Young man, you know that's not true," Thelma smiled, continuing, "I'm extremely thankful you're both OK. I heartily appreciate what you've done to help Zack, and I will be so relieved when you're both back in the States. I love you a bunch; now, may I please speak with your brother?"

"If you insist, Mom, but go easy on him; he's been through the ringer. Here he is." Evan smirked and handed the phone to his brother, sitting beside him, then rose and left the room.

"Hello, Mom," Zack said, feeling a flood of emotion bearing down. "It is wonderful to hear your voice. I do feel extremely guilty for the way I've been treating you. I don't deserve the help you're giving the children when I've been so mean. I feel certain Dad's told you some of what I've been through, but I'm resolved not to get back into that situation again. Every day I ache for Elaine. Will you help me track her down when I get back?"

"Well certainly, of course!" she exclaimed. "We are not judging you at all for your asking her to leave; you knew the situation you were dealing with. Obviously drug use is extremely destructive, but we can't help but mourn the loss of the wonderful young lady she was when you first met her. We'll work with you. Now, we want you back here. I'm hoping you'll meet us in Longview. We love you so very much! I have two youngsters here standing on their tiptoes wanting to talk to you. Danny's offered to be first."

"Thank you, Mom!" Zack responded sincerely. "Thanks again for helping with the kids; they can be a handful."

"Zack, these children of yours are absolute sweethearts. They've been nothing but responsible in your absence. We've been amazed at their foresight. We love them to death! Here they are," she finished, handing the phone to Danny.

"Hi, Dad," Danny said, suddenly subdued in a quiet little voice.

"Hi Son," Zack replied, realizing the hesitation Danny was expressing in his manner of speech. "I'm super glad to be able to talk to you."

"Yes, we were afraid those men with guns would kill you; we saw them taking you away. Later we saw the black SUV two more times at McDonalds when two of the men were buying food. Did they feed you McDonalds?"

"Yes, they did!" his dad replied. "What made you think that, and how did you know it was them?"

"It was a black SUV with two aerials on the back of it, and the guys looked the same only not with masks on like when they had you. They bought way more food than two could eat and didn't eat any of it at the restaurant. We got their license number, too—at least Sissy did—and we've now given it to the police. So, were you scared when they were shooting at you today?"

"I believe when the shooting started it was happening so fast I don't think I was thinking about being frightened; I was thinking about how to get us all out of there. I do think all of us were scared to some extent, though. I'll tell you more about it when I get home. Your grandma says you've done pretty well in the past couple weeks. When did you find the money?"

"Almost as soon as we went into the apartment when they took you away. We were coming home to eat, and the cereal was about all there was there."

"Danny, it wasn't right that I didn't have more food for you or warmer clothes. I'm very sorry; I plan to do much better in the future. I was drinking way too much alcohol, and it was making me stupid.

"Because I'd been drinking none after they took me away, I became extremely sick for several days. When I started to improve, I realized what a worthless father I'd become for the two of you."

"Yes, well, Sissy and I've made a pact that we're never going to drink or use drugs."

"I'll support you in that! Are things OK at school?"

"Pretty much. We only missed the Monday after Grandma and Grandpa came. Today we went with Grandma and told the teachers we were moving to Texas, so we've missed today too. You don't need to worry; we'll get right back into classes as soon as we get to Texas because Sissy and I have made a pact about that too; we're both going to stay in school."

"Buddy boy," Zack said, "somehow you got your head screwed on right! I sure do love you. I need to talk to your sister, though."

Danny handed the phone to Sissy. "Hi," she greeted.

"Hi, sweetheart," Zack replied. "How's my beautiful little girl?"

Sissy broke into open sobs, and through her tears in her choked voice said, "Daddy, I was afraid we'd never see you again! Please come home as soon as you can!" She continued to cry so long Thelma took the phone from her.

"Zack," she said, "they do love you. You may have some fears to erase for them, but as much as they love you and need you, I don't think it'll be an uphill battle. Have you and your dad discussed our plans about going to Texas tomorrow? Are there things we need to do before we leave here?"

"No, Mom, I think we've covered most of that. This is important, though: I'm thinking seriously about my relationship with God. Evan, the people at the Salvation Army who helped me, and Herman, a fellow prisoner just like me who was working with me in the factory all are depending on God and believing He can help us. I'm believing in prayer; in fact, I'm beginning to think I'd be ungrateful not to trust in God. I've been through some amazing stuff and am still OK."

"Well that's great," Thelma replied, somewhat nonplussed that Zack would speak so openly about his faith. "We've always felt a relationship with God was a good thing."

"Yes, but Mom, it's more than a relationship; it's depending on Him when you're in big trouble and even when you're not," Zack insisted. "I've really missed the boat along this line, and Evan seems so right on track. He hasn't missed a beat helping me even though he's put himself in real danger."

"You may have done the same for him if he'd been in a tight spot."

"I doubt it. I wasn't even caring for Sissy and Danny properly. We'll talk about this more later; I don't know how expensive it is for us to be making this international call. Tell Dad and the kids how much I love them, and I do love you, too! I'd better say good-bye and hang up."

"Well, then, good-bye, Son. I am so relieved you're all right and that you're doing so much better than you were. Bye-bye." Thelma couldn't help but smile as she hung up.

"Your dad sounded very much like his old self, didn't he?" she questioned the family.

"Yes," Jonathan responded, "I've been surprised at how calm both boys have been through this. Are you feeling a little better?" he asked, directing his question to Sissy.

"Yes, Grandpa, I'm fine. I don't know why I get all teary when even very good things happen."

"Sweetie, you're just tender-hearted. There's nothing wrong with that," Jonathan explained, grabbing her and giving her a big hug, obviously in good spirits himself. "Now we need to get packed, so we can be on the road very early tomorrow."

CHAPTER IX

SATURDAY, MARCH 13

The United States consulate in Belmopan encouraged Zack and Evan to remain as guests for their own security at least for the first night. The remainder of the day was spent with numerous calls for both Zack and Evan. Evan needed to plan with his workplace in Belize City, discuss Alice's work with both her and Jim Smith, call his superiors in Chicago, and attempt to get into touch with his landlord. Zack needed to talk with his former employer and landlord and received a call from the St. Joseph police inquiring about his knowledge about his abductors. He learned that his sudden leaving of St. Joe had been triggered by a failed crackdown operation on local drug activity by that police force and that they were now aware of the old warehouse where he'd been held prisoner. The consulate reported that the closing of the coffee/drug canning factory had netted eight more men involved in the drug cartel being imprisoned, but that the police had already released two of those for unexplained reasons. Altogether there'd been a total of sixteen arrests with two that had been picked up on the highway with the damaged radiator, the eight at the factory, and the six more that had been present at the shoot-out at the embassy gates.

"It makes you feel real safe that they've already let two of those monkeys go, doesn't it," Evan commented to Zack satirically as they sat ruminating in their room the next morning after a decent night's sleep.

"You bet!" Zack responded. "I've talked with Herman, and things don't sound good on that front either. He did get his cousin to call back, and he's reported that he's certain that the drug outfit is essentially holding his entire family hostage at the farm. The cousin said he'd anonymously reported it to the police twice, but there had been nothing done. Herman asked the consulate if they could help him with the situation, and they've evidently said that if his family were here in the compound, they could act by giving asylum and that they'd be willing to do so, but they had neither the jurisdiction nor the facility to go out to the farm and to bring them in. I wonder how soon we can leave this place."

"I asked Gregg that question last night," Evan replied. "He couldn't give anything official, but he suspected the embassy would want to bring in a small plane and fly us out to Guatemala City. He seemed to think the embassy would pick up the tab for that flight but that we'd be responsible for the cost of the flight from there. He thought we'd likely be here a few days for all that to happen."

"Have you considered how the fellows yesterday knew where we were?" Zack asked.

"Yes, I think it is very likely that the heavyset policemen at the traffic check got my license plate number and name and that either he or someone at the police station had access to my address, the car license, and driver's license, and the fact that there were two other occupants in the car. They were then able to track us down by the following morning. I suspect that the car that was out by my house yesterday morning and followed us was chiefly a spotter to keep track of us until they could call in reinforcements and that we got out of there just in time. I really shouldn't have said anything about Alice being my fiancée to that policeman!"

"You don't realize how precarious your situation is with a corrupt police department unless you experience it, do you?"

"No, and that is the problem when it comes to Herman's family. He can't depend on the police to reliably help him, especially if they've already been notified and have done nothing."

"Maybe we should do something."

"Probably, but there's an obvious risk. I hate to ask Josh, but I don't know how we'd get it done without him. He left the Humvee here for repair of the bullet holes and a new tropical forest camouflage paint job. Gregg took him home last night; they seemed pretty confident that his license plate number wouldn't have been compromised, but they'll get him a new number in any case here through the embassy."

"I believe that if we wouldn't help Herman, there's no one else that will or could. Let's talk with him about it first. I saw him down at the cafeteria half an hour ago talking on the phone."

The brothers set off to find Herman and located him in his embassy sleeping quarters.

After their greetings and morning pleasantries, Zack asked, "What would you think about us attempting to bring your family back here for asylum? We don't know if it is possible. We'd have to ask Josh to help us again, and I know the embassy could not be involved. Is there a way into Punta Gorda other than the main highway?"

"Oh, thank you, thank you," Herman responded. "I've been trying to come up with a way to get them out and praying about it but didn't think to ask you. I'm afraid anyone in the cartel would be aware of the Humvee now."

"Well, Gregg's already getting it repainted so inasmuch as there are several in the country, I'd doubt they'd suspect this particular one already again. Is there a back way into Punta Gorda, so we wouldn't have to approach from the main highway?"

"You'd need to go on the CA-13 down through Guatemala. There's no good road south out of Punta Gorda, so to get there you'd need to get to Jelacte somehow. It's a very small place. I've heard there's a trail through the forest and pastures there between the CA-13 highway and Jelacte, but I've never been on it. Maybe the embassy has a good map."

"Why don't you check that out and I'll try to get in touch with Josh," Evan directed. "I think we need to keep this under our hats even here in the embassy."

"I agree, but I think we need to let the consulate know something. I don't want to be stranded here because we've acted without permission. I'll go talk with the consulate about this and see if I can find out anything official about our exit plan while you do that then," Zack suggested.

As Zack went to the front desk of the embassy, he was greeted with a pleasant smile by the receptionist. "Were you able to sleep well last night?" she asked.

"I slept great," he replied. "Is the consulate available to speak to me?"

"He has a meeting later this morning, but I think he's free now. I'll ask."

Zack stood as the consulate entered and offered his hand. "You'll remember me as Zack Taylor from yesterday," he said, grinning.

"Of course, of course," the consulate replied, directing Zack back to the office and shutting the door, "you and your friends had a most memorable entrance, but I'm glad you gave your name because I do get you brothers confused. What can I do for you today?"

"I was here concerning the timeframe of our returning to the States."

"I bet you're more than ready to get home, and we're working on it. We want to get a plane in here to transport you both, but I'm afraid with all the paperwork it's going to take about a week."

"My brother and I are considering attempting to go down to Punta Gorda with Herman Hernandez to retrieve his family. Would that action jeopardize our relationship with you?"

"Well, if you're asking my advice as to the safety of that for you, I must advise against it. After all, one of our overriding missions in this office is to promote the safety of US citizens. However, should you leave our care and then return with additional asylum seekers who are in real danger, our welcome and assistance remains as you return here.

"Thank you," Zack continued. "At this point, Evan and I aren't certain if the attempt will be feasible, but we're considering it and don't want you to be left out of the loop as to our plans. We would need Josh, the Humvee owner, to help us, and Evan's working on that as we speak. We feel that the fewer people who know about this the better. Also, I need to thank you for getting the temporary passports for us so quickly."

"You're welcome. Please weigh the risk. I will discuss this with no one," the consulate cautioned, completing the interchange by directing Zack to the door.

That afternoon the three embassy guests gathered in the brothers' room to discuss their plans.

"Josh is totally in with us," Evan reported. "He's coming over tomorrow to talk with us about it."

"Well, when I talked with the consulate this morning, he told us it was an obvious risk but that it would not prevent us from getting their assistance once we returned here. He was firm but pleasant," Zack added.

"My report's a little less encouraging," Herman offered. "I was able to get a very good map, but it looks like the path we want is little more than a trail through the jungle. It is a two-track road and would be impassable in the rainy season. Since it's not rained for a couple weeks now, we could probably make it in the Humvee, but it will be very rough going."

"Are we able to contact your family in any fashion to let them know we're coming?" Evan asked.

"My cousin does not think so. The telephone line has been cut, and none of the family is entering or leaving the farm—only the cartel vehicles. My wife grew up in Belize City, so she's going to be feeling the frustration of being out of contact acutely! Her parents were English and had difficulty accepting me as a farm boy marrying their daughter. They're both deceased, and she's an only child; her other relatives are in England. My dad is seventy, but he's been in good health. He loves the farm, and it may be difficult suddenly to get him to leave. In a way, coming in to them as a surprise might be a good thing. They would have no time to prepare to leave and would therefore have little likelihood of doing something to make the cartel men suspicious of their going. Here's the map."

Both Evan and Zack leaned over the map.

"Where's the farm?" Zack questioned. "If we go through Jalacte, we'll still be on the Southern Highway a while, won't we?"

"Yes, we'll be on the southern highway for several miles, but we can get back off before we get to my place here," Herman said, pointing out the farm location. "We could come in through the back fields and also leave that way should someone be watching up at the front gate. If there were a full moon, we could drive through the fields without our headlights warning guards. A daytime contact would be easier as far as traveling in and out, but would be a greater risk as far as being seen."

"Going the western route through Guatemala would take how long to get there from here?" Evan asked. "How much difficulty would we have crossing the borders?"

"It was a couple years ago that I was across the borders, and it only took a few minutes each time. When we cross back into Belize, it will be unlikely there's anyone at the border at all. I'd say the trip down there as far as travel time should not be greater than six hours one way. It depends on the condition of those back roads and trails; making progress there can be terrible if they're full of puddles or potholes. Are we going to plan to return the same way we came?" Herman responded.

"Josh will certainly need to weigh in on all these plans," Evan offered. "He's a good planner with much more experience in covert operations than any of us. Zack and I will be going to give firepower and manpower in case they're needed."

"And moral support, too," Zack added. "What were the children's names again?"

"Angel's my thirteen-year-old son, and Jessica is my ten-year-old daughter. My wife's name is Ardine."

"How do you think they'll feel about going to the US suddenly?" Evan asked.

"I think mainly excited." Herman replied. "We'd talked about it some after my brother was killed. My wife initially wanted to go to England, but we knew finding work for us would be more difficult there than in the States. The consulate said they'd pay for my flights and the flights of the family if they could show up here. He also said we'd have to stay here several weeks while things are arranged through the immigration system. My family will forever be grateful to you both for your help if this all works out—well, for that matter, even if it doesn't work out."

"Let's pray for the best," Evan said seriously.

"Let's not just say we will pray, but pray," Zack inserted. "Herman, you pray."

The following morning, the three men eagerly waited in Herman's room for Josh's coming.

"How soon do you think the Humvee repair will be finished?" Herman asked, directing his question to Evan.

"I heard it was to be a rush job," Evan replied. "I still suspect another day or so. Josh will know when he gets here. If we tangle with the drug cartel again, he'll need to have it repainted again," he chuckled. "Here he comes now."

"Good morning gents," Josh greeted. "So what's the plan again?"

And so the discussion of timing, routes, locations, and fallback plans began and lasted several hours. It was decided they'd be able to leave in two days, only Josh's family and the consulate would be told, that they'd leave the embassy very early in the morning and hope to be back that evening, and that Josh would gather the necessary supplies and bring them back to the embassy the night before leaving to ensure an early departure.

CHAPTER X

SUNDAY, MARCH 15

The trip from St. Joseph, Missouri, to Longview, Texas, was begun before light in the windy chill. Thelma and Jonathan directed the sleepy children to the waiting vehicle, bucked them in, and wrapped blankets around them warmly. Jonathan drove while Thelma dosed in the passenger seat beside him. The family had passed through Kansas City before the younger members of the crew started to awaken.

"I believe I'm already hungry," were Danny's first words. "Do you think we could break out the nuts yet, Grandma? Where are we? How long have we been sleeping? Grandpa, are you tired of driving?"

The questioning was so typical of Danny that both grandparents were laughing so hard they had difficulty addressing his inquiries.

"Let's see," Jonathan responded, "we're about half an hour south of Kansas City going down through the western edge of Missouri on Interstate 49; you've been sleeping between two and three hours, and I'm fine driving; I actually enjoy it. Is Sissy awake, too?"

"Yes, Grandpa, but I'm still a little sleepy."

"We've gone far enough we could stop and eat should you wish," Thelma offered.

"I'd be happy with those nuts and water," Danny replied. "I don't want to get out of this nice warm blanket; it looks cold outside."

"OK, in that case we'll wait and stop in Joplin," Jonathan said. "I bet your dad came down this very road when the drug cartel men took him to Belize."

"Yeah, it's scary thinking that in any van we see on the highway people could be prisoners. Grandpa, do you think all these men that do these kinds of things are going to hell?" Danny asked.

"I'm glad I don't have to make the decision as to their being in hell or not. The Bible tells us not to judge people. Judging is for God to do. He's the only one that knows their hearts," his grandfather chuckled.

"I wouldn't have trouble judging and sending them to hell!" Danny exclaimed. "Taking people prisoner and making them your slaves isn't right."

"Yes, but look at it this way," Thelma intervened. "Should your dad who was drinking too much alcohol and who was being unkind and uncaring to you children have to go to hell? He'll say now that his action wasn't right."

"No, he's seeing what he did was wrong so that makes it better," Sissy countered.

"That is where we are with the drug men. What they are doing now is wrong, but in the future they may do what is right and be sorry for their actions. Only God can know that. We ourselves just need to work on doing the right things," Jonathan contributed. "This is a pretty deep subject so early in the morning."

"Danny thinks subjects like this are important," Sissy said as if her brother's thoughts were of overriding value. "We've been wondering if God was really paying attention to us. We sang 'Birdie in the Apple Tree' and were thinking about it. We decided He may have been neglecting us."

"I think it was Dad neglecting us," Danny stated confidently. "God gave us a dad and a mom, and neither of them were doing their jobs right."

"I agree, Danny," Thelma responded. "However, look at it this way: if your parents had been responsible, you and your sister wouldn't have had the opportunity to show what you could do in a difficult situation. In a way, you've become stronger in spite of it."

"Yes, but we could have been really hurt because of it, and we were sad and frightened when it was happening!" Sissy exclaimed.

"You're right," Jonathan concurred. "Nevertheless, you've come through this intact. There's a Bible verse that says, 'All things work together for good to them that love God.' That's pretty hard to believe, but it is there."

"So if it is in the Bible, it's got to be true?" Sissy asked.

"Yes, generally we believe that. People argue about it, but over the years I'm surprised at how often I find it is right."

"Your dad will likely be telling you a lot more about the Bible when he comes back," Thelma related. "I nearly dropped my teeth yesterday when he told me he believed in prayer and that we need to have a close relationship with God."

"What made him say that, and why are your teeth loose?" Danny wondered.

"My teeth are fine—it's just a saying. I think he's been with his friend in the prison factory who prays, and the Salvation Army people who helped them, and even Evan who is now pretty serious about his Christian religion," Thelma answered. "If it takes Zack being a better Christian to get him on track and to keep him on track, I'm all for it."

"That would be a change," Sissy agreed. "We hadn't been to church before last Sunday in I don't know how long."

"Do all Christians go to church, Grandpa?" Danny asked.

"Pretty much."

"Does the Bible say they need to go?"

Jonathan caught Thelma's eye, and they both grinned. "I believe it says Christians ought to gather together to encourage one another," he replied.

"What do you think I ought to do when I grow up?" Danny asked.

"That's a very good question and hard to answer," Jonathan fielded. "What made you ask that?"

"Dad agreed yesterday it was good for me to stay in school, and if you stay in school, you need to study to do something."

"I think you do your best work if you like your work," Thelma contributed.

"I like everything in school, so that doesn't help."

"Actually, that's a wonderful starting place. Whatever you do as an adult will require a good grade school education. As you go through the years ahead, there will be plenty of time to figure your future out based on what you find you like and what you're good at," Jonathan added.

"His grades are great, and he's right about liking school," Sissy said. "Some of our liking school I think was because it was warmer there than at home, and the food was better."

"Well, perhaps all children should live in cold houses with minimal food so that school would be better appreciated," joked Thelma.

"Oh, no!" exclaimed Danny, taking her seriously.

Sissy, understanding the situation, placated, "It could have been worse," then added, "we actually never really went hungry; we just didn't have many food choices. Do you think Grandma Denton will be able to cook for us?"

"Your Grandmother Denton is a fabulous cook," Thelma informed.

"She makes better apple pie than my wife!" Jonathan exclaimed.

"You are instantly in the doghouse," his wife rebutted, grinning. "She believes in three balanced meals a day, so if you don't stay busy and active, you'll be gaining some weight."

"Sissy is skinny, and she needs to gain weight. I need to grow," Danny observed. "Grandpa, what do I need to do to help myself grow faster? Dad's a big fellow, and I'm one of the smallest guys in my class."

"There's not a lot you can do except eat properly and get plenty of sunshine and exercise," Jonathan responded. "I suspect you'll be like your dad and uncle; when they were your age they were also small, but when they became about twelve they started growing, and we thought they'd never quit. They were some of the larger boys in their school when they graduated from high school. Whether you grow or not is something that can't be controlled unless it's clear out of line, so you should not worry about that. There are plenty more important matters to think about."

"I'm glad to hear that. I kept worrying about him not growing well," Sissy considered. "I really like not having to worry about things. How much farther is it to Joplin? I'm getting very hungry."

"I'll pull off at the next exit that looks promising for breakfast. We don't have to wait until Joplin. How does a Waffle House or Denny's sound?"

"It all sounds like food, and I'm all for it," Danny agreed. "Grandma, do you have trouble digesting your food?"

"No, sweetheart, why do you ask?"

"Well, old people have problems sometimes, my teacher said. Grandpa, can you tell us about when you were a boy? Tell us something interesting."

"I grew up on a farm near Collinsville, Illinois. Collinsville is just east of St. Louis."

"I thought St. Louis was in Missouri."

"It is. On the east side of St. Louis is the Mississippi River, and east of that, some of the city of St. Louis spills over into Illinois. They name it East St. Louis. Collinsville was a little east of that. Our farm was about four miles out of town. We raised horseradish. Do you know what that is?"

"Yes, it's real hot. Dad had some, and he put it in sandwiches; Sissy thought it was too hot. I liked it."

"A little is good. I liked a little, but too much is too hot," Sissy corrected. "Dad and Danny put on a lot; that's what he's remembering."

"Most of the horseradish raised in the United States is raised right around Collinsville," Jonathan continued.

"Did you have any animals on the farm?" Sissy queried.

"Yes, we had three or four milk cows, one or two horses, chickens, turkeys, a dog, and several cats."

"But there weren't any pigs, sheep, or ducks?" Danny asked.

"No, we didn't have any pond near the house or barn, so ducks and geese would have had no place to swim. My mother did not like the way pigpens smelled, so there were no pigs. Most of our farm was used to raise the horseradish. The chickens produced eggs, the cows gave milk, and we would butcher some of the calves for meat. Oh, and I forgot, I did raise rabbits, and we would eat them as well."

"Oh, dear, how could you eat the little bunnies?" Sissy worried.

"Do you like to eat fried chicken?" Jonathan asked.

"Yes," she replied in a tentative voice.

"All meat we eat comes from some animal. It is important to be kind to the animals you own, but they are all for our use or enjoyment. For us to have meat on the farm, it was much less expensive to raise the animals and to eat the ones we raised rather than buy the meat," Jonathan instructed. "I raised the rabbits and I would get attached to them. It was a lesson I had to learn to kill them and prepare them to eat."

"So did you eat the horses?" Danny asked.

"No," Jonathan chuckled, "people in the United States don't eat horses, but they do in Europe. My dad had grown up on the farm, and they'd used horses to do much of the work when he was small. He loved horses, so we always had one or two that we could ride. He was very particular in the way they were handled and trained. About the only work they would do was sometimes we'd ride them out to the pasture to bring in the cows for milking."

"What did you do with the horses when they died?" Danny persisted.

"When they got old, my dad would sell them."

"What happened to them then?"

"They were old and had difficulty walking. We knew they hurt to move, so we sold them to a rendering plant that would kill them and use their bodies for things like dog food and the hooves for glue."

"I don't think I wanted to know all that," Sissy complained.

"Here's an exit, so let's stop and eat. Is everyone interested in the Waffle House? There's one here."

"Yes, yes!" Sissy exclaimed. "Grandma, may we have syrup?"

"Why, certainly, darling, why?" Thelma wondered.

"Dad made pancakes for us sometimes, but then he'd have forgotten the syrup and say it wasn't good for us anyhow. We'd put sugar and butter on the pancakes," Sissy informed.

"I'm confident they'll have it available here," Jonathan encouraged. "Besides sugar and syrup are pretty much the same thing. Some of it is not damaging."

"Yes, I read they're both highly refined carbohydrates," Danny intoned as the four of them moved out of the SUV and into the restaurant laughing.

CHAPTER XI

SUNDAY, MARCH 14

The Taylor grandparents with their charges continued on the road to Texas. They drove straight on south, heading into Arkansas. "We'll get to see a little of the Ozarks on this trip," Jonathan announced. "Do you children remember your trip your family made to Longview when you were small?"

"I don't remember riding," Sissy responded, "but I was surprised when Danny told me he remembered the grandparents and the house being on a main street. I thought he'd have been too little to recall that."

"Well, the house will not be the same. Soon after you were there, they moved to a different part of town and into a much larger house. We couldn't understand why they'd want to have such a big house, and we asked them about it. Your Grandpa Denton said he wanted a garden and that the yard at the former house wouldn't allow it, that they needed to move to a safer part of town, and that the new house was to be bought at such a good price they couldn't pass it up. For their age, they stay very busy doing things," Thelma informed. "Actually, that big house is going to be very handy with us being there, at least until your dad gets back."

"What did they say when you said we were coming?" Danny asked.

"Oh, they can't wait until you get there."

"Why haven't we talked to them on the phone?" Sissy questioned.

"They're both pretty hard of hearing; they thought talking to you directly when you arrive would be better," Thelma answered.

"How old are they, anyhow? Why don't they have hearing aids?" Danny asked.

"I believe they're both in their mid-seventies. They were not young when your mother was born. She's their only child, and they have been extremely sad that she is not part of their life anymore. They didn't know your mother had left your dad until we called and told them after you found us. Now they are heartbroken about that as well. We'll really need to love on them to help cheer them up when we get there. I know they want to be with you!" Thelma advised. "I haven't asked about the hearing aids; some things are sort of a private thing, and one must be cautious about being too snoopy."

"Sissy says I'm too snoopy," Danny recounted.

"Yes, I'm right!" Sissy defended.

"Why do I ask so many questions, Grandpa?" Danny asked.

Jonathan laughed, "Probably because you realize there are many things you don't know and that you believe other people have the answers. Asking questions is not bad; it helps you learn. You just need to make certain that the questions you ask are actually questions you can't answer yourself with a little thinking. Your grandma's right, though: some questions you shouldn't ask because they're too personal, and if you ask them it may make the person you're asking uncomfortable or embarrassed. Boys your age can get by with more questions than grownups can, but you should work on not asking too many private questions. However, it is better to ask questions than to be afraid to ask. People who won't ask questions or who will not listen to the answers that are given often have more problems than those like you. I think most of the questions you ask are good ones."

"Will you tell me if the questions I ask are not good ones?"

"Sure. However, because I'm your grandpa, there's almost no question you can ask me that you shouldn't. I'll tell you, though."

"So, should I tell him when I think he shouldn't be asking things?" Sissy wondered.

"I think you've been doing your best to help him out," Thelma answered. "The two of you working together have been doing very well. Now that you have us we'll try to help, but what you've been doing has been working. You'll just need to watch to see that you don't get irritated with one another. Back to your grandparents Denton—what do you think about staying with them?"

"We don't know very much about them, so it is hard to say," Sissy answered.

"We like you, so living with you might be better," Danny added.

"That's why we're talking about this," Thelma explained. "You now do know us, and we love and know you, so it would at this moment probably be better if we could ask you to come live with us instead. However, we have two problems. First, the place where we live is too small for all of us. It is a nice apartment near the beach, but one of the rules is that there can be no children living there. We talked with the Dentons about this, and they understand the situation and have agreed for us to stay with them at their house at least until your dad gets back. If it appears you'll be staying in Longview permanently, we may eventually leave our apartment in Florida and come to live in Texas, but that would be several months away."

"Why doesn't your apartment want children?" Danny inquired.

"Children can be noisy and unpleasant. In places where there are many retired people, those older people often don't want to hear the noise or deal with the children," Jonathan replied. "We actually like children and miss some of the noises they make, but it has been a good place for us to live, and the rule hasn't been an issue for us since we had no grandchildren."

"So you think that in this big house there will be enough room for all of us?" Sissy worried.

"Oh, yes," Thelma reassured, "There are at least six bedrooms in the house—maybe seven."

"Why do they need so many?" Danny pondered. "They can only sleep in one or maybe two at a time."

"You're correct, and actually they mainly now only live in one end of the house where the kitchen and study and two of the bedrooms are. They shut the doors to the other end of the house. We were down to visit them two years ago and were able to see the house. It is very nice with a large yard and trees. Your Grandpa Denton loves to work in the yard and keeps a well cultivated garden."

"Are there neighbor children?" Sissy asked.

"I don't think we know," Thelma smiled, looking at Jonathan. "Did you see neighbor children while we were there?"

"I don't recall," he answered. "I'm pretty certain I saw a nice swing set in the backyard next door," he continued slowly. "Say, look children, we're coming up to enter Arkansas. See the sign that says 'Welcome to Arkansas the Natural State'?"

"What is a natural state?" Danny questioned.

"I suppose it means it is in its original condition, that it hasn't been changed," his grandfather replied.

"So that must mean all the other states are unnatural?" Danny grinned.

"Maybe," Jonathan laughed in exchange. "This road is certainly very winding. A little change to make this road wider and straighter would be a good thing." The road did curve along a stream with overhanging cliffs on the opposite side.

"A wide, straight road wouldn't be as pretty or interesting," Sissy observed.

"No, but it would be faster and safer," Danny argued.

"I think you're both right," Thelma placated. "Too often, improvement causes us to lose some nice things."

"After we get down past Fayetteville, there's some new road through the mountain that is beautiful in another way. It has big high bridges across lovely little valleys that are amazing to see," Jonathan added.

"Yes, that road is nice, but with this road you can enjoy the pretty stream and the rock cliffs," Thelma maintained. "It does slow us down, though. Getting back to the subject of staying with the Dentons—we'll all need to work very diligently to not make too much work for them since they are as old as they are. They will not be inclined to complain because they would not wish to make us feel bad, so we'll need to start as soon as possible trying to understand how we can help them the most. I'm suggesting that the four of us should sit down after a day or two and talk again about how we can best help. Your grandpa Jonathan and I will then talk things over with them about how we can make things go the most smoothly."

"How soon will we start to school?" Sissy asked.

"As soon as we can get it done," Jonathan replied. "Your Denton grandparents told us they'd ask some of their young friends who had children in school about the best place for you to be. They seemed to think maybe a private school might be better. We'll see what they've found out when we get there."

"I don't think our dad can pay for a private school," Danny interjected.

"Yes, I mentioned that to them," Jonathan explained. "They said we'd want to talk about it with your dad, but that they thought they could easily afford it."

"Often you have to wear uniforms to private schools," Sissy informed.

"You're right," Thelma agreed. "but I think I've heard that even at many of the public schools in Texas you must wear uniforms."

"Is Texas different from the other states?" asked Danny.

"In a way, yes," his granddad answered. "Texas is the biggest state in the lower forty-eight, and it is the only state among them that was at one time its own country. It is now the second most populous state in the nation and has one of the best run economies of all the states. Texans are known to be very proud of their state, more so than people in the other states."

"Hawaii was once its own country," Danny informed.

"You're right," Jonathan agreed, "but I stipulated in the lower forty-eight so that leaves out Hawaii and Alaska. Do you know who owned Alaska before we did?"

"The Eskimos?"

"Well, the Eskimos and Alaskan Indians owned it first, but it was a Russian territory, and the United States bought it from the Russians. It happened in 1867, and we paid Russia seven point two million dollars for it. Although that was a lot of money back then, it seems a frightfully small amount for an entire state now."

"So why did the Russians sell it so cheaply?" Danny asked.

"Because they were afraid the British would take it over and make it part of Canada. The United States leaders were hoping to be able to include British Columbia with Alaska and have the entire northwestern coast of the North American continent, but the British and Canadians saw that coming and within a few months formalized British Columbia as a territory in Canada."

"Grandpa, don't you think that would be neat if all of Canada was part of the United States?"

"If the two countries were one and they had good government I think it would be OK, but they are separate, and over the years have been good friends with no major conflicts between them. If we start coveting their territory we will end our friendship, and that would damage all of us. We need to stay friendly and appreciative of the Canadians working together with them to keep us all safe. In the same way we need to work with the Mexicans to keep our relationships friendly, so we can work with them. One of the big problems there is how much power the drug cartels are gaining across Mexico, Central America, and South America, particularly in Columbia. Texas has a long border with Mexico, so that problem concerns the Texans more than it does the people in other states."

"Is Belize part of Mexico?" Danny questioned.

"I know, I know!" Sissy exclaimed. "We studied the seven Central American countries in Social Studies just a couple weeks ago. Belize is the only Central American or South American country where the official language is English because it used to be a British colony. Its border touches the bottom of Mexico, and the west side of it touches Guatemala."

"Cool," commended Danny, "So Dad will have to travel all the way through Mexico to get to Texas?"

"He'll likely fly. Your uncle Evan has a car down there in Belize, but I think it is only rented and supplied by his employer, so they'll both be flying home when they can. If they don't call again today, we'll call them again tomorrow to see when they can get back."

Conversation continued on varied subject until Thelma introduced the Scrabble game. Jonathan then stopped the SUV, allowing her to move to the middle of the backseat so the three of them could view the travel board together. The children quickly recognized the need to use the double and triple word spaces to enhance their scores. The roads were clear, and the farther south they traveled, the warmer the day became. They all enjoyed the time together, forging lasting bonds.

Late that evening, they arrived at the Dentons' home in Longview, parking in the drive beside the house. "I hope they approve of us," Danny worried.

"They'll love you both," Thelma reassured. "Come on in and we'll introduce you."

They walked to the front door, standing in a group after ringing the doorbell. They were greeted by Dr. Denton with his wife standing close behind him. "You have finally arrived!" he exclaimed enthusiastically with a big smile. "We were about to send the police out to see if you were lost somewhere; we've been waiting all day to get to see you."

"We're glad we're here too!" Danny exclaimed. "We were afraid you might not like us or feel that our coming would be too much work. I'm Danny, and this is my sister, Sissy. We will try very hard not to be too big a burden for you in spite of your advanced ages."

"Well, hello, Danny and Sissy," the doctor said warmly, suppressing a smile. "We appreciate your concern, but we're not worrying about that at all. The Taylors have told us what capable youngsters you are. Hello,

Jonathan and Thelma," he continued, shaking their hands. "You're looking good. So the trip's gone well?"

"We had a super trip!" Sissy answered. "Sometimes Danny has an awful lot to say, but he means well. I think your house is beautiful," she commented, looking around appreciatively while formally shaking Dr. Denton's hand.

"Do you remember us at all, sweet girl?" Mrs. Denton asked, stepping back as the group entered closing the door behind them.

"A little," Sissy admitted shyly. "Danny also says he remembers you a bit. We remembered your old house. It was on a busy street, and you kept the door locked so we wouldn't go out."

"We are delighted that we can see you again. We're so sorry to hear about your daddy's problems and your mother being gone. We're just heartsick about that. Has she written to you at all?"

"Not that we know of," Danny answered loudly. "Am I talking loud enough for you both to hear me?"

"You don't need to be quite that loud," Dr. Denton responded. "We both can hear pretty well in conversation especially if you look right at us and we can see your lips. However, if you're in the other room or on the phone, it's a lot more difficult to pick up what you're saying. Don't worry about it; we'll tell you if we can't hear you. The best thing you can do is look at us directly when you speak. When did you last hear from your dad?"

"Yesterday. People were shooting at them."

"How do you feel about that?"

"I think the men are mean. Do you think they should go to hell? Grandpa Taylor thinks it's too early for us to say. He thinks they still might get sorry for being so mean."

"Young man, it sounds to me that Grandpa Taylor is right. I agree with him. It is wrong what the drug men are doing, but often their punishment is not only going to hell. When we do evil things, we can get into trouble here from God's punishment before we die. Not only are they likely to get put into prison or get shot themselves, but there may be other very sad things happen to them like illness from drug use. This is called the consequences of sin."

"Do you think Dad is being punished now because he was drinking so much beer and liquor?"

"I think that your sister is right about your ability to ask a lot of questions," Henry Denton responded, delaying his answer. "However, the honest answer may well be yes," he chuckled. "Let's ask him about this when he returns to see what he thinks. This is a pretty serious matter for us to be talking about so soon after you've come. I bet all of you are about ready to go to bed."

"We are," Danny answered for the group and then asked, "Do you think it would be OK if Sissy and I slept in the same room? We're used to that. Do you have any pets? Are there any children that live close? Have you decided on our school yet? Do you think Grandma Denton is a good cook?"

The room filled with laughter as Sally Denton fielded the questions. "We have a bedroom with twin beds; I thought you might want to be together at least for a while. We have a cat that spends most of its time outdoors or in the garage, there are children that live next door about your ages, and I'm a fabulous cook. Your Grandpa Denton will be in extremely hot deep water should he suggest anything else! Finally, we'll talk about school tomorrow; we want to talk to your dad about it."

CHAPTER XII

Monday, March 15

The four men had planned their mission to start at 5:00 AM and were able to leave the embassy only a few minutes later. Although they'd all had good night's rests, they were quiet as they drove the miles to the Guatemalan border. The air was warm and muggy with a dark heavy cloud cover. Arriving at the checkpoint, the guard looked over their outfit and started giving instructions in Spanish to Herman who was driving. After he'd finished talking, Herman reported that the guard was assuming they were going hunting, that he wanted to see their guns, that he wanted to see passports, car permits, hunting permits, and that he also was saying that with the expected rain, it would probably be a miserable day for hunting.

"Tell him we're not hunting in Guatemala, but that we're going down into southwestern Belize. I have four rifles here I can show him," Josh said, reaching into the back, straining to pick up four unloaded hunting rifles in their cases. "Does he want me to get out and show them to him or does he want me to hand them out?"

"He wants you to get out and show them one at a time," Herman translated after speaking to the man again. "We all need to show him our passports, too."

"I hope he doesn't have a problem with these temporary passports the embassy issued us," Zack worried.

The guard looked weary but recognized Josh from previous passages through the checkpoint and grinned and commented, pointing to the Humvee.

"He says it looks like you have a new machine," Herman translated again.

"Yeah, tell him it's the same one. I just had it repainted," Josh responded.

The guard looked over their papers, opened the gun cases, examining the contents, and waved them on.

"I hope he doesn't report us to the drug cartel so we have them alerted," Zack worried, again recalling their suspicion of the last checkpoint.

"I think that's not likely," his brother reassured, "because this fellow's Guatemalan, and I've been told at least at this border crossing the guards are pretty straight. I think its fortunate he didn't ask if we had any other guns to declare. Actually, I think he was supposed to do that but didn't."

"I think it's more of God taking care of us," Herman commented. "I am worried about the rain, though. If it starts to rain hard, we'll be having difficulty getting up and down that road. Much of it is gravel, I think, and we'll have to ford a couple streams. Because it's been dry they'll be small, but if there's much rainfall, it's going to be tough."

"OK, OK," Zack interrupted, "here we are again. We need to pray the rain doesn't stop us and thank God for our ease moving through the checkpoint."

"Amen to that!" Evan exclaimed. "I'll pray. God, we need your help. We need to get Herman's family out, and we don't want the rain to hinder us. We're trusting in you. Amen."

"That was short," Zack commented.

"Prayers don't have to be long to be effective," Herman defended. "Evan, what time did you say it was forecast that it would start raining today?"

"Around two this afternoon. Hopefully we'll be in and out of the gravel road by then. However, that weather report applied to Belmopan, and I couldn't seem to get any forecast for Punte Gorda,"

The men drove on down the nearly deserted highway and after four hours made the turn onto the road back into Belize. Initially the surface was paved, but it soon gave way to gravel with multiple potholes that had not been graded over. Herman drove carefully, but the ride was bumpy and rough nevertheless. "If it rains, all these holes will be filled with water," he observed.

They arrived at the Belize border fording a stream. There was no border guard, just a sign on a fence post announcing, ENTERING BELIZE. The road did not improve, and if anything became smaller, appearing to having had even less traffic. Their speed decreased, and mile after mile they swerved, dodging the old ruts and potholes. The small village of Jalacte was little more than a cluster of houses. They'd forded three shallow streams over rocky waterbeds before finally arriving at a paved road coming into Aguacate. However, the paved road was still filled with potholes, and the travel continued tediously and slowly on past Blue Creek. Several miles further on the road became gravel again, but was in better condition than the paved road had been. Finally they came to another paved road, and Herman announced, "This is the Southern Highway, and we're at the Dump. It won't be too much farther."

True to Herman's word he soon turned, taking a right off the main road. "We're coming into the farm from the back," he informed. "We'll get off on a trail behind the farm where there's a hill from which we can look down on the farm and see whether there are any vehicles around the house."

The ride became even bumpier, and Herman brought the vehicle to a stop before the crest of a hill. The four men got out, walking up to the top. Josh carried his binoculars, and when they reached the hilltop, handed them to Herman, asking, "So what can you see?"

"There are two vehicles that are not my family's," Herman reported slowly. "There's one in the yard by the house with a couple men standing beside it. I think one of them is my dad. There's also another vehicle out on the road by the front drive of the farmstead right near the cabin where my brother lived. I don't think we should go down there while there's a vehicle in the yard. We can't drive down there without being seen."

"I think we could walk down there under cover of the trees at the side of the farm, don't you think?" Josh queried.

"Sure, but we don't know how long the SUV in the yard will remain there. Not long I hope. Hey, it's starting to back up now. I think its leaving."

"OK, then let's start getting ready to move," Josh directed. "We'll all go back, get the guns, and start carefully down the hill. Herman, you're the only one that needs to go into the house. Do you think all your family will be able to walk back up here to the Humvee?"

"Yeah, Dad will be a little slow but he's tough. I would actually like you to be with me as I go into the house. I can't be certain there's not someone there with the family."

"Right," Josh agreed, "I should have thought of that. How close to the house can the rest of us get and stay invisible?"

"Actually we can get into the barn from the back. We can even go from there to the chicken coop without being seen from the house. However, the distance from the coop to the house is wide open."

"Which side of the house has fewer windows, and in which rooms are people likely to be looking out of the windows?" Josh asked.

"There are only bedrooms on the north side," Herman explained.

"So you fellows will be waiting in the barn while we go in," Josh said to Zack and Evan. "Herman, could they go up in the loft and give us some fire cover from up there while we go in?"

"Well, yes," Herman considered, "there aren't any windows in the loft low enough to look out, but there are cracks between the boards in the siding they could use."

"Let's hope none of this planning is necessary. The fewer gunshots the better since we want to draw no one's attention. Is that house over to the east the closest farm?" Josh asked, looking through the binoculars Herman had handed him.

"Yes, an elderly couple live there in the house. It is their farm, but the neighbor farther on up the road farms it," Herman replied.

"Let's do this then," Josh said, turning and starting back to the Humvee. "Let's all get the vests on and pick up our guns." At that moment, a heavy gust of wind came up with a few drops of rain driven in its path. "I've only got two thin rain jackets," he continued.

"You and Herman wear them," Evan directed. "Zack and I will be in the barn anyhow. These vests are some rain protection, too."

The men donned their gear and quietly set off down the hill in the cover of the trees. The wind died down and a gentle rain began to fall. As they neared the farmstead the rain became heavier, and they were all happy to get into the barn. Zack and Evan climbed the ladder to the loft, positioning themselves with their guns to overlook the yard behind the house. Herman and Josh stealthily moved on up to the chicken coop and then on to the house. Josh crouched to the side as Herman knocked on the back door which was in a screened porch. Ardine, Herman's wife, answered the knock, cautiously approaching the screen door, but then immediately recognized her husband. She fumbled with the lock on the door, saying and weeping quietly, "Oh, Herman, you're alive, you're alive! Where have you been?"

When the screen door was opened, Herman stepped in and took her in his arms. "Shhh," he whispered, "I love you. Are any of the drug men here?"

"No," she answered, "but they're to come back in an hour or so. One just left a few minutes ago and said he was driving into town. We needed some salt and sugar, and he said he'd bring it back. These people are horrible. They beat up your dad day before yesterday because he didn't hurry fast enough to catch a couple chickens for them."

"I'm here to take all of you away," Herman said quietly. "I'm with three armed men, so we need to leave as soon as possible. Let's get the passports and birth certificates and a few clothes. Are the children all right? Why don't you go in and tell them I'm here. We must make as little disturbance as possible; it appears you have a guard out at the front drive."

"So we're going to leave everything?" she asked.

"I think it's too dangerous to try to take anything. I'm planning to take us all to the United States. I've talked with them about it at the US embassy in Belmopan."

"You dad's not going to want to leave this farm."

"I don't want to leave it either, but I want us to stay alive! Go ahead in," he said, motioning Josh on into the porch and following his wife into the house.

"Everyone, come into the kitchen," Ardine called out. "Come quietly and immediately; I have a great surprise for you!"

"Just a minute," Jennifer called back. "I'm finishing ironing my dress."

"Stop now and come!" Ardine replied firmly.

"Daddy!" Jennifer squealed as she entered the room, rushing to hug her father and also breaking into tears. "We were afraid we'd never see you again—that they'd killed you just like they killed Uncle Juan!"

Angel and Herman's father, hearing the commotion, entered the kitchen as well.

"Dad!" Angel exclaimed, also hugging his dad, and Herman's father simply walked to his son, quietly putting his arms around the three of them with tears running down his eyes.

"We need to leave here immediately," Herman said. "Your mother thinks the drug cartel men will be back here shortly and we need to be gone. I'll tell you what's gone on with me when we're all loaded up. You need to get your coats and heavy shoes on because we're walking out to the back of the farm where we have transportation. There are three friends of mine with me here to help us." Herman stepped to the porch, motioning Josh in. "This is Josh, who's in charge; the other two are in the barn covering for us. Your mother is getting our passports and birth certificates. We're going to the United States."

"Dad, can I get the family picture album?" Jennifer asked.

"Yes, honey, but that's about all. Wrap it in plastic to keep it dry."

"Son, are you certain I should go? I'll slow you down," Herman's father asked.

"Dad, I've thought about it. Seeing how these people behave, I believe that to leave you here would be certain death. We only have to walk up to the back of the farm. I'll help you if you need it. Do you have the animals shut up anywhere? We should let them out as we leave."

"They've taken away the cattle and goats—even the dog. All we have is about fifteen chickens; we can let them out as we go by the chicken coop. Every day all of us have been doing the farm work. They have not allowed the youngsters to go to school. They've been demanding that all of us work in the fields every day. We'd be working today except that they knew it was going to start raining."

"In that case we need to be thankful for the rain, but we need to get started because the trail behind the farm's soon going to be impassable if we don't. Can I help you?"

"Pick up my briefcase behind the couch," his father directed. "I'll get my coat and umbrella."

The family was rapidly ready to go, and Herman realized his wife had suspected the possibility of such a rapid departure inasmuch as she had the bare essentials preassembled for the trip. Angel had the wrapped family Bible and a framed family picture, Jennifer had the picture album, Herman's wife had a bag of clothes and candy, while he was carrying his father's briefcase. Herman wondered if he'd ever be back as they all walked out of the home he'd known his entire life. They stopped at the chicken coop, opening the gate to the yard and proceeded on to the barn where Zack and Evan had already made it out of the loft and were waiting. Herman made brief introductions between his family and friends, and they continued in the rain on up the side of the farm among the trees. As they reached the top of the hill, they saw the black SUV heading into the farmhouse yard behind them.

"I know this is going to be a tight fit with eight of us," Josh commented as they approached the vehicle. "For now Herman's still driving, you brothers sit by the windows with your pistols ready. The ladies can sit in the middle, and Angel and I will be in back. Herman, get us out of here as soon as possible without getting us into the ditch."

Indeed, with the rain the trail was much more treacherous than formerly. Herman wound the vehicle up and around the hills now splashing through puddles. "How do I engage the four-wheel drive?" he asked.

Josh explained and asked how much further to the highway.

"About two miles," Herman answered.

"Good, we'll make better time then," Josh commented.

"If they catch us, it will probably be there, though," Herman responded. "When they find us missing, they'll look there because it's really the only way and main route out of town unless you're flying or on a boat."

"Go as fast as you think is safe," Josh again directed. "They'll have to drive pretty fast to find us."

A few minutes later the Humvee moved onto the highway, increasing its speed. Herman drove and talked with Ardine, white-knuckled beside him, and Evan on the right. Behind Evan was Mr. Hernandez with his arm around the silent Jennifer and Zack to her left. Angel was engaged in back with Josh, who was showing him the guns but keeping a close eye on the highway behind them. Herman was attempting to summarize to Ardine the events of his life since he'd been taken away from the farm. As Evan listened to the recounted events, he realized Herman was leaving a good bit out of his story that might increase her fear and attempting to insert a bit of humor.

"There's an SUV bearing down on us pretty rapidly from the rear," Josh reported. "Oh, they're slowing down a way back," he continued.

"We're almost to the dump where we turn off," Herman responded. "Let's see if it turns, too."

Sure enough, as the Humvee turned left back onto the gravel road to Blue Bird, the SUV did as well.

"Herman, you're doing great," Josh commended. "Keep going at the highest reasonable speed. They don't seem to want to get too close."

Herman sped along the gravel road at seventy miles an hour. The clouds became darker, and the rain started to fall much more rapidly. Mile after mile they traveled with Josh, unable to see the following vehicle at times, but then it would reappear, also traveling at their rapid speed.

With a large bump they lurched back onto the paved section of road, and Herman had to slow with the increasing numbers of potholes.

"They're hitting some of these holes pretty straight on and getting closer again," Josh informed.

"Let me know if they're close enough for you to shoot," Evan said.

"I really hate to take any shots at them without good reason to be confident that they are actually our assailants," Josh countered. Suddenly, from the rapidly rear approaching SUV, gunshots rang out, rattling off the rear of the Humvee. "Well, that answers that question," Josh immediately said. Everyone put their heads as low as possible. "Evan, I'll tell you when and if I think it's safe to lower the rear window. With the rough road, the rain, and the fact that it appears they have at least three in the vehicle able to shoot, I don't want that window open unless it's necessary."

Herman increased his speed but then began to sense that the Humvee wanted to hydroplane, and he had to slow again. The SUV swerved behind them with obviously the same difficulty. Jennifer whimpered beside her granddad, and Angel sat rigid and still, watching the road behind along with Evan. The Humvee splashed through Blue Bird and headed on around the frequent potholes to Aguate. The rain continued to pour, and the cloud cover remained heavy and threatening. Lightning flashed, thunder claps could be heard over the sound of the road and engine, and Herman forged on. "God help us, God help us," he prayed.

Ardine looked at him in wonder. "When did you start praying?" she asked.

"While I was in the factory prison," he replied. "I'll tell you more about it when things aren't so tense. It's very important."

"Ten more kilometers to Augate," Zack noted, reading an advertising sign. "I don't know if it'll be better or worse with us going through the town."

"I'm not looking forward to the rest of that unpaved road with all the rain," Herman commented. "And those fords will already have a lot more water in them."

"Yeah, I know, but we have a lot more clearance than the SUV so when we get there we'll splash rapidly on through unless is looks impossible," Josh encouraged.

The ten kilometers crept by and they moved rapidly through the town, seeing only a few cars on the streets. When they were back on the paved road, the SUV suddenly sped attempting to pass them. Herman swerved to the right to prevent its passage, and it swerved back to the left, attempting to pass on that side as well. There was more gunfire, but no sound of bullets hitting the vehicle. Herman swerved again, missing a very deep pothole and the close SUV, not seeing ahead, dived right into it. The group in the Humvee heard the bang and crunch of the SUV, but it still came on though somewhat farther back. They arrived at the first ford, which, as Herman predicted, was heavily swollen in comparison to earlier. Herman gunned the motor, and they indeed splashed on through but not without the vehicle losing its traction momentarily. However, the momentum of the machine carried it on through, and they slowly ground up the low but long rise on the other side.

"They started across but then backed up!" Josh crowed. "They're just sitting there. I actually don't think they could make it even if they tried. I'll keep watching, but I think we've lost our followers."

"Praise God!" Zack contributed. "Now we need the rain to stop."

However the rain didn't stop; it continued to pour heavily. Herman drove carefully attempting to avoid the now overflowing potholes. There was so much water on the road that some of the holes were invisible, and he would drive right into them with a resounding jar in spite of his caution. They came to a section of road with little, if any, gravel on it, and the clay like soil began to adhere to the tires, making it increasingly difficult to steer. On one downhill section, the Humvee started to slide and then continued slowly, moving them smoothly into a wet ditch by the road.

"Well, here we are in one piece," Evan commented, pleasantly attempting to keep up the spirits of his cohorts. "I think it's get out and push, even though we'll all get sopping wet."

"Josh, would you mind taking over the driving?" Herman asked. "I'd hate to tear up this transmission getting us out."

"No problem, pal," Josh replied, "With a shove, I think we can make it especially since it's downhill."

"Mom, do we kids need to get out?" Jennifer queried.

"Yes, everyone out except Dad," Herman answered for his wife. "Every little bit will help."

So all but Josh and Mr. Hernandez got out, sloshing through the water and weeds to the back of the Humvee.

Josh had his window down, calling out, "Everyone push on the count of three!"

They pushed. The wheels spun, throwing mud all over them, but they kept on pushing, and little by little the machine started to move back onto the road. They were all so elated that they'd been successful that no one complained about the mud and wetness but got back in laughing and cheering.

"That's the first time I've ever done that," Zack commented with a chuckle.

"It wasn't my first time at all," smiled Herman's dad. "When I was young and we couldn't get a car unstuck, we'd use a team of horses."

"Remember Grandpa's horses?" Zack asked, addressing his brother.

"You bet. We had a blast just being led around the barnyard. He was really patient with us. He'd hobble along with the rope in hand, which we thought were big stuff."

"So you lived on a farm?" Herman questioned.

"No, our granddad did; we were city boys."

Josh had come to another ford, which didn't seem as treacherous as the last, and drove through fairly slowly. Once through, he stopped and backed through again.

"So you like playing in the water?" Evan laughed .

"No, I'm hoping to wash off some of the mud from the tires. I think I may be able to steer a little better," his friend answered, continuing to drive back and forth through the rushing stream. He then continued on.

"Has it helped?" Zack asked.

"Yes, a bunch," was the reply.

"Cool!" Angel contributed from the back, where he was now riding with his dad.

"I'm getting cold. Can we turn on the heater?" Jennifer suggested.

"Sure, lady," Josh answered gallantly. "Anything for a lady!"

"We don't feel very ladylike wet and covered with mud," Ardine laughed. "But we're glad to be moving. So, I guess we're on our way to the US embassy in Belmopan? Why are we going this way? We should have stayed on the main highway."

Explanations were given, and they drove on through the rain in the dark afternoon with Josh dodging potholes. There was an audible sigh of relief from the adults as they reached the CA-13, making their way north.

"I'm hungry. How about stopping for some food?" Josh offered.

"I don't feel fit to be seen," Ardine objected.

"There's an El Pollo in Santa Elena," Evan suggested. "It's a little out of our way but not much. We can order to go. It's going to be pretty late by the time we get back into Belmopan. I don't think the cafeteria at the embassy stays open very late."

"Great plan," Herman agreed. "Maybe you're tired of fried chicken," he said, turning to his wife.

"We're so glad to be off the farm we'll eat most anything. We've not been allowed to leave there for three months now. The longer those thieves were there, the more restrictions they made. We were afraid to sneeze!" Ardine exclaimed.

"We're both free." Herman said, putting his arm around her shoulder. "Yes, we're all free, and what a blessing it is. We as a family need to thank these men for their help. It wouldn't have happened if they'd not all been a part of it."

"I don't feel I've done very much today to help," Zack considered.

"Don't underrate yourself," Herman corrected. "You got the ball rolling to come get us in the first place, you supplied manpower and protection today, and who knows without you we may still be back in the ditch," he finished laughing.

"It was Josh's guns and vehicle that allowed it to happen, though," Evan contributed.

"We're really glad you came," Jennifer added seriously. "Every day we were afraid. Living that way is no fun!"

"We were afraid they'd shoot Grandpa two days ago when it took him so long to catch the chickens. They laughed and shot the gun up in the air just to frighten him. It was awful," Angel recounted.

"We have a new life ahead of us, so let's be thankful and attempt to forget the past. Sometimes forgetting is partly a matter of talking about it and saying how things made us feel, though" Herman added wisely.

The rain continued steadily as they followed the CA-13 and then turned west toward Santa Elena. After getting the meal, they headed back to the border and on to Belmopan. The border crossing was easy inasmuch as they were reentering residents, and there was no question as to the validity of their papers. It was a weary muddy crew arriving at ten-thirty at the embassy gate. Fortunately they'd been able to phone ahead, and the guards were expecting them.

That night Herman slept with his family about him.

CHAPTER XIII

TUESDAY, MARCH 16

Zack and Evan sat in the Embassy cafeteria feeling restless but compensated by going over their plans for leaving Belize.

"So we're to be picked up here tomorrow and taken to the airport here in Belmopan? At what time?" Zack asked.

"About 2:00 p.m.," Evan replied. "They plan to fly us out at two thirty and don't want us hanging around the airport any longer than necessary."

"I think we'll probably do OK here with the embassy watching over us," Zack worried. "I'm not so sure about our layover in Guatemala City. We actually don't know the extent of the reach of this drug cartel; I feel pretty confident they hate us for what we've done to them here, exposing them as much as we have. They're pretty certain to be vindictive."

"I think we've got enough cover," Evan responded. "We're to be met at the airport by US embassy security stationed in Guatemala. We'll be kept in the Admiral's club, spend no time in the lobby, and escorted directly to security for the airline flight on which we're leaving. We'll board as soon as we arrive at the gate. I'm so glad Alice is able to be going with us. They were able to get a substitute teacher for her just yesterday, and I was able to get tickets for her on our flight online yesterday evening."

"I hope the embassy is OK with her going with us," Zack commented.

"Yep, I'd covered that with them right after we arrived and told them about it again yesterday when I found it was a go. My task today is to get back to Belize City to pick up what I'm taking from my apartment and to collect Alice and her things. I'll need to go buy some suitcases; I'm hoping you'll come with me. I only have one large case and a small carryon. We all three can take two large cases and each have a carryon. With all nine suitcases I believe that'll be adequate space for the things Alice and I need to take. One of the embassy security guards has been assigned to go with us this afternoon at one-thirty. Josh is planning to come pick us up to make the trek. The embassy thinks law enforcement has been quite successful in gutting the cartel's strength here. They've now picked up ten more fellows from Punta Gorda and six more from Belize City. What did Herman learn yesterday when he talked with the consulate?"

"He was told it looked like they'd be waiting here at least a couple more weeks. I talked with Dr. Denton yesterday, asking him if he'd consider being Herman's sponsor. He agreed, but I'm not certain that will be necessary with him seeking asylum. Herman's planning now to come to Longview since I'm planning to be there for a while, especially since my children are getting enrolled in school there. It's going to be a big challenge for him to be in another culture, but he seems very up for it. I've been surprised how much his children don't seem to be dreading going to a new place. I think they've been so frightened and fearful the last several months that saying good-bye is going to be easy. Even his dad seems optimistic about the move."

The trip to Belize City went without a hitch; Alice hadn't seen Evan since the momentous ride out of town and was overjoyed to see him. Zack felt painful remorse seeing their love and remembering the brightness of his early relationship with Elaine. Jim and Linda Smith were with Alice, assisting in the packing and agreeing to help Josh with the disposal of all their remaining personal effects. Zack could see the parting of Alice and the Smiths was difficult, but they all covered the challenge with jocularity until a few tears at the end were shed between the ladies.

After the four were back in the Humvee headed to Belmopan, Zack, sitting in front, turned and asked, "Well, Alice, how do you feel about having your school year being cut short and going home early?"

"It feels like I'm not in control but rather that circumstances are running my life," she replied.

"We were already planning to leave, so it has chiefly moved dates ahead. I've been here for three years, so it's a bit similar to leaving home. Jim and Linda are like my immediate family; they are even-dispositioned, always looking for a way to be helpful to others, and they're an inspiration to spend time with. We'd considered having the wedding down here, but that's certainly not going to happen now. It was more of a pipedream than reality anyhow since it would have been such a distance for most of our family and friends. How are you feeling about getting back home?"

Zack answered hesitantly, shifting to the center of the seat, "I'm more than thankful to be getting back to the US. I'm certainly looking forward to seeing the children and also am extremely thankful that they're now in good hands. However, I know I'm going back to face my past, which is my lack of a college degree, the poor treatment of my children, the damage of my alcoholism, and the situation with my wife. I don't know where she is or even if she's alive. Our folks have let me know they'll help me attempt to track her down."

"Don't be too hard on yourself," Evan commented from his seat beside Alice in the rear. "We'll all be facing change, but we'll all be around to help each other out. On the phone the other night, Alice and I agreed that it would be good if I would attempt to get a transfer in my firm to Dallas. We have a major growing office there, and I feel fairly confident that it could happen. That would allow us to be closer to her parents and ours as well inasmuch as ours are definitely planning on moving to Longview. I do want to suggest that you look into going back to school. Dad mentioned that idea to me on the phone yesterday, asking me how he thought you'd feel about it. It sounds like both sets of grandparents are more than enamored with your kids; I'm sure they'd help you manage your school schedule."

"I would love the opportunity, but I don't really see how it could be a possibility. I do have a family to support. I don't know if there are any schools around Longview where I could pick up my engineering even if I were able to consider it," Zack objected.

"Dad said LeTourneau University is there and that they have a great engineering department. He and your father-in-law apparently both think it has great academic standing."

"If the academic standing's too high they likely won't let me in; my study habits were pretty poor when I was at Normal," Zack countered.

"Yeah, well you never know unless you try," Evan persisted. "Dad also said there's a technical state-run school over in Marshall, the next town east. It would likely cost less, but it sounded to me from what Dad said that Dr. Denton's offering to foot your tuition cost if you can get into LeTourneau. Dad thinks he sees your education as a safety net for the grandchildren."

"He certainly wouldn't be looking at it as an investment, considering my lifestyle track record!" Zack exclaimed. "It's a fact; I don't deserve help like that. The Dentons have always been more than kind to Elaine and me as a couple, and we soundly turned our backs on them. I let their daughter slip into drug abuse."

"Dad says they seem to be seeing it differently. He says they feel part of your predicament was caused by Elaine rejecting the path of right living, not influencing you to a responsible lifestyle, and finally taking an easy way out with drugs. Partly, also I think they're looking at their wealth and wanting to see it put to immediate good purpose. Dad says they're pretty despairing of ever seeing Elaine again with this much time elapsed since anyone's seen her or had contact from her, but they haven't given up."

Zack sat quietly, digesting the comments. "To be very honest," he said, "I absolutely would love to go back to school, but I'm fearful about a bunch of things. I'm afraid of being rejected by a school should I apply, I'm afraid of failing if I get in, I'm afraid of myself being strong enough to stay away from alcohol, I'm afraid of what people would think about me taking in-law money to go to school, and I'm afraid of what has happened to Elaine. This just about sums up my life right now!"

Silence reigned a couple minutes. "I think that's actually some pretty clear thinking," Alice said slowly. "Much of the time most of us are unwilling to admit to our fears, men in particular, so we don't identify them and deal with them appropriately. You're now in a position to deal with what you're facing because you're identifying it."

"Hey! Hey! Are we bashing the male sex?" Evan asked, laughing.

"Yes, to an extent," Alice answered. "In our culture, men feel a need to be independent, which in itself is worthy but adhering to it too strictly leads to denial of fear, which prohibits clear thinking. Late adolescent men are particularly prone to this, and it makes them vulnerable to doing unwise if not stupidly foolish things."

"Boy, I certainly agree with that; I'm a case in point," Zack laughed. "Evan, maybe we both need to listen to what she says."

Evan rolled his eyes then winked at Alice, asking, "So resident expert, once we identify the problems, the fears, what do we do then?"

"We analyze them one by one. Some fears are real and valid and must be acted upon immediately or soon, but most are pretty indistinct or nebulous with multiple facets requiring a many-pronged approach."

"So what kind are mine?" Zack wondered, thinking out loud. "Let's see, the first one was I'm afraid of being rejected by the school should I apply. That falls into the nebulous category, I suspect, so what's my multipronged approach?"

"Several things," Evan replied, "you need to recall your stellar high school performance, which still remains on your high school transcript, and the sports trophies you won at that time. You do have one and a half semesters of credit at Normal, which you need to send to LeTourneau to see if they'll accept. I'm pretty certain they'll accept A and B grades and possibly some C work, but you didn't have much of that until the last semester. Finally, even though you're ancient in comparison to me, you have a commanding physique that may stand well for you should they meet you. For a college dropout, your speech is actually downright acceptable. Our parents made certain of that."

"Another thing," Alice said slowly, considering her words as she moved ahead, ignoring Evan's jibe at his brother, "you do have your years of work experience, which stand as some value for life lessons. Many universities have you write an autobiography to acquaint the admissions evaluators with your background and experiences, and inasmuch as LeTourneau is a Christian university, the admission evaluators would look positively on your conversion experience from unbelief to belief. It would likely be imprudent to enumerate all your past failings but helpful to give God recognition for the things you believe he's done for you."

"I can do that," Zack said quietly. "It all sounds so reasonable. I should probably hire you as a guidance counselor."

"She's special, isn't she?" Evan bragged.

"OK, my next fear is of failing if I am accepted," Zack continued.

"Well, think of it this way," Alice responded. "We know you've been out of the education loop a good many years, but people older than you are in colleges all the time. Most universities evaluate all new students and some reentering students to determine competence, especially if the service is requested. They can then fit a remedial program to your needs, giving you some insight into your strengths and weaknesses."

"What she says makes sense," Evan added. "However, as I went through the college classes, I realized many, if not most, of the classes stood alone. You didn't have to know a bunch to start right, but you did well if you buckled down the first day to learn the material and then kept at it. I know math's not that way; it does require a good grasp on previous classes, so you'd need to bone up on your algebra and trig, say, before you'd take calculus. It would be work of a different nature than you've been doing the past number of years, but it would just be work. You did it before and you could do it again."

Josh, sitting quietly as he drove spoke up, "I hate to interrupt your planning, but I'm afraid I should have had one of you fellows driving. I think I see someone following us, and I should likely be in back."

The others turned to see a black luxury model car following at some distance.

"Great scot!" Evan ejaculated, "Are we never going to be rid of these fellows?"

As he gunned the Humvee aggressively, Josh instructed, "I'm going to speed up dramatically and see if we can lose them in hopes that I can stop, and we can change seats. Evan, I'd like you driving; I'd like to be in back where I can have access to the guns. Evan, can you call ahead to the embassy to tell them of our new problem? We're about twenty mikes out from Belmopan."

The vehicle flew along the highway, reaching greater than 100 mph, and Alice began an audibly whispered prayer.

"We're not losing them," Zack reported from his turned position in front. "In fact, they appear to be drawing closer. They may be fearful now of losing us."

Zack finished his call, and Josh instructed him to get out the guns, to hand one to Zack, to give a pistol to him, and to ready one for himself.

Stopping her prayer, Alice said, "At this speed twenty miles will disappear quickly."

At that moment, they passed a police car sitting along the side of the road. It immediately turned on its flashing lights but pulled in behind the black car, which continued to race along, ignoring the police signal.

"Call the embassy again," Josh directed. "They need to let the police know what's going on."

Evan did so, and less than ten minutes later two additional police cruisers entered the highway behind the first with the lead cruiser passing the black car. With increasing traffic as they approached town Josh had to slow, and the black car darted down a side street with the two back cruisers in close pursuit. The third police vehicle simply followed the Humvee as it made its way to the embassy. Again, the gates were open as they entered and quickly closed behind them, and the guards stood beside the Humvee doors as the four moved into the compound while the guards spoke with the escort police.

Inside the building they were met by the ambassador, who shook his head, saying, "There are certainly more of these fellows than we had expected. The police already have the three that were following you in custody. Someone had to have been in surveillance of either the engineer's apartment or his fiancée's apartment for them to have picked you up so quickly. We're going to be glad to have you out of the country tomorrow!"

"We can't thank you enough for your help so far," Zack replied. "We are concerned about security in Guatemala tomorrow. My brother Evan here says you've been taking that into consideration for us."

"Yes, but we'll also have some American embassy guards at the Guatemalan airport on hand while you're there during you layover. By the time you're in Dallas, the regular airport security should be adequate. Who will be meeting you in Dallas?"

"Our dad will be meeting us; he's a pretty able fellow and has a carrying permit," Evan offered. "However, given Zack's recent abduction in St. Joe, we know we're going to have to be vigilant. I'm based in Chicago, but I'm truly hoping we'll be off their radar once we're back in the US."

"Well, I'd contact both the Dallas and Chicago offices about the situation. We're struggling with these organizations here and would hate to see them gaining ground there."

"I would like to offer my thanks for your help as well," inserted Alice. "I'm the engineer's fiancée," she added with a twinkle in her eye.

"We're glad to be of help," he responded politely. "I would like to meet with Mr. Josh Ash in my office, if you can excuse us."

CHAPTER XIV

MONDAY, MARCH 17

Sissy awoke before everyone after the first night in Longview. She climbed out of her twin bed and walked to the window, which looked out onto the front lawn. She noted the quiet street in a cul-de-sac and the fact that the leaves were budding on the trees. The pavement was wet, but there appeared to be no frost, which was a marked change from Missouri. She could hear birds singing through the window pane, and she looked for a way to open the window. Turning the latch, she was able to get the sash up eight inches and no farther, but even that was not entirely satisfactory with the screen preventing her from putting her head out. She watched a squirrel scurrying across the grass, stopping to dig and then turn the object of his successful search in his front paws as he chewed. She looked down at the front walk and the carefully cultivated flower beds not only in the yard beneath her but across the street as well. She could hear cars on a nearby street, but there were none within her view.

"Hey, Danny," she whispered loudly. "Are you still asleep?"

"Sort of," he responded. "I haven't opened my eyes yet. I was dreaming that Dad was home and that he wouldn't talk to us. We were still back in the apartment in St. Joseph. He came into the room and just sat and cried. We couldn't do anything to stop him; he sat there and cried, and we wanted to cry, too. I even feel sad now, and nothing has happened this morning that is sad."

"That is a bad dream," Sissy consoled and considered it quietly as she gazed out at the peaceful view. "Your dream was probably right that Dad is sad. We both think he's sad because Mommy left, so maybe we need to help him find her. We did find the grandparents"

"Good idea!" Danny exclaimed, jumping out of bed with eyes wide open and running to the window. "We could get the grandparents to help us; we wouldn't have to start by looking all by ourselves. Hey, look, there are squirrels really close!"

"You need to be less noisy," Sissy warned, "You'll frighten them away. See, they're both behind the tree now. I don't know if Dad's ever tried to find her; I think he's been trying to keep her from finding us. Remember, we heard him tell her he never wanted to see her again if she was using drugs."

"Maybe she's quit and can't find us. The grandparents didn't know where we were."

"If she were looking for us she'd likely have contacted her parents, and they didn't know she was even missing until they were told so after they'd found us."

"Actually, we found them; they didn't find us, but you're right," Danny agreed. "But since they didn't know she wasn't with Dad, they hadn't looked for her as if she were missing. Let's talk to them about it this morning. Do you think they're up yet?"

"I haven't heard anything yet, but this house with all these thick carpets is very quiet," Sissy answered. "Let's go down and see."

The two children headed down the long hall and down the stairs. As they reached the bottom of the stairs, they were in a large room but could hear the muted sound of voices around the corner. Dr. Denton was talking.

"Sally, do you think I should go wake anyone up yet? It's seven-thirty."

"They got in pretty late last night; let's wait another half hour and see if they don't come out on their own. I know you; you can't wait to start teasing those children."

"We're here!" Danny heralded, rounding the corner into the kitchen. "We want to talk."

"Well, good morning! Good morning, sweethearts!" Sally exclaimed. "Come have some breakfast. How does eggs with biscuits and gravy sound?"

"Good morning to each of you," Sissy replied primly. "We both would think that would be a wonderful breakfast."

"Good morning woolly heads. Did you sleep well last night?" Dr. Denton asked.

"We slept great!" Danny answered for the two of them. "Good morning, we think we ought to be finding our mommy now that we're here. Can you help us?"

"Well…. I can see that your wheels are turning in your head already so early in the morning," his grandfather replied. "Your grandmother and I have discussed this, and Dr. Taylor and I had talked about it on the phone before you came. Your dad asked him to help him find her, so we'd been waiting for your dad to get back to start looking."

"That actually makes it easier," Sissy considered. "I didn't know if Dad really would want her back with us because he told her to leave."

"That's not exactly what he said," Danny corrected. "He said she needed to leave and stay away as long as she's using drugs."

"We think, though, that she's probably still using drugs since she's not tried to come back," Sissy said. "I thought you would be angry at Dad for asking her to leave."

"Oh, no!" Sally exclaimed. "We love your mother, but we also realize the danger of having a drug-using parent raising children. It is difficult if not impossible for them to be responsible; too often their decisions are not based on what's good for the family but rather how to keep getting the drugs. Additionally, there's always the bad example they set. We don't fault your dad at all about that."

"Why does he want help to get her back if he asked her to leave?" Danny asked.

"What do you do you think about this, Henry?" Sally asked.

"I think your dad has made some big changes in his thinking since he was captured only a few weeks ago," Henry replied slowly. "While he's likely not sorry for asking your mother to leave with her using drugs, he's ashamed of his treatment of her before she started using drugs. He wants to ask her forgiveness, and he thinks he's done the wrong thing by making it impossible for her to reconnect with you and him. Some of what I'm saying is speculation, but I do know he has asked for help in finding your mom."

"Here is your food, children," Sally said, setting plates in front of them. "Are you happy with milk?"

"Oooo, we like milk," Danny claimed. "This food smells so good!"

"Here are some orange quarters, too," Sally added.

"Thank you so much! Grandmother," Sissy gushed taking her first bite, "this is so good. I need to learn how to make this; can you teach me?"

"Sure, sweetheart," Sally answered. "Oh, here are the Taylors. Come in and have some breakfast; we're having biscuits and gravy. Does that agree with you?"

"Good morning, Sally; it sounds wonderful," Thelma replied. "Is there anything I can do to help? We apologize for sleeping so late."

"No problem," Sally said, bustling about setting out more flatware and napkins at the kitchen table. "Pour yourselves some coffee. Cups are by the pot by the sink, and the sweetener and creamer are behind them. I'll have your plates dished up as soon as you have a seat. I've made plenty. It's fun to have a crew to cook for; I grew up in a large family and miss the comradery of mealtime and fixing a larger quantity of food."

"You should have had Zack and Evan to feed," Jonathan commented. "They consumed huge amounts of food as they were growing."

"Yes, the refrigerator always seemed empty when they were at home," Thelma laughed.

"Oh, you don't know how good it will be to see those boys again!" Sally exclaimed and then teared up. "I can't wait to feed a meal to them," she smiled through glistening eyes.

"We've been talking about finding Mommy," Danny said as silence had settled on the table with the eating adults. "Grandpa Denton says he's waiting for Dad to come back before we start. Sissy says she thinks Mommy is still using drugs or she would have contacted her parents if she couldn't contact us. I think she might be right. What do you think, Grandpa Taylor?"

"I don't know that we have to wait," Jonathan replied. "Unfortunately, I suspect Sissy is right. Sally and Henry, when have you last heard from Elaine?"

"We last heard from Zack and Elaine about three years ago. We knew Elaine had been in a drug rehab program, but then they stopped replying to our letters. Our last contact was when Elaine sent us a letter telling us not to contact them, not to call, and not to send gifts to the children."

"Yes, Zack had called and told us the same thing when they were still in St. Louis," Thelma informed.

"I believe none of us knew Zack and Elaine were separated until the children contacted us," Jonathan observed.

"That's right. We'd have attempted to track down Elaine had we known she was alone," Henry added.

"How can we help Dad find Mommy, then?" Sissy asked. "It sounds like the last we know about her was in St. Louis. Did she have friends in high school or college she may still know and talk to?"

"Good question," Sally said. "Here again Zack would know better than we do. Henry, do you remember the names of any of Elaine's high school friends. Some of them came to you for dental services, didn't they?"

"Yes, let's see. There were the Arnett twins that had those braces so long who were in her class, but I don't think they were particularly close to her. Jill Robinson was a good friend as I remember, and she spent a lot of time with the Briley girl. Do you remember her first name?"

"Oh, yes, it was Alexandra. The problem is these girls are likely all married, and we don't know their married names now," Sally replied.

"We can possibly search for them on the internet," Thelma suggested. "Do you perhaps have any of Elaine's old yearbooks from high school or college? They might jog your memories as to names. Especially the high school surnames could be tracked locally in a phone directory attempting to contact the girls' parents to get current married names."

"Maybe we should hire a detective," Danny inserted. "They probably know how to do this better than we do, but I guess that would cost money."

"You're right, buddy, but it's a very good idea," Jonathan responded. "We probably ought to at least try ourselves before we involve someone else. It may not be difficult if we make the attempt. I actually have no idea as to the extent of the expense; it would likely depend on the amount of time and effort the investigator would have to put in."

"Another idea would be to contact the police or the hospitals in the St. Louis area," Henry contributed. "I don't know if the HIPA laws prevent us from finding a missing person. We would need to consider that."

"What are HIPO laws?" Danny asked.

"Law protecting our personal privacy," Henry replied, smiling. "It actually stands for Health Information Portability and Accountability—HIPA. They were written to protect us from having our information get to the wrong people; however, they often hinder the proper access of families to the information they need."

"I think we need to have a plan," Sissy said. Let's make a list of things that might help and each do one or two of them. Grandpa Taylor, why don't you ask Dad for his permission for us all to go ahead and work on this and let him know what we're doing. You could also find out what's involved with contacting the police for their help in St. Louis. Grandpa Denton, why don't you find out what we can learn from the hospitals in St. Louis and if there's ever a reason they'd let us know if Mommy has been there. You could also find out how much it would cost to hire a detective. Grammy Denton and Grandma Taylor, you work together and

I'll help to see if there are yearbooks and make a system of contacting all the possible names we can find."

"What am I to do?" Danny asked.

"You can help the grandpas just like I'll help the grandmas," Sissy directed as all the grandparents started chuckling.

"Why are you laughing?" Sissy asked.

"Because, dear, you're being so freely directive," Thelma responded for the group.

"I'm sorry. Was I being unkind?" Sissy queried.

"No, you were just being yourself. We love you the way you are," Thelma replied warmly. "I think we also ought to come up with an easier way to identify ourselves as grandparents for you since we're all together. Sally and Henry, do you have a preferable way for the children to address us?"

"It's a great idea," Sally responded. "I've never wanted to be granny, but grammy, grandma, or grandmother without the Denton would all be fine. How about you, Henry?"

"Nix on gramps, but grandpa, grandfather, or pop pop would be OK."

"Do you have a preference, Jonathan?" Thelma persisted.

"No, but I think it's a good plan," he answered.

"Let's have the Dentons be grammy and pop pop, and you and I will be simply grandma and grandpa. How do you think that'll work, children?" Thelma concluded.

"It's fine with me," Danny responded. "That reminds me, Sissy and I were going to change our names, too. Remember, Grandpa, I was going to be Dan, and Sissy was going to be Brenda. I think we all forgot it. What does everyone think?"

"I think it's going to be easier for you children to make that change than for the rest of us," Sally said hesitantly.

"I have a rule for this," Henry inserted confidently. "I believe as far as it is reasonable we should call individuals what they wish to be called. However, in this case I think their dad should have a say in this matter as well. Let's do this. Let's all stick with the current names until Zack returns and follow his direction. How does that sound to everyone? I know he named you Brenda and Daniel, but I think it would be good to have him on board with the change."

All were in agreement. However, in her heart Sissy wasn't sure she still wanted to be Brenda, so this took her off the hook. She wasn't fond of Sissy, but it seemed comfortable somehow. Danny, on the other hand, much preferred Dan and started to think of ways to convince his father that the change would be good should it be frowned upon.

"We need to talk about school," Dr. Denton directed. "I've contacted the public schools here in our district and am feeling uncomfortable with them as a choice. On looking at their academic standing by reviewers, our district appears to be weak. For a charge, the children could attend a public school in the adjacent district, which would be better academically. Another option would be a private school over on the north side of town, but it's a significant drive over there."

"Wouldn't that cost too much, Pop Pop?" Danny asked.

"It would cost more, but the school is not unreasonably expensive," his grandfather replied.

"Maybe Dad couldn't afford it," Sissy cautioned.

"Like so many things having to do with you children, your dad's wishes must be taken into account," Dr. Denton continued. "However, your schooling needs to be taken seriously. We can get you lined up for school at least for the rest of this year and I can pay for it. I've made plans for us to go to the private school this afternoon and for us all to visit with their principal. We can then drive around town a bit so you newcomers can get your bearings; maybe we could even stop in for some miniature golf, if it's not too late."

"That sounds fun," Sissy offered. "Are all of us going?"

Jonathan looked at Thelma, and as she nodded he said, "It sounds like something we could have fun doing together. It's been several years since Thelma and I have been here, and enough has changed that we could stand some updating. We could all go together in the Durango, but I'd need to go get it unloaded before we go."

"Do we know when Dad is going to get back?" Sissy asked. "Has anyone talked to him?"

"I talked with him this morning about six o'clock," Henry said. "Zack thinks they'll be coming into Dallas at 8:00 tomorrow evening. It'll be Zack and Evan and Alice. They're to fly to Guatemala City and then on up to Dallas. I thougt perhaps we'd all like to go to the airport and meet them even though it would make a late night for us."

"Oh, how exciting!" Sissy squealed. "We can meet Alice and Evan! When are they going to get married?"

"We don't know," Sally said, smiling at the enthusiasm. "We'll ask when they get here. Perhaps we can all take a long nap in the early afternoon, so we won't be so weary with the late trip. Henry, you and I are not as young as we used to be. Will we all fit into one vehicle?"

"We probably ought to take two cars," Jonathan said. "The three of them will have too much luggage for us all to fit into one. Do you youngsters think you can handle another trip so soon after yesterday?"

"Yes, yes, yes!" Danny crowed. "We can! We can! How long will the trip take? Will we stay overnight in Dallas? I read about the Dallas Zoo and fairgrounds; could we stop there?"

"I think meeting the boys and Alice will be enough excitement for one day," Thelma answered. "The trip takes two-and-a-half to three hours each way so we'd need to leave by 4:30 or 5:00 0'clock. Unfortunately we'd be driving through Dallas at rush hour, so it could even take longer, especially if there's an accident. If it takes a half hour to pick them up, we may well not get home until midnight. Perhaps some day this summer we can take a trip to the zoo and see some of the other sights in Dallas."

"There's a very nice zoo in Tyler," Sally contributed. "It's much closer; sometime we'll have to do that. Thelma, I can hardly imagine how relieved you'll be to have both of those boys back safe and sound."

"You're right," Thelma responded. "Tears start to come when I'm even thinking about it. Additionally I haven't met Alice, so this is going to be an extremely momentous event!"

"We haven't talked to Dad much, and we really want to talk to him more," Sissy said quietly. "I know you've said he's changed, but I worry about it."

Thelma held her close and whispered, "We're here with you in case things don't go well, but I'm going to be surprised if it doesn't turn out much better than your fears. I've talked with your dad, and I could hardly believe the things he was saying."

"Henry, what time should we all be ready to go visit the school?" Jonathan asked.

"I set it up for 2:00 PM. Do you think that'll be a problem?"

"What are we going to do until then?" Danny asked.

"We will unpack our clothes, empty the Durango, and make our beds," Jonathan directed.

"Then you can explore the backyard, get acquainted with the dog, and we'll have a light sandwich lunch right at noon," Sally added. "I know you children have been used to organizing your own time, so we'll all need to work together to make it so all of our schedules are not problematic."

"Yes, Grandma said we'd all have to work on that," Danny smiled. "I think it's fun to have meals together. This has been the best breakfast ever!"

The children were awed by the yard, the dog, and the swimming pool. The ladies watched them trample through the yard which included the vegetable garden bed, the flower terraces, and the fenced-in pool. The azalea blossoms were just starting to open, and the buds on the deciduous trees were greening. The bright morning sunshine was warming the day; the gaiety and enthusiasm of the children was nearly palpable through the window.

"Such delightful children," Sally commented quietly as she watched. "It's nothing short of amazing with the problems Elaine and Zack have experienced."

"I don't understand it either," Thelma agreed. "It's as if they have an innate tendency to do the correct things. I think I just keep expecting them to revert to being normal, quarrelsome kids. I do recognize that Zack was harsh in his discipline, and I don't think he offered them adequate love, but they seem to be functioning very well. It is humorous and delightful that they seem to have such an interest in church although they've attended almost none. I certainly have found being around them a joy. I know I need to have faith, but I do fear Zack may slide back into the same patterns he started back in college. It was like a switch turned; he was a great student, good athlete, respectful youngster, and suddenly all he could think about was doing his own thing, spending time with Elaine, and having little to do with us."

Sally replied slowly, "Elaine was the same way. She'd been an honor student in high school. She was active on the debate team and collected an extremely pleasant group of friends. It was amazing to us that she wanted to go clear off to Normal to go to school, but we had no valid reason to prohibit it. Looking back we see it was the beginning of some very damaging choices. With Zack's background, you'd have thought he'd be the ideal boy for her to meet, but it seemed as if the two of them simply influenced each other into wrong decisions! I know we've gone over this before, but it does remain extremely troubling for all of us. We've prayed and prayed for them; perhaps this is what it's taken for them to be back on track. I agree one is tempted to be fearful, but Henry says we need to take each step day by day and trust in the best. He definitely wants to see Zack back in school and is willing to help pay for it. I've asked what if Zack reverts and the money's wasted. Henry says we can't let fear dictate our actions; we need to trust God and pray."

Thelma put her arm around Sally, saying, "We've been fairly casual about our Christian faith, but these events are shaking us up. I feel that if we'd been more concerted in our commitment in the past, the boys would have had a better example. As we make plans to move here within the year, part of the move will need to involve stepping forward in the paths of faith. Evan has been a huge encouragement to us over the past year, and I think Alice is a wonderful blessing. I'm so looking forward to meeting her and spending time with her. I think you'll find her a delight as well; have I shown a picture of her to you?"

The morning moved on, the tasks were completed, lunch was eaten, and the group arrived for the school interview. Dr. Denton introduced all present to the school principal, Mr. Jamison, and informed him the children's father would now likely be in town late the following day. Because it was Wednesday, they agreed that if the children were to enroll it would be Monday before they would start, so their father could speak to Mr. Jamison as well on Friday. Mr. Jamison moved the group out of his office and seated them all in a circle in a nearby vacant classroom.

"If we're all comfortable, let's begin," he started out. "Do any of you have any questions or concerns before I launch into a description of the school?" he asked, expecting the usual quiet diffidence.

"I have many questions," Danny informed. "Exactly how much a day does the school cost, and will my dad be able to afford it? Do you have a good library, and are the teachers kind? Is there a dress code, and if so, how much do the clothes cost? What time does school start, and what are your rules when someone is late to school?"

Mr. Jamison grinned and attempted to field the questions. "We charge by the month. Tuition is $200 per month for the first student and $150 per month for the second child. Not knowing your father's ability to pay, I cannot know what he can afford. We have a great library; many of our families have contributed many good books to it. We emphasize kindness in our teachers; most students love their teachers and find the end of a school term sad because they will not be seeing their teachers regularly. There is a dress code, and we'll give you a book describing it and listing the prices of ordering them through the school, should your family wish to do so. School starts at 8:30 a.m. each weekday and ends at 4:30 p.m. The policy for tardiness is in the school rule book. Are you expecting that to be a problem?"

"No," replied Danny, "but it is quite a ways from our house to here, and I'm afraid Pop Pop and Granny, as old as they are, may be having trouble getting us here on time."

"Your father can likely help out with that as well," the principal conciliated.

"He's not done so well in the past," Danny added. "We had to get ourselves to school on time. Maybe he will do better now than before."

"Please let me apologize for all his questions and arguments!" Sissy exclaimed.

"It is just fine," Mr. Jamison grinned again. "I do believe he's engaged in the process of education."

"We've got the tuition and timely attendance covered, sir," Dr. Denton said, winking at the principal. "Go ahead with your planned information."

For the next half hour they walked through the building and grounds, and the group was introduced to the various employees. During recess, they were introduced to probable teachers who were so welcoming that both children were ready to stay when it was time for the visiting group to leave. Danny was hopping up and down with excitement as they reentered their vehicle. "What do you think we can tell Dad to get him to let us come here?" he asked, climbing into the SUV. "Do you think he'll like it as much as we do?"

"I think you'd just like any school," Sissy commented wryly with a smile. "I did like it too, though. What did you think about it, Grandma and Grandpa Taylor?"

"I though it looked well-managed," Jonathan replied. "Henry, what did you find about its academic standing?"

"The students seem to do well on the standardized tests, and the high school graduates are doing very well," Dr. Denton answered. "I think at least for this year it is our best option. Now, who do we think will be our miniature golf champion? Sally and I haven't played for years, so we don't stand much of a chance."

"To my knowledge, Jonathan and I have never played either regular golf or miniature," Thelma answered.

"We haven't either," Sissy laughed, "so that means we don't have any idea who the champ will be."

"How much will it cost?" Danny asked.

"Well, for all of us, maybe twenty to thirty dollars, but we can afford it," Sally answered. "You let us do the worrying about that."

"I don't think I'm worrying," Danny answered. "I just want to know so I can decide if we can do it again. Grandpa, did you know that golf stands for 'gentlemen only ladies forbidden'? Maybe the ladies should play one game and we should play another."

"I doubt that's true," Sissy said.

"Yes, I read it in a sports magazine," Danny claimed. "Golf started in Scotland, and they put the letters on signs to forbid the ladies."

"Yes, I believe he's right," Jonathan agreed. "I'd read that somewhere myself and had forgotten it. However, I think it will be more fun if we all play and compete together."

CHAPTER XV

THURSDAY, MARCH 19

Zack sat restlessly in his seat after boarding the plane in Guatemala City, thankful there'd been no problems in the terminal, but wanting to get off the ground. Ten minutes earlier, the pilot had informed them that the plane was not meeting all its safety checks and that there would be at least a thirty-minute delay while they determined the problem. The temperature in the cabin was rising slowly, and he chuckled to himself as he watched his right heel shaking with nervous energy. He intentionally held the heel still and said to Evan sitting beside him, "My body knows I'm anxious whether I do or not! I'm tied up in knots! I think if I could be doing something rather than just sitting here it would be easier."

"I know," his brother replied, "we feel like birds on fence posts, vulnerable to being picked off with a shotgun."

"Yes, it's that and other things as well," Zack said. "I know I'm ill at ease with the expectation of meeting both sets of folks and even the kids. I've made a mess of things."

"You're going to get tired of me telling you to forget the past and to focus on the future, but I think it's important for your functionality," Evan commented.

"I agree, but it's difficult," Zack responded and moved on into thinking about how each of the parents and the children would behave at the moment of reunion. He wondered how best he could communicate his new resolves to each of them. The recurring wave of guilt washed over him as he thought how poorly he'd managed things with the children. What did his parents think about him? He considered how kind they'd been in their phone conversations, but he felt extremely vulnerable, worthless, and chagrinned as he thought of his past behavior. He gazed out the airliner window now delighted with the onset of motion and the pilot informing them that the safety check was clear and they were moving into the takeoff flight sequence.

As the plane lifted into the air, Evan punched him in the arm, saying, "One more step toward the good old USA! I may never get back down here to Central America again, but it's been a good chapter in my life. The job all in all went well, I met Alice, and think how very fortunate that I was here where the drug cartel brought you! I'm giving God the credit for that; you probably ought to as well."

Zack punched Evan's arm back lightly and turned his face toward the window to regain control of the sudden surge of emotion he felt before answering. "You're right, bud," was all he felt safe saying. Suddenly he felt overcome with weariness and realized that his constant state of vigilance that had become his way of life since the kidnapping now was ending. He leaned his head back in the corner of the seat and the cabin wall, stretched his legs under the seat in front of him, and quickly drifted off to sleep aided by the steady hum of the motors.

Evan eyed his sleeping brother and whispered to Alice on his other side, "How do you think he's doing?"

"Well, I think," she whispered back. "However, you fellows are so much alike you may be able to answer that question better than I can. I believe the main way we can help him is to keep him busy doing things that are moving him forward for self-sufficiency; however, he seems pretty much like a self-starter to me."

"He used to be that, all right. He was enthusiastic about nearly every project we engaged in and wouldn't stop until it was finished. It was a surprise to see how little motivation he seemed to have once he and Elaine were together. All he wanted to do was drink a beer, watch TV, and complain about how little money he had. He seems like the fellow I grew up with again now," Zack continued whispering.

"How long do you think you'll be able to stay in Longview?" Alice asked.

"About a week. Why?"

"My folks texted me back in the airport that they would like to drive up from San Antonio to get me and to have the opportunity of meeting you and your parents. What do you think?"

"Wow! That would be great. I suspect we'll need to clear that with the Dentons. Even with the limited acquaintance I've had with them, I doubt it'll be a problem. So, in all this change, when should we set the wedding date?"

"Now that we know it'll be in the States, I think it should be in San Antonio at my folk's church. I do wish we knew if you were going to be able to be transferred to Dallas. I'd like to know where we'll be setting up housekeeping."

"We're going to have fun no matter where we'll be. I'm sorry about the difficulty. I did send an e-mail to my supervisor yesterday about a possible transfer. He did not want to hear about it because he wants to keep me in his office; he had several projects he was thinking about involving me in, and my moving would thwart those plans. In his reply he said he'd inquire about the transfer for me and that he suspected the company would jump at the chance to move me since he knew the new office in Dallas was landing new projects more rapidly than they had anticipated."

"Oh goody!" Alice exclaimed, "I can't wait to tell my parents! I asked Mom how much time we'd need to get the wedding together. She said if I were buying a wedding dress off the rack and if I were not using a caterer to make the cake, we could probably get it done in six weeks. What do you think about that?"

"So we wouldn't have a cake?" Evan asked.

"No, we'd have a cake. Mom's got a friend who'd already offered some time ago to make me a cake when we married. She'd been disappointed with our talk of marrying in Belize. Now, however, she'll likely be delighted to do it. I've seen and tasted some of her cakes; she does a lovely job."

The two whispered on with their plans while Zack slept.

The two-car caravan was moving toward the Dallas/Ft. Worth airport. The ladies were together with Thelma driving the SUV, and the men were with Dr. Denton driving his car in the lead. Danny was strapped with his seat belt in the middle of the rear seat, or he'd have been bouncing against the car roof liner. "Pop Pop, what's the population of Dallas?" he asked. "Is it bigger than St. Louis or Kansas City? How big is the airport? How will we be able to find Dad in the airport?"

"Well, let's answer these questions one at a time," Henry answered. "Dallas is bigger than either Kansas City or St. Louis. The Dallas/Ft.Worth area has about six million people in it. The airport is very large and is in the middle between the cities; consequently, coming from the east, we'll have to drive all the way through Dallas. We'll find your dad and uncle near the baggage claim area in the airport terminal building. There are conveyors that bring out the suitcases from the various landing airliners for the passengers to pick up, so if we go to that specific baggage claim we'll find them there."

"If we're inside, where do we park the cars?" Danny worried.

"There will be a big parking garage nearby for us to use. However, should we arrive right on time we can simply wait outside for us to pick them up and to get them loaded. We'll see how the traffic goes through Dallas; we might not have any extra time. However, if there is a lot of extra time, we might want to stop and get a bite to eat," Henry answered.

"Do you think we can afford for all of us to eat at a restaurant?" Danny questioned.

"I appreciate your concern about spending money," Jonathan laughed. "We are not being extravagant, and often to get things done appropriately and pleasantly one needs to spend some money. Too often, people spend money without consideration of how much they have, and that's when they get into trouble. Being a good caretaker of your money means not spending more than you have, but it also means not hoarding money when you need to use it for a good purpose. We don't want you worrying about spending money, but we do appreciate your concern and want to encourage you to always be vigilant not to spend it unwisely. One of the important things to remember is that all of us can see a lot of things we want that we don't need. However, there are some things we really do need. The key is to see what we do actually need and what is only an unnecessary want and then to spend our money on the needs first and spend the money on the wants if there is plenty left over."

"So, buying this car and paying for the gas so we can go get Dad would be a necessary need," Danny said, attempting to apply the lesson. "Stopping for food if we don't need it would be a want that we should only spend money for if there is plenty. How about when Dad spent money on the beer, and there wasn't much money left for us to have food? Was the beer a need or a want? He sure acted like he thought he needed it."

"He was addicted to the alcohol; he felt bad if he didn't have it," Jonathan replied. "Beer, alcohol, and drugs would always fall into the want category. However, once you're addicted to them, it is more difficult for your brain to make that correct distinction. Because you feel badly if you don't have them, you begin to believe it is a need. The only way to be certain you never become addicted is to never use them. Some people can use a lot of the stuff before they become addicted, but others don't need to use very much before they get into trouble."

"Sissy and I have a pact to never ever use them!" Danny exclaimed. "Now, will Dad still be addicted to beer when he comes back?"

"When your dad couldn't get his beer when the drug men had him, he became very sick," Jonathan responded. "When he became better after the illness, he realized what had caused the sickness, and he realized how poor his judgments and decisions had been while he was drinking so much. He's now decided, like you, to never drink beer or alcohol. He knows that even if he drinks a little beer he's likely to get back into trouble, so he plans to stay away from it entirely."

"I believe God will help him with this," Henry added. "In fact, I think we can give God the credit for getting your dad captured, off alcohol, and now back home sober. This has been a frightening way for this to have happened, but it appears to have been for the best. We all need to pray now that God will give your dad the strength to stay away from the beer."

"Do you think God could help Mommy?" Danny asked.

"Yes, we do," Henry continued. "In fact you grandmother and I have been praying for her daily for several years now that she'd be freed from these drugs."

"God doesn't seem to be doing much, does he?" Danny complained.

"Not so far, but we must not give up hope and stop praying. I'm trusting we won't have to wait much longer now that we have a plan to get back in touch with her. When we talked yesterday with the St. Louis police they seemed quite helpful, saying they would not only look through their system and list her as a missing person, but also give our name to the hospitals and the drug and alcohol abuse centers that exist in the area that might have record of her. They're to call us back in a few days," Henry answered.

Traffic did become increasingly congested as they entered the city, and even though they could use the HOV lanes, they crept along at a slow pace through the city center. However, as they neared the airport they still had forty-five minutes to spare, so they stopped at an ice cream parlor before going on to the airport parking lot. By the time they all walked into the terminal and found the appropriate baggage claim conveyor, the whole group had become unusually quiet and took seats in the waiting area along the windows. Passengers from the flight were just starting to arrive.

Thelma was the first to recognize her boys as they rode down the escalators some distance away. She stood and rushed to them as they were attempting to decide which baggage claim area was theirs. Thelma reached Zack and grabbed him around the neck, sobbing incoherently, "I was so afraid we'd never see you again!"

Zack hugged her in return. "I was afraid of the same thing," he said, blinking away the tears. "God has been good to me giving me another chance. It is wonderful to see you!"

The other adults gathered around, and introductions were quickly made of all to Alice when Zack asked, "Where are the kids? Did you leave them at home?"

The grandparents all appeared nonplussed and looked back at the seats where they'd been waiting. There the two children were sitting with their arms around one another weeping quietly. Zack ran to them, kneeling down in front of them and taking them into his arms one on each side. "Children," he said, "I'm so sorry for the way I treated you! At times I couldn't sleep at night knowing how irresponsible I was. Please forgive me! I promise this will never, never happen again. I love you both so very much!"

"We were frightened for you and without you!" Sissy exclaimed. "We're glad you're back, and we forgive you! We think it's wonderful you escaped from those horrible men!"

Danny continued to hug his dad and weep. Finally, he said, "Dad, you must never leave us again. Do you think the men who took you away will go to hell? I sort of wish they would, but I probably shouldn't think that. Are you going to help us find Momma? Pop Pop said you would."

Avoiding discussion of his captors' eternal rewards, Zack answered, "You bet I'm going to work on finding your mom. That is number one on my agenda now that I'm here. Are the two of you ready to meet Evan and his fiancée, Alice?"

"Yes! Yes!" exclaimed Sissy, hopping away from her father's arms and looking up at the other adults gathered around them. "Hello, Uncle Evan. You sure do look like Dad!" she said, holding out her hand to shake with him. "And this is Alice?" she continued, unabashedly offering her hand to her as well.

Alice shook her hand and then knelt to give her a hug. "What a young lady you are!" she enthused. "I think we're going to be great buddies."

Zack stood while Danny continued to hold tightly to his hand. "Those introductions were easy," he said. "and Danny, this is my brother Evan; he's been looking forward to meeting you."

Danny offered Evan his right hand as he continued to firmly hold on to his dad with the left. "Hello, Uncle Evan," he said, "I did want to meet you. Grandpa said you'd made better choices in your life than Dad did."

"Hello to you, too," Evan quipped. "I'm glad to see someone here in this group appreciates me. They all seem to be running to Zack first. I probably need to put you on my payroll just to improve my PR!"

"What's PR?" Danny asked.

"It's public relations. It's the people you hire to make certain people know your good character," Evan smiled.

"I don't think you'd need that," Danny rejoined. "I think that to hire me would be a waste of money!"

Everyone laughed as they moved over to the baggage claim conveyor to collect the suitcases. As the group moved on out to the parking area, Evan was conscripted to drive the SUV carrying the ladies, and Zack was to ride in the back of the Dentons' car with his children beside him. Thelma spearheaded the arrangements, saying, "We ladies and Evan need to talk wedding plans, and you children need to bring your dad up to speed with your adventures!" The placements were satisfactory with all, so the trip home began with uniform good spirits, with the family first stopping at a restaurant for the evening meal.

"Thank you so much for coming after us," Zack began as the SUV exited the restaurant parking lot. "You likely can't know what a relief it is to get back into the US!" From his position in the middle of the rear seat, his arms were around a child on either side. "I cannot tell you how great it is to see these kiddos again," he continued, giving both a hug and choking up as he did so.

"You likewise can't imagine how relieved all of us feel to have you back!" his dad exclaimed. "It is as if you're back from the grave! Henry and I agree that it as if your life is starting again; we're hoping you feel the same way. We really want to be supportive of you to get things back on track."

"Yes, Evan's talked to me about it, and I'm pretty overwhelmed about what you both have in mind. I'm dealing with what I feel is responsible and what is just. I'm fearful of taking you up on your offers because I might fail. Evan says I need to be confident and positive, but I don't feel that way."

"That sounds like honest talk to me," Henry responded. "We know for you to get back on the path that can benefit your children and you the most will take a good bit of stick-to-itiveness, but we think you can do it, and we'll be here to help."

"Dad, we started looking for Mommy yesterday," Danny said, hesitantly bringing up the subject again.

"Yes, we talked about it with the grandparents, so we all started working on it," Sissy continued, attempting to protect Danny from his dad's disfavor if it were forthcoming.

"Oh, really? How's that?" Zack questioned.

Danny explained the different assignments, and Sissy continued with the progress that had been made in two short days. "Pop Pop says the police in St. Louis were very helpful," she concluded.

"So what did they say, Dr. Denton?" Zack questioned.

"They said they'd call back as soon as they'd reviewed their missing persons lists and coordinated that with any local hospital inquiries and people listed in drug and alcohol treatment programs. They seemed optimistic they could help if she'd been in the hospital; they also encouraged us to call back in case we didn't get a call from them," Henry said. "I think we should call back again tomorrow. I'm their main contact since Elaine's my daughter."

Zack gave a long, worried sigh. "I hope she's OK," he said slowly. "I've had terrible dreams of attending her funeral, of being with her in a hospital and my being unable to help her, and of her being involved in criminal drug-related cases without a lawyer and me being unable to afford one. The dreams never end well and always leave me feeling inadequate."

"Well, we've been praying for you and things are working out. We'll pray for her too and that we have the proper insight as to how to find her,"

Henry said quietly. "Rest assured we don't fault you for asking her to leave with her persistent drug use. We do, of course, wish you'd have told us, but I'm suspecting you didn't because you didn't want her to find you."

"That was true at first, but later I think it was plain old thoughtlessness," Zack admitted. "Please forgive me for that," he finished.

"We do," Henry assured, "and we're so thankful to have you and the children back."

Silence reigned in the vehicle as they moved on through the city and out onto the open interstate. However, things were not quiet in the SUV. Alice, Thelma, and Sally were enthusiastically making plans, and Sally had gotten on the cell phone to invite Alice's parents up for the weekend to pick up their daughter and meet the extended family. Evan, who was smiling at their chatter, quietly held Alice's hand over the console.

"This is going to be a lot of guests for you, Sally," Thelma cautioned.

"Oh, but it's going to be so much fun!" Sally responded. "I've dreamed of having the house full, and now it's happening. We're going to need to put your two sons in the same room. Do you think they'll mind that?"

"No, not at all," Evan inserted. "We were together at my place in Belize City and again at the embassy."

"My folks could get a hotel room," Alice suggested.

"Oh no, not unless they'd be more comfortable by themselves," Sally remonstrated. "I think it friendlier and more fun for us all to be together."

"You must let us help with the cooking, cleaning, and washing," Thelma encouraged.

"And I need to be helping, too!" Alice added.

"Yes, yes," Sally laughed, "That will be part of the fun of it!"

"We fellows can help, too," Evan contributed. "Mom, I can make beds, do washing, and clean house. I've been on my own for several years."

The conversation continued as bonds of friendship were formed and plans were made of the upcoming visit and more distant arrangements for the wedding. Unlike the men in the Denton's car who rode silently with the children and their father asleep in the backseat, the occupants of the SUV had a steady flow of conversation until they pulled into the Dentons' drive in Longview. Upon arrival, Zack and Evan carried the sleeping children into the house, placing them in their beds. Evan was asleep within minutes of being in bed, but Zack lay awake into the wee hours of the night going over the day, thinking about his future and attempting to turn the situations in his life over to God. He recognized the rollercoaster of his emotions as he thought of the wonder of his escape, the loss of Elaine, the good condition of the children, the fear of resuming the alcohol addiction, and the challenge of resuming his education. Finally, at three in the morning he drifted off to sleep.

CHAPTER XVI

FRIDAY MARCH 20

"Dad, are you awake?" Danny hesitantly asked from his position just inside the doorway of the bedroom Zack and Evan shared.

Zack awoke groggily, saying, "I am, sort of. I didn't get much sleep; it took me a long time to get started. How are you, buddy?"

Danny moved over to the bed and asked, "Do you have a headache, and are you sleeping here by yourself?"

"No, your Uncle Evan was here; I think he's cleaning up in the restroom over there," Zack replied, pointing to the door at the opposite end of the room from the entry door. "Why did you wonder if I had a headache?"

"Because you always used to, and you'd be grumpy in the mornings."

"Come to think of it, I haven't had a morning headache for the past several weeks. It was probably all that beer I used to drink. I sure hope you're smart enough never to behave the way I did. Why don't you hop in the bed here beside me? What made you wake up this morning?"

"Oh, I first wanted to make certain you were actually here and that getting you at the airport yesterday wasn't a dream. I didn't know where you were sleeping, so I started down the hall to check each room. Fortunately, your room over here was the first one I came to and here you are," Danny said, crawling over his dad and situating himself sitting snuggled up to his dad's shoulder with his back against the headboard. "I have things I want to talk about with you."

"So what sort of things are those?"

"I want to talk about school, about my name, about your name, and about you getting a car."

"When did you turn into such a question box?"

"I think I've always been one," Danny laughed. "I was always afraid to ask you much. You always got mad."

"Oh, help us all!" Zack responded, laughing as well. "What about school?"

"You're supposed to go there today and talk with the principal, Mr. Jamison. We can start Monday if you approve, and Sissy and I both like the school. I asked about how much it would cost, and Pop Pop said he'd pay for it at least for the rest of this school year. I guess we could pay for it with the money you left in the cereal box, but you might need that for something else. Sissy and I gave that money to Grandma and Grandpa to keep for us. We were afraid we'd lose it."

Zack sighed, "Sure, I'll go talk with Mr. Jamison. I don't see why you shouldn't get started back to school as soon as possible. I can work it out with your grandfather. So who's Pop Pop and who's Grandpa? Is Dr. Denton Pop Pop?"

"Yes, and your dad's Grandpa. We all decided that to keep things straight. We also talked about my name being Dan instead of Danny and of Sissy being Brenda. Grandpa said we should ask you before we changed for good. I was sort of hoping you might let us go back to calling you Daddy instead of Dad. I think it sounds friendlier. What do you think?"

"I think you're making my head swim," Zack chuckled, looking up at his son who was staring down at him with an intense worried look on his face. "I like to hear you call me Dad because it makes me feel like you're more grown up, but if you like Daddy that's OK with me. Someday not too far away you'll probably want to call me Dad because older children do use that word. So the answer to this is that I want you to call me either Dad or Daddy, whichever you want. I'm just thankful you're still willing to admit that we belong together. If you wish to be Dan instead of Danny, that's OK, too; I like them both. I'll talk Sissy's name over with her. It's funny; I'm all right with you growing up, but somehow it seems like she should still be my little girl."

"What about the car?" Danny persisted but was interrupted by Evan walking into the room in his undershorts.

"Hey, you're awake, and we've got company!" he laughed, addressing Zack while pulling a polo shirt over his head and donning some jeans. "What's this little geezer doing sitting in my bed?" he asked, reaching down and giving Danny a good tickle under his arms and sitting on the king-sized bed himself with his back against the headboard like his nephew.

"We were talking about important stuff," Danny explained, laughing. "I was asking Dad about him getting a car."

"That does sound heavy," Evan agreed. "What did your dad say?"

"I didn't have a chance to say anything," Zack answered. "Before I can get a car, though, I'll have to get my driver's license reinstated. Danny, I'm embarrassed to say this, but I lost my license up in Missouri due to a DUI."

"What's a DUI?" Danny asked.

"Short for 'driving under the influence of alcohol.' Our car was a rattletrap, and a fellow I knew at work wanted it. I knew I couldn't drive for at least six months, so I sold it to him. The six months are now up, so since we're in Texas, I need to see what I need to do to get my license back. This is one more good reason not to drink!" Zack finished.

"Do you need to call the state of Texas to ask them how to get the license?" Danny questioned.

"No, they'll have a local office here in town to handle all this. I just need to call them. I think I'm hungry, and I smell food," Zack finished, sitting on the side of the bed. "I'm going to clean up first, though. Why don't you fellows go down and scout out the availability of provender for us, and Danny, you come back up and report to me what the situation is."

"Aye, aye, sir," Danny stood up, saluting his dad. "The name's Dan, though, sir."

"Get out of here you little scallywag," Zack laughed, but Evan and Danny made their exit count by throwing socks out of a suitcase at Zack.

Walking down the hall and down the stairs, Danny grabbed Evan's shirt and whispered loudly, "Don't you think this is a cool house? It is so big and so nice, and there's a swimming pool out in the backyard!"

"Yes, it is nice, and yes I was able to see the pool this morning out our bedroom window. I wonder if it is heated. We could maybe go swimming today. However, on second thought I doubt that it is because I think you'd have seen water vapor coming up from it if it were warm on this cool morning," Evan replied.

"Oh, shucks!" Danny responded, "Let's ask Pop Pop anyhow."

The two rounded the corner into the kitchen and heard the shuffling of plates and silverware.

"Something's smelling good," Evan announced as they entered the kitchen.

"Yes, and your mother's responsible," Jonathan replied. "She demanded that she be allowed to do breakfast this morning for her boys, and Sally willingly agreed. I think the Dentons were pretty tuckered out by the time we got home."

"We've got eggs, bacon, cereal, toast, and monkey bread," Thelma announced. "The eggs and bacon are ready now, but it will be fifteen to twenty minutes for the monkey bread."

"Is my sweetheart up?" Evan asked.

"Well, it depends on who's your sweetheart," Thelma smiled. "If it's the lady who brought you into this world, who fed and cared for you for years, and who's always been there to love you through thick and thin, then she's right here, but if it's that little gal you've taken a shine for you picked up down in Central America, she's cleaning up in the restroom in by the guest room where she spent the night."

Evan walked to his mom, giving her a tight hug and saying, "You'll always be a sweetheart to me, Mother, but you've got to admit Alice is a delight."

Thelma, luxuriating in Evan's hug and returning one of her own, replied, "She's a doll and entirely worth waiting for. We are so pleased with your choice. It will be a delight meeting her parents; they've started this morning and will be here this afternoon sometime. When did you last meet them?"

"I'm going to go tell Dad and Sissy what's for breakfast," Danny interrupted and then raced out of the room and back up the stairs as Alice entered the kitchen dining area from the other direction.

"Good morning, beautiful!" Evan exclaimed. "Don't you look nice? We were just talking about your folks coming in this afternoon. When did I last see them? I guess it was at New Year's. You'd flown up to be with them for Christmas, and I'd been in Chicago and stopped in San Antonio for New Year's. We had a great time playing games and meeting her brother and some of the family friends. You're going to find them very much to your taste because they do like word games!"

Jonathan, who'd quietly been setting the table and placing the food from the counter on the table, said, "All this food is now ready to be eaten. Let's sit and talk while we eat. I agree with Evan; Alice, you look fresh as a daisy. Who'd know you were running from bandits two days ago? Alice didn't hear that there's also monkey bread coming later."

"I didn't hear, but I can smell it," she laughed.

"Here come the others!" Thelma exclaimed as they heard Zack and the children noisily thumping down the stairs. "Jonathan, do we have enough plates set?"

"I set for nine," he answered. "If the Dentons weren't awake, they are now," he continued, shaking his head and smiling.

"Oh, they're awake," Sissy informed. "They told us to tell you they'd be down in ten or fifteen minutes and to absolutely not wait on them. Grammy told me they'd slept like logs. Oooo, the food smells delicious! Good morning everyone! It is so fun to be here! Where do we sit?"

"Good morning to you, too," Thelma said, going down the line and giving each of the three a hug and lingering with her arm around Zack. "Let's have your dad sit at the end with one of you on each side. We'll save the other end of the table for the Dentons. There's nothing like coming in and taking over their house. We must all work not to let them overdo"

"Let's hold hands and say grace," Jonathan directed. "I am overwhelmed with thankfulness that we're all here together. Alice, will you do the honors?"

Prayer was said and the family proceeded to pass, serve, and devour the food with minimal conversation until Danny spoke up. "Sissy says I'm not to dominate the conversation, so I'll make my speech short. Dad said this morning that I could be called Dan. Is that OK with everyone?"

"We think it is fine," Jonathan answered after meeting eyes with Thelma. "Has a decision been made as to what we'll call Sissy?"

"I've decided that I don't want to change my name at home yet," Sissy answered. "Actually I haven't talked to Daddy about it, but I'm going to ask if I can use Brenda at school."

"Oh, I like that!" Zack exclaimed. "I was not wanting to tell you no, but I was dreading calling you something different here at home. Using Brenda at school will be fine. At what time today am I to meet with Mr. Jamison?"

"We need to check with Pop Pop," Sissy replied. "I think I heard him say one o'clock, but I'm not certain."

"I need to tell all of you that I'm feeling very anxious about Elaine," Zack said. "My bedroom door was ajar right before I came down, and I heard Dr. Denton take a call from a hospital nurse, and I think he was talking about Elaine. I did not interrupt because I was actually inadvertently eavesdropping."

"Well, this is a time to commit this matter to God together in prayer," Evan said, taking Alice's hand on one side and his dad's on the other. "Let's join hands again and I'll pray. 'Heavenly Father, things seem to moving so fast it makes us dizzy. We've just arrived here, and now we may have news of Elaine. Give us all wisdom as we deal with this matter. Help Zack and the children to deal with the emotional aspect of this. Be with Elaine; meet her physical, emotional, and spiritual needs. We commit this to you in prayer. Amen.'"

Everyone was silent as they heard the Dentons slowly descend the stairs. Everyone turned to look at them as the couple walked into the kitchen, passing the high island counter and standing with Henry's arm across Sally's shoulders. "We have solemn news," he said. "The Barnes hospital in St Louis called, and a nurse said Elaine was there as an inpatient and had been there a couple weeks. She's very, very ill. She had initially denied having any family, but when the police called the hospital looking for her, she admitted we were her parents and gave them permission to talk to us. The nurse gave me her doctor's phone number, so I called him right back and immediately got through to him as he was on morning rounds; he'd just been talking with the nurse. He told me Elaine has chronic active hepatitis B and that her condition was end stage. I asked about a liver transplant, and he said she didn't qualify because of her drug use and recurrent drug use treatment failures. He said they were starting arrangements to put her in a hospice because there's nothing else they can do for her in the hospital. I asked him if we could bring her home here if she wanted to come. He said there'd be some risk of her passing away on the ride home, but that risk would exist wherever she is, so, yes, we could bring her. I asked if we'd need an ambulance, and he thought that would be unnecessary."

Sissy sat quietly weeping, and Danny asked, "What is hepatitis B, and what is end stage?"

"Hepatitis B is a liver infection, and end stage means it is very serious," Zack answered.

"Can she die from this?" Danny wanted to know.

"Yes, she can, but where there's life there's hope," Dr. Denton instructed. "We can continue to pray for her healing, which in this case would be praying for a miracle."

"Am I permitted to go see her?" Zack asked quietly.

"I asked about that," Henry said. "I told the nurse that her husband was here and that he'd likely want to come see her. She said she'd ask Elaine and call me back within the hour. That was about fifteen minutes ago now."

"Well, technically that's not correct," Zack spoke hesitantly. "We're actually divorced. My boss in St. Louis told me that it would be foolish not to get a divorce because if I didn't, I would be responsible for her bills. So I did. I've felt guilty about it, but you need to know despite that I still think of her as my wife."

"I doubt that's an issue," Henry said. "It will depend on her answer to the nurse no matter what the legal relationship."

"We can drive the Durango up there and bring her back," Jonathan offered. "How soon can she come?"

"The physician didn't think they could keep her beyond Monday, but he also didn't think she could be released until then as well."

"I would like to be there to pick her up," Sally stated. "She'll need me to help with the long ride home."

Henry's cell phone rang, and he stepped into the living room to take the call. "It's the nurse," he mouthed as he moved out of the kitchen.

"I'm going to talk to the nurse too to find out what we need to take with us to care for her on the journey home," Sally said, following her husband.

The children had stood and were clinging to their dad. "I can't drive, but I'd like to go as soon as possible if she'll let me see her," Zack said.

"If you need to go, I'll take you," Evan offered. "There will only be room for two in the Durango if we put a bed in back. We may need to rent a car."

Henry stepped back into the room as Sally continued to talk with the nurse while writing out a list of needed items. "She definitely wants to see you, bud," he said, walking over to Zack and patting him on the back between the two children. "The nurse said Elaine broke into tears of joy when she heard you would come. You fellows don't need to rent a car;

you can take one of mine. We have two, so the ones staying here won't be stranded if you have one."

"I'm going to see what I can do about getting a license today," Zack announced. "I'd like to leave early—early tomorrow, if possible."

"Daddy, can we go with you?" Sissy asked.

Zack looked around the table for indications of guidance. Thelma responded by saying, "Children, I think we would all like to go, but this is one time most of us will need to stay here. Your mother is extremely ill, so the trip is going to be very difficult not only for her but the ones getting her as well. I'm staying here, and I'll be with you. We're expecting you to be in school Monday, so you'll have something to occupy your minds while your mother's being transported. I suggest we start making plans for school by getting you some supplies and uniforms today. I think it's unlikely at this point that your dad will veto the school. This visit with the principal today is likely going to be little more than a formality. Your dad's got a lot to concern him at this point."

Sally reentered the room, saying, "The list of supplies will not be difficult. Henry and I can run down to the durable medical equipment store and pick this up in a few minutes either today or tomorrow.

"I think we should go up to St. Louis on Sunday, preparing to bring Elaine back on Monday and/or Tuesday. Alice's parents will be here this evening, and I do not want to cut their visit any shorter than necessary."

"Henry, do you wish to drive my SUV to St. Louis, or do you want me to make the trip? I'm perfectly comfortable with the arrangements either way," Jonathan remarked.

"It's a long trip for me, but Sally can drive some. If Zack can get a license, it'll be easier. Let's see what works out for him today," Henry responded. "It's kind of you to offer; we could rent a larger vehicle, but that would be expensive. If Zack gets the license today, he can leave in the morning; Sally and Evan and I can go up Sunday morning."

"Well, it looks like we'll be here in your house, so your using our SUV balanced against our using your house—I think we're coming out ahead,"

Jonathan said, smiling. "I'll make certain it's all ready to go so you can get started early Sunday."

Zack and Evan went to the Driver's License Bureau immediately after breakfast. Fortunately there was no wait, and Zack was able to ask to speak with the local director privately. Zack explained his situation while the director sat patiently listening to him. After Zack had finished his synopsis of his past, his new commitment to sobriety, and the reason for his urgency in getting the license, the director continued to sit, thinking quietly. Finally he said, "I know who you are. I go to a prayer breakfast with your father-in-law, and he's requested prayer for you. Since you don't have your previous license from Missouri, I may have difficulty getting your information. Is there any chance you know your old driver's license number?"

"No, I don't, sir" Zack answered.

"Write down your birthday, your Social Security number, your full name, and your former address, and I'll attempt to contact the officials in St. Joseph. You take a Texas driver's instruction manual home with you now and study it and come back later this afternoon. You'll have to pass the written exam and a new in-vehicle driving exam before I can issue you even a temporary license. Unless there's something remarkable about your history, or unless I can't contact anyone, or unless you don't pass the exams, I believe we can make this happen. I am so very sorry to hear about Elaine's condition. I administered her driving test years ago when she was sixteen."

Zack was so amazed at the man's helpfulness that he sat a moment with his mouth open and then, smiling, said, "Thank you so very much."

The director grinned and remarked as he handed Zack the manual, "You really need to be thankful you're still alive. Now get out of here and get to studying this."

The rest of Zack's day went as well. He spent time going over the driving manual, swinging the children in the backyard, meeting with the principal, and going back to the license bureau to satisfactorily complete both portions of the test. He walked out with a temporary driver's license in hand. The introductions to Don and Sue Seymore, Alice's parents, would have been the beginning of a pleasant and comfortable evening if it hadn't been for the pall of Elaine's illness over the group.

"I think I can handle going by myself tomorrow," Zack told Evan out on the back porch as they stood and watched the children laugh and run with the dog in the backyard. "I do appreciate your offer to be with me, but I think you ought to be here with Alice and her folks the next couple days."

"How do you think you'll do traveling alone?" Evan asked.

"Do you mean will I have trouble passing the bars and not stopping to get a drink, or do you mean will I be able to stay awake, or do you mean will I get lost on my way from here to St. Louis?" Zack questioned, laughing.

"Well, I guess all of the above," Evan responded, smiling. "We laugh, but all are extremely important. Be open with me about when you think you need a drink. Call me anytime, day or night, and talk with me. You know I've never experienced addiction, but there's nothing I want more than to help you stay on the wagon. We can talk about your frustrations and pray for strength for you to overcome the desire to go back. I know you haven't bought a cell phone yet, so I want you to take mine. Alice will let me use hers if you call."

Zack sighed and said, "I don't want to be dependent on you, but I know I need to be. Fortunately, up to this point, I've not wanted a drink much. This situation with Elaine is big and depressing, so how I have felt may soon not apply—especially if I'm by myself. You're right about the cell phone. What I'll do is to check in with you every twelve hours or so; that way you'll know what I'm up to and if I'm still on track. I'll likely need your charger, too. I feel so ambivalent about this trip; I want to see Elaine, but I'm dreading dealing with her illness. Pray for me that I say the right things!"

"Well, let's start by praying now," Evan said. So in the twilight as the children raced about the yard with the dog barking at intervals, Evan prayed for Zack. He finished saying, "Lord Jesus, again I ask that You continue to give Zack the strength to overcome wanting alcohol and give him wisdom in knowing the right things to say to Elaine. We ask these things in Jesus' name, Amen."

"Thanks, bud," Zack sighed. "At the moment I'm feeling pretty up, but I know things won't always seem so positive. Even though I know Elaine's terribly ill, I'm relieved that she's still alive, that we've contacted her, and that she wants me to come. I'm going to try to leave about five in the morning so I can get there before visiting hours end tomorrow evening. Worrying about my starting to drink again makes me feel like a little kid."

"Rest assured I don't feel like you're a kid! You're my only big brother; I desperately want you intact to make my world feel right. If I feel that way, think how the children feel!" Evan expostulated. "I'm in this with you all the way; I know what you do is your responsibility, but I want to help if I possibly can."

"You're so kind; I feel guilty," Zack smiled, "but I know you've got my back. I do promise I'll call you if I feel tempted. Actually I'm praying that God will simply remove the temptation. He's done that for some people."

"Wow, that's positive," Evan responded, "I'll pray the same. Changing the subject, don't you like my fiancée's parents?"

"They're great. They were younger than I expected but are very pleasant. Do you think they're happy with you?"

"I do think so. We had a super time together last New Year's. I had a chance to meet Alice's younger twin brothers who are in college up in Idaho. They were a barrel of fun; we played basketball together for a couple hours each day, and they seemed surprised that they weren't able to walk all over me because they're both on the team up where they attend."

"Give me a hug and tell me good-bye. I'm going to read to these youngsters a bit after I gather them in and then tuck them into bed soon so I can get off early in the morning," Zack said, reaching over and giving Evan a side hug.

Evan responded in kind, saying, "Never forget how important you are to all of us. We'll all be in prayer for you and Elaine. I can't imagine how miserable I'd be if I were in your shoes with respect to Elaine."

Zack called the children in, and after getting them through their baths and their goodnights to the whole household, he took them into his bedroom, seating them on either side of him on the edge of the bed.

"We're going to have prayer together," he said. "I know we haven't done this before, but I should have had us doing this, so we'll start now. We have a lot to pray about; we need to thank God for getting me back here safely, for taking care of you while I was gone, for such loving parents and grandparents, and now I need us to pray together for me as I go on this trip in Evan's car that I'll be safe and that I can help bring your mother back without difficulty. Do either of you think there are other things we should be praying about?"

"These are a lot of things already," Sissy said. "I think we need to pray, too, that Pop Pop and Grammy will have a safe trip Sunday. We need to pray that Mommy gets better; she must be very, very sick. Do you think she will die?"

"What we've been told sounds extremely grim," Zack replied. "We can pray that a miracle will happen and that she'll recover."

"So if she doesn't get better, does that mean God is not answering our prayers or even the grandparents' prayers?" Danny asked. "We've been wondering in the past if He was doing very well at that, but we did get out of the problem we were in: being alone without you or Mommy."

"Talk this over with your grandparents," Zack fielded. "I couldn't believe how God answered the prayers of Herman and me when we were in the prison factory; I can't help but believe that He answers. I'm going to ask and leave it up to Him."

"I think we need to pray that God helps you get the right car, that school goes OK Monday, that Evan and Alice's wedding can be nice, that Sissy and I have fun at church tomorrow and make some new friends, and that we don't wear the grandparents out," Danny offered.

Zack smiled at Danny first and then at Sissy, who rolled her eyes and laughed. "I'll pray," he said before beginning. "You both say 'Amen' with me at the end." After the prayer, he took them down the hall to their room, tucked them both into their beds, and gave each a kiss on their foreheads, Sissy first and then Danny. Tears of thankfulness welled in his eyes as the simple routine reminded him of his fears in weeks past. In the dim light, Danny saw the tears and asked, "Why are you crying?"

"Because I'm so glad you're all right!" Zack answered. "If I couldn't thank God, I don't know what I'd do. I love you both; I'll see you Tuesday or Wednesday," he finished, softly shutting their door.

Zack headed to bed himself early and surprised himself by immediately falling asleep. He slept soundly, not even awakening when his brother came to bed much later. However, at 3:00 a.m. he awoke, restless to get out of bed. He crawled out quietly, gathered his traveling gear, and attempted not to disturb Evan. Just as he was moving toward the door to leave, Evan spoke up, "Are you planning to leave without saying good-bye?"

"I'd hoped I wasn't waking you," Zack whispered.

Evan stood and walked around the bed to give Zack a big hug. "Drive carefully and call me if you need me," he whispered back. "God be with you and bless you!"

CHAPTER XVII

SATURDAY, MARCH 21

Starting out on the trip, Zack felt he was embarking on his life a second time with the freedom of driving alone along the dark, nearly-deserted highways. The Dentons' car moved smoothly and the miles slid by. He caught himself gritting his teeth and felt frustrated with himself for being anxious. He knew he was lonesome and wanted to see Elaine. He attempted mentally to brace himself for her appearance because he'd been told she had lost weight and had yellow jaundice from the hepatitis. He analyzed his feelings. Was he fearful that she'd soon die? Was he angry at her for the situation into which her illness placed them both? Was he guilty for her plight and angry at himself for this whole sad affair? He told himself that Elaine's illness was a real fact that he must accept, that the past could not be changed, that his job now was to act faithfully in the present and to show Elaine the love that he'd failed to show in the past. He prayed out loud alone in the car, "Dear God, help me to do the right thing. I need your help here. Please give me the right words to say when I see her. Help me to be able to share with her the hope that I have in You! Please help her to understand what I say. Please, heal her!" He was so lost in his thoughts that it seemed very little time had passed before he'd crossed the Red River and was moving on through Oklahoma past Beaver's Bend and into the Ozark road switchbacks. The sun was rising as he neared and crossed the state line into Arkansas. To combat his sleepiness, he stopped in Fort Smith for breakfast and coffee.

In the restaurant, a flirty young waitress approached his booth, saying, "Hi good-looking, what's it going to be this bright morning?" and handed him a menu.

"Regular coffee," he ground out, taking the menu while frowning and feeling irritated with her for being so familiar.

"Are we feeling a little grumpy this morning?" the girl responded saucily.

Zack smiled, saying, "Probably. I'm not feeling real cheerful because I'm on my way to St. Louis to see my wife who's very ill, but I can at least be pleasant."

The girl's face turned red, and she said, "Well, now look who needs to apologize! I'll be right back with the coffee, and you look over the menu."

When the waitress returned with the coffee and to take Zack's order, he attempted to clarify his situation. "I may have problems, but that does not excuse me for being brusque. Thanks for the coffee, and I'll have a couple eggs and toast."

"No problem. Is your wife getting better? Is she in a hospital?"

"Yes, she's in a hospital, and unless there's a miracle, she's not going to make it. I've recently begun to trust in God, and I'm asking Him for her healing."

"Oh, my goodness!" the girl replied. "I'm so sorry! Facing something like this is very sobering. I don't pray, but it seems like a good thing to do."

"I think if I'd done a lot more praying in the past and a lot less trying to have fun, I may not be in this place," Zack said enigmatically.

The young lady looked at him perplexed and went off to get his additional order, but when she returned with the food she said, "My mom's a Christian and goes to church where they have a prayer chain. I'll ask her to put you and your wife on it. What's her name?"

Zack looked at her, considering, and answered, "Her name's Elaine. Thanks. You're young. Go to church with your mom. Make God part of your life; don't assume that if your mom prays that it's enough. We each need a relationship with the Lord. I'm learning to do it, and you can too."

The girl looked at him briefly and turned to go but then stopped turning back. "You're right," she said. "Things aren't going well for me at present, and that would be a good place to start. Thanks."

The highways from Ft. Smith on to St. Louis essentially were all Interstate except for a few miles in Bona Vista near the Arkansas-Missouri state line, and Zack made good time traveling. He thought of his conversation with the waitress and wondered at his unaccustomed openness with her. He considered her blatant flirty initial comments and realized he was no longer wearing his wedding ring that had been taken from him when he was abducted by the drug cartel. Even though he'd proceeded with the divorce he'd continued to wear it, but he now recognized its visibility had advantages; he also knew Elaine would notice if the ring were absent or present. When he arrived in Ft. Leonardwood he stopped to look for a replacement believing there would be a pawnshop in a military town, and was not disappointed in finding a suitable one. The shop clerk asked him, smiling, "Are getting married soon, sir?"

Avoiding a direct answer, Zack answered, "My ring was stolen a few weeks back, and I'm just replacing it. This one is simple and plain and looks the same as the old one."

"Was that around here?" the clerk inquired, preparing to accept Zack's payment.

"No, although it was in Missouri; it was up in St. Joe," Zack replied. "Is jewelry theft much of a problem around here?"

"Not really. Most of the items that come in here are from hard up soldiers or students. I bet this ring you're purchasing came from some kid who decided he didn't want to still be married."

"That's sad."

"Don't you know it?"

"Oh, how well I do!" Zack responded. "I've done enough dumb things in my life to fill a bathtub, but I'm getting back on track. I'm here to tell you that I've recently turned my life over to God, and it's making a difference. Thanks for your service," he concluded, walking to the door and glancing back to give a thumbs up to the clerk who was looking at him with a quizzical open-mouthed smile.

Zack stopped at a Subway for lunch and noticed that the wind was coming up and the temperature had dropped. He checked the cell phone for the weather to find that rain and sleet were predicted for St. Louis that afternoon. He'd not packed a coat or jacket in Texas, so he found a Good Will store to see what they might have on hand that would suffice. The only thing in his size was a nearly new, black leather jacket with a forty-dollar price tag. He was hesitant to spend the money but didn't want to waste additional time shopping. While paying for his purchase, the clerk commented, "I looked at that jacket for my husband, but it was way too big. I compared the price for it at Macy's, and the sale price they had was for one hundred fifty dollars. You're lucky you can wear it!"

"I was worrying about the price, so that makes me feel better," Zack laughed. "I see the weather's to get colder, so I'm attempting to be prepared."

"Oh, really? Colder here?" she asked.

"Well, I'm on my way to St. Louis, and there's rain and sleet predicted for there. I suspect it'll be colder here as well, though," he replied.

"Thanks for the warning," she smiled as he left the store.

Zack hurried to the car in the increasing wind gusts and resumed his travel in the deteriorating driving conditions. He finished the trip, arriving at the hospital at four in the afternoon despite the drizzle and sleet. He called Evan to tell him he'd arrived, that the trek had gone well, and to ask for him to pray that he'd handle his conversations correctly with Elaine. "I dread seeing her, but I dread not seeing her," he told Evan again.

"I can believe that," his brother answered. "I'll talk it over with Alice. We will pray about it. If she has any words of advice, we'll call you back very soon. Don't wait on us, though; go right on ahead. Be confident; you've a good head on your shoulders!" Evan laughed, "Whoever thought I'd be the one telling you that? It sounds like your line to me when we were in high school. Nevertheless, get bustin'! Remember, I've got your back! Bye."

"Bye," Zack punched the disconnect button on the cell phone and started to walk toward the hospital from the parking area. Each step seemed like a mark on his path to doom. He entered the front door of the building and looked for an information counter in the lobby.

"Good afternoon, sir. May I help you?" the elderly man behind the counter asked.

"Yes, I need to visit my wife, Elaine Taylor," Zack responded. "I do not know the room number nor the floor."

"Have you been here before?" the man inquired.

"No, I'm just arriving from out of town."

"Is she expecting you?"

"Yes, but she doesn't know the time I'm arriving."

"With our new security arrangements, I need to make certain that you're an approved visitor," the man continued. "Please pardon the delay while I call her nurse and get clearance for your visit. When I have that information, I'll make up a visitor tag for you so that this process will be unnecessary in the future." He dialed and waited for the nurse and explained the situation when she came to the phone. Hanging up, he grinned and said, "The nurse knows the patient is expecting you. She says your wife is currently asleep but the nurse is certain she'll be extremely glad to see you. Please give me just a moment while I get this name tag finished. Now, we've also available wristbands if you would prefer. They're water resistant, and you don't have to change them when you change clothes."

"Sure, I'll take the wristband," Zack agreed. "We're expecting her to be discharged on Monday, so I won't need it more than two or three days. Do you need my name?"

"No, but understand that you keep this band on while you're in the hospital so we know you're a visitor. For all I know, down the line we may need everyone to not only give their names but their driver's license numbers as well!" the man exclaimed, laughing. "Here's your band; let me help you put it on," he continued, holding the band out over the counter. He then gave Zack the room number and directions to the appropriate floor.

Leaving the helpful gentleman, Zack continued to dread every additional step. Arriving at the indicated room, he pushed the door open quietly and stood gazing at Elaine. He could not believe his eyes. His once beautiful wife was nearly unrecognizable. Her formerly blond, luxuriant hair was oily, thin, and stringy. Her face was yellow, drawn and wasted with weight loss. Her right arm lying across her chest was thin and wrinkled, but her abdomen appeared swollen and protuberant. Zack felt faint and slowly and quietly moved to a chair at the foot of the bed, sitting to maintain himself. He sat there watching her breathe panting short breaths. A heavy weight of guilt settled on his chest as he considered their lives together and, more recently, their lives apart. He wondered what had transpired in the months and weeks they'd been away from each other. How long had her condition been this bad, and how long could she last like this? He felt hopeless and remembered his newfound faith. "God, help her! Help me!" he breathed. "Help me know what to say." He then stood by the bed feeling lost, just staring.

As if sensing his presence, Elaine stirred and opened her eyes wearily. A glimmer of a smile flitted across her face. "Oh, you've come!" she whispered, and tears formed in her eyes as she reached up with her thin arm.

Zack knelt by the bed holding her right hand with both of his. He was near tears himself as he answered, "Yes, sweetheart, I'm here. I hate that you're so ill! How are you feeling today?"

"I was afraid you wouldn't come," she said. "I couldn't believe we would be together again after so long; I was afraid I'd die and never see you again."

"I should never have sent you away," he said heavily. "I've been miserable without you. I was a horrible husband, and I became a rotten dad."

"Don't talk anymore for a bit. Give me a kiss on the cheek and not on the mouth and hug me for a while without talk," she begged pleadingly.

Zack shifted his position, complying with the kiss and the hug and keeping his position for a full ten minutes until the nurse walked in.

"I see you made it," she said breezily to Zack. "I told you earlier he'd show up, didn't I?" she continued, addressing Elaine. "I'll be back later to give your meds," she finished, abruptly leaving the room.

"I need to ask your forgiveness for not helping better in the home," Zack started.

"It is good to hear you say that, and I do forgive you for that, but I still believe you did the correct thing by having me leave. I simply was unable to leave the drugs alone, and you and the children didn't need to have them in your lives. How are Danny and Sissy? Are they OK? Dad said they were fine and that he and Mom were enjoying them hugely."

"Whatever else has been wrong, they seem to be very, very well. Did your dad tell you what all has happened to the children and me in the past few weeks?"

"No, what happened? He just said you'd only gotten back from Belize a couple days ago. What were you doing down there?"

"It's a long story, and my knees will wear out if I stay down here on the floor," Zack laughed, getting up and pulling the chair over close to the bed so he could hold Elaine's hand. "I'll start from the beginning, but I don't want to tire you out too much."

"If I get tired, I simply go to sleep. Keep watching my eyes; when they close, stop talking so I won't have missed anything. I went to sleep on the nurse this morning when she was handing me my medications. I just conked out on her with her holding the cup of water out to me. We both had a good laugh over it; they've all been so nice to me here, and you could immediately see how relieved they all were to find my family was coming. Enough! Get started on your story."

Zack began his recital of events starting with his poor and deteriorating behavior prior to the abduction and continuing until Elaine obviously drifted off to sleep a few minutes later. After watching her sleep and feeling he was about to drift off himself, he walked out to the nurses' station to ask if it was permissible for him to spend the night in her room or if he needed to go get a motel room. The ward clerk told him to wait in the room and she'd check with Elaine's nurse, so he walked back to the room but stood in the hall beside the door. The cheerful nurse soon came bustling down the hall toward him smiling and reaching out her hand in greeting.

"Hi. I'm Amy," she began. "Sure, you can stay on the overstuffed chair by the bed; it folds down to be fairly comfortable. You might sleep better at a motel, but I know Elaine well enough to know that she would much rather have you close by; she has been in so much better a frame of mind since she knew you were coming. She told me she could hardly believe it and could hardly wait for you to show up. We all were frustrated with sending her out to a nursing home on hospice."

"I should have been here," Zack said quietly. "Thank you for your kindness."

"Don't guilt out on me," the nurse responded, overriding his humility. "Elaine's been real open with me about her past. She has enough guilt for the two of you, and I agree that she has the best interest of the children at heart by not having been with the three of you. However, she needs you now. Per her physician, she's deteriorating rapidly. Do I understand that in a day or so, you are still prepared to take her home? I talked with her mother yesterday morning. That's what she said."

"Yes," Zack answered, "her folks are coming up from Texas tomorrow with an SUV large enough to take her back on a bed. We'll all go back there together."

"I'll have the hospital social worker talk with you about discharge then for Monday morning. It is Saturday, and she's gone now, but she can meet with you tomorrow morning to get arrangements made for Monday. You'll likely have questions about medical services available in Texas after you get back. She'll be able to help you with that much better than I. Unfortunately, I do believe you'll need hospice, and that's generally arranged through a nursing service. Like I said my name's Amy, and I'll be around until seven tonight. The night nurse is a fellow, and his name is Mark. He's a great guy and will give good care. He'll be new to Elaine, though; he mostly only works this floor on weekends. I'll be back tomorrow. I bet Elaine's asleep now, isn't she? I'll wake her up at five-thirty to attempt to get her to eat. Perhaps you can help me get her to swallow something!"

Zack looked at the cell phone. "Oh, that's only twenty minutes," he said surprised, "I'm going to go call the children, but I'll be here." The nurse walked away, and Zack sat in a small waiting area near the nursing station thinking about how to best talk with Danny and Sissy about their mother. He dialed, and Dr. Denton answered.

"Hello, Son, how are you doing?" was the greeting that astonished and somewhat confused Zack.

"Well, Dad, I'm well. I'm calling to give a report on Elaine. I'll want to talk to the children, too."

"Are you by yourself, or is Elaine there with you?"

"No, I'm out in a waiting area; she's sleeping in her room. The nurse plans to wake her up in a few minutes to feed her supper. Dad, she looks bad! I think I almost didn't recognize her." Zack stopped, realizing his emotions were about to overcome him and attempting to compose himself while there was silence.

"Son, are you still there?" Henry inquired.

"Yeah, Dad, I'm here. I'm just having difficulty talking. Elaine was delighted to see me and is also looking forward to you and Mom coming, but she is extremely weak. She fell asleep after I'd only been here about twenty minutes. The nurse was very friendly and caring concerning her patient; however, she was open about a bad prognosis. Are the kids anywhere nearby?"

"I'm in my study. Sally's gone to the family room to bring them in here. They've been playing Uno with Evan and Alice and her folks. You're aware that little gets past them, aren't you?" Henry asked, chuckling.

"Yes, I need to walk a straight line," Zack replied. "Thanks for loving them and for being so forgiving of me! I do owe you and am looking forward to having you here tomorrow. Be careful on the trip."

"Oh, that's something I was to tell you. Evan's decided to come on up with us. Alice and her folks have decided to go on back to San Antonio tomorrow morning. Evan's planning to drive my car back on up to

Chicago from St. Louis. Evidently his work wants him back soon, and he thinks that this may portend well for him being transferred to the Dallas office."

"Great, then you'll have another driver. I'll see him tomorrow, too. Please give my folks my love and tell them I'll call back later tonight. I think I hear my kiddos!"

"Yes, they're here," Henry laughed. 'Keep you chin up. You have our prayers. Bye now. Here they are!"

"Hi, Daddy," Sissy greeted, "how is Mommy?"

"Hi yourself, gal; she was super glad to see me," Zack hedged.

"Do you think she will be able to come here to us?" Sissy persisted.

"Yes, that's what we're planning. Her nurse indicates that she can travel, but she gets very sleepy after being awake only a short time. She doesn't seem to be hurting; she's just weak and tired. She went to sleep while I was talking to her about what's happened to us. She really wanted to hear what I was saying, but she went to sleep anyhow. How have things gone for you and Danny since I left?"

"Oh, we've been fine. It was nice this morning so we played outdoors; we met the children on our street who were a lot of fun. The littlest one is only three years old, but some twins are my age: a boy and a girl named Bonnie and Kenny. I can tell we're going to be good friends because they both like to read; they also go to the same school we're to start Monday. Their mom said we might be able to car pool with them and that she'd talk with you about it when you came back. I told her Mommy was sick; she seemed surprised and sad. I don't think Granny and Pop Pop have told her about what's happened to you or us; I don't think they know each other very well because they just moved here from Ohio. They live two houses down the street. This afternoon it was raining, so we stayed inside and read. Grammy has a lot of books for us to read that belonged to Mommy; I think there are more than a hundred. I started on some Nancy Drew books, and Danny is reading a series called the *Sugar Creek Gang*. Have you ever read those?"

"Wow! It does sound like you've been busy and aren't missing me a bit! Yes, I read several *Sugar Creek Gang* books when I was about your age," Zack exclaimed.

"No, you're so wrong, Daddy," Sissy replied. "We did have fun, but we do not want to lose you again. You are so different since you're back that you're like having a brand-new special daddy. How are you doing without the alcohol? Have you been drinking any?"

"You shouldn't have to be asking that question," Zack replied, chagrinned. "I'm happy to report that I'm doing OK. It is sad to see your mom so sick, but it was so good to see her and to know she was so glad I came. Your uncle Evan is praying for me about the alcohol, and he's being my accountability partner on the matter. It's all right for you to ask me about it, though. You pray for me about it and I'll ask God to give me strength not to drink even if I want to. I probably should be talking to Danny now too. Your Mother is to awaken in a bit to eat supper, and I want to be there with her to persuade her to eat since she's not had much of an appetite. I love you, honey."

"I love you too, Daddy. Give Mommy a hug for me, and tell her we can't wait until she gets here. We're fixing up one of the bedrooms with a hospital bed. Here's Danny."

"Hi, Dad!" Danny enthused. "Did you have a safe trip, did the car drive OK, did you find Mommy OK, and is she dying?"

"Hi, buddy," Zack chucked, "your Mom's very, very ill, and she was glad to see me and talk to me. I'm going to pray that she gets better, but she's awfully sick. One of the first things she asked about was the two of you; I was glad to be able to tell her you are both doing well. My trip up here was fine, but it's a lot colder here than there. It is snowing and icy here, but I didn't have any trouble. When I found it was getting colder, I stopped and bought a coat."

"Where are you staying tonight? Can you sleep there in the hospital, and what are you going to do for supper?" Danny quizzed.

"You don't ask one question at a time, do you?" Zack laughed.

"Well, I ask what I think," Danny replied. "Isn't that OK?"

"I suppose so, but it does keep the person answering the questions on their toes. I'll be able to stay here with your mom in the room. I don't know if there is a hospital cafeteria here or not that is still open; I'll have to check."

"What does Mommy look like? Does she look different?" Danny asked.

"Yes, she looks very different. In fact, I'm glad you asked that; she looks so different that you and Sissy need to brace yourselves for that. She looks so very ill; I almost didn't recognize her."

"You have uncle Evan's phone. You can send us a picture. That will help us."

"Good idea! I'll ask her here in a little bit if she cares if I can send a picture to you. I'll actually send it to my dad, so you can ask him to see it. Oh, oh, here comes the nurse. We're planning to wake up your mom for supper, and I'm to help feed her. I need to go, but I love you a lot. We'll talk again tomorrow."

"Good-bye, Daddy, we love you too," Danny concluded quietly. "Tell Mommy we love her."

Danny rushed to the study to return the phone to his Pop Pop. "Daddy's going to send us picture of Mommy on Grandpa's phone," he informed. "I'll tell him to let us know when it comes; do you want to see it?"

"Sure, let me know," Henry answered, looking up from his book. "How did your dad sound; did he sound tired or sad?"

"He didn't sound happy, but he sounded OK," Danny replied, considering. "He said he'd call Grandpa back this evening. How are Mommy and Daddy divorced but still together? I thought when parents were divorced they were mad at each other."

"When people get divorced, it is always sad," Henry started, "but there are reasons that divorce happens other than when a husband and wife cannot get along together. In your parent's case, they essentially agreed that your mom's drug use was too dangerous for you children for her to stay in the home. Your dad asked her to leave and she understood why, so she left to not be near you while on the drugs. I believe your dad still loved her and still loves her now, and that's one of the reasons he was so depressed and drinking so much. I'm excusing neither her drug use nor his alcohol use, but because drug users tend to be so irresponsible and unpredictable, your dad was counseled to get the divorce for protection against bad financial decisions she could make while on drugs. She could have borrowed money and spend it, and he would have been held responsible for the bills if they were still married but not if they were divorced. I believe God does not want couples to divorce; I believe marriage is a sacred vow that we should keep. Nevertheless, I don't fault your dad for what he did."

"So do they now need to get married again?"

"It might be a good thing, but we actually need to leave that decision up to them. They're together now, and your dad's helping care for your mom. In a way, it is almost as if the divorce didn't happen. We need to focus on the good things—that we can be together, that your dad is safely back, and that we have found your mother. We need to turn the bad things over to God to allow Him to handle them—your mother's illness, the divorce, and all the changes there have been for your family."

"I think the changes are all good!" Danny exclaimed.

"I like the changes too but changes bring us the risk of new problems, and we want God's direction in what we do. He needs to help us make the right decisions."

"Do you think God will heal Mommy and make her well again?"

"God can do that, but He may not choose to do so. Here is a lesson that is always hard for us to learn."

Sissy, at that moment, entered the room. "What is hard for us to learn?" she asked.

"It is hard for us to learn that God is always good and that He is always just as well. Sometimes the justice overrules what we want. For example, we want your mom to get well. If she were to get well, that would be a miracle because it appears that she is not going to get well by herself or with the medical doctors helping. God may think it would be just for her to be punished for the wrong she has done by taking drugs which have caused her to get this disease. We have a difficult time accepting God's justice, especially when it is not what we want," Henry explained slowly.

"Who said God has to be just?" Sissy inquired.

"It is his very nature to be just. It is like His goodness; God is innately good. He can be nothing else," Henry smiled. "The Bible says God is just."

"Some people who don't do anything wrong get cancer and die young. How is that just?" Danny queried.

"I don't know that it is just except that there is sin in the world and because of sin, we all die." Henry fielded. "Because of the fall, the wrong decision of Adam and Eve, we all suffer the consequences. The justice for us in that is that God sent his son Jesus to die for us that we don't have to face the penalties for our sins but have the promise of heaven if we repent of our sins and accept Jesus as our savior. All justice is not accomplished in this life; we have to trust God for ultimate and complete justice," Henry replied.

"So even if Mommy becomes a Christian and does not use drugs again, she can die?"

"Yes, Son, all too true." Henry responded sympathetically.

"But she'll still be able to go to heaven, won't she?" Sissy inquired with shaking lips.

"That's right, sweetheart. We don't know how things will turn out. We can certainly pray for your mommy's healing, but we have to leave the outcome up to God meantime, thanking Him that we now know where your mommy is and that she's coming home to be with us now."

CHAPTER XVIII

SUNDAY AND MONDAY, MARCH 22 AND 23

Sunday morning came with Zack getting stiffly out of the bedside sleeping chair, cleaning up in the restroom, and attempting to get Elaine to eat. He was surprised about how much she did consume, but then was dismayed when she vomited up most of it in half an hour. The nurse assured him that this was a common event while Elaine went back to sleep. Throughout the day, in segments of time while Elaine was awake, Zack was able to relate in detail his experiences with the drug cartel, his escape, Evan's assistance, the children's resilient conduct in his absence, and finally his recognition of his need for God. He finished by again asking for her forgiveness. Elaine closed her eyes, and he thought she'd gone back to sleep again, but then she started speaking.

"Zack, that's a wonderful story; I'm very, very grateful that you and the children are OK. I do forgive you. However, even though I know you want me to agree with you about God, I cannot. I don't want to come back to Him in my tragic state with my tail between my legs. I know we did the wrong things when we left school and then when I started using drugs. I'm facing the consequences of my actions with my illness; I'm expecting to die, and I want to be brave. I'm just asking that you'll help me with that."

Zack listened with an aching heart. "I'll be here for you," he replied. "You'll hear me giving God the credit, but I don't want my new faith to cause a rift between us."

Elaine had not reopened her eyes and did not do so now, but Zack watched as tears slowly ran down both her cheeks, and she then did drift off to sleep. He felt a heavy weight on his chest, but also felt relief that he'd had the right words to say at a pivotal time.

Elaine's parents and Evan made good time arriving at the St. Louis hospital by seven o'clock that evening. The roads that had been icy in the St. Louis area that morning had cleared. Elaine was overjoyed to see her parents, and they were elated but dismayed to see her in her poor condition. Soon after their greetings, she went back to sleep. Zack had met earlier in the day with the social worker and understood the process of discharge the following morning. He discussed this with the Dentons as they went to a nearby restaurant for dinner together. He related his sadness at Elaine's specific rejection of his spiritual awakening, and they all agreed to commit the matter to prayer.

"We're going to go on to the hotel so we can get a decent night's sleep," Henry informed.

"Yeah, you'll need to show me where the car is so I can get on to the hotel as well," Evan added.

"You'll need your cell phone back, too," Zack said, handing it over. "The charger's in the car. Thank you so much for its use! I'll get one of my own as soon as I get back."

"Call Zack on our phone if you need to talk," Sally offered.

"I'm saying good-bye tonight because I'm heading out early tomorrow," Evan continued. "Do you think you'll try to make the return trip in one day or two?"

"It depends on how early the hospital releases Elaine. If it ends up being after noon, I think we'll stop on the way," Zack replied.

The brothers walked with the Dentons back to the SUV, hugging them goodbye and good night, and then walked on back to the parking lot to the car. "God answers prayer," Evan said, "even when things look grim."

"I know," sighed Zack. "I feel God helped me say the right things to Elaine even though I didn't like the content of her response. She likely thinks she's being responsible by handling this whole thing on her own. She always was the brave one, believing no matter what the situation she'd be able to handle it, at least that's what she always would say."

"This is a heavy thing for me to say to you, but you simply need to show her God's love," Evan stated.

"Yes, I agree," Zack remarked slowly. "Can we pray about it again before you leave?"

So the brothers stood in the cold, dark hospital parking lot praying together before Evan headed off for the hotel and Zack returned to the hospital room.

The following morning, Zack and the Dentons were pleasantly surprised at how soon arrangements had been made for their departure. The physician had preapproved the hospital discharge, and medication prescriptions were available at 7:00 AM. Elaine was loaded into the SUV on a comfortable air mattress, and the four were on the journey home by eight o'clock. Sally had requested the first traveling nursing shift, so she sat in back with Elaine while Zack negotiated the city traffic. The skin of Elaine's face had been reddened as they prepared to leave the hospital and all had attributed it to the excitement of the impending trip. However, even though she fell asleep soon after starting out, her face remained unnaturally flushed.

"I think she may have a fever," Sally commented, holding a hand to Elaine's forehead half an hour later. "I know I have a thermometer in those supplies I brought, but I can't reach them from my seat here."

"I'll pull over so we can get it," Zack responded. No sooner than the vehicle had stopped than Elaine started vomiting. Sally was prepared for that with towels and a basin, and when the temperature was obtained, it was one hundred two degrees.

"Apparently, the vomiting's pretty common," Zack informed, "but I don't think she's been having a fever."

"Sometimes I do, but this is higher than usual," Elaine reported weakly. "But I don't feel any worse than I generally do."

"Do you think we should be taking her back?" Henry queried.

"No, the doctor said there was nothing more that could be done there," Sally said firmly. "I will give her some antinausea medication and something for the fever, and we'll push on. How do you feel about that, Zack?"

"It sounds reasonable, but caring for someone ill is out of my judgment zone," he replied. "I'm glad you're here."

"Yes, please don't take me back," Elaine pleaded. "I do so want to see the children. I…." She dozed off.

Sally procured the gel antinausea medicine while the vehicle moved purposefully on down the highway with quiet occupants.

Danny and Sissy awoke that morning in high spirits, anticipating the experiences of the new school day. Sally had taken them Saturday to purchase new school clothes and supplies, so the opportunity to use the new educational accouterments heightened their expectations. Jonathan and Thelma both rode with them to the school, attempting to forestall any hitches in their enrollment. They all entered the school offices whereupon Danny took it upon himself to inform the secretary about his educational history. "This is the fifth school we've attended in the past five years," he said excitedly. "We started in Omaha, then we went to two different schools in St. Louis, and then we went to St. Joseph, and now we're here. My sister's in the fifth grade and I'm in the fourth. We both like school, and we both like to read. I don't think you were here last week when we came to visit the school. Do you remember us? My name is Danny Taylor, and I want to be called Dan, and my sister is Brenda Taylor, but we call her Sissy. She wants to be called Brenda here at school. These are our grandparents Thelma and Jonathan Taylor who have come to help us since our dad went to St. Louis to get our sick mother. Do you have papers we need to fill out?"

The lady at the desk smiled and nodded, saying, "Well, good morning! My name's Jennifer, and I'm glad to meet all of you. I wasn't here last week but I've heard you were coming, and your paperwork is all completed. It is here in two files right on this desk; apparently, your dad filled it out last week. We're still waiting to get your immunization records from the school in St. Joseph, but that is not a problem since the secretary last week went over the requirements with your former school nurse on the phone and found that you're both up to date. When you were here did you visit your classrooms, and do you remember where they are?"

"Yes, we were all here together," Jonathan answered quickly, forestalling Danny's reply. "Children, do you remember where the rooms are?"

"I'm certain we do," Sissy answered primly.

"Is it permissible that we walk with them to the rooms?" Thelma inquired.

"Sure," Jenifer agreed. "Will you be the ones picking them up after school?"

"Yes," replied Jonathan, "will that be at four-thirty?"

"Correct. The parents line up by the curb out in the large circle drive; we just ask that they don't block the street entering the school, so if the line reaches out to the street, drive on in and park in the parking lot."

Thelma and Jonathan walked to the children's rooms greeting the teachers and giving good-bye hugs to the children. As they made their way back out of the school, Thelma commented, "It almost makes me wish I were teaching again to see their enthusiasm."

"I'm suspecting the teachers will find them just as delightful as we do," Jonathan replied.

"This is going to be an extremely eventful day for them," Thelma commented as they reentered their vehicle. "They're in a new school for the first day, and their mother is returning home. It's going to be a busy day for me, too, finishing arranging Elaine's room, planning meals for the rest of this week, and doing some house cleaning. I'm going to call Sally to see if there's anything else she sees we'll need to have on hand when they arrive. What time do you think they'll get here?"

"Let's call Zack now," Jonathan replied, handing his cell phone to Thelma. "Dial Evan's number," he directed. "Evan loaned his phone to Zack."

When the phone was answered, Thelma was a bit taken aback that it was Evan she was speaking to.

"Hi, bud," she greeted, "I thought Zack had your phone. How are you doing this morning?"

"I'm super great!" was Evan's reply. "How's your morning going?"

"Oh, we're fine. We just dropped the children off at school. They were in good spirits. We're now planning our day, and I was intending to ask Zack when he thought they'd be arriving back here. Were you with them this morning?"

"No, I left early from the motel before the Dentons were up and about. Zack spent the night with Elaine at the hospital, and I haven't talked to them yet. The nurse last night indicated that every effort would be made this morning to get them going early, however. I'm making good time up to Chicago and hope to be there before noon. Call Dr. Denton's phone to talk with them. Zack will want to get his own phone as soon as possible I suspect."

"OK, we love you. Drive safely, and, say, we are so impressed with your Alice. She is a delight!"

"Yes, she's the light of my life! God is so good to me; I was just thinking about how fortunate I am to have her and to have you and now to have Zack back. I can't be thankful enough."

"No wonder you sounded so cheerful when you answered. You're a good son; both your dad and I are amazed at the positive influence you're having on all of us. I just hope Zack stays on track."

"I'm trusting God that Zack will do it; he's been very open with me so far. I think the longer he stays active taking care of Elaine and the children and working on his education, the less likely he'll be to backslide."

"Well, again we love you," Thelma concluded. "Let us know as soon as you find out when we'll be able to see you again. Bye now."

"Bye, Mom. I love you too and give Dad my love as well. I'm missing

Danny and Sissy already. Hug them for me. Pray for things to work out that I can be closer to all of you down there."

"He's a happy person to chat with," Thelma commented, plugging the phone into the charging cord. "He said to give you his love, and he said that Zack's being very open with him. He doesn't know when they left; he started for Chicago before the Dentons were up, and Zack stayed at the hospital. My phone's about run down, but I can call while it's charging."

"Did he say what he thought about Elaine's condition?" Jonathan asked.

"No, I didn't ask," Thelma answered. "I'll see what we can find out with this next call. Let's go to J C Penneys; Sally wanted me to get some mattress covers," she directed as she dialed again.

"Hello, Henry," Thelma greeted. "How are things going for you?"

"Well, good morning, Thelma," he replied. "Things are moving along here. We got off from the hospital in better time than we suspected. Not too far out Elaine upchucked, but she didn't want us to go back, so we're heading on and making good time while she's sleeping. Sally and I slept well last night, but Zack looks weary. He's driving though because he says it's something to keep him a little busy. He reported that Elaine was wakeful during the night anticipating the trip and seeing the children."

"Do you have any idea when you might get here?"

"No, we'll see how it goes. We'd like to drive on through and be there this evening if possible, but will stay in a motel if it seems prudent. We'll let you know as soon as any decision like that is made. We'll also keep you informed of our progress. I know the kids will be excited to know when their parents will be there. How'd they do getting to school this morning?"

"They seemed right in their element as soon as we dropped them off; I don't think they'll have any problem. Could I speak to Sally a moment? We're at the store, and I need to know if she needs me to pick anything more up."

"Sure, I'll give her the phone. She's sitting right by Elaine, so she may not speak up very clearly trying not to awaken her."

"Oh, then don't hand her the phone. Just ask her. You can tell me," Thelma said.

"She says she doesn't know of anything else," Henry reported shortly. "She says we'll make a list and call you should we have things we need, and she thanks you for picking up the liners."

"Tell Zack we love him and that if he's sleepy, he needs to let you drive."

Henry conveyed the message and reported the response, "He says, 'Thank you Mother for the advice,' and that he does love you back but is unused to such direct mothering."

"Tell him that loving and mothering are all part of the same ball of wax!" Thelma laughed. "Keep in close touch with us. I'll let you go now. Bye"

"Good-bye, we do hope to see you this evening," Henry ended the call.

"Zack's accusing me of mothering," Thelma chuckled to Jonathan. "In some ways he's the same as always."

"He always did have a charisma that made him enjoyable to be around; I'm glad it's still there," Jonathan responded. "What did Henry say about Elaine?"

"He said she vomited soon after they started but that now she's sleeping. They're hoping to drive on through today but will let us know if things change. Let's get going," she finished, opening her door and hopping to the pavement.

The SUV hummed along the highway quietly while Henry dozed in the front passenger seat, and Zack doggedly stared at the road with quiet determination to handle the anxiety-producing situation of transporting a terminally ill wife whom he realized he still loved. Sally sat in her narrow seat watching Elaine sleep mumbling and moving restlessly. Sally reached her hand out to take her daughter's hand in silent comfort. It seemed to make Elaine relax as she lay still for some time. She gazed at her daughter's face, aching about the visible ravages of the illness on this, her beautiful child, and watched worriedly as tears started puddling in the corners of Elaine's eyes. The girl squeezed her mother's hand, and Sally knew she was awake.

"Mom, I'm so glad you're here," Elaine breathed quietly. "I know you love me, but I am so very hopeless. I tried to quit, but I couldn't. Every day I would say I would quit, but then I didn't. Now I'm off the drugs, but I'm dying! How can you love me and be so kind?"

Sally prayed for guidance and responded, "Your father and I can't stop loving you even should we try, which we haven't. Your situation is a severe disappointment, but your value is not based on the situation. Your value is based on the wonderful creation that is you. We will pray for your healing, but even if we lose you, we will still love you. In spite of your illness, we will cherish the time that we can have together; I'm so happy to be here with you now."

Elaine opened her eyes and smiled tearily. "You are so sweet," she said and drifted back to sleep.

Zack, in the front seat, had heard every word over the hum of the vehicle and road noise. He now glanced back at his mother-in-law, catching her eye and crookedly smiling. "You're amazing!" he choked out in a whisper.

An hour and a half later Elaine awoke again, more alert this time. "How far have we gone?" she asked.

"We've been on the road about four hours," Zack reported slowly, computing the time in his head. "We're maybe about a third of the way there. How are you feeling, sweetheart?"

"I'm not nauseated right now. I, as usual, just feel overwhelmingly weary. It is so much trouble to move that even though it's sore where I'm lying, the soreness is better than the work of moving. I know that my skin will be damaged if I don't move, so I do try."

"Are you hungry at all, dear?" her mother asked.

"No, but I am thirsty."

We're approaching Springfield; we'll stop there. We need gas anyhow," Zack instructed. "What would you like to drink?"

"How about having some of that antinausiant medication now so you'll not have trouble when you drink?" Dr. Denton suggested.

"The trip is going better than I had feared," Elaine commented

"We've about eight hours more to go," Zack remarked. "Do you think you'll likely be able to tolerate the whole thing today?"

"If I'm sleeping this much, it won't be much different than being in the hospital; I slept most of the time there, too. I'd certainly like to see the children tonight if possible. It will be a dream come true," Elaine finished, tearing up.

"It's a dream coming true for us as well," Sally said quietly, patting Elaine's hand and then slowly reaching up and wiping the hair out of her eyes and resting her hand on her cheek. She then bustled about, getting the antinausea medication applied. "Zack, are you ready to have Henry spell you off with the driving when we stop?" she questioned.

"You know, I believe so," he responded. "I could spell you off with the nursing, too. Elaine, would you like to sit up for a while?"

"Not until I see how I do with the drink. I think I want some Sprite with ice."

Everyone chuckled. "That seems possible," Henry observed. "How far do we stay on Interstate 44?" he asked Zack.

"We'll stay on it until we get to US highway 69 in Oklahoma. Forty-four becomes a toll road in Oklahoma, but we're not on it too long. We could go a more eastern route, but we'd be driving down through some of the Ozarks. There's a mountain there with a number of switchbacks that we should avoid with someone tending toward nausea. It's a pretty drive, though. Sixty-nine takes you down to the Indian Nation Turnpike which reaches almost to Texas. It's a pretty straight shot."

The stop in Springfield was no longer than necessary, and travel resumed with the new seating. This time it was Zack holding the hand of sleeping Elaine. Henry played a quiet CD of classical music while both Zack and Sally dozed; then both moved into sound sleep, snoring lightly. Eventually Elaine awoke to say, "Dad, how are you're doing with the driving? Are you OK?"

Henry glanced back in the rearview mirror, replying, "Yes, honey, I'm doing just fine. Having you here with us reminds me of the times when you were younger that we all came up here to Branson and to Hot Springs in Arkansas. We had such great times, and you were so full of enthusiasm and the wonder of anything new."

Elaine made no comment, but Henry glancing back in the mirror again saw tears running down her cheeks. "Oh, gal, I didn't mean to make you sad; I was just enjoying the memories," he hurriedly apologized.

"No, it's all right what you said. They are good memories; I like them too, but it reminds me of what I haven't given to Danny and Sissy. That makes me angry at myself!"

"Those kids still have the future before them in which memories can be made. At present, they're full of energy and find delight in even the smallest of pleasures. We had a fire in the fireplace Friday morning, and you would have thought they both had been given expensive gifts. You're correct that things haven't been ideal for them, but they are extremely resilient. Right now, the concern on their front burners is your illness; they are praying for your healing and processing what it may mean for them should you die. They constantly amaze me. It is so much fun having them with us."

"Oh, Dad, you're so positive in the face of this horrid situation. I see myself as coming home to die. I'm glad I'm here with you, but I have difficulty seeing any benefit in this to you. Thank you for your love even if I feel I don't deserve it. How far along are we?"

"We're another four hours down the road; do you think you'll be able to hold out for another four hours?"

"Since I've been asleep most of the time, I do not see a problem. I suppose I should get into the wheelchair and use the restroom wherever we stop. That's going to be a challenge in a public restroom!"

"We can all help should you need it. Shall we awaken these snoring people? I'm actually just coming down into McAllister; we should be able to find a good clean place to stop and rest."

Sissy and Danny were full of enthusiastic discussion about their first day back at school when Thelma and Jonathan picked them up that afternoon.

"My teacher complimented me on my reading and my penmanship," reported Sissy. "There is only one class for each grade, and there are twenty-eight children in my room now including me; the teacher says we're the biggest class in the school. Danny, how many are in your room?"

"There are only nineteen with me. Because eleven of them are girls, the boys seemed glad to have me to even things up more. Kenny was at school there, so it was fun having at least one person I knew. But he is not in my class. He is in Sissy's class. My teacher said I did well in my math, but she wasn't too impressed with my penmanship. One of the girls said she thought I was cute, and I found that embarrassing. Grandma, don't you think that was wrong for her to say something like that?"

"She may have just been trying to be pleasant to a new fellow," Thelma placated.

Sissy wrinkled her nose, saying, "That sounds pretty forward to me. Either she developed an immediate crush on you, or she doesn't have much common sense in the appropriate things to say. What did you do?"

"I was on the playground. I blushed and looked at Kenny, who winked at me, and we both laughed. I didn't look at her again. Fortunately, she seemed to avoid me the rest of the day."

"What's her name?" Sissy asked.

"Alexis!" Danny exclaimed. "Don't you think that's a horrible-sounding name?"

"I think the name's OK," Sissy considered. "Grandma, what do you think?"

"I rather like the name," Thelma responded. "Danny, I don't think you should read too much into Alexis' comment. I agree that I can see how it would be embarrassing, but if I were you, I would for now just assume she was trying to be kind and let it go at that. Not looking at her only makes it worse and bigger than it needs to be, and laughing with Kenny may have hurt her feelings. I guess had you simply said, 'Thank you; I look like my Dad' or something like that, it may have been easier for her and for you both."

"Wow, Grandma, I can learn some stuff from you! Did Uncle Evan and Dad talk about things like this when they were little?"

"We did have conversations like this, especially as the boys got into high school and started growing. It seemed like many of the girls were impressed with them, and they'd be asking me how to handle it. Have you children been worrying about your parents today?"

"I haven't," Sissy answered. "How about you, Danny? I think there was so much new going on with school I didn't have time to worry."

"You're right," Danny said. "Have you talked to them, Grandpa? Do you know when they'll be here? How early did they start?"

"They got started in good time, are planning to keep on traveling until they get here, and I last talked to them an hour or so ago. They were still up in Oklahoma, so it will be several hours before they arrive. Your mom became ill shortly after they started, but since then she's been sleeping most of the way. She's likely to be worn out after riding so long. I'm suspecting she'll have trouble doing much more than hugging you and saying hello tonight."

"She sure looked sick in that picture you showed us last night," Danny commented slowly, quietly, and sorrowfully. "How do you get someone to eat who is not hungry? Can you give them medicine?"

"I've heard there is sometimes medicine for that," Thelma answered. "I think I've also heard that it is often not very effective. We'll have to fix her some very appetizing food. You children can help me with that; do you remember what her favorite foods are?"

"She likes Jell-O salad with nuts and cottage cheese, baked chicken, and mashed potatoes," Sissy informed.

"Yes, she doesn't like stewed tomatoes, asparagus, bacon, or peanut butter," Danny added. "We'd make peanut butter sandwiches and she'd want to leave the room because of the smell! I really do like peanut butter and jelly; could we have a sandwich of those and milk when we get home?"

"Why certainly, buddy," Thelma agreed. "I'd baked some chocolate chip cookies for an after-school snack, but you could have the sandwich instead."

"Oh, no!" Sissy exclaimed. "We do want some of those fresh cookies! How about both?" she negotiated.

"I was planning on a late supper in case the travelers might make it in and be able to eat with us so both cookies and sandwiches shouldn't be a problem now," Thelma conceded.

"Do you think Momma still really loves us?" Danny asked, changing the subject. "I know Dad told her to leave, but it doesn't seem that she would do that if she really loved us."

"Only your talking to your mother can adequately reassure you of that," Jonathan answered. "In my conversations with your dad, he mentioned several times how important it was to your mother that she get home here to see you as quickly as possible. I understand your worry, but you need to talk with her about it."

"We both worry about this," Sissy said slowly. "Do you think that is natural, Grandma?"

"Oh, absolutely!" Thelma exclaimed. "I think it's as normal as rain! Every child wants the confidence of the love of both parents. When you were younger, you felt it from both of them, but in recent months and years you've had your faith in them tested. Fortunately, I see things currently remarkably improving. Both of you wait and see. I believe that your parents are coming around to be the emotional support you need. Also, the two of you need to realize that you have the full love of two sets of grandparents."

Danny, sitting behind his grandmother, reached up and patted her lovingly on her shoulder and with a big grin said, "You're the best!"

"Here we are, back in Texas," Henry informed as he drove across the Red River bridge. "How does it feel?" he asked over his shoulder, addressing the question to Elaine.

"I feel tired, but knowing we're closer home feels good," she replied.

"We're going to put the two of you in the Jack and Jill rooms at the end of the house," Sally explained. "We've put a hospital bed in one of the rooms, and Zack will be right close by in the next room. The children are still rooming together, and I've left it that way since they were used to it. They're upstairs near our room, and Jonathan and Thelma are in the room across the hall from us. That room is large and has a private bath; they wanted to stay downstairs in the guest bedroom, but that room is small, and we're planning on them staying a considerable time to help care for you, so I insisted on the larger space to which they've agreed."

The conversation continued and as the subject changed to future plans, Zack announced, "I've decided to enroll at LeTourneau University to take my first courses during this summer's session. Although I'm looking forward to getting back into school, I'm feeling concerned that I won't be able to accomplish the work well. Evan's been so optimistic about me being able to handle it that I'll really feel I've let him down if I don't do well."

"So is it going to be mechanical engineering?" Henry asked.

"No, electrical engineering moving on to computer technology. The courses will take me three full years. I may be able to cut off most of one year if I take summer courses."

Elaine started to weep.

"What's wrong, honey?" Zack asked, holding her hand awkwardly.

"We never should have quit school," she sobbed quietly.

"I know," he agreed, "but we did. I'm so thankful to your dad that he's helping me with this. It is so good that I feel as if any minute now things aren't going to work out. I keep telling myself to trust in God that things will be OK."

"You don't sound like the same guy I married," Elaine commented wryly. "You always said, 'Trust me; I can handle it.'"

"Don't you think this way is better?" he laughed.

Elaine stared at him blankly and sighed. "I wish I knew," she said enigmatically.

Zack looked at her, winked, and responded, "Trust me it's better!" The conversation ended, and Elaine returned to sleep until they finished the journey.

CHAPTER XIX

MONDAY AND TUESDAY, MARCH 23 AND 24

As the Durango turned into the drive, the children rushed from the front door yelling. "Mommy! Daddy!!"

Zack opened his car door and unfolded himself, kneeling to hug both children and whisper in their ears, "Give her a hug, but be gentle."

The children clambered into the backseat side by side while Elaine laboriously lifted her upper body from the mattress, awkwardly reaching to hug them both simultaneously. They were all in tears.

"Oh, Mommy, it's so good to see you!" Sissy exclaimed.

"We were afraid you were gone for good," Danny added. "Are you able to get up?"

"Not by myself," Elaine admitted. "However, with help I'll get into the house! You both are such sweethearts. Your dad told me how well you'd done when you were by yourself. I'm so proud of you!"

Elaine struggled weakly to slide from the mattress onto the seat in the SUV while Zack collected the wheelchair and then lifted her into it. The children filled their arms with the paraphernalia from the journey handed out by Henry then joyously followed Zack and Elaine through the gate into the backyard, following the sidewalk along the back of the house to the back door and into the kitchen, on through the family room and down back the hall into Elaine's bedroom.

"Wow, what a nice big house this is," she exclaimed. "I am so tired, though. Children, where are your rooms?"

"We're together in bunk beds in a big room upstairs at the other end of the house," Sissy informed excitedly.

"Aren't you afraid so far away?" Elaine asked.

"No, Pop Pop and Grammy are just down the hall from us," Danny explained. "We feel really safe in this house with all the grandparents and family. It is wonderful! Mommy, are you ready for your surprise?"

Elaine smiled at his enthusiasm saying, "Of course!"

The two children went to the built-in desk and carefully lifted a white dish towel draped over a bowl of oranges and roses while turning to see their mother's response.

"How did you remember?" Elaine exclaimed. "Both are my favorite! Thank you, thank you, you little darlings!"

"We don't know how we remember; we just remember," Danny answered, fielding her question in a concrete fashion. "We thought of the times you would stop us and let us smell the roses in the park when we lived in St. Louis and how often you would eat an orange for a snack, so when Grandma asked us what you liked, she helped us get these for you."

"We're glad you like them," Sissy added. "Now what can we do to make you more comfortable?"

Elaine looked at her daughter nonplussed. "Oh baby, you are so grown-up; thank you for your concern. I am horribly sorry that I'm so exhausted. Zack, do you think you can help me get into the bed?"

Danny moved to the controls at the side of the bed, pushing the button to lower it while Sissy laid back the covers and Zack carefully lifted her into the bed. Sissy arranged the fresh pitcher of water and water glass on the rolling bedside table while Danny placed a bell beside the pitcher along with a box of tissues. "Mommy, you're to ring this bell for Dad in the night if you need him," he instructed.

Zack pulled up a chair beside the bed holding out his arms. "Children come here," he said. "This is the first time we've all been together in a long, long time, and I'm so grateful I hardly know what to say." The children stood one on each side while he continued, "I think I need to pray thanking God! I know none of you are used to me doing something like this, but I'm changing my ways, and this is part of it, so let's close our eyes while I pray. 'Wonderful God, thank you that we're all together. Thank you that Elaine has made the trip safely here and that we have could find her. Thank you for both of these delightful children. Thank you that you have brought me back safely from Belize, thank you for our families who are helping us. Please help Elaine to get well! We ask these things in Jesus' name, Amen.'"

When Zack and the children opened their eyes, Elaine was already asleep.

"We'll let her sleep," Zack instructed quietly.

"Can we give her a goodnight kiss?" Sissy asked, whispering.

"Of course. Then both of you go find your grandparents and give them goodnight hugs and kisses, and I'll be up to tuck you into bed."

"Daddy, I love you," Danny said, clinging to his dad, "but Grandma said we could have some ice cream and cookies before bed. Is that OK?"

"Sure, you go ahead. I'll be there in a bit. Tell Mom to fix a small bowl for me."

The children left, and Zack sat in the chair quietly looking at his sleeping wife. He felt a rush of panic and attempted to squelch it by thinking of the children and the safe trip, but realizing that was not working, he decided to analyze his own fears again. What was he afraid of? He decided that it was his fear of inadequacy in the handling of a sick and dying wife. How could he make the children understand? How could he forgive himself for being a part of allowing this to happen? He thought of Evan's advice to focus on the future, and rose from his chair to go join the children. He would plan for the future after the children were in bed.

Both sets of grandparents were in the dinette having some of the evening snack, and the children were happily consuming the ice cream. A fire crackled warmly in the raised fireplace by the table, and all were listening raptly to a story Jonathan was relating from his childhood on the Illinois farm. Zack took his place behind the bowl of ice cream, listening to the completion of his father's yarn and Danny's persistent questioning following it.

"Why didn't you stay on the farm when you grew up, Grandpa?" he asked.

"I guess I liked school, and my parents wanted me to have a better education than they did," Jonathan replied. "I went to Normal, finished my college work, and then decided I wanted to do postgraduate work. While I was working on my master's degree, I met your grandmother. We were both graduate assistants; she was in the math department and I was in the English department. After we married, we both got our doctorates in education and moved to the Chicago area to teach. I had liked the farm, so as the boys were growing up, we'd go back often in the summer times."

"Where did Grandma grow up?" Sissy questioned.

"I grew up in Chicago," Thelma answered. "My parents were Polish; my maiden name was Lucashefski," she smiled. "My dad worked in the stockyards long hours, but we had very little money. I was an only child and was a good student. When I was given a scholarship to Normal to pay for much of my college tuition, it was extremely exciting. I worked first as a waitress in a sandwich shop while I was in college. When I became a graduate assistant and met the handsome young Mr. Jonathan Taylor, I was in hog heaven!"

"I didn't know hogs went to heaven," Danny laughed. "Why did you say that?"

"It's just an expression," his grandmother replied. "I hate to end this fun occasion, but I suppose we all ought to get to bed."

"Mom, you're right," Zack agreed. "Kids, go on upstairs; I'm coming right on up. Brush your teeth," he smiled, "but you probably don't need to be told. Mrs. Denton, is there anything specifically I need to be doing tomorrow to be helping out here around the house?"

The conversation went on hold as the children moved around the table kissing and hugging each grandparent in turn and headed upstairs. "Zack, you go ahead and make your own plans," Sally answered. "Thelma and I have things covered here. We've been discussing it. The two of us with our husbands' help can accomplish all that needs to be done including much of the nursing for Elaine. You go right on up with the children; they have been so excited to have you both back, but I know they need to get on to sleep because they have school tomorrow."

"Thanks, Mrs. Denton," Zack said as he stood.

"That's too formal!" Sally complained.

"OK, Mom," Zack responded, leaning over to give her a resounding smack on the cheek. "How's that?"

"Better," she laughed.

"Good night all, then," he replied, heading toward the stairs. "I'd like to take the children to school tomorrow. May I borrow one of the vehicles?"

"Sure, Son," Jonathan replied, "you don't need to ask."

Danny and Sissy were still in the bathroom brushing their teeth but with their pajamas on when Zack arrived at their room. He waited to give them hugs and kissed them soundly before praying with them again. When he'd finished, he stood and leaned against the bunk bed quietly.

"Daddy," Danny asked, "can you sing 'Birdie in the Apple Tree' to us?"

Zack cleared his throat, saying, "This was what your mother sang. Are you certain you want me doing it?"

"I don't think she can do it, so maybe you can," Sissy explained.

Zack started singing, quietly finishing the song and somewhat surprising himself that he'd remembered all the words.

"Wow," Danny complimented, "I didn't remember that you could sing so well, Dad."

"Thanks, bud," Zack chuckled as he headed to the door. "I'm going to be taking you both to school tomorrow, so I'll be up to wake you in the morning. I love you both!"

"We love you, too," they chorused as he pulled the door nearly shut.

Zack walked the long upstairs hall hearing the muted conversations of both sets of parents in their bedrooms as he passed. It was a comforting domestic atmosphere. "No wonder the children feel safe here," he thought as he headed down the stairs crossing the family room, going down the back hall, and entering Elaine's bedroom to check on her. She was moaning in her sleep, so he sat in the chair watching her as he planned the day tomorrow. He'd go take the children to school, get a cell phone, and look for a car. He'd go to the university campus and talk to someone in admissions if possible.

"What are you doing here?" Elaine asked, sleepily opening her eyes.

"Well, I came to check on you and got to thinking about tomorrow," he admitted.

"I'm glad you're here; we need to talk. I know we've been together much of the day, but I didn't want to talk about things in front of my parents."

"What is it?" he queried.

"I've been thinking about what's happened to you and how you're so different. We always used to feel the same way about things as far as religion went, and now we don't. I decided when I went to college that I didn't want to be a Christian, and I haven't changed my mind. I'm glad to have you love me and take care of me, but I don't want you trying to convert me. I don't think I believe in God, let alone Jesus and all those miracles they said he did. Is there anything more foolish than turning water into wine?"

Taken aback, Zack responded, "Wow, that's hard to hear. I know you're absolutely right that I've changed my view of Christianity since we were together. I can't help wanting us to be on the same page in this matter. Of course, I cannot make you believe what you do not believe. I just know our former belief system of leaving God out of things was certainly not working for me. I feel like it's a miracle that I'm not wanting beer and liquor like I did in St. Joe. It is amazing to me as I think back how it was clouding my thinking. I was acting a fool. It's true that in the afternoons after I'd been at work during the day, I'd start thinking I shouldn't go pick up any more alcohol, but as soon as I'd get off work, I'd head to the bar or store because I just felt I had to have it. I never ever wish to experience DTs again, so that helps, but I do believe not to feel that craving is a miracle."

"I'm glad you're doing better, but that doesn't change my mind. I also wanted to tell you that you need to be making plans for when I die. I detect that you're hoping I'll be healed, but that's just not realistic. You and the children need to be preparing for my death. If you can accept that it's going to happen, I think you'll be able to be more prepared for it when it does."

Zack took a deep breath, saying, "You're right; I'm struggling with this. I can't help but pray for your healing, but I must prepare for your likely end. I know the grandparents have talked to the children about this and encouraged them to pray for you; I can't control that. I don't want to take away the hope that any of us have. Do you have any suggestions as to how you think I should handle this?"

"Well, I suspect you can't stop them from praying, especially since we're here in the folk's home under their roof, so I guess I mainly would want you to be making plans for your life and for the children's lives with the consideration that I won't be here. I want you and the children to be safe and happy. After I die, I want you to get married again. Also, I don't want us to get married again; you shouldn't be saddled with all my old hospital bills. Will you promise me these things?"

Zack stood and stepped up to Elaine's elevated bed, taking her right hand in his left hand and wiping the hair back from her forehead as he said, "Those are big promises to make. Let me make a bargain with you. I will promise to intend to remarry if you pass away if you'll allow me once a week, say on Sundays, to bring up the subject of your relationship with Christ."

Elaine looked at Zack, grinned, and in an atypical burst of energy exclaimed, "In some ways you might be different, but you're still a weasel! I guess I can agree to that if you don't make your sermons too long." She then was quiet, and as Zack watched, she drifted back off to sleep.

He continued to stand by the bed holding her hand, but finally released her hand as his shoulder started aching and quietly stepped to the next bedroom, leaving both doors open. He moved on into the shared bathroom, brushed his teeth, undressed for bed, and crawled in. He lay awake feeling anxious but, remembering Evan's encouragement to pray, started praying for his fear of inadequacy, lack of constancy, Elaine's illness, and the children's well-being before he drifted off to sleep. He awoke on the dot at 6:00 AM, hearing the grandfather clock down the hall in the family room striking the hour. He felt unexpectedly refreshed as he hopped from bed to check on Elaine since he hadn't heard her bell throughout the entire night. She was still sleeping soundly, so he awakened her, offering to help her into the restroom before he went to get the children up.

"I did sleep better than I expected," Elaine reported. "Thanks for coming in here; I really do need to use the restroom, but I feel frustrated that you should have to help me."

"Let's just focus on getting the task finished," Zack encouraged. "Your mom and mine will be here to help you though the day, but I think this is my responsibility now. I'm glad to help; it makes me feel worthwhile. I'm going to take the children to school. Do you think you'll be able to eat any breakfast?"

"I'm not hungry but I'll try," Elaine responded as he lifted her into the wheelchair and pushed the chair into the bathroom. "Could you get me a fresh drink of water now?"

Zack attended to her needs, soon placing her back into the bed after he'd straightened the sheets and plumped the pillow. "The kids and I'll be back down in a bit to say our good byes," he said in parting. "I'll be gone several hours. I'm going to look for a car to drive, get a cell phone, and try to talk with someone in admissions at the university."

"You need to go get a haircut first," Elaine admonished. "You look a little rough."

"Yeah, I'd better shave and get dressed before I go start on the children," he answered, going back into the restroom to continue his morning toilet.

As he was finishing, Thelma, in the hall, knocked on his bedroom door. "Hey bud, are you awake?" she called.

Zack came to the door, wiping his face with a towel, saying, "You bet, Mom," and gave her a hug and kiss.

"You smell good," she responded, returning the hug. "How's our patient?"

"She's awake; go talk to her. She said she'd try to eat something; maybe you can offer her some options. I'm going up to check on the kids," Zack said, throwing down his towel and hurrying away up the stairs to the children's bedroom at the end of the upstairs hall. He stepped into the room and stood watching his sleeping children. As if sensing his presence, Sissy opened her eyes, looked at him, and smiled. Zack's heart gave a lurch of love, and he grinned back.

"Good morning, Daddy!" she exclaimed. "It is good to see you! How's Mommy?"

"She slept quite well," Zack reported. "Mom was talking with her when I left. They were deciding what she could eat."

"We didn't get to talk with her very much last night," Sissy contemplated aloud.

"Yes, I know," Zack agreed, "but you'll likely be able to talk with her more this evening. This morning you'll be having breakfast, and we'll need to go on to school, so there won't be much time to be talking now. How'd you feel the first day of school went?"

"Danny and I believe this school is the most fun of any school we've ever been at. Did you know that they have prayer at the beginning of every class?"

Zack chuckled, "Well, actually I didn't know, but I'm not surprised. So you're praying several times a day, aren't you? Did you know that in the past in the United States that in almost every public school, teachers and pupils prayed and said allegiance to the flag every day?"

Danny, who had by this time had awakened, sat up speaking, "Morning, Dad! Why did they stop doing that?"

"There was a lawsuit by someone who didn't like the praying, and the

Supreme Court decided that it wasn't fair to non-Christians to have to pray in the public schools. That all happened before I started to school; I just heard about it," Zack answered, stepping over to hug his son.

"Was that a good thing or a bad thing?" Sissy questioned.

"I think we need to care about what people feel they are being forced to do. However, with the overwhelming majority of Americans being Christians, especially at that time, I think the decision of the court was an unfortunate move because without prayer the system automatically teaches young people that prayer doesn't matter and that God is not so important. We live in a country that needs people with a strong sense of right and wrong. Learning about Christ and his pattern of living accomplishes that, and I think it should still be happening in all the schools. I think I'm an example. Had I been more immersed in Christian ideals, perhaps I'd have been more responsible in the way I treated your mother and would have been readier to recognize the danger of drowning my sadness by using too much alcohol. Hey, I'm talking too long. You both need to get up and get going."

"We know, we know!" exclaimed Danny, hopping from his bed. "It will be so fun having you take us. Can you come in and meet my teacher?"

"Remember, I did meet her last Friday," Zack replied. "However, if you'd like me to come in, I will do so. I'll have to check at the front desk to see what the rules are in that regard."

"Will you come see mine, too?" Sissy questioned, also getting out of bed. "She's very pleasant, and I believe she likes me. She has three children, all of whom go to the school, but none of them are in my grade. Danny, you go change in the bathroom first while I brush out my hair. Dad, you don't need to wait on us; we'll be right down. I want you to see the new uniforms Grammy helped us buy. Grandma may need your help with the breakfast."

Zack laughed at being so summarily dismissed and dutifully headed back downstairs to the kitchen. His mother was busily setting out boxes of cereal, frying eggs and hash browns, and gathering up plates and silverware. "I can set the table," he offered. "Did Elaine decide on what sounded good to her to eat?"

"She said she wanted eggs and hash browns," Thelma reported. "I'm a little dubious as to how well that'll agree with her stomach, but I'm making it. Anything will be better than nothing. You might offer her some of that antinausea medicine before she eats."

"Sounds like a good idea," Zack answered, finishing laying out the items on the table. "I'll go talk with her; the children will be down in a few minutes. They're all excited about showing me their new clothes."

"They're so appreciative of everything. I think the school is going to be a good fit for them even though it's late in the school year," Thelma responded.

The morning was blustery, cloudy, and chilly but that didn't seem to blight the children's spirits as they headed out to the school. Zack paid the requisite visits to the two teachers and was met with friendly praise of their participation and attitudes. He felt proud but almost guilty of their good reports, feeling he'd contributed little to their good behavior. As he headed back to the house, he decided to ditch the guilt and just be thankful to God for the blessing of still having them in his life. On arriving home, he found both sets of grandparents gathered around the kitchen table finishing their breakfasts and savoring their coffee.

"Hi everybody," Zack greeted, entering the room. "This appears to be an august and pleasant conclave. Do you have some wisdom to impart for me?"

"We have experiences to relate, but we're a little reluctant to label it as wisdom," his father-in-law responded.

"Well, I've a couple things to do today and would like some input," Zack continued. "I think I need to get a car and a cell phone. Who has advice?"

"I think Henry keeps *Consumer Reports* magazines for car recommendations," Jonathan suggested.

"They have listing of reliable vehicles for each price range including used models. Had you anything in mind?"

"No, I don't need anything fancy—just something that will last me through school but be safe for the kids, too."

"They publish the list your dad mentioned every year," Henry informed. "I'll get the issue from my study and you can look it over. *Consumer Reports* also did a recent article on the best cell phones and cell phone services, so you may wish to check that out as well before you shop."

"What do all of you think about me using some of the money from the gambling to buy things?" Zack asked.

"It's so out of character to hear you asking for advice that I'm a little surprised," Thelma answered. "I think it would be OK. Even though I think gambling is wrong and unwise, your obtaining the money was not illegal. Of course, some of it may need to go for taxes, so some should likely be held back."

"The children were extremely careful with it. I believe in the time they were alone, they spent less than a couple hundred dollars of it. When we first got to them, Danny would almost grill us over each expenditure. I never expect him to be a spendthrift if he continues on this tack," Jonathan added, smiling.

"Yes, Dr. Denton told me about their frugality when he gave me some of the money I was to use on my my trip to St. Louis as he got it out of his safe. I just know it's all I have, and I don't want to use it all up," Zack worried.

"Why don't you come into my study and we'll have a money talk," Henry offered. "That's where the magazines are, and we can do some planning there."

"OK, but perhaps I should be checking on Elaine first," Zack hesitated.

"No, Son, let me go check on her," Thelma interjected. "She did eat a reasonable amount of the eggs and hash browns, but then went right on off to sleep. I suspect she's still asleep. She'd very much enjoyed the good-byes from you and the children, and afterwards she ate and had a bath . I think she was pretty exhausted with all that activity."

Zack trepidly followed his father-in-law into the study, seating himself behind Henry who was shuffling among his *Consumer Report* magazines in a shelf above his built-in desk against the wall.

Henry turned, handing two magazines to Zack. "This one discusses cell phones and service provider options, and this one contains the automotive recommendations," he informed and then returned to his seat in front of his desk turning in his chair to face Zack. "Now, I don't want to insult your intelligence by not recognizing that my helping you out financially is awkward for you. I trust I can handle this so it will not be a divisive thing between us, but it will take you trusting me too. I don't want you feeling like I'm watching every penny you spend, but I don't want to be foolish in my largess. Here's my plan: I don't want you to expect to pay for food, household expenses, Elaine's medical expenses, or yours and the children's school tuition. I'm going to give you five hundred dollars a month for your incidental expenses. I'd like to suggest that you set up your own bank account so that I can have that money deposited directly into it. I do not consider this a loan to be paid back, but I'd like to feel comfortable asking you to help me with tasks around the house and in the yard. However, I realize that your schedule will be full fathering the children, caring for Elaine, and especially when you start taking classes. Finally, and this is the difficult part of what I want to say, if you return to alcohol use or restart neglecting the children, all of this will end. Do you think you can live with all these?"

"Dad, it's more than fair," Zack said quietly. "I'm concerned that this is likely going to encroach on your retirement with you being so generous."

"Actually, that's not going to happen," Henry responded. "We had a good fund set up for Elaine's college education. When she stopped school the money was by no means consumed so it has been sitting there increasing in value in the meantime; we've never considered it as part of our retirement, hoping there'd eventually be a time she would return and be willing to go back to school. That seems unlikely now."

"My fear is that I won't meet your expectations, but I promise that I will try. Evan's promised to be my immediate go-to person when I'm feeling tempted, but I think this is also an opportunity to enlist you as an accountability partner as well. I would suggest that we set a weekly time to talk over my plans, goals and accomplishments, inviting your insight into how you think I'm functioning. Would that be possible?"

"Of course, Son," Henry replied. "That would be pretty invasive into your personal life, but accountability always needs to be a two-way activity, so I'd need to ask for your comments on areas where you see me functioning less than effectively, too. Maybe we could regularly meet at 7:00 AM on Saturdays. How about both of these things?"

"I doubt there'll be much for me to say in that regard," Zack laughed, "but OK. Another thing I do need to tell you, though, is that Elaine's said she doesn't want us to be remarried. I was pretty disappointed about this, and I don't know how you'll feel about this."

Henry sat in thought about this information before he said, "Well, we can't control what she does. Why do you think she's saying this?"

"I think it's because she still does not want anyone to be able to charge me for her medical bills."

"How do you feel about the issue?"

"She's likely right about the bills, but I'm disappointed; I thought the children would feel more secure knowing the marriage was indeed intact."

"Are you going to feel awkward caring for her personal needs?"

"I don't believe so. It presently seems in most ways like we've never been divorced."

"Have you talked with your parents about this?"

"No. Do you think I should?"

"Yes, I guess I do. I'd like your permission to talk it over with Sally. However, I think that in God's eyes you're still married despite the legal divorce, so the personal exposure is not an issue. I'd like to talk this over again with you after I get Sally's take on it. You should see what your parents have to say about it."

"Thanks for your understanding. Sure, talk with her mom; I will see what my folks say."

"OK, are we through with our conversation? If so, I want to get that money out of the safe for you, so you can go set up that bank account. You can also go read those articles before you head out. Do you wish for me to come with you?"

"You're welcome to come; I'd asked Dad to come already."

"Three fellows would probably be too much. I think I'll rake some leaves in the azalea beds then. You have a good time together."

The two men went their separate ways from the study with Zack giving the automotive article to his father to read first and heading to his own room to review the telephone article. He quietly checked at Elaine's door to find she was still asleep before he entered his own bedroom. As Zack was finishing the article, Jonathan came down the hall and stood at the open door.

"Hey, bud, are you ready to go yet?" he asked. "Henry gave your filthy lucre to me to deliver to you," he continued, smiling.

"I'm ready, Dad. What'd you think of the article?"

"It seems pretty straightforward. You can read it while we drive, but mostly it's a list of the best models in each price range, so if we use the information it will be a matter of looking around to see if we can find any of the suggested models at the various lots or dealerships."

"Thanks, Dad, for helping me with this," Zack acknowledged. "I'll enjoy your moral support in negotiating a car price; I never did particularly enjoy this process, and after I settle on a price, there's always the taxes, title, and insurance to deal with."

"That's two of us," Jonathan agreed. "But I think we'll do OK."

CHAPTER XX

TUESDAY, MARCH 23

Zack drove the new vehicle to pick up the children from school that evening. Both he and his dad had been satisfied with the purchases and felt that their day had been well spent.

"Wow, Dad," Danny enthused, "I like this car. How long do you think it will last? Do you know what size an engine it has? How fast will it go?"

"Danny, do you remember what Grandpa said about asking questions?" Sissy warned.

"He said to be certain the questions I ask aren't ones I can answer myself and that I shouldn't ask questions that would embarrass someone. I can't answer any of these questions. You aren't embarrassed about them, are you, Dad?"

"Not at all, Son," Zack replied. "However, keeping the questioning down to one at a time in general is a good idea. If you were asking someone other than me, a question not to ask would be, 'How much did it cost?' Most people would find that too nosey. Now, to answer your questions, the car will last longer if we take good care of it. It has thirty thousand miles on it, and I would hope we could put one hundred-fifty thousand on it before we would need a different vehicle. The engine is rated one hundred eighty horsepower, and I don't know how fast it will go. The speedometer goes up to one hundred ten miles per hour, but I'm not inclined to see if I can do that."

"Why not?" Sissy asked.

"Because going over the speed limit is against the law. There's no reason I need to be going that fast. We have a car that will do very well at the speed limit. Running it too fast is liable to damage it anyhow. How did school treat the two of you today?"

Sissy replied before Danny had a chance, saying, "Dad, school's so much fun that the day is over almost before you know it. You look different; you have a new haircut, don't you?"

"Dad," Danny asked before Zack could answer, "When will I start growing? Grandma said you and Uncle Evan were small when you were my age and then you suddenly started growing."

Initially ignoring Danny's questioning, Zack replied, "Thanks for noticing my haircut; do you think it looks OK?"

"I think it looks great; it makes you look younger somehow," Sissy replied.

"I decided a decent haircut makes you feel better about yourself, too," Zack agreed. "Now Mr. Question Box, I think I started growing rapidly at about age thirteen or fourteen. You're almost eleven, so I'd say you've got a couple years to go before your growth pattern would mimic mine. However, none of us can control how tall we get or what we look like; you may not have the same type body Evan and I do."

"I don't want to always be little and scrawny," Danny complained. "I want to look like you."

"Yes, I think you look really great, Daddy," Sissy agreed. "I hope I can marry a guy that looks as good as you."

Zack, feeling uncomfortable with the sudden adulation, decided to turn the conversation. "I don't care how good or poor someone looks; what really counts is the way they behave. I'm ashamed of the way I've behaved in the past few years; I hope neither of you does like I did. Each person, however, no matter what body God gives them, can do their best to take care of it. That means eating the right amount of the right kinds of food, keeping clean, and keeping active."

"Do you remember the pact that Sissy and I made, Dad?" Danny questioned. "The one where we said we would always be together, that we'd finish school, we'd not drink or use drugs, and find our family?"

"You mentioned it; I think it's great, but the last one doesn't need to be there anymore, does it?" Zack replied. "I wish I'd done something like that when I was your age."

"You probably didn't think about it because you weren't in the same bad situation we were in," Sissy observed. "Say, how's Mommy done today?"

"I wasn't home much. Your grandmothers cared for her most of the day. They said she ate a good breakfast, kept it down, but then ate almost nothing for lunch and slept almost the entire day."

"I hope she can talk to us more this evening," Sissy said pensively. "We just barely said hello last night and good-bye this morning."

"I know," Zack agreed. "Let's trust there'll be time while she's awake for you to spend more time with her. Do either of you have schoolwork tonight or things about school we need to talk about?"

The conversation continued until the three arrived at the house whereupon they were greeted by all four grandparents anticipating feeding them after school snacks and hearing the events of their school day. Elaine was still sound asleep so the children played in the yard while Zack reviewed the messages from the teachers, looked over their schoolbooks, reviewed the materials he'd obtained at the university, and started considering a summer term schedule. After supper, the three of them went in to check on Elaine again and were almost surprised to find her awake with the head of the bed elevated, her hair combed, and a bit of light makeup on.

"Boy! Don't you look all spiffed up?" admired Zack as he gave he a gentle kiss on the cheek.

"Did you do all this on your own?"

"No, your mother was my beautician," Elaine smiled weakly.

"She sure did make you look better," Danny commented brashly. "Don't you think Dad looks good too with his haircut? Not only does he look better tonight, but he can sing too. We were surprised when he sang us a song last night."

"How are you feeling, Mommy," asked Sissy, walking to the opposite side of the bed holding her mother's right hand in both of hers.

"Well, right at the moment I'm feeling fairly well," Elaine answered. "But I have some good days and some bad days. If I take the medicine regularly I do better. Some of the reason I'd get so ill was because either I'd not have the medicine or I'd be too sick to remember to take it. However, all of you need to accept the fact that I'm unlikely to last very long; that's what the doctor said."

"We want you to get better," Danny stated flatly. "We don't want to think about you dying; we are all praying you'll get better."

"Sometimes prayers are not answered," Elaine informed.

"Yes, we know," Sissy responded. "Pop Pop told us that. He said sometimes it has to do with God's justice; I'm still praying though. I'm asking for God's mercy because that's part of God, too."

Elaine caught Zack's eye. "Well, the two of you seem to have dealt with this subject before. I just want you to be prepared for the worst. You will miss me after I'm gone, and I want you to be as prepared for it as possible. I'm so very, very glad to be seeing you now; I'd been afraid it would never happen again this last time they put me in the hospital." She reached up and touched Sissy's cheek and reached her left arm toward Danny, who was at the foot of the bed. "Come up here closer, Sonny, and give me a hug."

Zack stepped back, making room for his son. Danny slowly moved toward his mother and awkwardly leaned over, attempting a hug around her protuberant belly. He rapidly stood again to say, "Mommy, I don't remember your middle being so big!"

Zack placed a cautioning hand on his son's shoulder, saying, "That's part of the illness. Her liver is being damaged by the germs and consequently leaks fluid, which fills up her abdomen."

"Oh. Mommy, did I hurt you?" Danny worried.

"No, buddy, it's OK. Thanks for the hug; I love you," Elaine reassured. "Tell me about what you children did after your Dad was taken away by the drug cartel men."

The children recounted their day-by-day experiences, including their visits to McDonalds, the consignment shop, the bookstore, the grocery store, and eventually the library. They kept mentioning Mrs. Jonas and her assistance to them, and ended with the initial meeting with the grandparents. As the recounting was completing, they all recognized that Elaine had gone to sleep.

"She sure doesn't give much warning when she goes to sleep," Danny commented quietly.

"No, Son," Zack agreed. "I'm glad she was able to hear your story, though."

The following day was Wednesday and the first visit by the hospice nurse, a gracious Hispanic lady who spoke English with a marked accent. Zack had taken the children to school and come back to the house where he'd waited with the rest of the family for her arrival at nine o'clock.

"Hello, I'm Meezes Moreno," she said in introduction. "I am here to take care for Meezes Taylor. I am an American citizen growing up een Corpus Christi, Texas. I do speak the Spanish if you need. How eez the patient?"

Both sets of parents and Zack introduced themselves, and Zack explained the family's arrangements for Elaine's care. Sally then led the nurse with Zack and his mother following. Elaine was sleeping as they entered but awakened as the nurse spoke to her. As Mrs. Moreno asked her questions she had difficulty answering, so Zack assisted in the answers, but as the interview progressed, Elaine seemed increasingly blank until Zack finished the answering by himself as Elaine returned to sleep.

"She's been very drowsy, but when she's been awake she hasn't been having this much trouble talking," Zack observed to the nurse.

"I am not surprised to see her have the trouble," the nurse answered. "She look better than I expect from the reports from the Hospital

Washington. Liver disease patients will have fuzzy thinking that come and go. This is sad case with her being so young. It is very good she has loving family to help care for her. Does she swallow the medicine?"

"Yes," Zack replied, "she said that before we brought her here she would get worse because she didn't have the medicine, but we've been certain she had it right on schedule."

Mrs. Moreno continued with a thorough assessment walking out with the group saying as they reached the kitchen, "Coulda we stop here and talk about the future?"

"Of course," Sally agreed, "could I get us all a cup of coffee? Mrs. Moreno, would it be possible for our husbands to join us?"

"The coffee is a nice idea," the nurse replied. "Yes, yes, let the men come."

Zack stepped into the study to bring Jonathan and Henry while Sally hurriedly set out the cups of coffee. The group listened to the nurse's explanation of what hospice could provide for Elaine and the support they could offer the family, including counseling for both the adults and the children should they need it. When she'd excused herself and departed, Zack continued with the parents to discuss their handling of the situation; then each went their separate ways. He made his way back to Elaine's bedroom, taking a seat to contemplate his role in her care, the appropriate management of the children through the coming weeks, and then his thoughts moved on to his next project of schooling. He walked across the hall to his own room, shut the door, and called Evan on his new cell phone. Evan didn't answer the phone, so he left a voice message and a text as well. He picked up the LeTourneau catalogue and the notes he'd made from the previous day's interview with a school advisor. Looking at the various class offerings made him feel anxious to get started; he saw the summer session began in early June, so he worked filling out the application paperwork needed for enrollment at that time. After a couple hours, he began to feel restless, and inasmuch as Evan had not returned his call, he checked on the sleeping Elaine and went to find Henry to see if there were some chores he could do.

He found his father-in-law and father both in the backyard raking leaves out of the terraced azalea beds between the house and the swimming pool.

"May I help with this project?" Zack asked.

"Well, I only have two leaf rakes," Henry responded.

"That means you need to hand yours over to Zack and go take a rest," Jonathan laughed.

"I suspect that's possible," Henry replied, doing as instructed by going to the sidewalk behind him and sitting on a folding chair. "This reminds me of a quote I heard years ago. 'Work fascinates me; I can sit and watch it for hours.' I feel plumb lazy sitting here."

"I think you likely have an overly developed work ethic," Jonathan chided.

"Yeah, while we're all here, you'll need to share your tasks," Zack added. "I was getting stir crazy in there filling out the school application forms. How come all these leaves are falling here in the spring time anyhow?"

"See those trees above you?" Henry instructed. "They're red oaks, and they hang onto most of their leaves until they start to bud in the spring, so I have to rake these beds both in the fall and the spring. The azaleas will be blooming within the next couple weeks, and they look much nicer with the ground cover plants not covered by dead leaves."

"This is a big yard," Zack observed. "Have you been doing all the work yourself?"

"Much of it," Henry admitted. "Sometimes I hire someone to mow or weed, but I do most of it myself. I can pretty well keep the front up to snuff, but this big back area gets away from me from time to time, especially if we're doing any traveling which has been less lately."

"Please let us help with it," Jonathan said slowly. "I'm still working on a textbook revision while I'm here, but I'll need breaks from that on a regular basis. I enjoy yard work; it's one of the main things I've missed since we moved to the planned community down in Florida."

"Yes, and I'll need to justify your hospitality while I'm here, too," Zack added. "What are some of the things that we should be making plans to do?"

Henry started to talk when Zack's phone rang. "It's Evan," he reported, as he laid down his rake and headed for the cement steps to sit and talk.

"Hi, fellow," he greeted. "Thanks for returning my call. What's going on in your life this morning?"

"Hi yourself," Evan replied. "I've been in a meeting much of the morning, but the good news is that I'll be able to move down to the Dallas office, just not as soon as I'd hoped. It won't be until July, so I'll have to live out of a suitcase likely between the wedding and the time I can move."

"Maybe you should just keep your apartment up there and have Alice come stay with you until you can move," Zack suggested.

"Well, yes, that could certainly be a possibility," Evan said, brightening considerably. "We could then move together and leave her things at her parent's house until we move. Your head may be useful for something other than a hat rack after all."

"We met with the hospice nurse today," Zack reported. "She wasn't very optimistic about Elaine's condition."

"That's not good."

"While the nurse was doing her evaluation, Elaine became unable to answer, so I had to take over. She'd been quite lucid until then. I find it frightening; it's bringing the reality of her deteriorating health to reality in my mind. It's depressing."

"That's understandable. How are you handling it? Are you craving alcohol?"

"No, actually, I'm not, and I'm awfully grateful for that. I've thought about the problems and I'm trying to stay busy. I've mostly finished my application paperwork for LeTourneau, and right now I'm out in the yard raking leaves."

"I see you've a new phone number; I am assuming this is a cell phone?"

"Yes, this is the first call I've had. I also was able to get some wheels yesterday. It's a white five-year-old low-mileage Toyota."

"Great, how are the kiddos doing?"

"They're fine. I found out this morning hospice will pay for counseling for them if they need it. I'm not certain they do; maybe we should have them talk with someone as a preventative thing."

"Talk it over with the folks. With their teaching experience, they should be able to help. You know I'm praying for you daily."

"Don't quit; I do need it, but there are many blessings here as well. Mom and Sally are so great with Elaine. Caring for her is heavy, but they're right here to help me. The worst thing I suppose is Elaine's refusal to consider spiritual things. She did agree to allow me to bring up the subject again Sunday mornings."

"Oh, really, how'd that happen?"

"Well, I made a deal with her; I wouldn't push her to get us to remarry now and would consider remarrying should she die if I could talk to her about her faith once a week."

"Mmmm, that's interesting."

"Yeah, it's a little unorthodox, but I think my priorities are right."

"You're there; I'm not. I'm here to support you."

"Have you talked with Alice recently?"

"Every day! We've set the wedding day for late May on the twenty-ninth. It's a Saturday; go ahead and tell the folks."

"That'll make everyone excited and happy. It'll work out for me too because my first day of classes will be at the beginning of June."

"I'm counting on you being the best man."

"I'll be delighted, but it is possible I'll need to be here with Elaine."

"Yes, Alice mentioned that. We decided to declare you the best man if you can be in attendance or not. I'm having a fellow from my work by the name of John Anderson stand up with me as well, so he can fill your duties if you're absent. I need to be getting back on the job, so give my love to all. It's great to have you on my radar again; it makes life seem intact."

"Bye now, then," Zack said, finishing the conversation and pressing the 'off' button on his phone. He stood thinking about the conversation before going to discuss this news with the parents. He wished he could feel more excited about his brother's wedding, but the sadness of Elaine's illness weighed heavily. "Focus on the future and the good things," he told himself.

Both sets of parents were now sitting on the back porch drinking iced tea and hoping for Zack to share the information from Evan's call. They were delighted with the wedding date news and the confirmation of Evan's eventual move to Dallas. When Zack mentioned that he was asked to be best man, Sally immediately suggested that she and Henry would watch Elaine so Zack could attend the wedding. Zack thanked her, stating that it would depend on her condition at the time. He didn't think he should promise to be there should she be rapidly deteriorating.

"Additionally," Zack continued, "I need to be making a quick trip to St. Joe to close up the apartment there by the end of this month. I'd need you to care for Elaine then. I'd been thinking Dad and I could drive up there, but on consideration since there is so little I'm needing to bring back, I believe I may just fly on up there and bring back the few things we need in order to be there less time. The furniture in the apartment is in such poor repair I doubt it's worth bringing down here, so all I'd need to get is some of my tools, my guns, and clothes."

"I'm doubting your guns are still there," Thelma said. "I didn't see any in the apartment when we were there with the children. There were no tools there that I saw either. We brought all the children's clothes they were still able to wear."

"No, the guns were in a storage locker down in the basement of the apartment complex, and the tools are at the shop where I worked," Zack explained. "The only other thing would be the dishes and cooking utensils, but again I doubt they're worth the cost of transporting them down here. I think I'll box them up and take them to Goodwill. If I stay here I won't need them"

"You should try to see Mrs. Jonas while you're there. I have her phone number and address," Jonathan suggested.

"Yes, Dad, I'd thought of that, and I do want to do that," Zack agreed. "She was a godsend to the kids, and I do need to thank her in person!"

"Don't you have any wedding gifts or anything in the apartment that you should be keeping?" Sally asked.

"Unfortunately not," Zack admitted reluctantly, "I believe Elaine took anything of value to the pawnshop before she left to get extra cash for drugs. When I finally recognized what had been happening was shortly before I asked her to leave." He sighed heavily, leaning against a porch pillar. "Dad, may I use your laptop to look for plane tickets?"

"Sure, Son, and say, that's something I've not thought of mentioning earlier. I did see your laptop in one of the drawers in the chest in your bedroom, so that wasn't stolen. I'd certainly be willing to make the trip to St. Joe with you, but I do think it's reasonable to fly. We could take you to Dallas or Shreveport if that would make it cheaper for you."

"Thanks, Dad, I'll compare prices and consider the cost."

"Don't forget to check on Southwest out of Love Field," Henry advised.

CHAPTER XXI

THURSDAY, MARCH 25

Zack took his place by the aisle in the small plane the following morning, having been able to schedule a flight out of the regional airport at a good rate. The window seat beside him was empty, and he hoped it would stay that way giving him more room. The flight appeared to be nearly full, and the seat stayed empty despite what appeared to be a crowded flight. However, the last person to enter the plane—a voluptuous, amazingly beautiful young lady who stepped down the aisle—stopped. Zack realized she was waiting for him to move so she could take the vacant seat beside him.

"Good morning," he greeted, standing so she could pass in front of him.

"Good morning," she replied, "Are you from around here, or are you here on business?"

Somewhat surprised by the direct questioning, Zack responded slowly, "I'm new to the area."

"My name's Alexandra Manly, and I grew up here. My maiden name was Briley. The Brileys are a large family, and even though Longview's grown a good bit in the past fifty years, I know and recognize most locals. I was pretty certain I'd never seen a good-looking fellow like you around. So what brought you to our fair city; do you have a new job here?"

Zack found the woman disconcerting with her generous figure and sinking neckline, but to be polite he replied moving his left hand onto his knee to prominently display his wedding ring, "Hi, I'm Zack Taylor. My wife grew up in Longview but has become extremely ill. I've brought her back here to be close to her parents as we all deal with her illness."

"Oh, how tragic! What was her maiden name? Would I know her?"

"Possibly, her dad is Dr. Henry Denton, a retired dentist, and her name is Elaine."

"You don't say! I knew Elaine when we were in high school together. In fact, she was in a group of about five of us girls that hung around together. So you married Elaine Denton? All the rest in our group were in awe of her; she was so beautiful and accomplished. Actually, I wondered then if she'd ever get married, her standards were so high. She always said the guy she married would need to be handsome, athletic, loving, righteous, studious, and fun. You must be something to have caught her eye. Where did you meet, and what's wrong with her?"

"I'm from the Chicago area and was attending the university at Normal when we met. I think she must have lowered her standards. She has a condition the doctors call chronic active hepatitis, and they feel there's nothing more they can do."

"How sad! That's not contagious, is it?"

"Well, they say it is blood-born, so we can be around her with little risk."

"Oh, good then, I'd like to see her when I get back. I'm only going to Dallas for a couple days. Would that be possible?"

"I suspect so. Her appearance has changed drastically from the ravages of the disease, and she has difficulty staying awake, but if you'd like to see her, call her parents to check on her condition. I'll give you their phone number. I'm hoping to return on Monday: I'm going up to St. Joseph, MO to close our household up there. The children and I have been going through some rough times recently, but praise be to God things are straightening out."

"How many and how old are the children?" Alexandra persisted.

Zack answered her questions, feeling very uncomfortable with her interrogation but not knowing why. He picked up a tattered airline seat magazine attempting to divert the conversation by looking busy, but she persisted.

"How are you going to support yourself while you're in Longview?" she asked.

"I'm enrolling at the university to complete my degree in electrical engineering or computer science," he answered.

"LeTourneau's tough; who'll help with the kids?"

"My parents are retired and live in Florida; they're also in Longview now helping with the care of Elaine and the children. They're planning to move here to continue to help, and of course, the Dentons are in Longview as well."

"I may be able to assist with that!" Alexandra enthused. "I'm a real estate agent and would love to show them some houses!" she continued shuffling in her purse for a business card. "I'll give you this, but I can give them one too if I see them during a visit to Elaine."

Zack was feeling suffocated by Alexandra's effusiveness and looked around for an escape. "You need to excuse me for a moment," he said, unlocking his seat belt and heading to the restroom at the rear of the plane. He stayed in the facility as long as he felt could be polite and not contribute to the discomfort of anyone else on the plane. He attempted to analyze why he was finding Alexandra so distasteful. She'd said nothing truly objectionable, but she just seemed dangerous. He finally headed back to his seat, telling himself that it was a short flight to Dallas and almost anything could be born for a limited time. Alexandra remained true to form, and it was with restraint that Zack finally said good-bye to her as they were disembarking. He wanted to jump and shout for joy.

The flight from Dallas to Kansas City International was quiet and without incident. Zack rented a car and headed for St. Joe, prioritizing his activities for the coming few days. On the way, he called Mrs. Jonas and invited her out for dinner that evening.

"Oh, Zack Taylor," Belle said in response to his request, "I'd love to go with you, but my daughter and I have plans this evening. My brother-in-law is going to be here in town with us for supper. It would be very convenient for you to join the three of us. We all met your children and loved them so much. We'd like to meet you too. How are they doing?"

"They're doing well," Zack replied. "You're likely to think I was a horrid father with them being left like that, but I'm so thankful for what you did that I'd like to meet you."

"Well, you come then. We'll be eating about six if my brother-in-law gets here on time. Do you need our address?"

"No, Dad gave it to me along with your phone number. Thank you for the invite; I'll look forward to seeing you." Zack hung up, hoping he wasn't taking advantage of people who'd already been so kind to his children.

On arriving at the apartment building and walking into his rooms, Zack realized he currently was living in a different world than the world he'd been in before he was abducted. He cringed as he looked around the dingy space where he'd lived and housed his children. He'd stopped by a U-haul agency, purchasing cardboard boxes, and began to fill them with items to be taken to Goodwill. When he'd filled the rental car with his boxes, he made his first stop at the police station to check in with them since they'd said they wanted to interview him when he returned. The detective who had been working on the drug cartel matter was not available, and his stand-in greeted Zack warmly, but said he knew very little about the case, and that he'd give the responsible detective Zack's contact information. He thanked Zack for coming in and excused himself.

Zack's next stop was his former employer's shop where there was sincere amazement by all that he'd returned.

"We thought you were likely a dead man when you didn't show up," his boss said after greeting. "Man, you sure look good. You've lost weight, but you just look healthier."

"Decent nutrition instead of a bunch of beer is good for my body," Zack admitted with a smile. "I honestly don't know how you put up with me.

"Grumpy people who smell like alcohol can do good work," the boss admitted. "We've been up a tree several times since you've left not knowing what to do with a difficult problem. Do you want your job back?"

"No, I've decided to go back to school. I'm just here to pick up my tools. Does anyone want to buy some of them?"

"We do have a problem," the boss confessed. "I told the fellows they could have your tools, but that if they took them should you return they'd have to give them back. I did make a list of them and know who has what so if you can come back tomorrow after I've had a chance to talk to the ones who have them I can give them the choice of returning them or paying for them at replacement price. Does that sound fair?"

"It sounds reasonable to me," Zack agreed. "I'll stop in around 11:00 AM then. Will that work?"

"You're not the old Zack, are you?" the boss said. "The old Zack would have thrown a mean fit about this."

"You're right I'm not," Zack replied. "Getting abducted, going through alcohol withdrawal, coming to my senses, being a mistreated prisoner, and seeing Jesus Christ work in my life has made me a changed fellow."

"Stick with it then," the boss said. "and anytime you need a referral as to a good worker you can list me."

"Thanks, that's more than kind considering the fellow you did put up with. I'll see you tomorrow," Zack concluded as he headed back to the rental car.

Zack unloaded his boxes and asked if Goodwill had a truck that could come to the apartment to get his furniture. He was told a truck was available but not until next Monday and that pickups for donations were not made on the weekends. Zack explained that he was leaving on Monday so the lady at the desk said she talk to her drivers who at present were gone and that she'd call him back that afternoon to let him know if they could rearrange their schedule or make an exception. Zack knew he could rent a U-haul trailer but there was no hitch on the rental car. He headed back to the apartment, filling up the rest of his boxes, getting his guns out of the storage room, packing clothes in the empty suitcases he'd brought from

Longview, and calling the airline about the regulations of transporting his guns. He was hot and sweaty at five thirty, so he hurriedly showered and arrived at the Jonas home right on time but with wet hair.

Belle came to the door on his first ring. "You're right on time," she said. "I'm so glad you called; we've been hoping to meet the father of those delightful children."

"Thank you, I agree that they're little cracker jacks, but I need to again express my appreciation of your assistance to them," Zack replied formally.

"It was our privilege. Let me introduce you to my daughter, Esther, and my brother-in-law, Mike Jonas. They both met the children and were here at the meal we had together just before your parents arrived."

"Oh, I know," Zack responded, "Danny and Sissy have described in detail the meal Esther prepared; Danny remains convinced chicken picatta is his all-time favorite food."

"It was very, very good," Mike agreed. "It's nice to meet you. Your daughter was impressive with her young sleuthing abilities the evening we ate together. Belle's pretty much filled us in on your wild adventures during the abduction."

"Yes, I've talked with both your mother and father on a couple occasions since they left St. Joe, so we know more about you than you know about us. We did pray for you after your abduction came to light and felt your rescue and safe return were an answer to prayer."

Esther had been silent until this time but now remarked, "Yes, your escape was a miracle in our eyes, but the change your mother has reported in your outlook on life was no less than miraculous as well."

Zack was taken aback at this open discourse on his behavioral change, but he said, blushing, "I can only agree. None of it would have occurred if I'd been living my life right."

"Esther has chicken and noodle casserole for us this evening," Bell directed, "so let's get seated and continue or conversation at the table before it gets cold."

"Wow, if it's the same recipe she fixed a couple months ago it's delicious," Mike commented.

"It is; I made it because you'd liked it," Esther laughed.

Belle directed Mike to pray for the meal and little conversation ensued until after the plates were filled. Then she turned to Zack, asking, "How is your wife doing since she's arrived home?"

"At first, I thought better; she's eating some, but she's sleeping much of the time. Fortunately, she seems to have little pain. A couple times this week, though, she would just blank out and not be able to respond. We had a hospice nurse in a couple days ago, and she seemed to think that was to be expected. The outlook appears to be grim. She takes her medicine regularly, but the physician in St. Louis didn't give us much hope. I haven't talked to the folks today about how things have gone, but I'll give them a call later."

"We're also praying for her," Esther said quietly.

"Thank you," Zack said, looking at her and speculating on how much he should reveal. "I think only prayer will change her physical condition. She is so appreciative of being able to be home and seeing the children, but she does not wish to have anything to do with Jesus or prayer for her healing. This is very good casserole; no wonder Mike likes it. What are the little green things that taste so good?"

"They're green olive pieces," Esther laughed. "They accomplish in this meal somewhat the same thing the capers do in chicken picatta."

"What was the culmination of the search for the drug operatives?" Mike asked, changing the subject.

"We think the organization down in Belize is now pretty well gutted. I think the group here in the US escaped the sweep they planned here in St. Joe, and I worry about the cartel attempting to track me down with my move to Texas. Danny told me your line of business; do you think there's anything I should do to protect myself and the family?"

"I'd say mainly for you to avoid being anywhere near locations where they would be located. It's my understanding that you won some money from them gambling. Unless it was a huge amount, I'd think they'd likely have other fish to fry rather than to track you down."

"Because they took us through Houston, I'm inclined to think they may have a base there," Zack responded. "I'm planning to avoid that area at least for several years. It's between three and four hours away from Longview. I have guns that I'd stored in the storage area at the apartment complex that I'm taking with me. I've had a carrying permit in Missouri, but I'll have to find out what I need to do in Texas to keep that current. I went by the police station here today, but the detective that oversaw the cartel sweep here that failed wasn't in. His replacement told me he'd call me if he needed me."

"Even if he doesn't call, I think you should talk to him," Mike advised. "You need to tell him what all has happened to you and your concerns about Houston. He or his contacts in Houston may need to contact the Belize law enforcement people to attempt to identify the actual cartel. You need to let them know you'd be willing to give any information you would have that they might need."

"Thanks, I'll do that. Have you had problems with things like this in your town?" Zack asked.

"No," Mike answered, "our community is a peripheral suburb of Kansas City, and we've been fortunate not to have experienced this element.

"How are you getting along with your move?" Belle asked.

"I was able to get most of the items I don't wish to keep boxed up and over to Goodwill today. They have a van to pick up furniture, but it was not available today. The lady said she'd call me back if they could help me, but I've not heard from her. I may have to rent a truck for the task. I can't hitch a trailer to the rental car."

"I'm in my pickup, and I'm free tomorrow morning," Mike offered. "We'd likely need to make several trips if there's very much."

"I hate to take advantage of you, but thank you so much!" Zack exclaimed. "Now I really feel indebted to you. There isn't a lot; there are two beds, two dressers, four counter stools, four chairs, an old couch, a couple end tables and an old coffee table. I think a couple loads would do it. None of the items are in good enough shape to warrant care packing."

"Do you think we could help?" Esther asked.

"We could clean out the cupboards and mop the floors," Belle suggested.

"I was planning to do that on my own," Zack admitted. "I was hoping not to lose my security deposit. It wasn't very spiffy when I moved in, so I was hoping the manager would not set the bar too high."

"We'll make it a work day together," Esther laughed.

The conversation drifted on, and when Zack looked at his cell phone and realized it was nine o'clock, he recognized he'd failed to call the children before their bedtimes and needed to check in on Elaine. He quickly excused himself and gave his good-byes, arranging with Mike to meet at eight in the morning.

The apartment seemed bleak, bland, and shabby when he returned to it. He pulled out his cell phone, dialed, and greeted his father. "Hi, Dad, how are things going for all of you today? How has Elaine done today?"

"Hi, Son, things are not too terribly good here. Elaine's not had a very good day; she's hardly been awake at all, and she's eaten almost nothing. We could get her to drink, but she says even the thought of food makes her nauseated. Your mother and Sally are at their wits' end. I think she does better when you're here to encourage her. How are things going for you?"

"They're going better than I'd expected. I've been able to clear most of the small stuff out of the apartment, and even though Goodwill is unable to send a truck to get the furniture, I've got that covered tomorrow morning because Belle Jonas' brother-in-law's going to help me move the furniture with his pickup. He's a chief-of-police down in a town near Kansas City and was able to give me some good direction as to my issue with the drug cartel. Additionally, my boss is rounding up my tools and was very encouraging about offering to give me a recommendation. I ate supper with the Jonas family; they're certainly extremely kind. I hadn't realized you and Mom were in such close contact with them. The children couldn't have happened on to better folks. I'm sorry it's been a difficult day for Mom and Mrs. Denton; please express my love and appreciation to them. I'm pretty well tuckered out, so I'd like to talk with the kids before I keel over. Are they still up?"

"Henry just walked out of the room and down the stairs from tucking them in, so I'm certain they're still awake; I'll walk up and give them this phone. We all love you, and I'm tickled that things are going so well for you. Are you're still hoping to come back Monday?"

"Yes, I'll rent a room near the airport because my flight is at six in the morning. I've gotten so much done already I could have come home tomorrow, but I don't want to have to pay for the ticket change."

"Here is Sissy. Good-bye, we love you, bud," Jonathan finished, handing the phone to Sissy.

"How's my favorite daughter?" Zack asked.

"She's fine," Sissy replied a little sleepily. "How are you? Did you get to meet Mrs. Belle Jonas?"

"I certainly did. In fact, I had supper with Belle, Esther, and Mike. We had a great time; they are very pleasant people. Did you have a good day?"

"We had a great day. After school we played with Bonnie and Kenny for a while in their yard. When their mom walked us back home, she invited us to go to the Tyler Zoo with them tomorrow. Do you think we can do that? Grandma said she thought it would probably be OK, but that she wanted to clear it with you, so you'd need to talk with her about it. Will you do that?"

"I see no problem with that," Zack answered. "I love you; you sleep well. I wish to talk with that brother of yours now."

"Hi, Daddy," Danny greeted cheerily, not sounding the least bit sleepy. "So did you say we could go to the zoo?"

"Sure thing,"

"Did you go back to the building where they had you tied up?"

"No, I don't actually know where it is. I'm certain the police know, but the main fellow in charge of the operation dealing with those criminals was not available today; I'm hoping to talk with him soon. Did school go OK?"

"It was fun, but nothing special happened."

"Most days are like that."

"We miss you,"

"I like that; I'm missing both of you too, but I'm going to say good night. I do love you!"

"Love you, too. Good night," Danny said, finishing the conversation.

CHAPTER XXII

FRIDAY, MARCH 27

Zack awoke to ready himself in his barren apartment for the activities of the day. After shaving and showering, he dismantled the beds and was gulping down some cereal and milk when Mike arrived. The couch, table, and chairs completed the first load, and the men made the first run to Goodwill. By the time they'd returned to the apartment, the ladies had arrived with their cleaning equipment and were waiting to get started.

"You folks are making a difficult task a social event," Zack laughed. "Here I am embarrassed about the pitiful condition of my digs, and it's just a chore to be completed for you. I can't thank you enough."

"We think it's a good cause," Esther said.

"I'm just glad we were all free this morning," Belle agreed. "With Mike here to help, we can wipe this task out. No bigger than this place is, it should only take a few hours."

"By myself it would have taken all today and likely some of tomorrow," Zack commented. "I'm not used to this kind of help."

"Buck up and enjoy it," Mike laughed. "What do you want on the next load?"

"Let's take the beds and two of the side tables," Zack replied.

"Why not all three of the mattresses too?" Belle asked.

"I'm planning to sleep here tonight and tomorrow night; I'll need a mattress. Besides, Good Will won't take mattresses," Zack admitted.

"Then how will you get rid of the mattresses?" Belle asked. "You can't get it into the rental car, and you need it out of here. You should plan to come over to our house tonight to sleep. We have three bedrooms, and although Mike stayed in the third one last night, he's going back home this afternoon, and it will be empty."

"That sounds reasonable to me," Mike said, agreeing. "If you can't take the mattresses to Good Will, maybe we should haul them to the dump. I hope my comment's not offending you."

"Not at all," Zack replied, "these mattresses are dump material." The men began carrying out the beds, hauling them down the stairs and stacking them into the pickup. When they'd delivered the second load, Zack and Mike returned to find Esther using a carpet cleaner and Belle washing the walls and woodwork. It was late morning by the time the third load consisting of the mattresses to the dump was finished; Mike said his good-byes to all and headed home while Belle admitted she had a church committee meeting at noon and left.

"The carpets and walls are finished," Esther said, "so it's mostly the cupboards, counters, and kitchen floor we need to finish up."

"This place is going to look much better than when I moved in," Zack noted. "I'd never have done this good a job by myself. However, I can finish this up; you don't need to stay here."

"I like to see a task completed," Esther remarked. "Besides, I've been wanting to ask you some questions and didn't wish to broach the subjects while the others were still here."

"I'm good at answering questions," Zack chuckled; "I'm just not certain how accurate the answers will be."

"Oh, you'll see that with my questions the answers can be as accurate as you wish to make them," Esther responded enigmatically. "First of all, why do you think we're all giving you so much assistance here?"

"That's a question I think you can likely answer better than I can," Zack smiled, dipping his cloth into a pan of soapy water as he washed the floor of the space under the sink. "I guess I just thought you were being kind."

"We are being kind, but our motives are more ulterior than that, and I for one wish to make a clear break with them. Last night before you arrived, we'd been discussing your situation, the condition of the children, the tragedy of your wife's health, and your recent separation from alcohol. We decided that if you were to have a difficult time staying on the wagon, it would be now while you were alone in St. Joe where much of your drinking had occurred. Our intent was and is to keep you busy and interacting with us as much as possible. What do you think of that?"

"Well, so far your strategy seems to be working. Actually, for you to be telling me is a little patronizing, but in honesty I think I deserve it. I think it is fine, and I think I need to say I'm thankful one more time."

"We all do want to see you succeed in overcoming the alcohol, not only for the sake of the children but for yours too. I feel what we're doing is rather an invasion of your privacy, but I do want you to know we've no malicious intent. How do you feel you're doing handling the urge to drink?"

"You don't mince words, do you?"

"No, I think this is about the most important thing in your life right now."

"At this point, I'm doing well. I'm doing much better than I may have suspected. When I was having Elaine go through drug addiction programs and seeing her fail time after time, I developed a pretty fatalistic idea of addictions, a belief that they were nearly incurable. I knew over time I was addicted to alcohol myself because of the many times I planned to quit and then wouldn't follow through with it. However, after I was dry, after I went through DTs, and then when I became right with Jesus Christ there's been, up to this point, no trouble at all. I'm afraid to take a drink and do plan to be a teetotaler the rest of my life. My brother's being my accountability partner, and we're talking about my sobriety regularly. You're right about it being important; Jesus and alcohol abstinence need to be my basics. If I keep them in place, I can turn my life around with education, caring for the children, and being the necessary support to the children. I'm extremely fortunate to have such helpful parents, children, and in-laws. Elaine's deteriorating health is my biggest heartache. To see her now, you'd never believe what a joyous, wonderful person she was. It gives me a sense of nausea to think of what the drugs have done to her. Well, you certainly received a long response from that question, didn't you? I've never discussed all this so openly with anyone else except my brother Evan."

"Thanks for your transparency; it makes it easier for me to be transparent. So what are you planning for this afternoon and all day tomorrow?"

"Well, I thought I wouldn't be finished with all this cleaning and packing up and moving until sometime tomorrow, so since I'm so far ahead of schedule I've not given it any thought," Zack laughed as he finished up his current cupboard shelf and started on the next. "Your plan to help me has given me more free time which undermines the effectiveness of the interventions all of you made."

"Yes, I realize that, so I thought I'd offer you some suggestions. Mom and I would like to invite you to go the Kansas City symphony orchestra concert tonight. We have tickets and an extra one. Mike has season tickets but he can't attend, so it wouldn't cost you. What do you think?"

"It sounds like fun; it's been a long time since I've attended any classical concerts, but I like classical music. How dressed up will the two of you be?"

"Oh, we like to dress up a little, but there are attendees in dressy casual and even blue jeans there all the time."

"I can do a little better than that," Zack smiled. "Let me take you down there in my rental car, and that way I'll be feeling like I'm contributing a bit. Now, what else do you have up your sleeve for an agenda of business for me?"

"You catch on quickly," Esther admitted, blushing slightly. "We agreed we'd invite you to go to church with us tomorrow morning and then invite you for lunch afterwards. Do you think you can stand that much of our company?"

"I haven't been to church in years," Zack said thoughtfully. "Despite my recent renewed faith, there really hasn't been an opportunity. Yes, that would be great. Why don't you let me take the two of you out for lunch after the church service? I'd invited your mom out for dinner last night but that didn't work out, so let me take the two of you for lunch tomorrow."

"My shift starts at 5:00 PM tomorrow, and I generally like to take a nap before it, so that'd be fine. We'll ask Mom what she'd think. What did you find out last night about your wife's condition?"

"My dad said she'd had a bad day. He thinks she eats better when I'm there. She slept most of the day. I feel I should be going home as soon as possible, but I'm reluctant to attempt to change my airline tickets. I feel very inadequate when I care for Elaine. It doesn't seem like there's much I can do; I certainly can't bring her back to health. That is the big problem. The children are actively praying for her recovery even though she tells me she doesn't want them doing that. She wants me preparing them for her death. I guess that may be reasonable, but it's not a very bright prospect."

"I've dealt with a lot of liver failure patients having worked on a general medical floor most of my career. Many of them do sleep a great deal, and they often have periods when they don't think clearly. Do you think this is the problem?"

"No, it's when she's the most lucid that she seems most adamant against spiritual things."

"Mom and I have been praying for all of you. This gives us a better idea of the needed direction of our prayers."

The two finished cleaning the kitchen and Zack took Esther back home by midafternoon. He returned to the apartment to clean up and get ready. He thought about how long it had been that he'd been to a symphony concert, feeling guilty that he'd never given his children the opportunity to experience one. He resolved to make that happen in the future as he headed out. He stopped at a Subway and had a sandwich before going on to pick up Belle and Esther to make it to the performance in time.

The trip to Kansas City was marked by pleasant conversation as Belle recounted family times of the past, discussing events in her life before she's retired from teaching; Esther contributed some amusing stories from her nursing work, and Zack told of escapades he and Evan had carried out as youngsters.

"Then you met Evan's fiancée down in Belize?" Belle questioned.

"Yes, she came over to meet us that first night we were there," Zack replied. "She was teaching in the Salvation Army school there. Because she came back with us, her parents came up from San Antonio to pick her up so we could meet them as well. The family agrees that they are great people. The wedding's to be at the end of May in San Antonio. Alice, Mrs. Denton, and Mom are suddenly very busy attempting to get everything done with it being such a short time away. I'm to be the best man. However, my participation is a little dicey depending on the state of Elaine's illness."

"How does your brother feel about that?" Belle asked.

"He's OK with it; he says he'll just rely on the first groomsman to do my duties if I'm not there."

The conversation drifted on with an ease that surprised all three participants.

CHAPTER XXIII

SATURDAY, MARCH 27

Herman, Ardine, and their children sat around a small brown table in their room in the American embassy in Belmopan discussing the news they'd just received from the consul's office. "So we'll still be here another week at least," Herman told his family. "I know this sounds like a long time, but I was also told that the time we wait here is much better than if we're sent on to the US to have our asylum processed there. Apparently, there are so many asylum seekers in the US that they're having difficulty keeping up with them, and there's a big backlog. Documenting what's happened here with us having to leave the farm and all is easier here than if we were already in the US. The letter my cousin sent us two days ago is going to help too. He's found out that more men from the drug cartel have moved onto the farm and that there are apparently about twenty of them and that they are farming the land and the neighbor's land as well. He's anonymously notified the police but sees that nothing is being done about it. Obviously, it is not safe for us to return. My biggest concern is what we will do for money."

"Can't you get work in the United States?" Angel asked.

"Yes, the American consul says with this waiting I'll be able to get a green card."

"What's a green card?" Jennifer asked.

"It is the American permit that says I can work there," her dad replied. "Until I can get a job, though, we don't have any money, we don't know for certain where we'll live, and it is difficult to plan."

"Perhaps we should be thinking of attempting to go to England," Ardine suggested.

"Maybe," Herman admitted, "but with all the problems England and Europe are having with their asylum seekers and refugees, I think we'll do better in the US. Also, we're already here in the American system, and they seem willing to help us. I'm going to make this a matter of prayer for all of us. Additionally, Zack and Evan did say they'd be glad to help us if they could. I'm going to call Zack Monday to see what he could do to help us. He did say he thought we could move to the town in Texas where he would be living. I suspect the consul will be able to help more if we have a plan."

"How much have you talked this over with your dad?" Ardine asked.

"He thinks it's a big problem, but he thinks we have no choice but to follow through as much as is possible with the embassy's direction, and that we will solve the problems as they arrive," Herman responded. "The consul's secretary told me to I could call Zack or Evan Monday to see what they would have in mind."

"Would your dad and I be able to get green cards, too?" Ardine questioned further.

"Oh, yes, I should have already told you that," her husband replied. "Even if the three of us can't get good jobs right away, we likely can do OK with three incomes."

"I'm really getting tired of being here in this building," Angel complained.

"Aren't we all!" his mother exclaimed, "but it is certainly better than being back there on the farm. I'm so thankful that we're all still alive. The people here are kind to us; I think with the cartel down there on our farm it is very unsafe for us to be anywhere in this country except here. This is so sad because I've lived here all my life, and for many years I was proud of the improved conditions that were developing here. To be cooped up in this building is a small price to pay for life in a safer place."

"I think not knowing what will actually happen to us is almost as bad as waiting," Jennifer observed.

"You are so right," her mother agreed.

"We have to move through each day as it comes," Herman considered. "We need to do what we can to plan for the future. The embassy here has several books to read on life in the US, so we need to read and pay attention to that material. Let's set up a reading assignment system and all read the books, and then I'll write up quizzes so we can check to see that we remember what's important. This will keep us busy and preparing."

Danny and Sissy were excited when they returned from the Tyler zoo. The four children had enjoyed one another's company as well as viewing the animals. The only misadventure had been when Danny had tripped on the walkway and stumbled into a cactus plant. He was still nursing incompletely removed spines from his left arm.

Bursting through the front door on arriving home, they were enthusiastic about their day, but the grandparents were quite subdued, listening patiently to their description of events. "Sssssshhhh," Sissy said, holding up her hand to her brother sensing the reserve of the elders. "What's the matter? Why are all of you so quiet?"

Sally and Thelma looked at one another, and Sally answered. "This has been a very difficult day for your mother. Again today she's eaten almost nothing, and when she's awake she's been crying asking where you were. We've told her several times, but then a little later she's asked the same thing again. She's also asked about your dad's whereabouts and says she has something important to tell him, but then the same thing happens all over again a few minutes later."

"We'll go talk with her," Danny said, suddenly subdued as well. "Is she asleep now?"

"She's been asleep for a couple hours now, so it should be OK to awaken her," Thelma answered.

The children tiptoed down the hall, moving silently into the sick room. "Hello, Mommy," Sissy said quietly, "Are you awake?"

Elaine opened her eyes drowsily. "Sort of," she replied. "Where have you been? I've been missing you. I kept dreaming that I'd lost you again."

"We went to the Tyler Zoo, and I fell into a cactus bush."

"You mean cactus plant," Sissy corrected.

"Yes, whatever," Danny agreed. "I still have some of the stickers; they're so little I can't see them, but they still hurt if you rub them."

"I'm sorry," Elaine replied vacantly. "Where's your dad? I have something important to tell him."

"Mommy, remember he went to St. Joseph to close down the apartment," Sissy explained patiently, realizing they were experiencing the same forgetfulness the grandmothers had mentioned. "This is Saturday, and he'll be home Monday. Can you tell us what it is you want to tell him? We can get Grandpa to call him."

"No, I need to see him to tell him," her mother answered weakly. "Where have you children been?"

"We went to the Tyler Zoo," Danny explained gently. "We had a good time. Do you not remember us talking about it just now?"

"Did we talk about it?" Elaine responded.

"Yes," Danny answered, choking up as he realized the inadequacy of his mother's memory. "I love you, Mommy," he finished and hurried from the room to avoid displaying his grief; he rushed through the house and straight to his room for solitude as he sped past the grandparents in the family room on his way.

As Sissy came back from her mother's side seconds later, Thelma asked, "Did something upsetting happen with Danny?"

"Yes, he saw that Mommy wasn't remembering anything. Did he go upstairs?"

"He was through here before we even could speak to him," Sally answered.

"I think he was starting to cry and didn't want us to see it," Sissy commented sagely. "I suspect he wants to be alone. I wish Daddy were here;

we need him. He called so late last night we didn't say much. Do you think he is in danger there in St. Joseph from those drug men?"

"He's talked with the police there, and they think those men have all left the immediate area," Jonathan reassured her. "He also talked with Mike, Mrs. Jonas brother-in-law who's given him some advice as to how to do his best to see that we are all safe. Mike thinks there's little likelihood that those men will attempt to track him down anymore."

"Mike is a nice man," Sissy responded, feeling somewhat reassured. "Has Daddy called today?"

"No, but I think he will, or actually, there's no reason we can't call him," Jonathan said, pulling out his cell phone and dialing. The message went straight to voice mail so he dictated a message. "His phone's either lost its charge or he's talking on it," Jonathan explained to Sissy. "Let's give Danny a little more time and then we'll go out and play some games in the backyard."

"You're too old to play games," Sissy said primly but smiling.

"We're none of us too old!" Thelma exclaimed, joining the spirit of the moment. "Sally, you know how to play hide and seek or pig in the pen, don't you?"

"I do, I do," Sally laughed. "You men both need to come join the fun before it gets dark," she said, looking at Henry pointedly.

Henry rose from his chair, exaggerating his stiffness, saying, "A bit of exercise may be good for me but not too much."

"I'll go get Danny," Sissy offered, running up the stairs as the grandparents headed out the door to the back patio.

Evan, in his small apartment in Chicago, was feeling disconnected. He'd put in a long Saturday at work, starting in his office at 6:00 AM, and had been not broken for lunch trying to catch up on the tasks that had accumulated in his long absence. His immediate supervisor had stopped in at his office at five-thirty in the afternoon to commend him on his accomplishments during the last several days; however, having heard through the building doorman about Evan's weekend workday hours, he had kindly told Evan that he was giving him a deadline of 6:00 PM to get home and relax until Monday. Evan had complied but was so used to filling his free time with work that he was at loose ends. He'd attempted to call Zack but had been directed straight to voicemail, so he'd called Alice, but she'd not answered either. He then called his friend Jason who was to be Zack's backup at the wedding. Jason did answer, but he and his wife were just leaving the house to go out for dinner and a movie, and he was not free to talk. Finally, Evan decided to call his parents; he'd not talked with them for several days.

"Hi, Dad," he greeted, "this is Evan. How are things going down there?"

"Hi, Son, they're going pretty well. I'm out of breath from playing hide and seek with the children in the backyard."

"You may be having difficulty acting your age," Evan laughed.

"If I was having trouble, so were your mother and the Dentons. We were all out there together. The kids had been over to a zoo in Tyler, and when they came home Elaine was so forgetful asking the same questions that it had upset Danny, so we were all trying to brighten the mood. It was good exercise, and besides I'm entitled to a second childhood."

"Was the zoo a good experience?"

"Yes, except Danny fell into a cactus and got some stickers in his arm."

"Did Zack tell you that I'm for certain moving to the Dallas office?"

"Yes, we're delighted with your prospective move. He called late last night. We tried to call him this evening earlier when the children returned, but he didn't answer. I hope he's not in trouble."

"Yeah, me too. I tried to call only a little while ago and he didn't answer. So far he's been very available until tonight when I called."

"He told me he'd had supper with Belle Jonas last night and that they were going to help him with the move today. I think I might give her a call to see how things went. She might have some knowledge of his whereabouts."

The conversation moved on with discussion of the upcoming

wedding, particulars of Elaine's care, and more about Evan's move. At the conclusion, both men expressed their love and hung up.

Jonathan immediately called Belle and was disappointed when she didn't answer, so he sent her a text greeting her and asking how the move went and if she knew of Zack's location. Soon her text returned informing that Zack was with her at a symphony concert, and she'd remind him to call home during intermission unless it was an emergency. Jonathan texted back his thanks, assuring her it wasn't an emergency. It was then that he noticed on his phone that Zack had attempted two calls to him that he'd not answered while they were in the yard. At that point, he called Evan back to tell what he knew to keep him from worrying about his brother.

"Thanks, Dad," Evan responded after hearing the news, "I can't help but worry about the pup, especially with him being back in St. Joe. Can you believe he's at a symphony concert? I wonder how that happened."

"I'd suspect Belle engineered it," Jonathan chuckled. "She doesn't mind jumping right in whenever there appears to be a need. He'll call me back in a little while; I'll tell him you wanted to talk to him, too."

Later that evening after the children had been put to bed, Sally went to check on Elaine and found her bedsheets covered with vomitus and discovered that she was unable to arouse her. Sally called Thelma for assistance in cleaning things up, and they agreed to call the hospice nurse. They debated as to whether to call Zack but decided to wait until they talked with the nurse. Mrs. Moreno arrived, seeming just as confident and professional as she had on her earlier visit.

"So Meez Elaine vomit tonight?" she asked.

"Yes, we cleaned her up before we called," Sally explained. "She's hardly eaten anything the past couple days, so we are questioning where the material came from, but what has us more worried is that she is not actually talking with us. Her husband, Zack, is in Missouri taking care of business, and we're wondering if we should call him to come back early. His return flight is on Monday."

Mrs. Moreno checked Elaine's vital signs, duly recording them on her encounter sheet. "Have you given the antinausea medicine?" she asked.

"No, we waited to speak with you," Thelma explained. "Here it is; it makes her drowsy, so when she wasn't responding we didn't want to make it worse."

"Let's give it," the nurse directed. "Too much vomiting is worse than sleepy. Being the unresponsive often happens with liver failure."

"Should we take her to the hospital?" Sally queried.

"If the hospital could cure her, it would be good. Because, as we know, there is no cure, it will not help. We need to keep her comfortable."

"What do you think about us calling my son and getting him home here tomorrow?" Thelma asked.

"I do not think she pass away that soon. I think Monday ees OK. Does he know she ees worse?"

"Yes, we talked with him this evening," Sally contributed. "He asked us then if he should try to change his airline tickets, and we told him we didn't think so."

"Let's wait until the morning and see how she does," Mrs. Moreno suggested. "I will come back early at the eight o'clock."

"I think I'll sleep down here in Zack's bed then," Sally thought out loud. "I will let you out the front door, Mrs. Moreno. Thank you so much for coming. Thelma, you go on to bed; I'll not plan on going to church tomorrow again."

"Don't hesitate to call me for anything," Thelma cautioned Sally as they all walked to the front of the house. "Remember I'm here to help."

CHAPTER XXIV

SUNDAY, MARCH 28

Zack groggily climbed out of bed in his unfamiliar surroundings. He chuckled to himself about the cocoon of care Belle and Esther had given him since yesterday. Underneath, he felt somewhat guilty about accepting their kindness, suspecting he'd actually not needed it. He wondered had he been on his own if he would have wanted to go drinking; he didn't know, but realized as it was there'd been no temptation. He showered as he prepared for the morning at church and was completely dressed before opening his bedroom door to see if anyone was about.

Belle immediately spied him, greeting, "Good morning! How about some coffee and boiled eggs? I have toast and cheese as well."

"Well, thanks, I am hungry," he admitted. "I was thinking this morning about how much I enjoyed the evening. It was certainly different from nursing a series of beers in a bar," he continued, waiting for her response to that comparison.

Belle looked at him and laughed, "I see our invitation looked pretty transparent, didn't it?"

"Esther clued me in on your designs," he smiled. "I think she was feeling guilty manipulating me. It has made it easier to accept your hospitality knowing it was motivated by an ulterior motive. I recognize that it is kindness, and I appreciate it. At first I was a little chagrinned that I might need your help, but then I reconsidered and decided that a bunch of humility would do me well and that truly I need all the help I can get."

"Go ahead and eat," she said, setting the food in front of him at the dinette table. "Esther and I both teach classes at church, and that starts at nine forty-five. We'll just as well all go in one car since we'll be eating together. Are you certain you wish to spend the money to take us out? We could eat here conveniently."

"No, I wish to have the meal express my thanks for your super kindness to Danny and Sissy. Your assistance was a lifesaver to them. They mention it time and time again."

The three went on to church. Zack joined a middle-aged adult class; he said nothing during the discussion and felt awkward in the unfamiliar surroundings. He was glad when the worship service started, and was able to sit beside Belle and Esther for a little moral support. He did enjoy the music and sang the hymns familiar to him from his youth. To him the sermon was engaging, but he struggled with the pastor's emphasis on forgiveness. *Should I be forgiving the men in the drug cartel?* he wondered. *I know I'd rather be shooting them.* He thought of Elaine, wondering if he'd adequately forgiven her, then wondered if he'd asked for her forgiveness appropriately, considering his behavior. He remained uncertain. The final blessings from the pastor warmed his heart.

The morning at the family's Longview household was quiet. Soft Christian music played in the kitchen as Thelma prepared breakfast for the children. She'd told them of their mother's problems during the night so they did not disturb her hoping to let their mother and Sally sleep longer.

"Grandma, do you think Mommy's getting worse?" Sissy questioned slowly.

"It does appear that way, sweetheart," Thelma answered. "The hospice nurse came last night, and she thought your mother may be better today. We'll see when she awakens. Your Grammy stayed with her most of the night. There's the doorbell; will one of you go answer it? It's likely the nurse again; she said she'd come back over this morning."

After Mrs. Moreno entered, the four of them walked down the hall. Thelma led and peeped into the room, opened the door, and ushered the rest in behind her and then closed the door. Mrs. Moreno walked to the bedside and gently touched Elaine's arm, saying, "Good morning, Meez Elaine. We are all here to see how you're doing this morning. Are you able to wake up to talk?"

Elaine slowly opened and focused her eyes on the line of people by her bed. "Good morning," she grinned, stretching, but a wince of pain crossed her face as the stretch ended. "I'm pretty much the same," she reported. "How come you're all standing around looking at me?"

"You don't remember feeling bad last night?" Mrs. Moreno asked. "You were very sick, so I come back this morning to check. I see you better, though."

The children greeted their mother by giving her gentle hugs and kisses, and Thelma sent them off to get dressed for church. "We'll leave by nine-thirty," she instructed. "The church is close, so we'll have plenty of time. Tell your grandfathers that your mother's better, so we won't need to call your dad this morning. I'm going to see if she'll eat something. I may not go with you."

Mrs. Moreno completed the tasks of her visit and left while Thelma prepared a light breakfast for Elaine, and Sally never awakened. Soon the children, Jonathan, and Henry were heading out the door.

The children had been at the church the previous Sunday with both Thelma and Jonathan. They enjoyed the children's classes during the first hour but attended the worship service with their grandparents, attentively listening to the sermon and music.

Evan bounced out of bed feeling enthused and invigorated for the day. He'd slept well after having watched a little TV the night before and then reading a novel until he'd fallen asleep. He called Alice before getting cleaned up, laughing and explaining his frustrations the night before about not being able to get in touch with anyone.

"What are you planning to do today?" she asked.

"I'm back to teaching the teenage boys' Sunday school class," he explained. "I no sooner let the church know that I was back in town before they conscripted me. It's OK, though; they're a lively and fun group. There's a good youth pastor in the church and they've connected well with him, so they're pretty well educated in Christian ideas and are old enough to ask me some good questions. I met them all after the Wednesday evening youth service. After church, I'm going to go for a bike ride for a couple hours with Jason; I'd like to go back to work and get some more things wrapped up, but the boss told me not to show up until Monday."

"Good, you need the rest. I have some wedding things to talk with you about, but my list is out in the car in the garage, and I'm still not dressed after my shower. Have you heard how Elaine's doing, and did you get in touch with Zack?"

"Yesterday Dad said Elaine wasn't eating and that Mom and Sally were worried. I don't think it sounds like she's doing too well. Believe it or not, Zack was at the Kansas City symphony with the lady that befriended Danny and Sissy. He wasn't answering the phone because he had it turned off. I'll talk to him later today." The conversation continued at some length until they both agreed they need to resume their responsibilities of the morning and that they'd talk more later in the day about the wedding.

After he'd cleaned up, Evan decided he needed to start on the process of making the move to Texas. He knew it was several months away, but the challenge of setting up a married household appealed to him; the whole process seemed like fun rather than a chore. He grabbed a pencil and a blank sheet of paper to make a list of things to do attempting to prioritize as he wrote. He listed: find apartment or house in Dallas or Plano, arrange for moving van, box up belongings, and notify utilities. He then started daydreaming about how he'd have Alice to help him with all of these tasks and how much enjoyment it would be doing them together, particularly the drive down to their new home.

After church and a pleasant lunch, Zack called to check on Elaine. As usual, his dad answered his phone and gave the report that she'd had a bad night.

"Do you think even now I should attempt to come home earlier?" he asked. "I'll be there by noon tomorrow as the ticket stands. I'm finished at the apartment, and I did get my deposit back."

"I believe your being here helps with Elaine, but I doubt that changing your schedule would accomplish much. Your mother-in-law was awake much of the night with Elaine. Sally slept late this morning, so even if we have another bad night, she can handle that part of it. Elaine's lack of memory as well as the extent of her illness were brought home to Danny yesterday. He ran to his room to mourn. We're attempting to dispel the pall of gloom over the house, and I think we're accomplishing it. The children did enjoy church this morning and have been agitating Henry to get the swimming pool open since it's been so warm."

"Maybe I can help him with that when I'm back."

"Oh, say, Zack, your friend from Belize, Herman Hernandez, called me last night wanting to speak with you. I gave him your phone number. Did he call you?"

"Yes, he called just a while ago. He says he's coming to Dallas next week and wants to know what, if anything, I've arranged for him. Have you discussed this with Henry at all?"

"Yes, but it's been a couple days ago. He said he has a construction job lined up for him then but no final arrangements on housing. Apparently the immigration service has a list of apartment owners who will allow immigrants to rent from them, but we don't have the list and don't know if there are any in Longview. As you may suspect, most of these are in the larger cities. How are the rest of Herman's family doing? I didn't ask."

"He said they were fine but getting stir crazy in the embassy. Apparently the report from his cousin is that a number of the cartel men are now working the farm. It would seem that the government could go in there and capture the lot of them; I suspect this means that the local police in Punta Gorda are being bought off by the cartel. Nevertheless, Herman is fearful of even stepping out of the embassy."

"How are you doing emotionally with the move and all, Son?" Jonathan asked.

"Dad, I'm doing OK, I think. I do have a heavy feeling that seems like a black cloud over my head. I believe it's mostly knowing Elaine is so ill. I'm trying to focus on all the good things, but the weight is still there. I deal with feeling guilty that Elaine started using drugs, but I know I really tried to help her. I feel guilty about the alcohol use. Evan told me to focus on the future, and I know he's right. Belle and Esther are committed to keeping me busy while I'm here, but amazingly I'm not itching for a drink. My plane leaves at six-thirty in the morning, so I'll need to get up by four-thirty to be an hour early at the airport. The only stop on the flight will be Dallas, so I'll hope to be back down there by noon. I guess Longview's my home now, so I should be saying I'll be back home by noon," he finished, chuckling.

"Here's our love, then," Jonathan replied. "Have a safe trip. Be certain to give Esther and Belle our regards. We'll see you tomorrow."

"Okay, Dad, I will. Tell everybody I send my love. Thank you for everything! I know I need your prayers; tell them all I need their prayers. Actually, I believe I'm already benefiting from it. Love you! Good-bye."

After reading a book Belle had recommended for a couple hours, Zack decided to go for a walk. As he was preparing to go, Esther was also leaving to go to work. "It was fun meeting you," she said. "I had a hard time reconciling in my mind an alcoholic dad with two such wonderful children. I now see you're not all bad."

"Don't kid yourself," Zack laughed. "If I'm anything but bad, it's because you're blind. I guess a little touch of God could account for some of the improvement."

"We all need a big touch from God," she said seriously. "Because you're leaving early in the morning, I'll say good-bye now. I may have to stay after work to complete my charting. Perhaps I'll be back. But don't count on it. Have a safe trip, and hug those two children for me."

"I'll hug them until they squirm," Zack smiled. "It was good getting acquainted; thanks for being so open with me. Good-bye." It seemed that the life had gone out of the room when she left.

"I'm so proud of her," Belle commented as she waved her good-byes to Esther through the big bay window in the living room. "Her work at the hospital is very demanding, but she carries on as if her load is light when I know it is not. She's been the head nurse on her unit since the fourth year she's been in nursing. The administration's attempted to get her to move into a more administrative position, but she knows she'd have less patient exposure, so she's continued where she is. St. Joseph's not a large city, so it's not uncommon for me to run into folks who have appreciated her care, know who she is, and have commended me for the care she's given. Are you hungry? I have several options for supper and several ideas about how we can occupy our time this evening. Was Elaine doing all right when you called?"

"I'm not hungry yet. Maybe I could eat in another couple hours or so. I know I need to get to bed early tonight to get going so early in the morning. I also need to turn this rental car in when I get to the airport. Elaine's not doing well. Her mother was up with her most of the night. I should be there to help them; they think Elaine does better when I'm present. However, I feel at a loss knowing what to do to help her."

"Likely your just being there helps her. That was what my sister said when she was dying. She had breast cancer and died in her early fifties. I would go up to the town in Iowa where she lived and stay with her during the last few months; we'd always been close, and she was very comforted by me being there, even when I could do almost nothing for her."

Belle accompanied Zack on his walk and then the two of them did nothing but talk and eat sandwiches until he turned in at eight-thirty. Belle seemed to have a knack for listening, and Zack continued to be surprised at how easy it had been to discuss his life while chatting with her. She'd been open with him as well concerning the pain she felt on losing her husband. Zack could see that even now, she was missing her spouse and admired her for her strength in moving on.

CHAPTER XXV

MONDAY, MARCH 29

Danny and Sissy as usual came scurrying down the stairs to the kitchen in good spirits.

"We've decided we are getting too old to share a room, Pop Pop," Danny said, addressing Henry, who was sitting at the head of the table reading the newspaper.

Henry smiled at the bright-eyed youngster, saying, "Somehow that doesn't surprise me at all. What alternative arrangements do you propose?"

"Sissy thinks I should ask you if I can move into the guest room down here, but I think I'd rather sleep with Dad in his room. Dad's room has a bed big enough for two."

"Daddy gets up in the night to check on Mommy," Sissy contravened.

"That's okay," Danny persisted. "If I wake up, I'll know what's happening. Besides, if I go into the guest bedroom, there won't be anywhere for the guests like when Alice's parents came."

"Those both seem like reasonable concerns," Henry agreed. "Let's ask your dad's opinion when he gets back today. He may or may not like Danny rooming with him. Do you think you'll get lonesome in that big bedroom at the end of the hall all by yourself, Sissy?"

"I don't think so," she replied tentatively. "It is a big room, and if he moves out I won't have anyone to help me clean it, but then because he's always leaving the towels on the floor in the bathroom, it actually might be easier. He can still come up there, and we can read and play games like we do now. I'm hoping sometimes to invite some of my friends to spend the night, and truthfully I wouldn't want them knowing we sleep in the same room. Danny, if you have friends over, where would they sleep?"

"In the guest room, I guess; they'd be guests. Guys don't do that as much as girls do, though. So Pop Pop, would that be all right?"

Henry smiled at the engaging youth, saying, "I suspect so, but let's talk with you dad. I'm the only one manning the kitchen this morning, so what do you two little yokels want for breakfast? I'm only preparing one thing, so you'll both need to agree as to what it is."

"Do you do pancakes?" Sissy inquired.

"Yes, with a pancake mix," Henry admitted.

"Oh! That sounds great!" Danny exclaimed. "Can we have peanut butter and powdered sugar on them?"

"Certainly, and that'll give you some protein as well. You'll both need to drink a glass of milk, too."

"How about chocolate milk?" Danny negotiated.

"Nope, white milk," his grandfather stipulated. "The chocolate in chocolate milk combines with the calcium in the milk in a process called chelation. When that happens, your body doesn't absorb the calcium, so you don't get as much benefit from it. Additionally, you'll be getting plenty of sugar with the pancake toppings."

"I actually like white milk with sweet foods," Sissy observed. "I think it makes the sweet taste not stay in your mouth as long. So when does Daddy get here?" Sissy asked.

"Early this afternoon," her grandfather answered. "I suspect he'll be the one picking you up from school today."

"Make sure he's on time," Danny directed.

Henry laughed, "You're on his case, aren't you?"

"There were too many times in the past when he didn't show up when he said he would. We'd then have to ask for a ride and wait a long, long time; a few times we had to walk home from school alone in the dark, but now he's doing a lot better," Sissy explained.

Breakfast was soon devoured, and the children gathered their necessities for school before Henry loaded them into the car. As they were pulling out of the driveway, they waved good-bye to Jonathan and Thelma, who were finishing their morning walk.

As Zack pulled his carry-on suitcase from the wheeled rack positioned beside the plane after he'd landed in the Longview airport, he noticed two Hispanic men ahead of him dressed in black t-shirts and tight jeans. Although he had very little recollection of the appearances of his old captors, he immediately became suspicious of these men with a sense that he had seen them before. He stayed back in the line watching them as they entered the terminal and then attempted to unobtrusively watch as they moved on toward the parking lot. They were met in the drive by a black SUV with two aerials and a Kansas plate. He quickly noted the number, and as he headed back to the luggage carousel, he wrote it down so as not to forget it. With a sinking feeling that the ordeal was not over with the cartel, he resolved to get to the local police station before going home to report his previous experiences and this presence of men he believed likely to be connected. He wondered if the children would remember the license plate number they'd acquired in St. Joseph but decided rather than to frighten them by asking about it, he'd first call the St. Joseph police to see if they still had that on record. He made the call while waiting for the luggage and identified himself, asking for Jesse Freeman, the officer who initially had led the unsuccessful sweep in St. Joseph and whom he'd not been able to meet and speak to the previous week.

When the connection through the station phone system completed, Zack heard, "Good day, Officer Freeman, what can I do for you?"

Zack replied identifying himself and explaining the nature of the call. "Do you have that Kansas license plate number?" he asked.

"Thank you for your call," Freeman answered. "I apologize for missing you when you were here. I should have the number. All that case's forms should be scanned into my computer; please wait a moment while I find it. Do you feel at the moment you're in immediate danger?"

"I can't be certain, but I doubt it. I suspect that they didn't even know I was on the plane. I was one of the first to board in Dallas, and I didn't see them then. They sat toward the front; I do remember some fellows getting on right at the last minute. However, they may have been watching me board. The SUV has driven off. My actual fear is that they've tracked me to Longview and that my family is in danger. I'm planning to call the police here as soon as I hang up with you."

"Good," Officer Freeman agreed, "I'll give them a call as well to support your concern; here's that number. It's Kansas SWP-392. Is that the same?"

"Yes," Zack replied with a choking sensation in his throat. "This past weekend, I talked with a fellow named Mike Jonas who's a chief of police down in Johnson county Kansas. He told me to talk with you and to also contact the police here and in Houston as well because I was taken down to Houston while I was held prisoner and put on the small boat to Belize there. Do you have any other suggestions?"

"That's good. Because this definitely looks interstate, I'm going to be calling the FBI as well. You'll need to be expecting a call from them. Do we have your current number?"

"Yes, it's this cell phone I'm talking on now."

"I've got that. I'll call you back if I need more."

"Thanks for your help," Zack concluded.

"Yes, thanks for your call; I'll get right on this. The sooner we can get these fellows off the streets, the better it will be. Bye now." He hung up.

Zack drove slowly, watching carefully for the SUV and attempting to make certain no one was following him. He used his GPS to go directly to the police station and stood at the information window to ask to speak with the detective in charge. There was no one at the window, but there were two empty desks. After waiting a couple minutes with no one appearing, he decided to call the station on his phone.

After the sixth ring, a lady's voice answered, "Longview Police, may I assist you? If this is an emergency you'll need to call 911."

"No, it is not an emergency, but it is urgent," Zack explained.

Elaine awoke from napping in the early afternoon. A feeling of peace she'd not been experiencing existed through her drowsiness when she realized that Zack was sitting in a chair beside her bed holding her hand. She looked up at him, realizing that he was quietly staring out the window across her bed. "I thought I'd lost you again," she said quietly.

Zack, startled, looked at her, grinning, "So, you finally did wake up. I've been here about half an hour. Mom and Sally have told me how sick you've been since I've been gone; I didn't want to wake you up. How are you feeling now?"

"Where have you been?" she persisted.

"I was up in St. Joe closing down the apartment. Apparently, you don't remember my good-bye and all. I just got back a couple hours ago. Mom and Sally said you'd been confused and vomiting. Do you recall that?"

"Faintly," she frowned, "I feel pretty good now, though."

"Super!" he exclaimed, leaning over and kissing her. "I've felt bad this weekend because I wasn't here Saturday, and that was when we'd agreed to talk about my new faith in Christ. Do you think you're up for that now?"

Elaine's gaze caught and held Zack's for a couple seconds, and she then looked at the desk and bookcase against the wall in front of her before turning her head to look out the window at the front lawn and trees.

Zack held his breath; his heart pounded in his ears waiting for her response.

"I've had something important that I wanted to tell you, but right now I can't think of what it was," she said, tearing up. "I wanted you here to tell you."

Zack watched the tears course her cheeks and squeezed her hand. "I'm going to be here," he assured. "You'll remember sometime. Have you thought anymore about your relationship with God?"

"Yes, I know I'm afraid of dying, but I tell myself that it is inevitable and that I need to take my chance that God doesn't exist and that everything will just end with death."

"My seeing what happened to me when Herman and I prayed wiped away my question of God's existence," Zack said thoughtfully, "but that doesn't solve the problem of unbelief for you. I don't know how to bridge that gap for you. I've been praying that you could believe."

"Thanks," Elaine responded quietly. "I know the children would be at more peace about my death if I could reassure them that they could look forward to seeing me in heaven. However, if I said I believe and didn't, wouldn't that be a lie?"

"Maybe so," Zack agreed. "I know the answer to that is that you should step out on faith and claim to believe, but that's easier to say than to carry out if you feel you're essentially overriding your conscience."

"Sometimes I don't even know if I have a conscience anymore," Elaine offered.

"I feel like I'm so ignorant about these things that I'm like the blind leading the blind," Zack admitted. "Would you be willing to talk to your dad about this? You and he used to be very close."

Elaine closed her eyes, and Zack again saw the tears flowing. "My dad loves me so much, and I know I've been such a disappointment to him that I'm afraid to talk with him."

"I don't think he'd be unkind,"

"Oh, I know that!" she exclaimed. "He's told me in the past that he's always willing to talk about things but that he won't force a conversation on me that I don't want."

"So he didn't make any bargains with you like I did?"

"No, but that's OK, I know you care. You're probably basically a little pushier than Dad," she smiled.

"Then I'm going to ask him to talk with you since I'm pushy," Zack persisted, taking advantage of the conversation and looking at her with an expression of question on his face.

"That'll be all right," she assented. "It needs to happen."

"You've been so out of it while I was gone I feared there'd be no time for us to have this conversation when I returned," he said.

"Yeah, it's interesting how a lot of the bad times, although they're very unpleasant at the moment, don't even seem to register much after they're over," Elaine murmured as she drifted back to sleep.

Zack continued to sit in the chair, watching her sleep and asking for help from God for wisdom in his dealings with her. Her breathing was at times erratic; he found this troubling. Sadness washed over him as he wiped wispy blond hair from her forehead. He slowly rose from the chair to find his father-in-law. *Too many problems*, he thought as he moved through the family room and on through the kitchen to the study. No one was present there, but he heard movement upstairs to so he decided to check that area; he found his mother in the laundry room folding clothes.

"Hi, Mom," he greeted, "do you know where Dr. Denton is?"

"Yes, Son," she replied, "both your dad and Henry went to pick up the children; they should be home any time now."

"Mom, I've got some serious stuff for us to discuss among the five adults. At this point I don't want Danny and Sissy involved. I don't wish to wait until after they go to bed, though."

"Your dad told me you saw the cartel men at the airport; I believe I can make arrangements with the neighbor a couple houses down to let them go play an hour or so. When they get home, I'll have a snack for them and call Mrs. Hudson. She's invited them over twice since they were there, so I doubt it'll be a problem, especially if I tell her that a new emergency has arisen. Remember that our American police departments are not the same as the ones in Belize."

"Yes, I know, but that doesn't keep me from feeling guilty that I've brought this danger to you folks and to the children as well."

"Son, we're all in this together. I agree that it is frightening, but we're not without resources. I understand you talked with the police about how we should handle this. What'd they say?"

"That's some of what I want to talk with us all about. Officer Gay, the one I spoke with, said we could defend ourselves even with guns if someone entered the house but that even if someone was on the lawn around the house, we'd need to rely on police protection. One of the problems I see is how big this house is and how strung out the rooms are. It's not very defensible."

"I see what you mean. Actually, when you think of it, American homes are mostly indefensible. I know Henry has a security system here, but I don't think they use it. Maybe it's used to protect the property when the Dentons are away. He has some exterior security lights, but I'm uncertain to how complete they are as to total perimeter coverage. With this demand for security, we need full coverage with cameras and monitors."

"You're right, and we need them tonight. I'm certain that can't happen. How soon do you think Dad'll be home?"

"Any time now. Did Elaine awaken when you were in there?"

"A little; she said a few things. She couldn't remember the important thing she wanted to tell me. She did agree to have a talk with her dad. I hadn't realized there was minimal communication between them."

"I guess I hadn't either, but now that you mention it, I see that it is likely a fact."

A door slammed below and excited voices were heard as the children raced from the back door to the family room. Zack grinned at his mother and called out, "We're up here. Are my favorite rug rats home to greet me?"

The children pounded up the stairs and into his arms. "Was everything all right in St. Joseph?" Sissy asked. "Did you see any of the cartel men there?"

Zack caught his mother's eye, saying, "No, but I did go to talk with the police there. The main fellow I wanted to talk with was gone, but I'm to called him later. Our safety is important."

"Did you get your guns, Dad?" Danny asked.

"Yes, they're out in the car; I haven't brought my things in yet."

"May I see them?" Danny asked.

"Yes, I'll need to clean them, and you can see them then. We can do that tonight."

"Would anyone be interested in some brownies and milk?" Thelma queried, changing the subject.

"Oh, great!" Sissy enthused.

"You children go ahead while I get my things out of the car," Zack directed. "I think I'll wait until supper to eat. Your grandparents and I have some things to talk about, so after the snack we'll see if you can go over to Bonnie and Kenny's house and play awhile."

The group moved down the stairs, and Jonathan followed Zack out to the car to help him unload. "Was it a difficult trip?" he asked.

"Not really; it was good. It's just this new appearance of the cartel that has me worried."

"Could you possibly be wrong about that?"

"No, the vehicle that picked them up had the same Kansas license number that the children saw."

"Not good," Jonathan replied with a serious look as he stood holding the gun cases while Zack picked up his two suitcases.

"As soon as the children go to the neighbors, we'll need to talk with the Dentons about how to deal with this. Do you think maybe we should all just try to leave here? That would be very hard to do with Elaine sick and all."

"Let's talk about it; going to stay at our place in Florida is actually not an option with our occupancy restrictions. We could rent a resort room down there in Fort Walton Beach, but that would be expensive. Who is to know that they couldn't track us down there? I'm suspecting it would be better to stay here where we already have the police involved."

The men crossed the back of the house, entering through the family room carrying the luggage to Zack's room and depositing it in the large closet. They then found Henry with Sally in the study, and they all moved to the front entry, saying good-bye to the children as they rushed out the door to be with their friends.

As the five adults gathered in the living room, Zack started by telling the group of the sighting he'd had of the cartel men at the airport and the discussions he'd had at the police station concluding by asking what they felt plans should be for the protection of the household.

"You need to know that before I bought this house it had been struck by lightning which damaged the security system, and I've never had it repaired," Henry offered. "The exterior lights are on a switch in the master bedroom, but while they cover a good bit of the perimeter of the house, they're not complete. We can put up some more lights on extension cords for tonight, though, and that would give more complete lighting."

"We do not know that the cartel has our address here. However, we need to assume that they do since they are in town," Henry commented. "I think we need to remain here, especially since the police now are fully aware of our situation. I know Officer Gay's dad and know the son's a sharp and responsible fellow like his dad."

"I believe one of us should stay awake through the night watching for any suspicious activity," Thelma suggested. "As far as we know, the cartel men will not know we're aware of their presence locally, so we have that in our favor. Because that is the case, we can likely all sleep in our usual beds and only go to safer locations if someone is sighted. That way the children would not need to know of the danger."

"I believe closets would be the best for safe locations," Sally contributed. "How about using the large closets down in the guest bedrooms where Zack and Elaine are sleeping?"

"Yes," Zack agreed, "I was worrying about Elaine being by herself, and we'd all be right there with her if these fellows show up. Those two bedrooms are actually the most defensible part of the house; unfortunately, because they abducted me with guns last time, I'm assuming they'll be armed this time as well if they show up. Henry, do you have any guns?"

"I have an old hunting rifle, which I haven't used in years. It's in a locked case in my closet."

"I'll clean it tonight when I'm cleaning mine," Zack directed. "I trust we won't need any of them, especially since we wouldn't be using them unless those fellows break in and enter the house. We can call the police immediately should we see any sign of them. Officer Gay gave me his personal number."

"Sally and I will assume the task of putting up the exterior lights," Henry suggested. "I know I'll need some new bullets for my rifle, so I'll go to the store and get those; will you need ammunition as well, Zack?"

"Yes, for both guns," Zack replied. "Dad, could you help me get them cleaned, and then maybe you could go with Dr. Denton to get the ammunition."

"I'll fix supper, and if you'll tell me where the flashlights are, Sally, I'll put them along with some water in those closets," Thelma contributed. "Oh, look, here are the children coming in now already," she continued, hearing the back door slamming and Sissy calling 'Daddy, Daddy!' in a loud hoarse whisper.

"We're all in here! What's the problem?" Zack questioned as the children rushed into the living room.

"We saw the drug cartel men on our street in front of the Hudson's house. We came right home to tell you!" Danny exclaimed.

"We know it was them because it had the same license plate number on it. What do you think we should do? Should we call the police?" Sissy added and questioned.

"Oh, kiddos, I learned they were in town when I saw the vehicle at the airport, and your grandparents and I were just discussing how we'd handle this while you were over at the neighbor's place. We have set up a plan and will all be working together to keep us all safe. Your seeing those fellows helps us know they know where I live; I talked with the police about all this just this afternoon, but I'll need to call them again about our new information. I don't want you children outside the house now without an adult."

"So much for secrecy," Thelma muttered with a wry smile as they dispersed to carry out their plans.

CHAPTER XXVI

EARLY TUESDAY, MARCH 30

Danny and Sissy were sleeping in their dad's bed, fearful of staying in their own room. Discussion had been made of moving them to another location, but their pleas to remain with the family had been heeded. Zack slept on a cot for the first watch of the night in Elaine's room, while Jonathan watched the back of the house from his upstairs bedroom, and Henry watched the front from the master bedroom. The change in shifts came at 1:00 AM, when Thelma went down to sleep in the cot beside Elaine and Sally took up the observation point for the front of the house while Zack surveilled the back. They had all moved through the house in the semidarkness avoiding turning on interior lights, allowing the external lighting to be adequate. Zack had only been at his post fifteen minutes when Sally quietly came across the hall into the back-upstairs bedroom whispering, "They're here sitting out in a car in the street." Zack and Sally rapidly walked back into the front bedroom, and Zack immediately dialed Officer Gay's number while Sally purposefully moved to awaken and move the others to the downstairs closets, excepting Elaine, who was sleeping quietly.

"Officer Gay here," was the sleepy response Zack received for an answer.

"Hello, Officer," Zack greeted, "this is Zack Taylor, and I'm notifying you that we think the cartel men are out in the street in front of our house."

"Yes, Mr. Taylor, I'm on it! I'll get some cruisers over there as fast as possible; I'll call them from a separate phone, and you stay on the line. Are you in a safe place?"

"Yes, we're all going to be down in the addition at the west end of the house."

"I assume you're armed?"

"Yes."

"I'm putting you on hold; don't hang up."

Zack watched through the window as the driver of the SUV got out of the vehicle and stood by its door looking at the house, but he then hurried down to his assigned position guarding the hall between the west bedrooms and the family room. He stood inside the cracked open door of the rear bedroom where he was able to look down the hall into a narrow view of the family room and past an external rear door in the hall.

Jonathan, who was guarding the front bedroom window beside Elaine's bed, reported, "Three men are out of the SUV, and they're all armed and wearing ski masks. One's heading this way, and two are at the other end of the house."

"Are you still there?" Officer Gay asked over Zack's cell phone.

"Yes, I'm here. Three men have moved out of the SUV and onto the lawn; they're armed and approaching the house. In fact, one's ringing the doorbell now."

"Well. obviously don't answer it. Our police should be there within five minutes. One is located at the front of the subdivision now, but I want all three there simultaneously when they arrive. I'm only about seven minutes away myself. Remember, no shooting unless they enter!"

"Yes, we're really hoping there will be no shooting!" Zack said fervently. "My wife and children are here as well as both sets of parents. Someone is pounding on the front door."

"Hang tight. We'll be there promptly."

Zack could hear Officer Gay's siren through the cell phone. He'd had it on speaker and now switched it back. In the silence, he could now hear Sally in the closet with the children praying, "God keep us calm in this difficult time! Help our men to stay alert and to know what to do. Bring the police here rapidly and safely!"

"One fellow came right up to my window a bit ago," Jonathan reported hoarsely. "I think he's casing the house to see if there are any open windows."

"There are two fellows in the backyard by the pool," Henry said from the window behind Zack. "Now there are three. They're running up to the back patio!"

Soon there was the crash of breaking glass and the sound of splintering wood. Zack realized the house was being entered. "Where are the stairs?" one of the men shouted as he ran into the family room. "Oh, here they are!" he exclaimed as he pounded up. Immediately behind him, a second man headed toward the hall where the family was hiding holding his gun in front of him.

"Halt!" Zack dictated tersely. "We're armed, and we'll shoot!"

Immediately the invader let off two rounds of gunfire, and Zack responded with one shot, taking the man down. The intruder landed with a scream of pain and cursing.

"Police!" the man upstairs shouted as he raced back down past his injured cohort. Zack switched his phone back on speaker listening.

"Are you still there?" Gay questioned.

"Yes, we're all OK, but we're still in the west end of the house. The police are now at the front, but the other two intruders have run back out of the house into the woods behind the house. I've shot one and he's down in the family room. They broke into the kitchen door from the back. The intruder in the family room's still alive and armed; he's groaning. When your men come in, they may still be in danger; he can probably see out onto the back porch. I can't get to the front door to open it for them. You could come in through the garage. Let me give you the code to enter the garage door from the keypad on the outside. The code's 86646."

"Hang on, I'll relay that information."

Zack heard the crackling of the police radio and switched his phone back off speaker. "Hey, Dad," he whispered. "I'm okay; are things all right in there?"

"Yeah, we're all scared silly. The police have gone around the other end of the house," Jonathan replied.

"I see police lights flashing in the subdivision over on the other side of the woods," Henry reported.

Zack could now hear the police at the other end of the house. Elaine was calling out, and Sally was comforting her. The groaning from the intruder stopped, and Zack heard a chair topple in the family room with appended swearing, but he could see nothing. Suddenly, the family room lights blazed on and the police yelled out their presence. There was only silence. Finally, Zack called out, "We're back here but the man in the family room is armed and alive."

No one moved. Zack heard Jonathan opening the window, removing the screen for Officer Gay to enter in the front west bedroom and talking with Office Gay, who then came around through the joint bathroom to stand behind Zack. "Do you think your intruder's to the right or to the left of out visual field?" he asked.

"I think he's to the right," Zack replied, "because that's where the table and chairs are, and I heard one fall."

Gay moved ahead of Zack down the short hallway, getting a visual on the man who was sitting on the floor with his back against a chair aiming his pistol toward the kitchen door where he knew the police were located.

"You need to put your gun down," Gay stated loudly. "You're surrounded by police front and back."

The intruder turned and shot toward the hall, but Gay had stepped back, and the bullet sunk into the drywall and studs. The kitchen police, however, immediately responded by firing two rounds with one of them hitting the man's hand and sending his pistol flying onto the carpet. He again shrieked in pain while the three police rapidly approached and secured him. Sirens were heard as an ambulance pulled up in front of the house, and Zack realized Officer Gay must have called them earlier for them to be arriving so soon. From the bedroom across the hall, Elaine, frightened by the repeated gunshots, wailed and asked what was happening. Sally explained the situation, telling her things were now getting under control. With this information, Thelma and the children burst from the closed closet.

"Hearing about shooting is much less scary than being in shooting," Danny pronounced. "Is Dad hurt?"

"No, I'm fine, buddy," Zack responded, stepping into the bedroom picking Danny up for a reassuring hug.

"Have they caught all three of the men?" Sissy wanted to know as she rushed to her father to be held in his other arm.

"No, the other two are on foot in the woods behind the house. Two of the police officers have left to go out there now."

"I can see flashing red lights on the street on the other side of the creek in the woods behind the house," Henry reported again. "It's probably more police; they need to be very careful because those fellows are armed and desperate!"

"All of you stay right here while I go check to see what's going on in the family room," Zack instructed. "Elaine, are you OK?"

"Yes, you be careful!" she exclaimed, now fully awake.

"God's taking care of all of us," Sissy stated, standing by her mother's bed. "Grammy prayed with Danny and me," she continued, attempting to encourage her mother.

Zack stepped down the hall and into the family room. Officer Gay and another officer were present, and the ambulance medics had the injured intruder loaded onto a gurney. Zack was amazed that he recognized the man who now had the ski mask removed as the one from whom he'd won the money in the card game.

The man looked at Zack in open recognition, yelling, "I'll kill you if it is the last thing I ever do! You have ruined my whole business and operation."

Zack looked at Officer Gay but said nothing as the man was wheeled through the kitchen and out through the front door screaming epithets. "Do you think I should be looking for some kind of ongoing protection for the family and myself?" he asked.

"Perhaps," the investigator answered. "I think we should wait to see what information we can garner from this man before we act. I'll be keeping in touch; at the moment, I need to be working with the officers attempting to catch those other two intruders right now. Stay alert; let no one in the house, and get the door that was broken secured. Let us know of anything else you see that is suspicious. I'll have an officer here within half an hour to offer you protection. I do think you're at some risk until we have those two fellows in custody. You've handed things well up to this point. Keep up the good work," he finished as he moved out the front door.

Zack returned to the family, turning the interior lights out as he went. "Dad and Dr. Denton," he said as he entered the bedroom area where they we still gathered, "we need to be fixing the door where those men broke in. Officer Gay went to help the other police search for those other intruders who went into the woods. How do you best think we can handle this?"

Jonathan responded, saying, "Son, why don't you and Henry go work on the door? He'll know what he'll want done to secure it and where the necessary tools and supplies are. I'll stay here with the women and children and keep guard from the back window. I see you've turned off the interior lights, and I believe we should attempt to keep them off as much as possible. Those fellows could certainly come back here at any time if they've found they're blocked in other directions. After all, their vehicle is still out there in front of the house."

Henry and Zack went to investigate the damaged French door and repaired it with unfinished boards that had been stored in the garage attic. They had barely finished their nailing when a female police officer rang the front doorbell. Henry let her in as Zack returned to the bedrooms to report on their progress. "Is everything going all right back here?" he asked quietly as he noted Elaine's eyes closed, and the children sitting wide-eyed by Thelma on the cot. "A police lady is here to watch things for us while several police are out looking for the other intruders, so we should all go back to sleep," he continued without waiting for a reply.

"I don't think we can sleep," Sissy responded. "This has been too frightening! It was worse than when the men scattered everything around in the apartment. The difference was that here we had Daddy and all the grandparents to be with us."

"Dad, may I learn to shoot a gun?" Danny asked. "You did a really super job. You stopped that man with only one shot. Do you think he's going to live?"

"Yes, I intentionally shot his leg, and the police shot his hand, so although he's seriously injured, he's unlikely to die."

"Why didn't you kill him?" Danny inquired.

"It is much better to use your gun to stop an intruder without killing," Zack instructed.

"This way he could still repent and get right with Jesus," Sissy added.

"What a great observation!" Sally commended. "We never want to get far away in life from our concern as to what Jesus would want us to do."

"But Jesus said for us to turn the other cheek when we get slapped," Danny worried.

"To be slapped is more like an insult," Henry contributed. "Jesus never told us to let someone kill you and your family without trying to do all you could to stop it. Your Dad handled this situation very, very well. We all need to be thankful that he had such a level head."

"I'm thankful we were all able to be together and work together to be as safe as possible, but I think we all need to get on to bed. You children do have school tomorrow." Zack persisted. "Danny, you go crawl into my bed, and Sissy, let me tuck you into the cot here. You can both give all the grandparents hugs before getting in."

The household returned to a semblance of normal as the grandparents went back up the stairs to their bedrooms, and the children got into the beds.

Zack knelt for a while by Elaine's bedside, held her hand, and finally whispered, "Are you really OK through all of this?"

Elaine squeezed his hand in the darkness, replying, "It's easier seeming to be inert. I love you for taking care of us all; you were certainly our hero tonight."

"Thanks, but I just felt I was doing what I should and could. I did feel more at peace than what I would have thought. Having Mom and Dad here seemed to somehow stabilize me. I do think that I'm a different person since I've taken up my allegiance to Christ Jesus."

Elaine squeezed his hand again, and he gave her a light kiss on the cheek before he went back out to check with the police officer. He then returned to his bedroom where Danny was already sound asleep with his arms and legs splayed out on both sides of the bed. Zack rearranged his son to the other side of the bed before climbing in himself. Sleep did not come immediately as he lay there reviewing the events of the past hour, attempting to see if there had been any way that things could have been better. The intruder's threat continued to run through his mind, and he entertained the fear that his life and that of his family may never be safe as long as the man lived. *Jesus, take this fear from me*, he prayed. *Help me steer a straight path toward You*, he concluded as he fell into steady sleep.

The family did not reawaken until 9:00 AM, when the police officer knocked on Zack's bedroom door, saying, "I just received a report from Officer Gay informing me that they've been able to incarcerate the other two intruders. They are being held for questioning. I've been told I'm no longer needed here, so I'll be leaving, but Officer Gay told me he'd be back in touch with you again before noon."

"Were any of the police hurt?" Zack asked, standing at his bedroom door in his boxer shorts and t-shirt trying to act awake.

"Although I'm not certain, I doubt it," she replied. "I've been listening to the scanner all night, and nothing's been said about it. By the way, Officer Gay thinks your whole family should remain here at the house until further notice. Do you think that will be a problem?"

"No, I don't think so," Zack replied. "I'll need to call the school and tell them not to expect the children. They're already late. I'm surprised we haven't already had a call from them. Thank you so much for being here with us; I've slept like a log! We'll stay right here. Can I show you out?"

"Oh, I know my way," she smiled, looking at his boxer shorts. "Just be certain to lock the door after me."

As the front door closed, Zack also heard the parents moving about upstairs, so he quietly called the school and attended to his morning toilet before joining his folks for breakfast.

"Are all of the rest of your crew asleep?" Thelma asked as he entered the kitchen.

"Yes, they're all still asleep, and with the excitement of last night, I'm going to let them awaken on their own," he replied. "Officer Gay left word with the police officer that was here last night that we should all stay here until he calls back, and she also knew all three were caught. I think they're interrogating them to attempt to determine if we appear to continue to be in danger. I've called the school to let them know the children won't be there today. How much do you think Elaine ate all day yesterday?"

"Not enough," Sally responded from her place at the table. "I believe she's simply slipping away from us. How much is she talking to you?"

"A little," Zack replied. "She talked a bit when I first came home and then a bit last night when you'd all gone to bed. I told Mom, but I don't think I told you that she wants to talk with her dad about spiritual things. Also, she couldn't remember what that important thing she wanted to tell me was, and she cried about that. How the brain works when we're ill is a curious thing, isn't it?"

"It is hard to understand or predict," Sally agreed. "Oh, dear, there's the doorbell; who could be coming over this time of the morning?" Zack walked with Sally to the living room, looking out the window to see if they could determine who might be visiting. A yellow Corvette was parked by the curb.

"I have no idea whose car that is," Sally commented as they moved on to the front door.

"Please let me answer," Zack instructed as he stepped in front, leaving the chain lock in place but cracking the door. "Hi," he greeted without letting himself be seen, "can you identify yourself?"

Alexandra Briley moved over, making herself visible in the crack while attempting to see the speaker. "It's me, Alexandra," she answered with a laugh. "Is that you, Zack? Are you expecting bandits this early in the morning?"

"Good morning! You wouldn't believe what's been going on here through the night," Zack laughed, unhooking the chain lock and opening the door. "Alexandra, this is Sally Denton, my mother-in-law. The two of you may have met before."

"Indeed, good morning," Sally greeted, "we've met, but it was several years ago when Elaine was in high school. Come on into the kitchen and have some coffee. Zack and I were sitting and chatting; the rest of the household's not up yet. It has been a long night for all of us. Sit right here at the table. I also have some powdered doughnuts if you're interested."

Alexandra seated herself, noticed the boarded door, and asked, "Wow, what did go on? Did someone actually try to break in?"

"Yes, they didn't just try—they broke the door. Fortunately the police responded quickly, and the intruders were arraigned. There were three of them, and they're all in custody now. That's why we're running so late. We're hanging out here until we hear more from the police. I bet you're here to see Elaine; she's not been awake yet, but I'll go check on her," Zack informed her. He then walked out of the kitchen using the broken door which still had an intact latch and out onto the back covered patio. He continued to walk around through the backyard to the back-hallway door. He felt irritated with Alexandra for not calling his in-laws before coming as he'd instructed her.

He stepped quietly into Elaine's bedroom, expecting to find her asleep, but her eyes were open, and she winked at him. "You've got company," he mouthed silently, picking sleeping Sissy up with her blanket, moving her to the adjacent bedroom, and putting her beside her sleeping brother before returning to Elaine's side. "It's Alexandra Briley; I met her on the plane to Dallas, and she's here to see you. Do you want me to tell her to come back some other time, or do you want me to help you get ready to see her now?" he whispered.

Elaine stretched and smiled, saying, "It's not as if I'm going to be better any time soon. Why don't you roll the head of my bed up, give me my toothbrush so I can brush my teeth, and let me put that mobcap over there on the desk on before she comes in."

Zack looked around the room. "I'll move this cot out and bring in another chair. Do you want me here while she's here, or do the two of you want to be alone?"

"Stay here at first, and if I say I'm hungry you can go get me some breakfast. You never told me you'd met her."

"No, I'm sorry; I forgot about it. There's been a bunch going on since I came home."

"I'm glad to see her; she was one of my best friends in high school."

Zack squelched the negative comments he felt about Alexandra, saying, "Great, I'll bring her right on back," as he carried out the cot, placing it quietly in his bedroom across the hall and going on out to the kitchen.

Sally and Alexandra were in conversation as he entered, Sally saying, "I know Elaine will want to see you, but I'm not certain she'll be up to it today. What'd she say?" she questioned Zack.

"She's ready to see you," Zack announced in reply. "Mom, why don't you go ahead and fix some breakfast for her; I'll come get it when she asks." Turning, he said, "Alexandra, come on out this way with me. We're avoiding using the family room because of the events of last night. I think the police are going to wish to examine the area more closely, and we're staying out until they do." They walked together around through the backyard.

"Oh, this yard is so, so lovely!" Alexandra exclaimed. "Dr. Denton certainly keeps it looking nice."

"Yes, he does," Zack agreed, "but I'm beginning to see that it might be almost more than he can handle; he's asked me to help me with it while I'm here. On another subject, please don't be too surprised about Elaine's appearance. I don't think she's too sensitive about it, but be prepared," he finished as they entered the small hall and then the bedroom.

"Oh my goodness, here you are!" Alexandra enthused as they entered. "I'm so, so sorry you're ill!"

Elaine gave her a wan smile, responding, "Yes, here I am. I bet you never expected to find me in such a pitiful state."

Alexandra went to the bedside, leaning down to give Elaine a quick peck on the cheek. "Maybe you'll get better. Zack told me you were very sick. Where did you contract such a horrible illness?"

"I was in St. Lois at the time, and I've been in and out of the Barnes hospital there having some of the best medical care available, but it is not working. Let's not talk about that, but let's talk about what you know about our friends in high school. Please bring me up to date with whatever you know. I haven't been in touch with anyone."

Alexandra, realizing the subject had intentionally changed, began, "Well, first I'll tell you about me, partially because I know more about myself."

Zack moved a chair close to the bedside facing Elaine and motioned for Alexandra to have a seat while he sat in a chair by the bathroom door.

"I went to school over in Tyler on the University of Texas campus there and finished a business degree before I came back home. While I was over there, I married Jim Goldsberry after my junior year. You probably remember him—one of the fellows on the golf team from high school. We were married ten months before I caught him in an affair and divorced him. When I finished school, I came back home and joined Dad in his real estate company. I've been working with him doing that ever since. I did get married again about five years ago to a man named Percy White, but we didn't have any children, and he blamed me for it. I finally persuaded him for us to do fertility testing, which we did. We found out it was his problem and not mine, but he still wasn't happy, so he divorced me a couple years ago. My marital success has been pretty spotty; I don't have any children, and I stay very busy at work."

"Have you given up on getting married?" Elaine questioned.

"No, I date some, but my expectations of finding Mr. Right are certainly dwindling," Alexandra replied. "Well, let's see, remember Janelle Robertson? She went to Kilgore Junior College and got her associate degree in nursing and then went on to finish her RN through UT Tyler. We reconnected when she moved to that campus our last two years. I'm the closest to her of any of our high school crowd. She married a fellow from Tyler, and they've stayed there. She works over at Mother Francis hospital in the ambulatory care clinics, and they have three of the most darling little boys. She now stays so busy with the family and her work and all that it's hard for us to spend much time together."

"Janelle was a very consistent student," Elaine commented. "Wasn't she dating Harvey Sailor when we were seniors? I thought they were almost engaged."

"Yes, but he dropped her at the end of that summer when he went off to UT in Austin. He didn't want to try to maintain a long distance relationship, and I can't fault him for it. She's happy with Donald, the father of her boys."

Elaine looked over at Zack, winking surreptitiously saying, "Honey, will you go get my breakfast? I'm getting hungry."

Zack stood, grinning as he said, "Sure thing. This conversation has been riveting, but I'll drag myself away. Your mother has been making it, so I'll be right back."

As soon as the door closed behind him, Alexandra sighed, laughed, and said, "What a hunk! I got on the plane in Longview barely making the flight on time last week. As I went down the aisle deciding on my seat location, this tall, very handsome man stood to let me in. I had no idea who he was until I pried it out of him. You really made a find! Did he meet all the qualifications you used to tell us your husband would need to have?"

Elaine looked serious as she replied, "He had some of them, but not all of them. I was feeling rebellious about having to stay in school, and he went along with me. We met, fell in love, and quit school while I was a sophomore. It was a horrible decision, and I feel it eventually led to much of the rest of what transpired. We quit having contact with our parents, and we decided against faith in Christ. We do have two delightful children, but mostly Zack's been with them the past three years. I'd started using drugs, but after failing rehab three times, Zack asked me to leave, which I did. I contracted the hepatitis from the dirty needles, and I have a form of it that can't be treated. Most hepatitis B can be managed, but I'm one of the few who will die from it."

"Oh, how tragic!" Alexandra exclaimed. "Zack told me you were seriously ill. How long have you been back together?"

"It's been only about ten days; Zack came up to the hospital in St. Louis with my parents, and they brought me back here. I have hospice care, and some days like today I do pretty well, but some days I'm sleeping and mostly out of it. Zack, my folks, and his folks are being so kind caring for me I can hardly believe it. Before I came here, Zack had been abducted by some drug cartel men who took him as prisoner to Belize. Consequently, he's back to a belief in Jesus, taking good care of the children, and planning to go back to school. I'm having difficulty seeing him as the same guy who sent me away from the house when I was into drugs."

"I'm assuming you didn't want to leave?" Alexandra questioned.

"Well, yes and no," Elaine replied. "I didn't want to leave the children because I did love them, but on the other hand I decided that my being around them using drugs wasn't good for them. I was tired of feeling guilty about my drug use—Zack always seemed to be bringing it up no matter whatever problem arose. He was grouchy and helped with the care of the children only minimally. I didn't realize it at the time that he'd started drinking. So I left."

"Is Zack still drinking?"

"No—when the drug cartel men took him, he went through DTs. That scared him, and when a fellow prisoner influenced him to Christ, he quit altogether. He doesn't seem to be having any difficulty staying on the wagon. Actually, he looks a lot healthier than when I left him."

Zack knocked on the bedroom door, entering with a breakfast tray. "Who looks healthier?" he asked, flashing Elaine a dazzling smile.

"You do," Elaine laughed.

"Wrong answer," he chuckled, setting up the tray on the bedside table. "You look pretty good today yourself, and I wouldn't want to be accusing you ladies of talking about me behind my back."

"You know we're here to be talking about people, so you should not expect to be the only taboo subject," Alexandra intervened saucily.

"I'm afraid you've about exhausted all appropriate victims' reputations if you're down to discussing me," he replied in repartee. "Well, holler at us if you need anything," he said, closing the door quietly behind him.

Elaine and Alexandra continued their conversation for another quarter of an hour, covering numerous of their mutual acquaintances' histories before Elaine, realizing her strength was dissipating, asked, "Alexandra, I know this is a forward thing to ask, but I'm recognizing I don't have much time left. I've told Zack I want him to remarry after I die, and I think the sooner the better. Will you check in on him from time to time after I pass? He may or may not be interested; you may not be interested considering our past, but I would appreciate it."

"My goodness, sweetie, you don't seem that likely to die soon!" Alexandra exclaimed.

"But I am, believe me!" Elaine pleaded. "Our conversation here today has been some of the best I've felt." Elaine feebly reached out her hand to Alexandra's forearm. "Just promise me," she slowly said weakly and drifted off to sleep.

The end of the conversation was so abrupt that it left Alexandra off guard. She sat gazing at the face of her old friend for a full five minutes before she silently rose from her seat and quietly made her way back to the kitchen through the backyard. The kitchen door was ajar so she knocked, seeing Zack and Sally at the table with their coffee and cell phones.

"Come right on in," Sally greeted, looking up. "Did you girls have a good talk? Zack told me Elaine seemed unusually alert. I'm so glad she was able to see you on such a good day."

"She seemed so alert most of the time I was having difficulty believing she was seriously ill," Alexandra answered. "However, when she became weary, she went to sleep very rapidly. She believes she's dying and won't be here long."

"We know that, but we're hoping and praying for a miracle," Zack responded seriously. "Sometimes she'll go to sleep right in the middle of her own sentence. She certainly seemed to enjoy your visit. I'm hoping you can return and chat with her again."

"I'll try to do that. Also, remember that I'd hoped to talk with your parents today about real estate possibilities, but since it still seems they're not available, I'll try to set up an appointment some other time."

Taking the matter in hand, Zack agreed with a smile, "Yes, an appointment would be helpful, even when checking on Elaine because we'd like to be able to have her as comfortable as possible for any of your visits."

"Thank you for coming!" Sally exclaimed cheerfully, following Alexandra to the front door totally unaware of Zack's intentional undercurrents.

Alexandra left wondering why Zack seemed to be holding her at such arm's length when Elaine had seemed to be so friendly and trusting.

CHAPTER XXVII

WEDNESDAY, MARCH 30

Danny awoke early the next morning having slept beside his dad. He stretched and wondered why old people like his dad made so much noise when they breathed. Zack wasn't snoring, but the sound of his breathing was audible, and Danny wasn't used to it. *It's better having him breathe noisily than not having him here*, Danny thought as he lay staring at the side of Zack's face with a night's growth of whiskers and the profile of his nose while luxuriating in the fact that, at least for the moment, his family seemed to be intact. Had he been with Sissy upstairs in their former shared bedroom, he'd have gotten out of bed to discuss the morning with her, but she'd slept on the cot in Elaine's room, and Danny didn't want to go in there lest he awaken his mother. He thought of the events of yesterday with the early morning shooting and then of the late breakfast. He'd been there when the police came about noon to scrutinize the family room where the shooting had taken place.

It had been like a bright, sunny, unseasonably warm summer vacation day when he'd gone with his dad and both grandfathers to Lowes to get a new kitchen door, and he'd watched the men hang and paint the new door. In the later afternoon, he'd helped the men remove the covering for the pool, and they'd all gone for their first swim in the chilly water. He thought how he'd wanted to be in the water but had been so afraid at first; however, with his dad's cajoling, he had been able to get into the shallow end, initially standing on his tiptoes and walking around. He also recalled how much fun it had been to have Zack throw both him and Sissy into the air time and time again to land with a splash. They'd enjoyed the time until after dark, continuing with the glowing light at the bottom of the pool. He thought of the fact that today was another school day and lay quietly wondering what the time was. He looked up at the slowly moving ceiling fan and the pattern on the wallpaper border, and again at the sleeping silhouette of his father. Propping himself on one elbow, he looked down at his dad's face, considering the best tactic for awakening him; finally, he punched Zack on the shoulder, asking, "Hey, Dad, can you wake up? Do you know that I love you very, very much?"

Startled awake, Zack looked at his bright-eyed son, thinking how unworthy he was of this child's love but how glad he was for it. "I do know that," he said as he grabbed the youngster, giving him a big hug. "I think it is a wonderful thing, too. I also love you in return; every day I'm thankful for you!"

Danny struggled out of the hug, leaning back against the headboard, saying and asking, "We need to go to school, but I don't know what time it is. Are you going to take us, or will it be Grandpa? What are you going to be doing today? Do you think Momma's getting better?"

Zack grinned and responded after looking at his watch, "Mr. Question Box, it's about six-thirty, I think I'll be taking you, I haven't organized my day's agenda yet, and I would say your mother seemed better yesterday than she did this past weekend. She spent quite a bit of time talking to an old friend of hers yesterday morning and then talked a while last night with your Pop Pop before she went to sleep. Are you ready to get back to school this morning?"

"Yes," Danny sighed slowly. "Yesterday was so much fun with all of us doing things together that I partly wish I weren't going back today, but every day at school is fun, so I believe I'm ready. What are we having for breakfast?"

"Well, let's clean up, get dressed, and go find out. Why don't you shower first while I shave?"

"Can I just sit on the counter and watch you?"

"OK this time, but then you'll need to hurry so your sister can use this restroom."

"If she's in a hurry, she can go upstairs to her own restroom," Danny instructed, complacently climbing onto a chair and seating himself on the counter.

Zack laughed at his directive son as he spread on his shaving lather and picked up the razor.

"How old were you when you started to shave?" Danny asked.

"Oh, I think I was about fourteen; with my hair being darker than Evan's hair, he didn't start until he was about seventeen. I think he was jealous about my need to shave."

"Was it fun having a brother?"

"It was. We were good pals for many years. Sometimes we quarreled but not very often. He was always easy to get along with. In ways you remind me of him, but I don't remember him asking so many questions."

Danny was quiet several minutes watching Zack; then he asked, "How old were you when people started confusing the two of you?"

"It was when I was a junior in high school. He became a sophomore that year and had become nearly my height. We looked so much alike that even though I always had darker hair, the teachers especially would confuse us.

"Why did Uncle Evan stay in school and you didn't?"

Finishing his shave, Zack splashed water on his face and dried it with a towel before answering. "Because I didn't have good sense! I certainly hope you can learn from my mistake. Do you think you can do that?"

"I hope so," Danny said, agreeably hopping down from the counter. "I'm going upstairs to get my uniform, underwear, and shoes. My toothpaste and toothbrush are up there, too. I'll be right back to take my shower."

Zack showered and dressed as Danny returned, humming to himself while he made his toilet. When they were finished, Zack stopped in Elaine's bedroom where he found her still sleeping, and awoke a drowsy Sissy, who immediately trudged upstairs to her own room. In the kitchen, Thelma was making French toast while Jonathan and Henry shared the morning paper over their coffee. Zack hugged and kissed his mother before pouring coffee for himself, generously adding cream and two teaspoons full of sugar and making a second cup for Danny consisting chiefly of milk and sugar with some coffee flavoring. They sat a few minutes with the men, but then Zack realized the table was not set and got up and conscripted Danny to help distribute the utensils, plates, and necessary condiments. As he was finishing, Sally and Sissy entered.

"Everybody's just in time," Thelma greeted, "because breakfast is ready. We're having milk, coffee, water, French toast, and ham if you want it. Zack, Sissy, and Danny, come take the food to the table while I get Sally's coffee."

"Oh no, dearie!" Sally remonstrated, "I can do for myself."

"Not this time," Thelma directed, "You just sit right down. See, I've already fixed it."

"Why is it called French toast?" Danny wondered.

"Maybe the French prepare toast that way," Sissy offered.

"I'm uncertain," Sally answered, frowning. "I believe we'll need to look that up."

"Dad could look it up on his cell phone," Danny suggested.

"No, no cell phones at the table," Zack announced. "I'll look it up for us after breakfast."

"Why no cell phones at the table?" Sissy questioned.

"It distracts us from the food and the conversation," her dad replied. "I'll want you children to follow that rule, so I need to follow it as well."

"I couldn't agree with you more," Henry said, folding the paper meticulously and laying it aside. "Jonathan, will you say grace?"

Everyone was seated with hands held around the table while Jonathan prayed; then conversation lagged while the food was passed and arranged on plates. At that juncture, Henry announced that Herman Hernandez had called earlier that morning informing that he and his family were to be arriving at the Longview airport on the afternoon flight on Saturday. "We can all go out to the airport to pick them up," he continued. "Herman said the US Immigration Service has assured him that his wife and father will have green cards as well as himself. They have very little luggage, so if we take two vehicles, we should be able to bring them all back."

"No, I'll stay with Elaine," Sally said. "There are five of them, and there'll be five of you, so that's ten—so even if you take the SUV, that's quite a few."

"I wouldn't need to go," Thelma considered.

"Mom, I think Ardine, Herman's wife, would feel more at ease if there were a lady involved," Zack intervened. "It's going to be a difficult but exciting thing for all of them. We need to make it all work as smoothly as possible. One thing that will help a great deal is that they all speak English. Herman's dad has a definite Hispanic accent, and Ardine has an English accent, but both are easy to understand. I know you have a job lined up for Herman, Dr. Denton, but we didn't know the other two would have green cards. Did you ask Herman anything about housing?"

"I did," Henry replied. "He said that since they don't have any approved housing here in Longview that they could rent an apartment or house for somewhere around a thousand dollars a month and that the immigration department would be reevaluating the situation within three months. They'll also pay for a couple motel rooms for up to a week to allow them a place to stay until they can move into a more permanent place."

"Herman's two children and wife seemed extremely pleasant the short time we had with them. I was amazed at how little they complained about the restrictive living quarters at the embassy, but their living situation at the farm had been so terrible that they were mostly grateful being out of there. When they move into the apartment or house, they'll likely need some furniture," Zack added.

"Beds especially," Sally contributed. "Henry, don't we have a couple twin mattresses stored in the attic that we could give them? I also think the folks at the church will help with this; we'll just need to ask."

By now most of the breakfast was consumed and the family dispersed, going their separate ways with the children gathering their backpacks and lunch sacks. Thelma and Jonathan started cleaning up the kitchen, and Sally went to check on Elaine. "Zack, I had a very good talk with Elaine last night," Henry remarked before leaving the table. "Did she say anything about it last night?"

"No, but she was already asleep when I went to say good night," Zack answered. "I'll make a special effort to talk with her as soon as I get back from the children's school. Thanks for the heads up."

"The conversation was a blessing to me, and I know it will be to you as well."

"So she's dropped her resistance to Christ Jesus?" Zack asked.

"Yes, but I wanted her to be able to tell you," Henry grinned.

Zack stepped to the head of the table where Henry was seated, saying, "Please stand up here, Dad, and let me give you a hug; I am so very appreciative of all you do for me!"

"Thanks, fellow," Henry replied, "but what I do, I do for all of us; it is my joy!"

Danny sat in the backseat on the trip to school being unusually quiet when his dad asked, "Why so quiet, buddy?"

"I'm working on asking fewer questions," he answered.

"I was surprised you didn't ask me about green cards this morning," Zack commented.

"I figured out from the conversation what they were for," Danny laughed. "Grandpa told me to do that. He said not to ask questions I could answer for myself."

"Good advice," Zack nodded.

"But don't we ask questions sometimes to see if people agree with us?" Sissy asked.

"Sure, but not too often," her dad reassured. "Children, there's something your Pop Pop told me this morning that I think you'll be delighted to know. Your mother has invited Jesus back into her life. I haven't talked with her about this yet, but I will as soon as I get back. We're now almost to the school; what I'd like to do as we stop to let you out is for you to stay in the car a little while I pray thanking God for this blessing."

Zack drove up in front of the school, and the three of them bowed their heads as he prayed. "Thank you Jesus for this day, thank you for these wonderful children, and most of all, right now, thank you that Elaine is recognizing you as Lord of Lords in her life. Be with Danny and Sissy this day, and may they feel your love. Amen." Zack leaned over, giving Sissy a kiss on her forehead while Danny, unfastening his seatbelt, popped up from the back to plant a kiss on his dad's cheek. Happy goodbyes were said as the children gleefully went to their classes.

On the way home, Zack was nearly overcome with tears as he considered this new development. *Why couldn't I have come to my senses earlier?* he wondered. *What if Elaine and I'd have stayed on the right track all along? We knew what was right. I can't focus on tha*t, he thought again, *I just need to keep moving ahead.*

He immediately went to Elaine's room on the return home, finding her sitting up in bed, dreamily staring out of the window. "How's it going?" he asked, walking over and planting a kiss on her forehead. "Your dad's told me you have some good news for me."

"Oh, he did, did he?" she smiled, turning toward him. "I suppose you wonder why now and not before."

"Well, yes, but that's not the important thing; the important thing is that you're committed to Christ."

"I'll tell you anyhow," she smiled. "I realized that I was kidding myself; I was scared silly of dying and the possibility of hell. I recognized I did believe, but I was too proud to admit it. Too long I've let what other people might think about me direct my decisions. Who cares what they think after I die or even now, for that matter?"

"Nobody," agreed Zack, kneeling beside the bed and putting his arms around her. "We don't want you to die; we want there to be a miracle."

"I'd like a miracle, too," Elain admitted, "but we can't assume it will happen. You probably need to content yourself with the fact that I've now given my allegiance to Christ. For me who vowed never to give in to being a Christian again, that's pretty much a miracle. Have you given any more thought to marrying again?"

"No, I'm thinking about your recovery. You've seemed better the last few days."

"The severity of my symptoms go up and down; I've seen it happen many times and would hope I was getting better, but then I'd get sick again and it would be worse than anything before. Yesterday when Alexandra was here, I was thinking she might be a good choice for you. She's beautiful, pleasant, from a good family, and I think she's attracted to you."

Zack looked into Elaine's blue eyes; seeing her sincerity, he decided not express the revulsion he felt for Alexandra. "I don't think I'm attracted to her," he said. "She just seems to rub me the wrong way. When I first met her on the plane, she seemed invasively questioning. I want to think about you getting well."

"Promise me that you will go on one date with her after I die. You don't have to marry her; just give her a chance."

"If I promise that, what'll you promise me?" Zack negotiated.

"I'll promise to love you until I die!" she returned.

"Oh, dear, that's hard to refuse," he laughed. "Maybe you can't stop loving me, especially if I behave myself, so at that point you're not promising anything." He leaned over to give her a kiss on the lips, but she turned away causing the kiss to land on her cheek.

"Zack, I'm not turning because I don't love you; it's because I do love you," she said sadly. "I want there to be no chance of you getting this disease."

Chagrinned that he'd forgotten the restriction, he said, "That's OK. I forgot. I'm thankful you can still love me."

CHAPTER XXVIII

THURSDAY, MARCH 31

Elaine had not awakened by the time Zack had returned home from taking the children to school. Sally had prepared some Malt-o-meal and a boiled egg for her and had it warming on the kitchen range, so Zack took it into the bedroom to see if he could awaken her and entice her to eat. He gave her a kiss on the forehead and attempted to arouse her, lightly shaking her shoulder, and noticed she was feverish. He called Sally and they checked her temperature, finding it was 103 degrees. They both spoke loudly to her, but there was no response.

"I suppose we need to call hospice," Zack said. "Do you think we'll need to give her some acetaminophen?"

"She can't swallow a pill, but I do have some suppositories," Sally responded. "I'll go get them now."

Zack busied himself straightening up his room, making his bed, picking up unneeded articles in Elaine's room, and emptying the trash. Elaine slept on, occasionally moaning. Zack climbed the stairs to the laundry room where Thelma was doing the wash and ironing.

"Mom, Elaine's running a high fever of 103 this morning and not waking up," he reported. "We've called hospice and given her some acetaminophen. Do you have any suggestions?"

"Oh, dear, here we thought she may be doing better," Thelma commented. "This is disheartening. Has her temperature ever been this high before?"

"No, and she can't seem to wake up either."

"Let's all go pray for her, Son. I'll get the men," Thelma comforted Zack, giving him a hug before leaving the room. "Let's all go pray in her room."

"The five adults gathered around the sick bed while Henry, with tears in his eyes, held his hand on his daughter's head and prayed. "Dear Lord, we thank you that when we have nothing to offer in the way of help, You are always sufficient. Right now, we also thank You that Elaine has renewed her commitment to You. She is Your child and we bring her need to You. We love You and trust that Your will shall be accomplished. Amen."

The doorbell rang and Sally went to answer, greeting Mrs. Moreno and leading her back to the sick room.

"Such high fever is not good," she pronounced after taking her vital signs and examining Elaine, while all the five stood against the wall waiting quietly.

"Has she had a cold or cough the past few days?"

"No, actually she's seemed better the past couple days," Sally answered. "She's been more alert and has seemed to have more stamina. We were hoping she might be improving."

"I will ask the doctor if I can collect a urine specimen to see if she has an infection there," the nurse informed. "I can take it to the lab today to have it checked. If it is OK, I will talk to the doctor to see if he wants to check Meez Elaine. I will call him now," she finished picking up her cell phone and dialing.

"I would be asking if we should be taking her to the hospital," Zack said when the nurse hung up, "but Elaine made me promise that we wouldn't take her back to a hospital."

"I understand," Mrs. Moreno said, nodding. "The doctor says to get the urine specimen and that he'll come see the patient at around noon today whether or no the urine look good. He is very kind to come on a day that he is in his office so soon. You will need to talk with the doctor about the hospital. Meez. Denton and Meez. Taylor, you canna help me get the urine while the men go now."

Dutifully the three men filed back to the family room, gathering around an old oak table. "I need something to do, something physical," Zack stated as he sat. "I don't do well sitting and waiting."

"Let's go work on the backyard," Henry agreed. "You can trim the hedge against the fence on the south side with the hedge trimmer; it's getting a little too heavy for me. I'll clean up the trimmings as you go."

"What can I do to help?" Jonathan questioned.

"We'll need to sweep around the pool, weed the groundcover in the Azalea beds, and I'd like to get some of the spring bedding plants in the ground. I also have a vegetable garden that needs tilling and planting over on the north side of the yard."

"You give us direction and we'll do it," Zack laughed, getting up from the table. "I'm going to change into some work clothes first," he continued, going down the hall to his bedroom.

After the men had vacated the room, the three ladies entered with Sally saying, "Obtaining that specimen was certainly not as difficult as I had imagined. You did a great job, Mrs. Moreno. Of course, I suspect you've had a good bit of experience, and had it been my task, it would have taken considerably longer."

"Yez, is part of my work," the nurse laughed. "I will get the urine to the lab now and will call you as soon as they check it. The doctor may not be right on time because he need to finish seeing his morning patients before he canna come. Good-bye."

"I'm going to sit with Elaine this morning, I think," Sally said, standing next to Thelma who reached out her hand, giving Sally a loving squeeze on her arm.

"I'm aching for you, sweetie," she commiserated. "I'll go up and finish the laundry. Please don't hesitate to call me if you need anything. I think

I'll also make some lunch for all of us; did you have anything particularly planned or is there anything I could fix for you that you'd like?"

"I saw that open-faced beef sandwiches were on the written menu we'd made, and that will be just fine. Thank you so much for your help," Sally answered as she slipped back into Elaine's room.

Dr. Spencer, the hospice physician, arrived at twelve thirty, just as the family was finishing their lunch. He'd greeted Henry at the front door, having been acquainted with him through mutual patients in the past. "So your daughter's started with a fever this morning?" he questioned. "The urine that Mrs. Moreno collected is fine. Let's look at her," he said confidently as Sally led him to the sick room with Henry and Zack following.

The doctor had his bag with him, got out his stethoscope, and started the patient's examination. "The fever started this morning?" he questioned.

"It may have started in the night, but this morning was the first we recognized it," Zack replied while Dr. Spencer continued his work. In attempting to look in Elaine's throat, he moved her head and she moaned loudly.

The doctor's face blanched, and he attempted to move her head forward with an even louder cry. He then examined her hands, which he noted to be chilly despite the fever, and her feet and ankles displayed a mottled rash. How long do you think this rash has been here?" he asked.

"It wasn't there this morning when we changed her bed," Sally replied. "What do you think it is?"

"I hate to tell you, but I think it likely is meningitis and the serious bacterial type; she needs to be in the hospital. We cannot care for her here."

"She made us promise not to take her to the hospital," Zack explained.

"We always try to honor a patient's wishes, but in this circumstance we don't have a choice. If what I think is true, your whole household is at risk from this disease, and we can better isolate her at the hospital than in your home."

Henry looked at Zack, saying, "We certainly know she wouldn't want her illness to put the children at risk."

Zack, with an anguished expression, looked at the physician, saying, "Of course, we need to do what's right."

"I'm calling the ambulance then, and we'll get her admitted to the ICU. You probably remember that our hospice uses Good Shepherd Hospital, so that's where she'll be."

"Thanks, Doctor," Sally said, "will you be the one caring for her?"

"Yes, she'll be admitted to me, and I'll be asking a neurologist to see her as well and probably an infectious disease specialist. She may need to stop in the emergency room first to expedite the initiation of her care. Cases like this need to be handled very quickly," he concluded, dialing his cell phone for the ambulance service.

Sally and Henry set about making plans for Elaine's departure while Zack went to inform his parents of the doctor's findings. He felt he was moving in a slow trance as he stepped down the short hall into the family room where they were waiting.

"It doesn't look good," he said first. "Doctor Spencer thinks she likely has serious meningitis; he's sending her to the hospital now; he doesn't think it's safe for all the rest of us for her to stay here. He says she'll be in the ICU; he's called the ambulance."

Jonathan stood, stepping toward Zack and placing his arm around his son's waist, "You'll need to go on to the hospital to be with her as much as you can; we'll take care of the children."

"Go change out of your work clothes because the ambulance will be here in just minutes," Thelma instructed. "Henry and Sally will be at the hospital, too, but you don't know how long you'll be there, so you should drive separately. We're here for you," she whispered quietly, going on into Elaine's room.

True enough, even though Zack hurriedly changed, the ambulance was bringing the stretcher down the hall before he finished. The EMTs efficiently loaded Elaine up onto the gurney, and Zack realized they were wearing masks. "Do we all need to be wearing masks?" he asked Dr. Spencer, who was packing his black bag in preparation to leave.

"Not right now," he was informed. "Once you get to the hospital you will, though, if she has what I'm almost certain she does. I'm confident enough of my diagnosis at this point to be requiring all medical personnel to be wearing the masks."

"Do you think our parents and the children should be treated with something?" Zack worried.

"Once I've confirmed the diagnosis, I'll let you know. We should know within a couple hours or even sooner." By this time, the ambulance and EMTs were already back through the house and moving up the front sidewalk. "I'll no doubt be seeing you at the hospital," Dr. Spencer finished, snapping his bag shut.

Henry and Sally were already backing out of the driveway to go to the hospital as Zack rushed on out to his car. He followed them as they carefully made their way across town and parked beside them in the lot behind the hospital. They went into the emergency entrance together and were rapidly greeted by a pleasant receptionist who proceeded to gather the necessary information. Before she had finished, a nurse appeared at the receptionist's elbow and greeted them, saying that the ER doctor would be with them shortly as soon as he'd finished his examination of Elaine and written his orders. She also asked that they sign a permission form for a lumbar puncture and gave them an explanation of the risks involved. Upon completing the paperwork for admission, they sat in the waiting area hardly saying anything. After twenty minutes, Zack could see that Sally was having difficulty maintaining her composure, so he put a comforting arm around her back. Henry sat in his chair leaning forward with his elbows on his knees and his hands cupped over his face.

"I'm afraid we're already losing her," Sally said. Zack patted her shoulder. "She won't have any resistance to fight something like this."

A young physician in scrubs stepped through the ER entry door. "Hi, I'm Dr. Harry Ansley," he greeted. "I talked with Dr. Spencer before your daughter arrived. We got started on her treatment immediately, and now the lumbar puncture is completed as well. We should have the report from that very shortly. We're going to get her moved to the ICU floor as soon as possible, and that's up on fifth floor. They have a waiting area for you up there, and I'll ask your daughter's nurse up there to contact you as soon as the LP report comes back. I know this illness is extremely serious, especially compounded by her end-stage hepatitis B." Turning, he asked the receptionist to direct them to the ICU waiting area and excused himself. He hadn't been gone more than three minutes before he came back again. "We have a hitch," he said. "The hospital has a rule that hospice patients cannot be admitted to the ICU; we're going to need to admit her to the IMC, which means intermediary care. The good thing about this is that someone in the family will be able to stay with her. One of the problems, though, is that the isolation room she'll be in is quite small. I feel confident that her care will not suffer being in IMC rather than ICU. The nurses there are well able to handle complex and unstable patients."

Zack looked at Sally and Henry and then turned again to the physician, saying, "You know, I for one was dreading having her in the ICU and not being able to be with her, so I think this will be a blessing. Thanks for letting us know."

"I believe she's already on her way to the floor," Dr. Ansley said, smiling again before returning through the ER doors.

"OK, let me get out of my cubbyhole here and I'll show you the elevators up to fourth floor," the receptionist said kindly, slipping through the door beside her desk and joining them in the waiting room. "It will take the nurses a while to get the patient settled into the room. Should you wish, there's a cafeteria on the second floor. Otherwise, you'll need to wait up on fourth floor in the chairs by the elevator until the nurses are ready for you."

The three exited the elevator, found the fourth-floor nursing station, and inquired about the room number for Elaine.

"Oh, the patient just came up and you're here already," the unit clerk said cheerfully. "Great! The patient is in room 475. You can wait back by the elevator in those chairs and I'll have the nurse come out and talk with you. She'll have to tell you what our respiratory isolation instructions are."

"Uuuh, she doesn't have a respiratory problem that we know of," Zack said slowly.

The young lady grinned. "Yes, but they suspect meningitis, and that's handled with respiratory isolation; I think it's because that's generally the way it is transmitted."

Zack and the Dentons waited for the nurse, who appeared in about twenty minutes. The time had seemed to move interminably slowly, but they had waited patiently. They listened to the isolation instructions, donned their masks and gowns, and moved on into the room. It was indeed small. *No wonder Elaine doesn't like hospital rooms,* Zack thought to himself as they attempted to arrange chairs for all three of them to have a place to sit. Elaine's breathing seemed uneven and at times gasping, but she was not awake. Occasionally she would moan, but most of the time the only sound was the labored breathing.

"What time is it?" Sally wondered. "How long did the ER physician think it would be before we could know?"

"Two-thirty now," Henry answered. "I think he didn't give us an exact time; he said the nurse would let us know."

"Let's ask," Zack suggested. "I'll go," he said, getting up and leaving the room and going to the nursing station.

He learned Elaine's nurse was busy with another patient, but the friendly young unit clerk said, "I'll call down to the lab and see if they have the report. Neither I nor the nurse can give you the report without the physician's permission, but I can find out how it is progressing."

As Zack stood waiting, she made a call to the laboratory, went back and retrieved a report from her printer, and paged Elaine's nurse, which resulted in getting instructions to call Dr. Spencer, and, eventually, she held the phone up for Zack to speak. "It's Dr. Spencer on the line," she informed.

"Hello, this is Zack Taylor," he greeted.

"Hi, Doctor Spencer here. You're Elaine's husband, right? The lab work's back, and the diagnosis is as bad as I suspected. However, the prognosis is worse than the diagnosis, as bad as that is, because her white count is extremely low; it appears her body's making very little effort to fight the infection. I will have the infectious disease physician come by and see her tonight. I'm so sorry to have to give you this news. I didn't talk with you about this at the house, but I need to ask if you wish her to be resuscitated should her heart stop."

"No, I know she didn't want that," Zack responded slowly. "What do we need to do for the family to attempt to protect them?"

"There's a dose of medicine that each of you need to take. I can call it in, but should you wish to have your own physicians do that, it would be fine."

"Oh, no, the children and I haven't been in town long enough to establish a physician; please do call it in for all of us."

"OK then, stay on the line and I'll have the nurse get everyone's age and weight."

"Thanks," Zack was able to say before he was put on hold. After giving his information, he returned to the room to give the horrible news to the Dentons. They took the information stoically, and he stepped back into the hall to call to inform his own parents.

"Do you want us to tell the children, or do you want to tell them?" his mother asked after the greeting and the sad disclosure.

"They'll need to know immediately, when they see she's not in her room," he said thinking out loud. "I think you'd better tell them. I'm not certain if they'll be allowed to come up here and visit; I'll check with the nurse."

"How does Elaine look?"

"Well, I think her fingers look bluer to me than when she was at home. She's quit doing any moaning though; I think maybe they've given her some pain medicine. I know Danny and Sissy will want to see her, so let me ask the nurse about hospital policies and I'll call you right back."

"How are you handling this, Son?" Thelma asked.

"I'm struggling, Mom, but I'll be OK," Zack replied. "I know this is terribly hard for the Dentons too, but they seem so at peace as they face this. Hey, here comes the nurse. Love you, good-bye," he concluded, hanging up.

The nurse informed him that hospital policy allowed children on the IMC floor during visiting hours, but children were not allowed to don gowns and masks to go into an isolation room. The children could only enter the isolation anteroom and view their mother through the separating door's window. Zack called his mother back, letting her know the restrictions, and it was agreed they would all come to the hospital after the children were picked up from school.

Zack felt the scene in Elaine's hospital room seemed surreal with the three visitors all dressed in yellow isolation gowns and light blue face masks. He sat quietly by the right side of the bed holding her cold right hand while Sally sat on the left doing the same thing. Henry had a chair at the foot of the bed where he sat with his eyes closed praying.

Within an hour Thelma called Zack, informing him that she, his dad, and the children were entering the hospital lobby and would be right up. He slipped out of his isolation gown, informed the Dentons and went out to meet his family. It was a subdued group that he met, and he could see by their red and swollen eyes that the children had been weeping. He knelt in the hall with one on each side and explained the rules to them. "We can all go into this tiny little room here," he said, pointing, "and your mother is in the next small room with Pop Pop and Grammy. Your mom's too sick to talk; she's not awake, but you can look at her. You can't go into the room and we'll leave the door closed. We don't want you to catch this same illness."

"Why can Pop Pop and Granny go in when we can't?" Danny asked. "They might catch the illness too."

Zack steered the children to the separating door, letting them stand beside the window. "See the yellow gown and blue masks they're wearing? Those are for the adults to wear to prevent the spread of the disease, but children aren't allowed to have them."

"Why is that?" Sissy questioned, supporting her brother.

"I think it is because the ones who made the rules knew that some children wouldn't follow the rules, so to keep everyone safe, they excluded the children from having the gowns."

"I bet there are adults who don't keep the rules!" Danny exclaimed.

"You're probably right, but these are the rules and we're not breaking them. Sadly, your mother is not aware that you're here. I'm certain that if she were awake, she'd be glad you've come, though."

The children and their father and then Thelma and Jonathan stood and gazed through the window. Finally, Thelma broke the silence, saying, "We think it would be a good idea if we went to Chick-fil-a for supper. Zack, please check with the Dentons to see if they want us to bring them anything."

Zack dialed his phone, taking the order from his father-in-law.

"So you didn't want to go in there? Is that why you called?" Sissy asked.

Zack gave the order to his mother before answering Sissy's question. "Yes. Do you want to see me put on one of the isolation gowns?"

"Sure!" the children agreed in unison, and Zack dutifully wriggled into the outfit, exaggerating the task, leaving the children giggling and the grandparents smiling. He then hugged and kissed them all, telling them to hurry back with the food.

No sooner had they left than the infectious disease specialist, a lady, came down the hall, greeted Zack, and asked him about the sequence of events of the illnesses. Zack answered the best he could, mentioning that there were medical records from the Barnes Hospital in St. Louis that were still at the house and offering to get them if needed. The doctor asked several more questions and reassured Zack she'd talk with him more after examining Elaine as she put on the isolation gown and mask. Zack followed her through the anteroom and into the patient room as she switched on the overhead light. During the examination the physician looked very grave, giving a worried shake of her head as she examined Elaine's feet and ankles, which Zack could tell were darker and more mottled in appearance than they'd been formerly. The specialist then asked the family to step into the hall, giving a blunt but kind explanation of the prognosis; she said there was no doubt it was meningitis, a life-threatening illness in the best of situations, but with the patient's diagnosis of chronic active hepatitis B, the chances of survival were low.

"How come her feet are discoloring and her hands are so cold?" Sally asked.

"This is caused by poor circulation in those areas that we believe are triggered by the toxins from the germs," the lady responded.

"Can you give us any idea as to how soon we can expect some improvement?" Zack asked.

The doctor looked at Zack with a fleeting expression of consternation, saying, "The prognosis is very, very poor; this illness is extremely aggressive, and with her poor initial condition, even with the antibiotics we've started, we could lose her at any time. Have you talked with Dr. Spencer about resuscitation should it be necessary?"

"We have, and he knows we don't want it'" Dr. Denton answered. "Elaine was very determined that she would not have to undergo that ordeal."

"I'll make certain that is in the chart then," the doctor answered before excusing herself.

Shortly after, Jonathan appeared with the meal, and Zack met him in the hall moving with him into the anteroom. "The infectious disease doctor was here, and she said Elaine could go at any time," Zack related, choking up on his emotions. Jonathan turned to him, giving his son a big bear hug and patting him on the back, saying nothing; then he stood by his side gazing through the window into the isolation room.

Finally Jonathan waved good-bye to the Dentons, and as they stepped back into the hall he said, "Son, we know this is difficult; I'm glad we're all here with you. Have you talked with Evan about this illness?"

"No, I called but got his voicemail; I did leave a message," Zack replied.

"I'll make several attempts too, then," his dad replied. "Don't hesitate to call us with any change in her condition even if it's in the middle of the night."

"OK. How do you think the children are doing with this?" Zack queried.

"They've been very quiet. We ate at the restaurant; of course, there were the requisite number of questions from Danny, but they both seemed subdued. They didn't show their normal enthusiasm, so I believe they're processing."

"They're such good kids," Zack commented.

"They're a gift from God to all of us!" Jonathan agreed. "Good-bye," he concluded, giving Zack another hug before heading back to the elevators.

Two hours later, Dr. Spencer came by on his late evening rounds. Zack and the Dentons were at the bedside. "The ID specialist called me after she saw Elaine," he said. "She was pretty grim; has anything changed since she was here?" he asked as he raised the bed covers examining ankles and feet.

Zack could see that the mottling was getting darker and moving up Elaine's legs. "We realize it is very serious," he said dully.

Dr. Spencer continued his examination and left, and the family sat listening to Elaine's labored breathing. "Maybe the two of you need to go home and get some rest," Zack suggested.

Jonathan looked at Sally smiling, saying, "I doubt either of us will sleep; we feel we should stay here if anything happens; I know visiting hours are about over, but I'll ask what the rules are in a situation like this."

"I'll go ask," Zack said, leaving the room and going to the nursing station counter where he was informed by the unit clerk that the nurse would soon come answer his questions in the room if he would wait there.

When the nurse appeared having gowned in the anteroom, she introduced herself graciously and said, "In situations like this, I believe it is fine for all three of you to stay. Unfortunately, there's not enough space in this room for any of you to make one of the sofa chairs out into a bed. Should you wish to have coffee, ask me and I'll get you some."

She was standing by Sally as she examined Elaine's arms and legs. Because of her isolation mask, Zack couldn't read the expressions on her face, so he asked, "What do you think of how she's doing?"

"I think her situation is extremely grave," she replied. "Please do not hesitate to notify me if there is any change at all. I know you can see that my gowning up each time I enter the room is a nuisance, but it is necessary, and you must not allow that to deter you from calling me. Especially, should you feel she's miserable or in pain, I want to know immediately."

"She seems entirely silent," Sally commented. "The only thing out of the ordinary is the episodic cessation of breathing, which will frighten me at times, but then she starts breathing again, and it seems normal."

The nurse felt Elaine's forehead, commenting, "My, she certainly seems hot; we have an order for acetaminophen suppositories. I'm going to get her temperature checked, and if it's over one hundred-two degrees, I'll give her one." So saying, she stepped from the room but was soon back with the thermometer and the suppository. "One-o-three point six," she reported, removing the thermometer from Elaine's ear as the device beeped. "Gentlemen, you may wish to step out while Mrs. Denton and I attend to the suppository."

Zack and Henry dutifully stepped into the anteroom. "How are you doing with this emotionally?" Zack asked Henry as they stood with their backs to the patient room window.

"I feel numb and heartbroken," Henry responded, "but I'd be feeling ever so much worse had she not made the step to renew her faith in Christ Jesus. At present, I can feel at peace with her passing even though I'd hoped against hope that she'd improve. How do you think you're doing?"

"Probably horribly," Zack admitted. "Honestly I'm mainly feeling guilty even though I know we tried to get her off the drugs. The doctors and nurses seem so grim about this illness that I can't help but fear that the end is very near. I feel hopeless, helpless, and fearful of the negative impact her death can have on Danny and Sissy. I think I feel too sad to weep right now."

"Remember, we're all in this together," Henry responded, putting his hand up on Zack's shoulder as they stood side by side.

"I know, and I'm grateful for it," Zack returned. "I think they're ready for us to go back in," he remarked as a knock was heard on the window behind them.

Once again they resumed their seats with Zack and Sally holding each of Elaine's cold hands. They noticed as the next two long hours passed that the episodes of breathing cessation were getting more frequent. They notified the nurse, who was frequently checking on her patient, coming and going quietly and efficiently. The time came when Elaine's breathing stopped but never resumed. Zack noticed it first, immediately going out to call the nurse. When he returned, both Sally and Henry were silently weeping. Zack knelt in the small corner space between them, putting an arm around each of their shoulders as the nurse checked for vital signs.

"I'll need to call the doctor," she said. "He'll likely have two RN's pronounce her death, and we'll do that should he wish. I am so very sorry! I'm going to record the time of death as eleven fifteen," she concluded, slipping back out of the room.

Zack continued to simply feel numb kneeling in his corner but finally stood to go call his parents. He stepped out of the room to make the call, remaining in the anteroom. "Hi, Dad," he greeted when the connection clicked in. "This is Zack.... Elaine's gone." A rush of emotion at that point overwhelmed him, and his tears started to flow.

"Oh, Son, I'm so sorry!" Jonathan responded. "I never expected it to be so soon." Now hearing Zack weeping on the line, he covered his mouthpiece whispering to Thelma. "Elaine's passed away."

Thelma reached for the receiver and, listening, heard her oldest boy weeping. "Zack, can you hear me?" she asked.

"Yes," he mumbled as he wept.

"Buddy, we love you," she said. "How do you want us to handle letting the children know?"

"I want to tell them," he replied, composing himself. "I'll do what I need to do here, and then I'll come home and wake them up."

"How are your in-laws handling this?" Thelma inquired.

"They're both weeping but seem resigned to this," he answered. "I'll call you if there is any hitch or delay in finishing things up here. I'm guessing it may take an hour or two. I'm glad we did go ahead and set up the funeral arrangements; it makes it easier now."

"We did get in contact with Evan," Thelma said.

"He wanted to be notified as soon as any changes in condition happened too, even in the middle of the night, so if you don't wish to call him, we will."

"Thanks—no, I'll call him. Bye now," Zack concluded.

CHAPTER XXIX

FRIDAY AND SATURDAY,
APRIL 1 AND 2

Danny and Sissy stayed home from school, and Zack made every effort to be with them as much as possible during the entire day. He did go with Sally to the funeral home for a couple hours in the morning to make arrangements for the service to be held in a small chapel at the Dentons' church. Elaine had wished to be cremated, but the family had agreed to have an open casket to allow the children to have better closure with their mother's death. The funeral was scheduled for Tuesday, with the viewing Monday evening. Sally and Zack found their tastes were easy to accommodate one with another, and the activity moved smoothly. In the afternoon the men borrowed a utility trailer from one of Dr. Denton's friends, and they and the children hauled some donated furniture for the Hernandez family to store in the Dentons' garage. Later, Zack and the children spent a couple hours swimming in the unseasonably warm weather, nearly wearing themselves out, but when the neighbor children, Bonnie and Kenny, joined them after arriving home from school, the fun started all over again, lasting another hour before Zack took his children in for baths and supper.

After the family had gathered for the meal and grace had been said, Danny asked, "Grandpa, are you and Grandma going to leave right away after the funeral?"

Jonathan looked at Thelma, smiling and saying, "We haven't actually discussed a date. I believe we're going to need to go back home if for nothing else to get some additional clothes if we stay here much longer. We brought mostly winter clothes. I think the Hernandez family may need help getting settled in, and we wish to help with that. We've talked this over with the Dentons, and apparently our welcome here is indefinite. Was there a reason you asked?"

"We don't want you to leave; we like you here," Sissy answered for her brother.

"Yes!" Danny agreed, "we like you right here, but I was thinking that maybe when you go back we could go with you so we could see the ocean."

"You've still six more weeks of school," Thelma responded. "The rules of the condominium complex where we live do allow grandchildren to visit for a couple weeks a year, so that sounds like a great idea. We'll need to go back down there sooner than that, though, to get the clothes. I'd thought of going back in seven to ten days from now and then again at the end of the school year. Our lease expires in July, so we'll plan to be out before then. Your grandpa and I have been looking for a place to move to here."

"Do you think the condo management would allow you to move out early if you could get things lined up?" Zack asked.

"We could move out early, but we would still have to pay the rent," Jonathan answered. "We've understood they're sticklers for keeping contracts to their full length. A single lady in one of the units passed away and they required her estate to pay the full contract, even though she wasn't there and the family had moved out all of her furniture and belongings."

"Don't feel that you're wearing out your welcome here," Sally contributed. "We're getting spoiled having you here with as much of the household maintenance and chores as you're doing."

"I like that we're all here together," Sissy emphasized again. "If you get a house can you get one very close to here, so we'll be able to visit easily?"

"We'll keep that in mind," Jonathan assured her. "We'll try to have one with a guest bedroom or two so you can come over and spend the night at times. Sally and Henry, do you think you'd like to come down to Fort Walton Beach for an early summer vacation?"

"We'd love to; it's been years since we've been down there. I remember how beautiful the sand and water were. Sally, do you know of a reason we couldn't be going?" Henry responded.

"No, it sounds like fun to me," she answered.

"Is there anything else we need to be doing to plan for the Hernandezes' arrival tomorrow?" Zack worried. "With them coming and the funeral and all, it seems like a lot going on."

"It is a lot," Thelma agreed. "We all need to be helping get the work done so that Sally doesn't overdo."

"Thank you, but I'm fine," Sally responded. "I need to stay busy right now anyhow; it keeps my mind occupied."

"Evan's flying into our airport Monday, so someone will need to go pick him up," Jonathan informed. "I think he'll be here around 11:00 AM."

"Alice and her folks are coming up to the funeral, too," Thelma added.

"Do you know where they're staying?" Sally asked. "I want to make them feel welcome to stay here; there's no sense in them renting a hotel room when we've beds to spare."

"Alice could sleep in my room with me!" Sissy exclaimed. "Her folks can stay in the guest room, and I guess Uncle Evan can sleep with Dad."

"Maybe," Sally said thoughtfully, "but that reminds me: the DME company is going to come pick up the hospital bed tomorrow morning. I called them today about it. Henry, do you think you and Zack could get the regular bed set back up in that room tomorrow?"

"Sure, Mom," Zack answered for his father-in-law. "We'll put the bedding on too. Evan will be happy to sleep there and I can keep Danny with me. We're getting to be pretty good sleeping partners, aren't we, fellow?" he asked, addressing his son.

"Sometimes you snuffle when you breathe, but most of the time I'm asleep and don't know you're even there," Danny smiled. "What's a DME?"

"Durable Medical Equipment," Sally replied. "They rent out things sick people need."

"The Hernandez family will be staying in a motel for several days," Henry commented. "If I have time Monday, I can take them around trying to locate place for them to live. Once that's decided, we can make plans to get the children into school. Unfortunately, they've been out of school several months this year."

"Why don't you let Thelma and I work on that?" Jonathan asked. "It won't take long to be getting Evan."

"Are we going to school Monday?" Sissy asked.

"I believe so," Zack answered. "You'll be out Tuesday with the funeral and all, but you don't want to miss any more days in school than is absolutely necessary. However, we're interrupting Dad's question for Dr. Denton. I'd be willing to go along with Dad to help Herman and Ardine, too."

"Well, let's see how busy I am," Henry replied. "There will be a good-sized crew around here with Alice and her folks coming. I just may well let you do that. The only problem is I'm better acquainted with the community than any of you are."

"It'll be a good opportunity for us to get to know things around here better!" Thelma laughed.

The conversation moved forward as the family made plans, but when the meal was finished, Henry asked them all to listen to him for a bit.

"We've talked about a lot of things being here together like this, but we've not talked about Elaine," he said. "Before we go our separate ways for the evening, I think it will be good for us to talk about her, how we'll miss her, and some of her good points. I know this will likely be difficult, but I believe it will help us all so I'm going to start and we'll go around the table. What we say does not have to be long. I think what I'll miss about her the most is her smile; even when she was a little tyke, any time she looked at me I just felt I had to smile in return. Her smile seemed to affect everyone in the same way." He turned to Sally who was seated beside him and nodded for her to continue.

Sally sat a moment contemplating her contribution and composing herself. "I believe what I'll miss the most is spending time with her," she said. "We used to have such great times together cooking together and even cleaning house together. She could make the dullest tasks seem fun."

Sissy was next in line; she started to speak, choked up, but started again. "What I've missed the most since she went away was her hugs and kisses. I always knew she loved us, I just couldn't understand why she needed to leave us. I hate drugs, I hate drugs, I just hate drugs!" she finished vehemently.

Thelma, next in line said, "I loved Elaine's beautiful smile too. She was just beautiful in the way she talked and walked. She was also kind; even when I knew she disagreed with me, she would be kind."

"I liked her quick wit," Jonathan continued. "Sometimes her responses were a little saucy, but the speed with which she could make a droll comeback was to me amazing."

Zack who was next in the table circle surprised himself with his composure. "This is hard to say because there are so many things. I think one of the important things, though, is how she interacted with me. She could make me see the lighter side of things. If I were discouraged and feeling hopeless, she'd help me see that things could be a lot worse; if I were grouchy, she'd help me see how foolish I was being. It seemed she did all this without even trying."

Sitting between his dad and Dr. Denton, Danny was last to speak. He stood to talk, putting his arm around his father's neck as he spoke. "I miss her singing so many songs to us and reading to us. When we were little and Daddy was not at home, she would read and sing." He could go no further but turned to his dad, burying his face in Zack's chest as he wept.

The whole family wept with him.

The next day dawned blustery and cold as a front moved in from the northwest, squelching the little spring heat wave. The family gathered for a late breakfast at eight o'clock with Thelma serving sausage gravy and biscuits, hash browns, and scrambled eggs. Henry had made a fire in the dinette fireplace, and the whole family, but especially the children, were basking in its warmth.

"Dad, what are we going to do today?" Danny asked after the food had been served.

"If it weren't so cold and rainy, we could have helped your Pop Pop plant his garden. We've never had a garden, and I think you'll enjoy the process of seeing one grow. When the weather warms again, we'll see when he's ready to do that."

"I think this is a good day for housecleaning," Thelma contributed. "Would you children and your dad consider cleaning the west bedrooms, Sissy's room, and the family room?"

"Sure, Mom," Zack answered. "You guys would help me with that, wouldn't you?"

Danny looked at his father speculatively, saying, "Are you certain you know how to clean? You didn't do much of it in St. Joseph."

Zack considered his options and replied, "Here's the deal: we can either all clean the four rooms as a team, or you and Sissy can go upstairs and clean Sissy's room and bathroom while I clean the west bedrooms and bath. At the end, we'll have my mom come and judge who has done the best job; the loser or losers will have to clean the family room."

"I think we better stick with the team thing," Sissy said emphatically. "That would be more fun."

"Besides, Grandma may be partial to Dad," Danny said, trying to maintain a straight face by looking down at his food but grinning anyhow.

"So a team it is then," Zack smiled smugly.

"This division of the work is a great idea, Thelma," Sally laughed. "Let's see if we can rope our husbands into the same plan. Since you've already done the breakfast, why don't you finish up in the kitchen and dinette here? Henry and I will do the study, front hall, and living room and dining room. Both couples can do their bedrooms. What do you think, Henry?"

"I think I'd rather be in here cleaning than outside working in the rain," he responded, looking out the back window by the fireplace. "My, this covered patio needs sweeping off," he noted further.

"Let us do that," Jonathan offered. "We'll do the guest bath and guest room down here too. Can you show me where the vacuum cleaner is located?"

"Daddy, could we maybe go to the library today after we finish cleaning?" Sissy asked.

"I should think so," Zack answered. "Are you needing something for school?"

"No, it seems like a good day to sit by the fire and read."

"Oh, wow, yes!" exclaimed Danny. "Dad, you could read to us in the family room. Pop Pop, could we start a fire in there too?"

"Why sure, sonny," Henry relied. "Actually, when your dad gets tired I'd like to hear you do some reading as well."

At four thirty that afternoon, the ones going to the airport for the Hernandez family gathered in the kitchen on their way out the door. "Don't forget that they are all to come over for supper," Sally instructed. "I know they'll want to arrange the hotel rooms for tonight first, but I'll have things on the table at six thirty."

"Do you need me to stay and help you?" Henry offered.

"No, I've got it," she replied. "All we're having is chili and salad and green beans, and the chili's been on the stove the past three hours. Just let me know if you're held up for any reason."

Once the vehicles were loaded, Danny, sitting behind his dad, asked, "Dad, do you think Jennifer and Angel will be nice to us kids?"

"I believe they're going to be pleasant but shy," Zack answered. "Remember everything is going to be very new to them. When we meet new people, we just need to expect that they'll be friendly and to be friendly ourselves."

"One thing you can do is to invite them to our place to swim in the pool; I'll bet they'd like that," Henry suggested.

"Danny, I don't have a very good handle on Angel's personality; I wasn't around him very much, but if he's anything like his dad, I don't think there'll be a disappointment in him for you despite the age difference," Zack finished. He then continued talking, asking about his father-in-law's ideas concerning hotels for the newcomers. Then conversation lapsed.

After a ten-minute silence, Danny asked, "Dad, when do you think you will get remarried?"

Suppressing a sudden rush of anger, Zack answered tersely, "Buddy, this is not the appropriate time to answer that question. Why don't you wait at least a couple weeks before you bring up that subject again!"

Henry, sensing Zack's emotional overload, commented, "Danny, remember how you said your Grandpa told you that sometimes questions are too personal? Well, this is one of those times. Don't feel that your dad doesn't love you because he does. He is, as expected, moving through a period of grief, and this is a subject that does not need an immediate answer."

"Oh, Dad, I'm sorry!" Danny exclaimed. "I should have known that!"

Silence reigned again until they reached the airport.

The small plane carrying the Hernandez family for their last flight leg from Dallas to Longview landed on time despite the rainy weather. Herman greeted Zack with a warm hug, and Zack proceeded to introduce both families to each other. Thelma made a special effort to welcome Ardine, and the family's two meager suitcases were loaded into the Durango. Zack's vehicle included Herman and Angel in the rear seat, with Danny, Henry, and Zack in the front seat and led the two-car caravan.

"We knew it would be colder here but not this much colder," Herman laughed as they tightened their seatbelts.

"You should have been here yesterday," Zack replied. "It was downright hot, and we went swimming. You'll experience a good deal more variation in the temperatures here than you did in Central America. We've several hotels for you to see before we go to the house for supper. Is there anything we need to stop for on the way into town that you need?"

"I don't think so for a couple days, except food," Herman replied. "We will find the hotel first and decide what we will need then. The immigration people told me my driver's license from Belize would work OK here for a while. The immigration is giving us money for food and lodging for a couple months, but there is no money for a car. We will need to arrange our living so we can use the city transportation. Immigration told us you have a bus service."

"We do, but our family plans to help you out as much as possible with transportation for the first several weeks, so you need to let us know when we can do that," Zack said.

"We're hoping to get your children enrolled in school within the next week," Henry said. "I understand they've missed a good bit already this year. In our schools here there are about six weeks left before summer break. Your job at Lowes is to begin this coming Thursday."

"I know you have the viewing on Monday and the funeral on Tuesday; we would understand if you could not help us with this sad thing happening," Ardine pointed out.

"Most of the arrangements for those have been made and it will indeed occupy some of our time, but you are a priority too. We all do appreciate the positive influence you have had on Zack and the care and support you offered him those several days you were at the factory together," Henry explained.

"God has been so good to me, and you are a part of that goodness," Zack said with sincerity. "My life has been turned around, and even though I'm grieving my wife's death, I thank God for His mercy."

"Well, praise the Lord!" Herman exclaimed, "Are you reading your Bible and praying?"

"I'm praying but not reading the Bible much," Zack answered.

"You must do that; maybe we can plan to do that together sometimes. I find it very helpful in my Christian walk," Herman instructed.

"You are a good guy, and don't you forget it," Henry laughed as the vehicle moved on into the town.

Henry pointed out places of interest, explaining to Herman the layout of the town. The group was soon at the first hotel where Herman and Ardine felt the two suites that could be rented would be very adequate for temporary housing and that there was little need to look further, and they all continued on to the Denton home for supper together.

The whole group was able to be seated around the dinette table, and Danny had made it a point to be next to Angel. "Did Dad tell you he shot a drug cartel man on Monday night?" he asked in a stage-whisper conspiratorially.

"Did he kill him?" Angel asked, astonished.

"No, he hit his leg and it took him down, though. The police shot him again in the hand, and they took him to the hospital. He's in prison now," Danny informed importantly.

"This is worrisome!" Ardine exclaimed, having overheard the boys' conversation. "I didn't think they'd be able to hunt us here!"

"The police were able to apprehend all three of the fellows that came after me," Zack said, entering the conversation. "Again I think it was God's protection over us that allowed us to become aware of their presence here in Longview and to be prepared for their attack on us before it happened. The fellow I shot was the head of the cartel, and the police here think after their interrogation that the US branch of the outfit is now defunct and of little danger to us. However, they don't know that for certain, and I think we'll still need to be quite vigilant."

"They don't appear to be defunct in Belize," Herman said. "My cousin down there says that there are a number of men running our farm and the neighbor's farm. He's informed the police anonymously, but nothing's been done."

"We'll need to let the police in Longview know that first thing. Officer Gay here in town has asked me to let him know anything we find out about the cartel. He seemed very willing to work with me and the FBI to help with this. He'll need to know about you being here and where you'll be living too. Rest assured our police here may not be perfect, but the likelihood that they're corrupt is extremely slim," Zack added. "That's one of the reasons you're here instead of still down in Belize."

"Those cartel men are just horrid!" Jennifer exclaimed. "We thought they were going to kill Grandpa Hernandez before we were rescued. They sent him into the yard to catch a chicken for supper, and when he couldn't catch one right away they started yelling at him and laughing. Then they started shooting their guns up in the air to frighten him; we were afraid he would die either from fright or them shooting him. They are just mean!"

"It's hard to avoid hating them!" Ardine agreed.

"When people are mean, how do you keep yourself from hating them, Pop Pop?" Danny asked.

"When people treat you cruelly, it is hard not to hate them," Henry answered. "You're right, though, Jesus told us not to hate our enemies but rather to love them. I think to keep from hating takes a miracle in our minds; we need to pray for our enemies and pray that God will give you love instead of hate."

"I think I'd rather just go on hating them!" Angel exclaimed.

"The problem with allowing ourselves to hate," Herman said, "is that it actually damages us. It makes us mean and uncaring. Jesus' instruction to forgive is a powerful part of His teaching; it frees us from becoming unkind and bitter people."

"Feeling angry at someone who has done something mean to you can be difficult not to do and may well take some time, but it is worth it," Zack agreed. "As I got my life back on track when we escaped from the factory, I still felt very angry about the way they beat me that day, but as I've focused on all the good things God's done for me, the anger just seemed to fade away. I still fear that those men could hurt me and all of us again, but I'm thinking about how God helped us to know they were here in Longview, and I'm trusting Him to continue to care for us."

"Wow, Zack, in times past when you were in college and then for years thereafter after, I never thought I'd ever hear you say anything like that," Thelma said in wonder.

"I still think I want to feel mad, and I want to hurt those men," Angel frowned.

"Son, I don't blame you," Herman said, placing a hand on his son's shoulder. "I'll pray about this; you think about what everyone's said and we'll talk about this more some other time."

CHAPTER XXX

Monday, April 4

Zack had slept poorly during the night, awakening several times attempting to will himself to return to sleep. Finally, at five o'clock, he carefully rolled himself from the bed quietly, avoiding arousing a sleeping Danny, pulled on some jeans and a t-shirt, and made his way to the kitchen in the silent house.

He started a pot of coffee and took the first cup out to sit on the covered patio savoring the flavor and facing the day. He first sat numbly thinking about the activities of the previous day: the experience of the whole family, the Hernandez family being in church together, the nice meal his mother had prepared for the group, the time they'd spent around the dining room table, and the quiet evening of reading with the children enjoying the fire on another cold and drizzly day. After he'd put the children to bed, he'd felt restless and had borrowed his father-in-law's rain slicker and gone out for a long jog through the nearby neighborhoods, but even with the exercise he'd slept poorly.

His mind drifted to Elaine's death, a topic in his mind's forefront. The disparity between his life as he was experiencing it and as he'd envisioned it in earlier days weighed heavily, and tears seemed to just flow without effort. He wondered if he were chiefly feeling sorry for himself, for his children, for her parents or for Elaine herself, the fact that there would be no more life for her to enjoy. He couldn't answer himself; he sat in misery. He decided to follow Herman's advice by going to get a Bible and to read a while. He knew where Sally kept hers on a shelf in the kitchen, so he grabbed it and took it back out to the patio where he decided to start reading from the beginning of the New Testament in Matthew. The first chapters dealing with the Christmas story, John the Baptist, and Jesus' temptations were interesting but not necessarily helpful until he got to chapter five, where he recognized the beatitudes. "Blessed are the poor in spirit, for theirs is the kingdom of heaven," he read. "Blessed are those who mourn, for they shall be comforted. Blessed are the gentle, for they shall inherit the earth," he finished, feeling amazed about such promises. He'd read them all before but now they applied to him, and he felt reassurance in their meaning and resolved to memorize them so he'd always have them.

"God, I'm here mourning," he prayed quietly to himself. "Help me to depend on these words and help me to let them help the rest of the family too. Thank you for Your comfort!"

The back door opened, and Jonathan appeared carrying a newspaper and a cup of coffee. "Mind if I join you?" he asked before setting down the cup.

"Please do. What are you doing up so early?" Zack asked.

"I could ask the same of you, Son, but I'm suspecting sleep was a problem. How do you think you're handling things?"

"I've had a good cry, but I'm depending on God's comfort from the Bible and I'm already feeling better," Zack smiled at his dad. "When you experience things, the words describing those things mean more. Do you want to come with me when I go to the airport to pick up Evan today?"

"No, your mom and I are planning to take the Hernandez family out to do some shopping this morning; they want to be at the funeral but feel they have no fit clothing."

"Give them my best, then. I'm going to take the children to school and go talk to Officer Gay before I go out to the airport. Do you know when Alice and her folks are coming in?"

"They said they were leaving early this morning, so I think they'll be here in early to midafternoon. Sally talked with them last night, I know. How long is Evan staying? Did he say?"

"He'll be here through Wednesday; his company made this a business trip so I'm to take him to Dallas early Thursday morning for him to meet the personnel in the office there to get acquainted and get a leg up on some of their projects. He seems enthused about the move."

"Oh, he's enthused about everything. For a fellow who never seemed very interested in dating, it's fun to see him looking forward to marriage and this new phase of his life. Until he went down to Belize, I was about resigned to him becoming a bachelor!" Jonathan laughed heartily.

"Dad, I'm so sorry I've been such a chump for you," Zack responded, turning the interchange serious again. "I know I've said it before, but I just feel it bears repeating."

"For now, let's say all's well that ends well," Jonathan replied sympathetically. "I'm sorry for what you've been through, but I'm terribly encouraged by the way things are now. Keep counting your blessings, best among which are Danny and Sissy. We are all here to cheer you on; we don't want to smother you, though."

At the airport, Evan and Zack greeted with a handshake and a hug. "How are things?" Evan asked as they climbed into Zack's white car.

"Well, they're decent," Zack answered, attempting to put his grief in perspective. "I'm dreading the funeral and even this viewing this evening; I think I'd really like to go into a corner with my shoulders hunched over and cry. I'm not the only one to consider, though. I do agree that Danny and Sissy will do better with the arrangements as planned. Sally has been so sweet to help me set things up there's not been a minute of discord. Part of this will be for the Dentons; they've been here in the community for many years, and their friends will wish to show their support."

"I'm here to help, so let me know if I can spell you off with the kids if need be or whatever," Evan offered.

"Thanks, they'll be glad to see you. Have you talked to Alice today?"

"Yeah, they left San Antonio at seven this morning, so maybe they'll be here by the time we get back to the house."

"Oh, really, I was going to invite you to go with me to pick up the children from school, but you'll want to be with Alice."

"I'd like that, and she'd probably like to go with us; let me check with her when she gets here and I'll let you know. What time do you get them and is school working out OK for them?"

"They're doing famously with school, and I'll need to pick them up at four."

"Are the Hernandez family doing all right?"

"Yeah, Mom and Dad took them shopping this morning for clothes; they all seem to have good attitudes. Henry arranged a job for Herman, and Ardine and Herman's dad, Joseph, are going to be job hunting; they already have green cards. They're all in a hotel now but will soon need to be moving into a rental property. They were understandably upset last night when they learned the drug cartel had been here Monday night— well, I guess it was Tuesday morning. I went by the police station this morning to talk with my main contact there, a fellow by the name of Officer Gay; he's contacted the FBI and he told me to expect a call from them in the next couple days. He seemed quite confident that our current level of danger was quite low, but he'd somewhat intimated that Monday when I went and talked with him and now this has happened."

"I'm glad you were armed when this all occurred. Back when Dad had us do that shooting practice so many years ago, I doubted it was more than a waste of time."

"Yes, it was fun but I felt the same. We were very fortunate in having our parents; they're so down-to-earth about almost everything."

"I think it is difficult for you to realize how much they grieved your separation and how much they're celebrating your return with the children. I know the loss of Elaine is bringing a pall over their happiness, but it isn't squelching it."

"Their kindness to me has been nothing but steady," Zack responded as the two continued toward the house.

Danny and Sissy rode to the viewing with their father discussing why a viewing was held and who would be there.

"Can we touch Mommy?" Sissy asked.

"We're going to get there earlier than most of the people, so you can touch the body," Zack replied.

"She'll look fairly normal and possibly a little better than before she died because the funeral home knows how to make dead people look good. If you touch her, though, her skin will be cold, so don't let that upset you. I'll be right there with you; of course, we won't want to disturb her clothes but leave her looking just the way she will look when we first see her. Should you wish you could give her a kiss, but that would be for you because she could not feel it."

"If she's in heaven, she might be able to look down and see that we kissed her," Danny objected.

Zack looked at his son and smiled. "You're right, but actually I don't know about that."

"I'll ask Pop Pop," Danny grinned. "He's my go-to guy."

As Zack walked to the funeral home, he suddenly realized that both children were holding his hands when he was approaching the front of the building. An attendant opened the door for them and directed them to the viewing area, where they quietly moved toward the casket, which had been lowered for the children to view. The three stood looking at Elaine, silently weeping.

"She does look nice like you said, Daddy," Sissy commented after some time.

"I think she has too much makeup on," Danny responded. "What do you think, Dad?"

"She never did wear much makeup except when she was getting fixed up for something formal, so it is no wonder that you have that opinion. Considering how much the illness altered her appearance, I think she looks fine. Your grammy had some old pictures of her for them to use to guide how they prepared her face; I think it is quite good."

"I think it is fine too," Sissy agreed. "She was actually prettier than they've made her look."

"I'm ready to give her a good-bye kiss," Danny said soberly.

"I am too," Sissy added, "but could the three of us just stand here and have prayer?"

Tears again started in Zack's eyes. "Sure thing," he allowed as one by one the two children bent over the casket and planted a kiss on their mother's forehead.

"I'll pray first," Sissy directed. "Dear Jesus, thank you for bringing Mommy back to us. Thank you for her decision to love you again. Help us to live our lives so that we can eventually join her in heaven."

"Dear Jesus," Danny prayed, "if Mommy can see us now, help her to know we love her and that we are missing her. Help her not hurt anymore and to be able to think right. Amen."

Zack attempted to control his emotions so that he could speak coherently. "Dear Lord," he prayed, "thank you for my children. Help us all as we deal with Elaine's death. Help me to be the kind of dad that these children need. Forgive me for all my horrible shortcomings. Amen."

The three continued to stand there for another minute or so before Jonathan and Thelma entered the room. Thelma slipped up to her son, giving him a one-sided hug, asking, "Zack, would you like a bit of time alone? We'll take the children out to the lobby."

"I'd appreciate that," Zack said simply, and the group moved out of the room, quietly shutting the door behind them. Zack knelt beside the low casket; he tried to keep his tears from dripping on the satin lining, but he bent over to administer his final kiss, saying, "I've never felt so inadequate and so guilty before. Sweetheart, I wish things had been different; I wish I'd treated you better, I wish there had been no drugs, I wish we'd done things better! I know you're gone and possibly only God can hear me, but I am so very, very sorry!" He continued with racking sobs, which finally subsided, but he continued to kneel, composing himself before ending his minutes of solitude. When he left the room, he was met by Henry and Sally. Recognizing his own benefit by being alone with the body, he offered them the same opportunity, which they readily accepted, and he moved on over to be with his parents and children.

"We've decided that about halfway through the viewing, we and the children are going to go get some ice cream at Dairy Queen if you approve," Jonathan offered.

Zack looked at the expectant children and managed a smile through his grief. "I think it will be fine," he said. "Evan will be here in about five minutes. He's planning to stay the full time, and I suspect Alice will be here too. There will be a number of people that I don't know."

The group waited until time to start the viewing before going in again where Sally and Henry were sitting in the front row near the casket. More flower arrangements had been brought in and the casket raised for the viewing. The family seated themselves behind the Dentons, with Zack by the aisle and Evan beside him with Alice. When the doors were opened to the viewers, one of the first to enter was Alexandra. She immediately walked over to Zack, giving him a smothering hug, saying, "Oh, you poor thing! I'm so sad that Elaine's already gone. Whatever are you going to do?"

Zack assumed the question was rhetorical and did not answer; he stood introducing Evan and Alice. While Alexandra and Alice were shaking hands, Zack caught a smirk and wink from his brother who had also stood.

"Oh, I must go see how she looks! Can you come with me?" Alexandra enthused, taking Zack's arm. "Do you feel they've done a decent job with her appearance?"

"I felt it was adequate," Zack admitted, moving up to the casket.

"Ooooh, I think she looks fabulous!" Elaine exclaimed. "I'd heard they do a great job with bodies, and now I believe it. If you don't mind, I'm going to stay close by; there are several Elaine's old school friends coming, and I want to be able to introduce you. You and your brother certainly favor one another; where did he meet his fiancée, and what kind of work does he do?"

"He was working on a project down in Belize; she was teaching down there at a Salvation Army elementary school and they attended church together. The wedding's going to be in a few weeks," Zack informed before they turned back. Zack stood near the front with Alexandra at his right introducing one after another of Elaine's old friends and classmates.

Evan, true to his word, was on his left taking in the situation quietly. When Alexandra stepped away for a few moments to introduce an acquaintance to the Dentons, Evan asked in a low whisper, "Does this woman think she owns you?"

"It seems," Zack sighed wearily. "There's more to the story; I'll tell you when this ends." He then continued chatting briefly and amiably with one stranger after another, most of whom were acquaintances of the Dentons, but if one of Elaine's friends appeared, Alexandra was right there to give introductions.

After fifty minutes, Thelma and the children came and patted him on the arm, telling him they'd be back in half an hour or so. Another forty minutes later, Alice and Evan suggested to Alexandra that they'd like to take her out for pie and coffee. The crowd had thinned considerably with only elderly people present so she consented, checking with Zack to see if he thought he'd be all right.

"Thank you," Zack replied graciously, inwardly relieved, "I'll be fine."

Evan was standing behind Alexandra, and he gave his brother a second wink. "We'll see you at the house," he said.

As Zack later left the funeral home, again with his children, he asked, "Well, how did you think it went?"

"It wasn't quite as boring as I had suspected it would be," Danny replied honestly. "There were more people there than I thought there would be."

"I think there were a lot of people there who love the Dentons, and they're sorry for them for the loss of their daughter," Sissy added. "What did you think, Daddy?"

"I thought it was nicely done, but it seemed very long to me. I'm glad it is over, but I think it was a good thing to do. How do you children think you will handle the funeral tomorrow?"

"We'll do OK," Sissy answered. "The best part of tonight was us praying together; it seemed like it just made us a real group, sort of like we're a team together."

That evening after Zack had put the children to bed, he went out on the back porch for some time to ruminate over the events of the day. Evan soon appeared, and they sat in companionable silence for several minutes. "So what's up with Alexandra?" Evan asked.

"She met me on the plane when I went back to St. Joe, and I told her Elaine was ill. She then came and visited Elaine, and Elaine enjoyed her visit immensely. Earlier, Elaine had asked me to be certain to remarry after her death, so when she became reacquainted with Alexandra who had been one of her best friends in high school, she asked me to promise I'd take her out on at least one date and consider her as a wife," Zack answered.

Evan was quiet.

"You were correct; the way she acted tonight, it was as if I were some of her property. I believe Elaine may have said something about that as well. The woman is pretty, she is socially adept, but she rubs me the wrong way. I didn't tell Elaine how much I didn't care for her old friend. I appreciated you getting her off my hands. How did you manage that?"

"We need to give Alice the credit for that. We were both racking our brains for a way to get you out of your misery when Alexandra was gushing about a new little pie shop and how she just couldn't resist an invitation to go there, so Alice took the bait and ran with it. I think Alexandra wanted us to taste the pie and to pump us for information, so it went well. She is actually quite pleasant when you don't feel you're in the sights of her gun," Evan laughed.

"In the past I might have been interested, but I'm not now," Zack said glumly. "I don't know how I can possibly handle a date with her."

"Give it a few weeks, take her out, be kind and gentle, and tell her exactly how you feel," Evan advised. "I bet Elaine was attempting to help you out; she certainly was not wanting you to be miserable."

CHAPTER XXXI

Tuesday, April 5

Zack awoke at five-thirty and knew he'd never get back to sleep. He'd agreed with Evan to jog together early in the morning, but as they had not set a specific time, he quietly scooted out of bed, put on exercise clothes, and knocked softly on Evan's bedroom door.

"I'm awake," his brother responded. "Go make some coffee while I get dressed."

Zack dutifully headed to the kitchen, considering the enormity of the day before him. A wave of grief washed over him as he placed his hands on the counter and leaned on outstretched arms, waiting for the coffee to move through the percolator.

"Buck up, man," Evan said, walking into the kitchen and putting his hand on his shoulder. "Today you only have to live one hour at a time. I can sympathize with you, but I can't give you empathy; I've never been where you are now. How long before the coffee's ready?"

"Here's for a good pal," Zack replied, pouring a cup and handing it to Evan. "Sit here at the counter. Do you think you want an energy bar or anything before we go?"

"No, Mom said she was making an eggs and sausage casserole for breakfast for everyone and some crazy bread, so I'll wait for that. Were you able to sleep last night?"

"All in all pretty well. I woke a couple times but went right back to sleep. I think I'm doing as well as can be expected."

"How about wanting a beer?"

"The thought crossed my mind yesterday after the viewing, but there really doesn't seem to be a craving; I just thought about it. Being around no one who drinks, not having it on hand, and not doing the shopping makes it a lot easier, I think."

"I'm ready to go," Evan commented as he set his cup in the sink. "I'll follow since you know the area better than I do."

"There aren't any sidewalks in this part of town so we'll have to start out on the streets, but there's a long trail about a quarter mile away that is quiet this time of day. We'll go there. How long do you want to run?"

"You decide; I don't mind. I just want to be back to be cleaned up by breakfast when everyone else is getting up."

"You mean up and slicked up for Alice when she shows up," Zack chuckled. "Well, that's all right, I'm glad you care."

As the front door slammed behind them, Alice sat up in her bed and could see the two men moving down the front walk and out onto the street beginning their run. She smiled groggily at their physical resemblance and felt cheered at their comradery. She tried to imagine how Zack was feeling but gave up on it, simply thinking of what her role would be during the day. *I'll focus on being supportive of the children and the Dentons*, she thought, *This is going to be an especially hard day for all of them.* She stealthily moved out of the bed, gathered her fresh clothes, and slipped into the restroom to shower and dress. When she'd closed the door, she started to hum a song, letting her mind drift over the words:

This is the day,
This is the day,
That the Lord has made,
That the Lord has made,
I will rejoice,
I will rejoice,

And be glad in it,
And be glad in it.
This is the day that the Lord has made,
I will rejoice and be glad in it,
This is the day,
This is the day that the Lord has made!

Sissy awoke to the sound of the shower and Alice's humming. It had been fun the evening before talking with her future aunt about things they'd be planning to do together in the future. Alice had spoken with her almost like an equal. She thought about the viewing and how her mother had appeared in the casket, feeling suddenly bereft. *Mommy will never come back,* she thought. *She will not be here as I grow up; I won't have anyone to talk to about things. Maybe Alice can help. I'll ask her.* She thought about the three of them praying together and her dad's prayer. *How can he be so different?* she wondered. *Can it really last?* She thought about the funeral and the dress she and Thelma were planning for her to wear. It was navy blue and made of a soft slinky material that made her feel very grown up. Thelma had also purchased some black shoes with a bit of a raised heel for her to wear. She wondered if Alice could help her do her hair today.

Jonathan and Thelma were already in their own bathroom chatting about the arrangements for the day.

"Help me see if there's any possible thing I can do for Sally," Thelma instructed, combing her hair. "I'll have breakfast on the table by eight. I just can't imagine how badly the Dentons must be feeling. However, they do seem to take events with amazing equanimity. I don't think I'd be able to do it. We won't need to be doing much cooking for the next several days: people have brought food for about ten meals, I'd say. With the funeral at three o'clock, I believe I'll just warm one of the casseroles up for lunch. Do you think we should have a sit-down meal or let people come and go as they so desire?"

"I'd ask Sally," Jonathan replied. "In time of significant emotional stress, a routine schedule can be comforting to some and to some it's a nuisance. You also need to let me know if you see something I can do for Henry. I'm certainly glad that Evan could be here. This visit with Alice and her parents has been a great time again to become better acquainted with them too. They did seem awfully weary when they arrived here, though."

"They'd both been very involved with their church's spring children's program," Thelma commented. "I think the schedule they'd all been keeping last week had almost done them in. I don't think Evan could have picked a sweeter young lady; did you notice how kindly she handled Sissy's request for her to sleep in her room?"

"Yes, I agree. She's a jewel!"

Henry and Sally had been up for some time but had stayed in the master bedroom and had seen the boys go out the front walk for their run. Henry was in an easy chair by the widow reading his Bible while Sally, after finishing her shower, was curling her hair by her counter in the bathroom. She stood and walked back into the bedroom, standing by her husband's chair with one hand resting on the chair back while she thoughtfully looked out at the street. "I never thought to see this day," she said sadly. "I'm telling myself, though, that this is not truly the worst day of my life. This is a day to celebrate that Elaine will be in heaven. As I look back on it, a worse day was the day we learned Elaine was using drugs and that she didn't want us to communicate with her anymore. I lived through that day, and I can live through this day."

"Yes, the day requires us to remain focused on the good, doesn't it?" Henry agreed. "I was overwhelmed by the kindness of the folks at the viewing last night. We are blessed despite our grief. This is a day for us to see ourselves as reeds bending before the will of God and giving Him the praise. Hold my hand, dear, as we pray. 'God in heaven, thank you for our blessings. Thank you for Zack and the children, thanks for all our kind friends, thanks for Elaine's return to You, and most of all thank You for the comfort and wisdom You impart so freely. Help us through this difficult day and we give You praise! We ask these things in the precious name of Jesus Christ. Amen.'"

Henry stood giving Sally a hug, and they moved out into the hall to begin their day.

Danny awoke when Zack and Evan returned from their run. They had attempted not to awaken him, quietly entering through Evan's door before going into the joint restroom with the door to Danny's room shut, but he was roused by the rumble of their voices as they chatted together. The sound gave him a sense of belonging and security, so he soon jumped from bed to make himself a part of it. "Good morning, guys!" he greeted, swinging open his door to the bathroom.

Evan was in the shower, but Zack was standing in front of the sink with a bath towel around his waist shaving. "Good morning yourself," he responded, rinsing the lather off the safety blade. "You certainly look all bright-eyed and cheerful this morning."

"Where have you been?" Danny asked.

"We were out getting a little exercise running," his dad answered. "Have you missed us?"

"No, I was sleeping," Danny laughed. "When am I going to get some muscles like yours?" he asked, eyeing Zack's arms as he continued shaving.

"All in good time, Buddy," Zack replied. "Say, why do you think God gave men more muscles than women?"

"So they could be strong and take care of the women, I guess," Danny answered importantly.

"Good answer, bud, and don't ever forget it. Our muscles aren't given to us to take advantage of women but to help them. Unfortunately, in our culture and in many cultures of the world, young men are unintentionally taught their muscles are present to show how strong they are in comparison to other men and to be used to take advantage of anyone that is weaker than they are. We need to be thankful for the bodies that we have, but we must not lord it over other fellows that are not as fortunate as we are. Men's muscles certainly can be used to earn a living for the family and to take care of our family and friends. You need to think of yourself as you grow older as being the champion of your sister, of any girl that needs your help, even guys that are smaller or weaker."

"Wow! Sermons already this early in the morning!" Evan exclaimed, coming out of the shower and toweling off. "It sounds a little heavy, but I couldn't agree with you more."

"Yeah, Danny was coveting my muscles, so I decided to give him a little balanced perspective as to the responsibility that a big healthy body gave him," Zack laughed. "Danny, do you need to brush your teeth? I'm finished shaving here."

Dutifully Danny picked up his toothbrush and started applying the toothpaste. "I still want big muscles," he said. "I don't care if there is responsibility with them. I'm certain I could handle that."

Evan and Zack looked at one another, laughing.

"He may be small, but that doesn't impair him having an opinion," Evan commented dryly.

With the turnout at the reception, the family had arranged for the funeral to be held in the main sanctuary of the church rather than in the small chapel nearby. The decision was fortunate because even the sanctuary was full. Zack and the children moved through the process numbly with all three of them appreciating the music and comments that were given. Evan was at Zack's elbow throughout, and Thelma kept an observant eye on the Dentons. There was an afternoon lunch in the church multipurpose room afterwards where Alexandra again made her presence known, but she fortunately had a property showing soon after the lunch started and had to leave. Zack sat with the children on either side of him and with the Dentons across a small round table from them. The meal was relaxed, and the atmosphere gave a sense that the troublesome part was now complete.

As guests were leaving, Sally asked, "Zack, were you in anyway disappointed with the service?"

Zack replied thoughtfully, "I was all right with everything that was done. How did you feel about it?"

Sally smiled, saying, "As sad an affair as it was, there was nothing I know of that we should have done differently."

That evening, the families gathered in the living room. The Seymore ladies, Alice and her mother, were accomplished pianists, so the two ladies played piano duets, enthralling Sissy and Danny. Alice then requested Evan to sing a couple hymns for the group that she'd previously accompanied for him at the Belize City mission. He graciously acquiesced, again enthralling the children.

"Man! Uncle Evan, you can really sing!" Danny exclaimed as the song ended.

"I'm no better than your dad. Have you heard him sing? We were both in high school choir, and he can read music much better than I can," Evan responded.

"A few nights ago he sang a little song for us, and that was the first we'd heard him," Sissy informed.

"I have some old hymnals," Sally offered. You fellows can sing a duet."

Zack felt uncomfortable but didn't want to be a cold blanket on the festivities. He tried to think of a gracious way to excuse himself.

Henry, sensing his reluctance, said, "I'll make it easy for us. Evan, you sing the lead and let Alice sing the alto. We'll put Zack on the tenor and I'll do the base. Let's pick an easy, well-known song to start with. How about 'Amazing Grace'?"

They found the page in the hymnal and all turned to it as they stood around the piano facing the keyboard while Sue Seymore gave them their respective pitches and played an introduction. Within the first phrase a good balance was set, and the children sat in open-mouthed amazement to hear the music from the family.

"Bravo!" exclaimed Jonathan at the close of the hymn. "I feel like I've been to church! What can you do next?"

"How about 'In the Garden'?" Thelma suggested.

So they sang:

I come to the garden alone.
While the dew is still on the roses;
And the voice I hear,
Falling on my ear,
The Son of God discloses.

And He walks with me and He talks with me,
And He tells me I am His own;
And the joy we share as we tarry there,
None other has ever known.

I'd stay in the garden with Him
Tho' the night around me is falling,
But He bids me go; thro' the voice of woe,
His voice to me is calling.

And He walks with me and He talks with me,
And tells me I am His own;
And the joy we share as we tarry there,
None other has ever known.

"How lovely!" Thelma complimented. "This is so much fun! See, Zack, this isn't so difficult, is it? Singing's a little like bike riding; once you learn to do it, the ability sticks with you."

"I must admit I did better than I expected, but I don't think I'll plan to go into performance," Zack responded. "Sally, do you have more of these hymnals, then maybe everyone could be singing."

"But we don't know how," Sissy complained.

"The two of you just sit on either side of your grandma Sally. She has a good strong soprano voice, and she'll show you where the words are on the page and you follow her voice," Zack directed, feeling chagrinned that the children were so willing but uninformed.

For the next fifty minutes, the families sang one song after another until Zack looked at his watch and announced the impending bedtime.

"Daddy, can you teach us to sing?" Danny asked.

"Actually, right now you've been learning. Doing it together makes it easy. As you get older and have an interest, we could get you some voice lessons."

"I think I'd like some piano lessons," Sissy added. "I love to hear Alice and Sue play!"

"I think that's a wonderful idea," Sally agreed. "I know a lady here in town that gives lessons, and I've heard nothing but good reports from her students and their parents. We'll talk more about this some other time when you're not being hustled off to bed."

CHAPTER XXXII

WEDNESDAY, APRIL 6

It was a subdued trio that sat in the car as Zack took Danny and Sissy to school the next morning.

"Daddy, what are you going to do today?" Sissy asked before the two got out.

Zack's initial first thought was, *I will no longer be caring for your mother*, but he thought better of voicing it and answered, "I'm going to spend much of the day working with the Hernandez family helping them settle in and look for an apartment or house."

"Are you going to pick us up?" Danny questioned.

Zack looked at his son, smiled, and said, "I will be the one picking you up most of the time from here on. I do want you be able to trust that I'll show up; I know that can only happen over time."

Both children gave him a dutiful peck on the cheek before heading off to the school door.

Zack, per previous plans, went directly to the Hernandezes' hotel to pick up Herman and Ardine. Upon arriving, he found the whole family in their hotel suite sitting around the table just having finished breakfast. "Have a seat while we finish Bible reading and family prayer," Herman directed. "Do you want a cup of coffee?" he asked and then began preparing it with Zack's affirmative answer. "Angel," he instructed, "go ahead and finish reading to the end of the chapter."

Zack sat, allowing the words of the fourth chapter of Philippians to wash over him.

"Finally, brothers, whatever is true, whatever is honorable, whatever is just, whatever is pure, whatever is lovely, whatever is commendable, if there is any excellence, if there is anything worthy of praise, think about these things," Angel read.

Wow, Zack thought, *that's what I should be thinking about! When I want to think about the bad things like my past or Elaine's death I need to turn my mind to these things.*

Herman prayed, and the family started cleaning the breakfast items from the table. "Zack, let's go down to the lobby to talk. Dad, will you come with us?" he asked.

The three men then walked down the hall before seating themselves in a quiet corner.

"As a family, we've talked over what we want to do," Herman informed. "We've decided it is not the right time to be thinking of buying a house, so we want to rent a three-bedroom apartment. We are very uncertain what our incomes will be, so we need to plan to live off only my income initially, saving the incomes from Dad and Ardine for a down payment if and when they have jobs. We will want to be within walking distance to a grocery store and public transportation. We understand the public schools will take the children to school on a bus. Finally, we'll want to be in the best school district for the children and preferably not too far from where you live."

"I'm afraid I'm not very qualified to help you with all of that," Zack said. "Let me call my father-in-law who knows the area and see if he can come with us to look and tell us where we need to go."

"I will want Ardine to come with us too," Herman said.

Zack made the call; Henry was more than willing to help, and soon the five were heading out, having left Angel and Jennifer at the hotel planning to make use of the swimming pool. "I think your best choice of schools will be in the Spring Hill area, except I don't know about city transportation up there," Henry said.

"I'll call and ask," Zack said. He made the call and reported that the buses only ran up Gilmer Road just past Hawkins street.

"That's about a mile from the school, but there's a grocery right near," Henry said. "There are a good many shops along Gilmer Road, so the transportation could get you there as well. Let's go see if there are any reasonable apartments in that area. Oh, say, Sally asked us all to plan to come to our house for lunch; she and Thelma have sandwiches in mind."

Three separate apartment complexes were found in the area, one of which seemed satisfactory to Ardine; she was especially pleased that the individual units were all on ground level so there would be no fellow dwellers above or below them. A three-bedroom unit had been vacated April first and was undergoing refurbishing but was to be available within a week. Zack then took his passengers to the Denton home, going on to the hotel to bring back Angel and Jennifer to join in lunch as well.

Gathered around the dinette table, the families discussed their findings. "Visiting the school seems like the next thing to do," Thelma suggested. "One of the big hurdles we had with Danny and Sissy was to have their immunization records. Do you have anything like that?" she asked, directing the question to Ardine.

"Yes, I've kept records from our health department, and I brought them with me in the Bible," Ardine replied. "Do you think they'll accept that?"

"They'll likely accept some of it," Sally contributed. "The rules as to what is required change frequently, so we'll take them by and see; we may need to take them to the county health clinic to get any other necessary shots that may be required. Even a physician health certification may be needed."

"Immigration required us all to have health exams in Belmopan," Herman said. "We'll take those records too."

"I'll plan to go into the office with you," Henry offered. "One of the ladies from the church works in the front office, and I may be able to make things go more smoothly. Let me call and see if there's anyone to help us this afternoon."

"Ardine, have you thought of what type of work you would consider?" Thelma asked.

"Before I was married, I taught school," Ardine answered. "That's been fifteen years ago, so I'd be pretty rusty even if I were hired."

"Yes," Thelma agreed, "but you have the experience and the education; you're also fluent in English. Do you speak Spanish?"

"Oh, yes. There are many Spanish-speaking residents in Belize, so a good portion of the population speaks Spanish, even though the official language is English."

"You may be able to qualify to teach Spanish then, with your education background. Sally, do you know anyone who would be up to date on the qualification teachers need in Texas?"

"Texas has some unusual rules; I've heard about teachers here needing to have courses in Texas history, but I understand that those can be taken after you start teaching if you're hired. There was a lady in Dr. Denton's practice who was a career counselor over in Kilgore College; we had a friendly relationship with her. If she can't answer our questions, I'm certain she can direct me to someone who could," Sally answered. "I'll call her this afternoon."

"What kind of work did you have in mind, Joseph?" Henry asked.

"I've always been a farmer, so I thought being a clerk in a hardware store or a feed store would be something I could do," he replied.

"I don't think they would hire two men from the same family at Lowes," Henry said, "but that wouldn't keep you from applying at Home Depot. Unfortunately, I understand that most employers are requiring people to apply online; I think it makes it very difficult for a prospective employer to get a reasonable evaluation of your abilities. It is easier to turn in the application, though, because you can go to the website online to turn in the application. Do you know how to do that?"

"He hasn't used the computer much, but he can learn," Herman offered. "We had a computer at the farm, but it was one of the first things the cartel men took after I was abducted."

"I have an old desktop computer I'm not using. Let me get that set up for your family," Henry offered. Zack, could you help me with that?"

The families completed their lunch together, and Henry set off to the school with Ardine and Herman, leaving Zack to deal with life on his own again. Evan had gone with Alice and her parents to consider the various areas in Dallas for housing as well as to meet the men in the Dallas office with whom he would be working. After delivering Angel and Jennifer back to the hotel and returning to the house, Zack walked back to his bedroom to decide what needed to be done first. He chose to call the university to find out if it would be permissible to audit the end of some of the math and science courses. He was told he'd need to come in to the university to get permission from the department chairmen, and he scheduled appointments to meet with them the following day. Because Henry had not returned with Herman and Ardine, he walked to the back-yard looking for something to do before he was to go back and pick up the children. The backyard looked like it was in pristine shape, needing nothing. Zack recognized his feelings of helplessness and hopelessness that he'd experienced so frequently after Elaine had left the home at his request. For the first time, he wanted alcohol. *God, help me with this*, he prayed, sitting down on a metal lounge chair on the back patio. *I'll go get some iced tea*, he thought, getting up to go into the kitchen. Thelma was baking cookies and the aroma of fresh baking was a friendly introduction as he entered.

"Mom, is there any of that tea we had for lunch left?" he asked.

"There is," she replied. "I'm surprised you're already thirsty after the two glasses you drank at lunch."

"Well, to be honest, I feeling at loose ends, and I was wanting some beer," he said seriously. "I'm feeling the same way I did when Elaine left."

"Wow! That's understandable," Thelma sympathized. "What can we do to help?"

"Keep me busy, and talk to me," he admitted. "I called LeTourneau University a bit ago to see if I could audit some courses, but I need things to do now."

Thelma looked at her son in consternation, saying, "I don't need anything done; perhaps Sally does. Your dad's in the study; check with him. Henry will be back soon, I think."

"Dad, do you have anything that needs doing for the next hour or so?" Zack asked entering the study.

"Let's see," Jonathan said, thinking out loud, "I know Henry was wanting to get started on the garden. I've not seen a tiller in his garage, so I suspect he spades up the garden unless he rents a tiller. You could take a shovel and go out and start that process."

"Dad, I've never had a garden," Zack grinned.

"I'll come with you and we'll look at it together," Henry instructed, rising from his chair; "A bit of exercise wouldn't hurt me anyhow. What's making you so ambitious suddenly?"

Zack blushed faintly but answered, "I'm wanting beer and thought staying busy would help."

His openness somewhat flustered Jonathan, who responded by saying, "Let's get spades out of the garage and go out to get started. We'll use the same general layout Henry did last year, and he can decide where he wishes to plant the various things. So in all these years, you've never planted a garden?"

"No, we've been living in apartments without access to a plot of soil since we left St. Louis. I don't think we ever had a garden while we were growing up," Zack replied.

"You're right, we didn't," Jonathan agreed. "After the two of you left for college, I had one for several years until we moved down to Florida; there's no place to have one there. In Illinois, I got a lot of satisfaction being able to raise several vegetables; you actually don't save a lot of money raising vegetables in a garden, but the things you raise are healthy for you, and you can be certain you're eating fresh food. Additionally, having grown up on a farm, I think I became accustomed to enjoying seeing things grow. Spading up an old garden bed is chiefly just turning the top layer of the soil over and the breaking up the large clods you produce. This is essentially what the farm implement plow does. A tiller does the same thing too, but it oftentimes has a difficult time accomplishing the task if there's too much grass sod in the garden bed," he continued as he demonstrated the process, starting in the garden corner and turning over several shovels full of soil. Zack moved to another corner, and the two worked companionably until time for Zack to go and pick up Danny and Sissy.

"Thanks, Dad, for your being with me," Zack said humbly as he laid down his shovel. "Not only was this a good occupation for my mind but it was fun being with you, and I can see how the process of gardening can be a pleasant activity."

Jonathan looked at his son, remarking, "Someday I wish you could explain to me how when you were such a highly motivated youngster you chose such a different path during your college days and then now after all these years you're like your old hardworking self again."

"I can't really tell you, Dad," Zack replied after considering. "You were good parents, and I always felt fortunate that Evan and I had such a good home, but I think I felt that there was an easier way to live life and that I was smart enough to make it happen for Elaine and me. I now know it was stupid thinking, but how are you going to make a kid believe that? I know we were all in church, but to me it was more of just the nice optional thing to do. I had no deep trust in Jesus Christ; I considered Him simply part of our culture. As I think back on it, I see my choices to have been selfish, lazy, hedonistic, and godless. How's that for a self put-down, but that's what I think. When I finally was forced into sobriety and faced myself, I recognized I had been totally unable to control the situations in my life. While I was held prisoner, I finally reached out to God realizing I wasn't so strong or smart after all. That was when I started making progress. I have a whale of a long way to go yet, but even now I'm benefiting from my upbringing and I thank you and Mom for it."

Jonathan shook his head, "You'll never know how many sleepless nights your mom and I spent. At this point I do not believe we hold that against you, though. We are heartbroken about Elaine, and I have difficulty also understanding how kind the Dentons are in all these. Looking back, I can say this, though, and I think your Mom would agree with me: we feel we were not attentive enough in your spiritual development. Maybe had we been more careful in our own spiritual lives, you'd have done better."

"Maybe," Zack agreed, "but look at the Dentons. You could hardly ask for parents that were more on track spiritually as far as I can see, but Elaine behaved the same way I did. I think you'll only likely get an adequate answer for your questions when you get to heaven and talk to God!"

"Yeah," Jonathan laughed, "but I'll be so busy thinking about other things then I'll probably forget to ask. Hey, you'd better get going. Don't let me make you late."

Zack considered their conversation as he drove to pick his children. *Each day is important*, he thought. *What am I doing today to help Danny and Sissy to do better than I did? What can I do to keep them from messing up like I have? I think*, he said to himself, *I need to daily set the best example that I can taking the most advantage of the opportunities that I have, and stay as positive as I can so they feel secure in my love. I need to approach life to be cheerful and happy so they find being with me is pleasant and that I enjoy what I'm about rather than finding it a chore.* The drive to the school was no chore; he arrived to join the automobile queue picking up the students and was delighted to see the smiling faces of Danny and Sissy as they raced to the car. *What if I'd fallen off the wagon and gone and gotten a drink earlier?* he wondered as the children slammed the car doors. "Did you noisy things have a good day?" he asked as they bucked their seatbelts.

"I did," Danny said excitedly. "We were studying Texas history, and I learned that in the Battle of San Jacinto, the United States army fought less than an hour defeating the Mexican general. Did you know they have a monument down near Houston to commemorate that? I want to go see it. We did fractions in math, and the teacher said in a few weeks we could even do some algebra. I got a one hundred on my spelling test even though we were gone yesterday. How well did you do in spelling, Dad?"

"I don't know about the monument, but I'm willing someday to go see it. My spelling was fair," Zack laughed, enjoying his son's enthusiasm. "How about you, Sissy?" he said, turning to Sissy.

"I didn't have a bad day, I just felt sad all day because of Mommy. I had a hard time not thinking about her and the fact that she's gone and can't get better. My teacher was very nice, though. I was not paying attention in health class, and she asked me to stay in for recess. I did, and she told me she was so sorry for our loss and asked me to come talk with her about things if I wanted to. I started crying, so she patted me on the shoulder and gave me some Kleenex. I felt better, but I still did feel sad all day. None of the other kids said anything about it; I think they were afraid anything they might say would be the wrong thing. The afternoon actually was a little better than this morning. Did you find a house for the Hernándezes?"

"I think they found a place not too far away from where we are. They all came over for lunch, and then Dr. Denton went with Herman and Ardine to talk with the Spring Hill school administrator about getting Jennifer and Angel enrolled. They hadn't returned before I came to pick you up."

"What's for supper?" Danny asked.

"I don't know, but the house smelled like cookies before I left," Zack replied. "How much homework do the two of you have tonight?"

"I have some from yesterday and some from today," Sissy replied. "I think it will take me about an hour or so to do it, I think."

"I have a three-paragraph report to write about the history of our county," Danny contributed. "Dad, do you think you could help me look that up online and see what we can find? Did you know our county is one of the smallest in Texas?"

"I do know that, but I don't know why. Maybe we can find out and you can put that in your report," Zack answered. "Here we are. After we have our cookies and milk, let's go to the table in the family room and wipe out this homework. After supper, we can do whatever we wish."

Forty-five minutes later the three were well-settled into their tasks in the family room when Zack's cellphone rang. "Hello, Zack Taylor speaking," he answered pleasantly.

"Why, hello, Zack! This is Alexandra; is this a convenient time to talk?"

Zack rolled his eyes as the children watched him.

"Who is it?" Sissy whispered. He held his hand up, palm facing her.

"Well, the children and I are in the process of wiping out their homework," he answered as he stood. "Hang on a moment." He placed his hand over the mouthpiece, instructing, "You both go ahead with your work. It's Alexandra, and I'm going into the bedroom to talk. I won't be long." He stepped down the short hall and into his room, closing the door. "I'm here again," he said into the phone. "I needed to get them continuing with their work."

"How are you all doing? Evidently you sent them to school today?" she asked.

"Yes, they went on to school and I think they're doing as well as can be expected. Sissy seems to be taking it harder than Danny, but she may just be processing Elaine's passing more rapidly than he is. They are both so diligent at school that sometimes I think I expect more of them than I should, although I've read that children often arise to your expectations. I don't want to limit them."

"They are such dears!" Alexandra enthused. "How do you think you're holding up?"

Feeling uncomfortable with her invasive, direct questioning, Zack answered noncommittally, "I'm doing fairly well. I'm trying to stay busy."

"Do you have anything planned for this weekend?" she asked.

"No," he answered, racking his brain for some excuse he felt he might offer.

"Well, there's a very nice winery up northeast of town that I'd like to ask you to take me to," she suggested.

Zack felt a surge of anger at her forwardness but covered it by laughingly asking, "Are you forgetting that I'm now a committed teetotaler?"

"Oh, dear, I forgot!" she exclaimed. "The food is very good there, though. You wouldn't need to drink, and often they have live music."

Zack considered a refusal but decided against it, telling himself that there was no benefit in delaying his necessary conversation with the woman. He would attempt to honestly and kindly lay his position out to her, hoping not to alienate her. Face to face would be better than over the phone, and he'd be keeping his agreement with Elaine. "I believe I can swing that pretty easily," he said slowly. "What time would you like me to pick you up; I assume you know how to get there?"

"Oh, I do!" she gushed. "It's such a lovely place! I'll text you my address, and I think if we leave at five-thirty it will be fine. I'll call in some reservations; do you think your children would want to come?"

"I suspect they'd be all for coming, but I believe they'll be fine here with their grandparents," Zack arranged, certainly not wishing to have listening ears as he waded through this social quagmire. "Thanks for your concern. I trust we can have a pleasant evening," he finished, hoping he wasn't being two-faced. "Good-bye."

"Great!" she responded. "Good-bye, now! I'm so excited!"

Zack hung up, feeling like a heel and went back to the family room.

"So, what was that secret conversation all about?" Danny asked.

"Well, buddy, I'll tell you, but first I need to remind you both that it is not good manners to ask someone who is calling, especially when they're on the phone. The less closely you know a person, the ruder it is."

CHAPTER XXXIII

FRIDAY, APRIL 8

By the time Friday evening rolled around, Zack was wondering if Danny hadn't been the one who was right. Never had he dreaded going on a date more in his life. He told himself that it was because he was so out of practice, but he knew it was partially that he simply felt uncomfortable in Alexandra's presence. He also recognized that he was fearful of being unable to kindly and adequately communicate to her that he did not want a relationship with her. He'd purchased some new boots to wear and donned jeans and a sport jacket he intended to wear with an unbuttoned shirt collar. Danny had watched his preparations, asking why he was dressing up for the occasion when he didn't need to impress Alexandra.

"It's a matter of being respectful of the lady when you go on a date with her to look decent and appropriate," Zack had said. "In a way it is also a way of respecting yourself to make certain that you look right." Danny hadn't looked convinced, but had said no more.

Zack pulled up the long driveway to a large two-story house at the address Alexandra had given him. He wondered if she lived with her parents. He rang the doorbell and was quickly greeted by his effusive consort.

"Good evening, Big Boy," she greeted. "Man, aren't you right on time? How do you like my house?"

"It's a lovely home," Zack complimented, looking about and, seeing no sign of any other residents, asking, "Do you live here all by yourself?"

"Yes, I've only been here a couple years. You know I divorced not too long ago and I didn't want to stay in the house where we'd lived, so I put it on the market planning to move into an apartment, but this house came available at what I thought was a great price, so I purchased it instead, somewhat as an investment. It's bigger than I need, but I'm enjoying it. Have a seat here; I'll run upstairs and get my jacket. My, you certainly look nice! You look all-Texan with those boots and jeans. Maybe you need a cowboy hat."

"I tried," Zack smiled, "but I decided to pass on that one. You look very nice yourself," he said graciously, even though he inwardly cringed at the livid red of her lipstick, the plunging neckline of her black dress, and the black polish on her nails. He took a seat in the proffered chair, waiting about twenty minutes and wondering what she could possibly be doing to take so long. Nothing was said as she arrived, and he opened the door to usher her out into the misty evening.

"This wet weather will make a mess of my hair!" she exclaimed as they settled into the car. "Men are so lucky they don't have to worry about these things! What did you do all day to stay busy?"

Zack went over the activities of his day, they discussed the emotional responses of each of his family members to Elaine's death, he reviewed for her the events of his life briefly, and she discussed her marriages, the people involved in her family's real estate business, and more information about her parents than he felt comfortable with. On arriving at the winery, they entered and were seated indoors as it was becoming chillier. The place was crowded, but the noise level was entirely suitable for conversation. After they'd ordered and were waiting on their food, Zack decided that he would wait until the drive home to cover the most essential portion of his mission.

"What kind of music do you like?" Alexandra asked.

"I guess I rather prefer classical," he admitted. "It always seemed when I was younger that I couldn't hear well enough to pick up the lyrics on a lot of the popular songs, so I didn't listen to pop much. I enjoyed high school choir and classical choral music, and I used to have a nice collection of old LP records with that on it. Recently when I was up in St. Joe, I went to hear a symphony orchestra; I enjoyed it immensely and kicked myself for not making that a bigger part of my life and the children's as well. What do you like?"

"Well, not those kinds of things. I like rock and some country, but I'll do easy listening for background music if I need to concentrate. The fellow that sings here live has a wide selection of things to sing."

The conversation drifted on, and Zack felt he was spending his time doing nothing. He enjoyed the food and the singing while doing his best to be animated in conversation without acting a fool. At one point, Alexandra suggested he might want to try just a little bit of her wine. Her comment started a low burn of anger in him that he did his best to tamp down. He pasted a slight smile on his face for a time. Sensing his reticence and interpreting it as grief, Alexandra suggested they go on home. Zack agreed, attempting not to seem overjoyed. For most of the miles, they road quietly until Zack started to speak. "I need to talk about something serious," he started out. "I appreciate your effort to be friends with me and to suggest this outing to further our friendship. To be open and honest, I suspect you partially did it at Elaine's request, but I don't know that. However, I do know that Elaine made me promise to go on a date with you, so I've fulfilled that promise. I value you being a friend to me partially because I don't have very many and partially because I believe that you truly cared for Elaine and were concerned about her. At this juncture, though, I don't believe I'm attracted to any lady; probably it is too soon after Elaine's death."

"Am I interpreting your comments to mean that you're not interested in going out with me anymore?" Alexandra asked.

"That's pretty much right," Zack agreed. "At present I don't see myself as having the time or the energy to do any dating. For the next couple years, I'm going to focus on completing my education and reestablishing a strong relationship with the children. In a way I need to prove to myself that I can be the type of person that can be a responsible husband, not the kind that takes the easy way out of everything like I used to. I do blame myself partially for the mess that Elaine was in. I know I need to forgive myself for that and that it was her choices as well that contributed to her problems; I'm dealing with that."

"With time you may change your mind about me," Alexandra said slowly. "I'll admit that I'm not ready to spend the rest of my life by myself, so if you do change your mind it should likely be sooner than later. Nevertheless, I hope you realize that with your history of alcoholism, you're a risk to a relationship. I decided I'd take that risk, so now I feel like I've been slapped in the face because I thought I'd give you a chance."

"I knew this would be a difficult conversation," Zack responded, "but I felt it needed to be dealt with given my promise to Elaine. I think you are a beautiful and capable lady; I simply don't believe I'm able to spend time with you."

"Well, you were right," Alexandra simpered. "Elaine did suggest to me that we get together. I hope things go well for you, but right now I'm feeling peeved that the evening's been such a bust. With a little time I may get over that, and I'm not closing the door in your face."

"Thanks," Zack said as he braked the car to stop in her front drive. "You've been very understanding of my position, and I appreciate that. I'll walk you to the front door."

"Please don't," she said. "I think that would be awkward. I'll go by myself."

Zack sat in the car and waited until she'd gone inside, closed the door, and turned off the front porch light before he drove on home to a quiet house. He let himself in heading back to his dark bedroom.

"How did it go, Dad?" Danny asked from the bedroom gloom.

"I thought you'd be asleep, buddy," Zack chuckled.

"No, Sissy said I needed to stay awake and find out if you were OK. I told her you'd be fine, but she was afraid maybe you'd be drinking and she would want to know if that were the case."

Zack reached over and hugged his son in the dark, saying, "I'm so very sorry you both need to be worrying about that, but I don't blame you for it. There was alcohol there where I was but I didn't drink any, and actually I didn't want any. Alexandra asked me to try a little and it made me mad. I tried not to act like it but I think she sensed it, so we left soon after that."

"Do you like her better now that you've had a date with her?"

"No."

"Good, then can I talk about your going on a date with anybody else yet because it has not been two weeks?"

"You're a monkey! Well, since I've already gone on a date and we've already talked some about that, it is likely only fair that you could say your piece on the subject. Why do you want to talk about it?"

"I know someone I think you ought to consider."

"You do? Who is that?" Zack asked, surprised.

"It is Esther, Belle Jonas's daughter. She's super nice, she likes Sissy and me, and she needs a husband."

"You wear me out!" Zack responded, rolling his eyes in the dark. "She probably thinks of me as that rascally drunk who neglected his children. I must admit she is a pretty lady, though. I can see why you and Sissy like her. She and her mom were extremely kind to me when I was back in St. Joe."

"They're coming to see us."

"What? When?" Zack asked incredulously.

"Next weekend. Belle called Grandpa tonight and he told us they're coming. They're going down to Houston to visit her sister and are going to stop here to see us on their way. Don't you think that will be super nice?"

"Yes, it will, but I don't want you to say anything about this to anyone—that is about Esther and me."

"Sissy and I have already talked it over, and we agree about it."

Zack sighed, "OK, then, no one else. I think we need to get to sleep," he finished as he adjusted his pillow.

"I do, too," Danny agreed sleepily as he turned to the wall. "I had trouble staying awake waiting for you to get home."

Zack lay in his bed suddenly wide awake. He reviewed the events of the day and the evening, he thought of his conversation moments ago with his son, and he considered his conversations with Esther when he'd been in St. Joe. Somehow the last thoughts left pleasant feelings, and he dropped off to sleep to dream of playing the cello proficiently at a symphony concert with his proud children sitting in the audience.

In a motel on the outskirts of Joplin, Missouri, Belle and Esther were settling into their beds sharing the same room after the first day of the beginning of their two-week vacation. They'd driven down from St. Joe that early morning, spending the later hours of the afternoon visiting the Precious Moments chapel and gift shop. They'd had a leisurely meal at a restaurant, and finished the day in their room reading and watching TV.

"What a lovely time we've had today," Belle commented. "I'm so glad you were able to schedule time off work for this trip together. Going places like this is so much more fun if you have someone to do it with. I do wish it had been a little warmer today and a little less rainy, but all in all it was great."

"Mom, I'm glad we can have this time together too," Esther responded. "It's nice to be able to plan to go all these places we've placed on our schedule rather than to tell ourselves we're going to go there some day. I bet it's been ten years since we were in Branson; I think the bed-and-breakfast you've scheduled there sounds like so much fun right on the river. The weather forecast is promising warmer weather so I'm imagining myself sitting out there on the deck watching the birds and boats with my book in hand and my feet propped up on a stool. This whole trip is such a change from my work schedule that even if we were to do none of the Branson shows, I'd be happy. How did Mr. Taylor respond when you contacted him about us stopping in to see Danny and Sissy?"

"Oh, I'm sorry I haven't already told you. You should have asked earlier. His response was extremely positive. In fact, after I told him we hoped to stop in he called back inviting us to spend the night with them. You remember they're all staying with the children's mother's parents, so after he told them we were visiting, they had asked him to call back to invite us to spend the night. Apparently they have a large home, and there's room for us to visit. He seemed to think that Zack and the children were doing as well as could be expected after the funeral. I went ahead and agreed for us to spend the night; I guess I perhaps should have asked how you felt about it before I accepted, but you were in the filling station when I talked. When you came back we had those cinnamon rolls, and I forgot to tell you."

"That's certainly OK, Mom. It'll be fun to see those livewire children. You didn't happen to ask how Zack was doing staying away from alcohol?"

"No, but Jonathan seemed so positive and delighted we could be coming I'm suspecting all is well on that front. He did say Zack was going to be auditing classes at a university nearby to keep himself busy now that he wasn't caring for Elaine."

"So what night are we staying there?"

"Well, actually the invitation was for one or more nights, as many as we were able to spend. I told them Friday a week from tonight and said I'd call back with any change in plans or to confirm our date again. To an extent, it will depend on how well this visit with Janie goes."

"Are you expecting Aunt Janie to want us to be there less time?"

"No, the problem would not be with her; it would be with her new husband, Patrick. We don't know him very well, and even though Janie has been begging us to make this visit, I haven't heard anything from him. I may just be borrowing trouble saying something like this, but I'm wondering how he feels about our coming. Please don't interpret these comments of mine to be negative about him because I know Janie's a lot happier now than she'd been after Sam passed away."

"Well, maybe we could spend a couple nights in Longview, then," Esther said.

"Honestly, child, are you more interested in seeing Danny and Sissy, or is it Zack you want to see?"

Esther looked at her mother, wishing she weren't feeling a slight blush rise to her face. "You're too intuitive for my own good!" she exclaimed. "To be honest, I've thought about him and have come up with this conclusion: I'll be friendly, but I would want to see him have at least a couple track years of sobriety before I consider any significant relationship with him. I couldn't run the risk. He seemed so sincere when we spent the time with him, but I've seen too many alcoholics that can't stay on the wagon."

"I couldn't agree with you more!" Belle agreed. "Being single has its heartaches, but marriage to the wrong person is much worse. I will agree to pray with you about this, and we can both pray for Zack."

"I think this is very likely a moot conversation, Mom. He hasn't expressed the slightest interest in me."

"I agree," Belle laughed, "but thinking back at how dedicated Danny was to get you married off, I strongly suspect he'll bring the subject forward even if his dad hasn't given it a thought."

CHAPTER XXXIV

FRIDAY, APRIL 15

It was a beautiful spring morning with lovely green lawns and banks of fuchsia and white azaleas in full bloom along Zack and the children's drive to school. Danny and Sissy had awakened excited about the coming of Esther and Belle knowing they'd be arriving shortly after they returned home from school.

"Daddy, do you think I should invite Esther to sleep in the extra bed up in my room like Alice did, or do you think they should sleep together in the guest room?" Sissy asked.

"After they arrive, you may ask her that," Zack responded. "I think either way would be fine."

"Dad, are they going to stay one night or more?" Danny asked.

"I'm not certain," Zack answered. "Originally they'd said only one night, but that won't make a very long visit, especially if they leave early in the morning tomorrow. I do know that Esther doesn't have to go back to work until the evening shift on Tuesday, so I would think they could stay a day or two and get home in plenty of time. They may wish to see how smoothly the visit goes before they make a commitment. There's a symphonic band concert at the Belcher Center on the LeTourneau University campus they might like to attend tomorrow night. Let's just wait and see and invite them."

"Maybe we could get Esther to cook some chicken picatta for us while she's here," Danny suggested.

"You're going to put her to work, aren't you?" Zack laughed.

"It's probably not polite to ask people to do things when they're guests," Sissy objected.

"It depends on the person," Zack explained. "Some people as guests very much want to enter the spirit of celebrating the time together, and if they know how to do something to make the time more enjoyable, they're all for it."

"I think Esther's that kind of person," Danny stated. "Besides, Dad, you haven't had her chicken picatta, and I think you just must taste it. It's the best thing I think I've ever eaten!"

"Well, here we are at school. We'll take all these things into consideration one at a time," Zack instructed, laughing. "Have a fun day now, and don't forget to absorb some knowledge."

The children gave him good-bye kisses and sedately walked together up the way to the school door, deep in mutual conversation. Zack watched them move along in their uniforms feeling so proud of them, and a wave of sorrow washed over him as he wished Elaine could see them and enjoy their bright, cooperative personalities. He drove silently on down to the university to attend the Friday classes and labs, feeling grateful that his thoughts could be occupied with something other than his loss.

Esther and Bell arose early the next morning and went quietly about their packing and morning toilets. Belle's sister, Janie, who they were visiting was an invalid who lived in a west side apartment with her husband. Janie had chronic obstructive pulmonary disease and was oxygen-dependent but continued to smoke—although she fortunately made it a practice to avoid smoking in the room with her oxygen. The apartment had a small balcony where she would step out to get her nicotine fix. Belle and her daughter spoke in low whispers, attempting not to disturb their host and hostess.

"Mom, how do you feel Aunt Janie's health is doing in relationship to last year when we visited?" Esther asked.

"I don't see much difference," Belle responded. "What do you think? You're the nurse and likely have more insight into changes than I do."

"I agree; to me she seems about the same. I certainly wish she would stop her smoking, though. Even though she smokes outdoors, this apartment fairly reeks of the odor. I think it's mostly because of her clothes. Of course, Ben's cigars don't help much either. It's sad to see her so confined; she's only a couple years older than you, but the difference may well seem like fifteen years when you consider her disability. How old was she when she started smoking?" Esther finished with a question.

"I'm not certain; I did know she snuck around with an occasional cigarette when she was in high school. She was in Columbia, Missouri, in college and only came home occasionally; I don't recall any smoking during those times. She married soon after college, and they moved down here to Houston, so I know she was smoking heavily the first time she and Richard came home; my mother threw a fit about it and rather ruined that visit. I've taken a pretty cautious stance on the issue since then, and we've always had a great relationship. She's such a dear and caring person otherwise; the fact that she was unable to have children was one of her major heartbreaks in life."

"I have real difficulty understanding the lure of cigarettes," Esther responded. "I've probably cared for too many people gasping for air in their attempt to stay alive. Changing the subject, are you OK with our plans to go see San Jacinto before going on up to Longview?"

"Certainly; I feel I'm pretty sketchy on Texas history, so I think this would be a good chance to gain some knowledge about it. Everyone is aware of the Alamo, but I understand that for Texas independence, the battle fought here at San Jacinto was decisive. I think it would be fun to be going to this with Danny; he's so enthusiastic about everything."

Esther laughed, replying, "He is that! Sissy lets almost nothing get by her too. She's less expressive than he is, but her mental cogs are always turning. She's developed more filter in the things she says than he has, but she's amazingly sharp. We'll need to pay attention today to what we see so we can tell them all about it this evening."

The two ladies quietly packed their suitcases, stripped the sheets off the bed, remaking it with clean sheets, put the soiled sheets in the washing machine, turned it on, and slipped out the door. It had rained during the night but the pavements were drying, and the mostly blue sky was bright with a few fluffy clouds.

"What a gorgeous day to be sightseeing!" Esther exclaimed as they were getting into the car. "I always think of Houston as being so hot, but you can have some pretty wonderful days this time of the year."

"I agree; the weather is beautiful," Belle responded, getting behind the wheel, "but I'm not particularly fond of all this green pollen on the cars."

"I can put up with that to have these lovely azaleas," Esther said, nodding to a gorgeous yard they were passing. "You need to get on Interstate 45 for a little way before we turn east to go to the monument."

The time at the monument passed swiftly; soon it was noon, and the ladies started on their journey up to Longview. They made good time, pulling into the Dentons' drive at four that afternoon. Sally and Thelma met them at the front door, warmly greeting them inviting them in and offering iced tea and cookies. The four sat talking at the dinette table with Henry and Jonathan soon joining them, having finished their backyard gardening project for the day.

"Zack and the children will be arriving soon," Thelma mentioned. "They generally get here about four-twenty. Danny and Sissy are extremely delighted that you're making the effort to come and visit them. The two of you are some of their favorite people."

"Well, the feeling's mutual," Belle replied. "I do not think ever in my life I've met two children that immediately caught my attention in such a riveting fashion. After the first fifteen minutes with them, they had burrowed a place in my heart."

"You certainly acted upon your response in an effective way," Sally contributed. "None of us can thank you enough for the part you played in assisting them to contact us. After hearing the story, I just feel that God was guiding you to them at the library and then again for them to have attended the same small church with you on that last Sunday they were alone."

"We also do appreciate your taking Zack under your wings when he was back in St. Joseph," Jonathan added.

"We were glad to do it," Belle said. "I have to admit I was curious to see how such sharp children could be raised by an alcoholic father. Once we met Zack, it wasn't difficult to understand. While there had obviously been a marvelous turnaround in his demeanor in the time between our meeting the children and his visit back to St. Joe, you could understand how the children were so alert."

"Zack was surprisingly open with us about his previous problems and his current problems when he was there," Esther added. "We've been hoping Elaine's death won't influence him to drop his resolve to avoid alcohol."

"He's being open with us as well," Thelma replied. "Most of the time it doesn't seem like much of a temptation, but he lets us know if it is and stays busy. Did you know he's already auditing classes at the university in preparation for getting enrolled full time for this summer session? Part of this is his intentional staying busy, but his pattern in the past was that if there was a task to be done, he wanted to be getting it done."

"I hear car doors closing; they're here," Sally announced as the children noisily slammed the gate and came running up the back walk entering the dinette through the patio door.

"Hello, everybody! Hello, Mrs. Belle and Esther!" Danny exclaimed, going first to Belle and giving her a hug.

"Hi, Esther," Sissy said with shining eyes, "We've so very much wanted to see you again." She started to give Esther a handshake but thought better of it and gave a warm hug instead, which was cut short by Danny's boisterous hug around the two of them.

Zack stood in the open door grinning at the warm reception his children were giving the ladies. "There appears to be no question as to us wanting to have you visit," he said. "It's really great you would stop in to see us. How did your drive up from Houston go?"

"We had a safe and uneventful trip today," Esther reported. "After we left my aunt's home this morning, we spent some time over at the San Jacinto monument; the day was lovely, and we enjoyed it."

"You went to San Jacinto?" Danny said. "I was just telling Dad a few days ago that I wanted to go there. What was it like?"

"It was more than we expected," Belle answered. "We knew you would probably be interested, so we picked up a book about it for the two of you and took some pictures for you to see."

"Let's do this," Sally interrupted. "We stopped these ladies as soon as they walked into the house and have been talking ever since. They haven't had a chance to refresh themselves or be shown to their room. Why don't we do that first so they've some time to freshen up before supper? Let's talk more about these other things at the meal or afterwards."

"Grammy, I'd like to invite Esther to stay in my room if she'd like to. I asked Daddy, and he said I'd need to ask her. Is that all right with you?" Sissy asked.

"Of course, darling, that is fine. The choice will be hers."

Sissy turned to Esther with a pleading look.

Esther laughed and said, "That sounds like an adventure with just the two of us girls. I'll go out and get my suitcase, and you can show me the way to your room."

"Let me help you with the luggage," Zack offered. "Danny, you can come help."

"Yes, Dad," Danny said excitedly. "May I carry Miss Belle's case?"

"Why yes, young man, thank you so much," Belle replied.

"Bring her things to this downstairs guest room," Sally directed. "Belle, let me show you the room.

"Again, we're so glad you've come. Do make yourselves comfortable; we're hoping you'll spend more than one night with us. The boys will be right in with your things. We'll plan to have supper at six, so there's a little time if you feel you need a nap."

"Oh, what a nice cozy room!" Belle exclaimed as Sally directed her into the guest room. "Thank you, thank you. I'm letting Esther decide on the length of our visit; she's the one that needs to be back at work. You couldn't be making us feel more welcome, though."

"I know the children will have many things they'll want to show you," Sally said, smiling. "Therefore, there's very little I need to say. They'll be explaining the full nine yards."

Esther was not getting the same encouragement to rest that her mother was. Sissy was carefully ushering her up the stairs, carrying her small overnight bag as Zack followed with a larger suitcase. Danny, who was wheeling Belle's case into the guest room, was still downstairs. "When we first came, Danny shared this room with me," Sissy explained as they walked down the hall. "Now I have it to myself except when he comes up to visit and play. See how big it is? There's plenty of room for the two of us, and we have a bathroom that we don't have to share with anyone else. Dad, please put her suitcase up here on this counter."

Esther looked around the spacious room, contrasting it to the apartment she'd helped Zack clean. "It is nice and big," she agreed. "No wonder you wanted me to see it and to share it with you. The hall we came down is long; do you worry about getting lonesome here?"

"Not at all," Sissy replied decisively. "Since we've been here, both sets of grandparents are just down the hall, and Dad's down at the other end of the house. I've felt very safe here except for the night that the cartel men came and Dad shot one. We all went down to his room that night and the next."

"Oh, yes!" Esther exclaimed, "Your grandfather told my mother about that happening. I bet that was extremely frightening. Do you worry they'll come back?"

"The police don't think so since all those fellows involved were apprehended, but we're trying to be vigilant nevertheless," Zack said, entering the conversation. "Unless you ladies need me, I'm going to go change clothes and check the air in the car's tires. One of the sensors indicated low pressure. Sissy, please do let Esther get some rest if she needs it," he finished, walking back down the hall.

"Are you tired?" Sissy asked. "I'm so glad you're here. I have a lot of things I thought about that I want to tell you; I just hope that I can remember them all."

"Well, if you forget some, you could always write a letter to me telling them," Esther chuckled.

"Oh! That sounds like fun. Could I get your address? Wait, I already have it. Your mother gave us these cute little billfolds when we were in St. Joe and put her address and phone number in them for us. Is this it?" she asked, holding up the card she'd removed from the billfold.

"Sure thing," Esther replied, examining the card. "We could be pen pals and write letters regularly."

"My! Yes!" Sissy enthused. "I almost never get letters. Would you like to see some of my recent homework?"

"Certainly," Esther agreed as the two of them took seats in front of Sissy's built-in desk, with Sissy pulling a large stack of papers out of a lower drawer.

"This is the math," Sissy said, holding up the first clump of papers. "I like to make my arithmetic papers neat; it makes it more fun."

Esther leafed through the completed assignments and tests, saying, "Gal, these are lovely; you do make them tidy. I'm impressed with all these one hundreds too! Does Danny do well in math too?"

"Yes, he actually probably does better than I do. He seems to understand math just by looking at it; I must think and try, but his papers are not as neat as mine by a long shot. Here are my art pictures, which I think are fun to do too. Did you like to draw?"

"I didn't mind it, but it wasn't my forte." Esther replied. "These are beautiful; they're certainly better than what I produced at your age. What does your dad think about them?"

"He likes them; he's saved a couple he likes the best and keeps them on his desk down in his room. Here's the history paper I wrote on the treatment of slaves in the South before the Civil War. That was really gruesome! Some of them were treated OK, but some of them were treated worse than we would treat animals now. I can't imagine how horrible it would have been to be a slave even if I were treated well."

"That's true," Esther agreed, reading the complimentary note Sissy's teacher had written on the first page. "Did all your classmates write on this same subject?"

"No, the assignment was just something about the Civil War. Dad helped me find some of the material; he was very pleased with the paper, and all the grandparents liked it too. They're all very interested in everything we do. I hope they're not spoiling us. Do you think they are? We went from having no one to having all these people who love us so much. I don't want to become too selfish so that I don't care about others."

Esther looked at the kind, intense child in front of her, smiled, and said, "A lot of love never hurt anyone. By the fact that you concerned about not becoming spoiled likely means that you're in little danger. One thing you need to remember, though: all your grandparents loved you and prayed for you even before they could have much contact with you. I suppose, your dad loved you too but was falling down on the job with his drinking."

"Yes, we knew that, but he was so strict and at times unkind that we were afraid of him. He's so different now since he came back. He's like the dad we knew when he was at home when we were little before Mommy went away. We have all kinds of fun with him now, and he seems interested in everything we do. He makes certain we get our work done, but he's not mean doing it. I do think a lot of it was the beer; he smelled like beer all the time except in the morning, and then he was complaining about a headache and had bad breath."

Esther laughed, "I'm glad he's better. You do realize that Jesus Christ changes people, don't you? He may not remove your bad breath, but he does give us the strength to be kind. I have bad breath often in the mornings too. I just try to get my teeth brushed as soon as I get up in the morning so as not to offend anyone."

"Here are my spelling tests," Sissy said, holding up another pack of papers neatly clipped together and handing the lot to Esther. "We're going to have a spelling bee at the school next week, and I'm looking forward to it. I think I'll do well, but we're doing it with the fourth graders, which includes Danny. He's good, and I don't want the my little brother to show me up. I have to tell myself to be proud of him because he's my brother, but sometimes I like to win!"

"That's understandable," Esther smiled. "I never had a brother or sister, so I haven't dealt with the same feelings."

"Dad has a brother, our uncle Evan. He's very nice; I think you'd like him. He looks a lot like Daddy; his hair is just blond. Dad says that when they were little, he and Evan competed in school even though Evan was a year younger, so Dad understands. Evan's getting married in San Antonio to a lady named Alice in six weeks. I think the wedding is going to be so exciting; Dad's going to be the best man, and Danny and I are going to be junior bridesmaid and junior bridegroom. Boy, I do wish you could be there too!"

"So Evan was the one down in Belize who helped your dad?"

"Yes, Uncle Evan was working down there at the time; that's where he met Alice, his fiancée. She's very pleasant too. She's been here a couple times, so we've been able to meet her. In fact, she and her parents were here for the funeral, and Alice stayed up here with me like you're doing. We had the best time; I know you'd like her too."

"Don't you think that it was extremely fortunate that your uncle was down in Belize when your dad got out of the factory prison and that they were able to get out of the country?" Esther asked.

"Grammy Sally says it had to have been the hand of God; I think she's right! Danny worries about forgiving the cartel men who shot at Dad and the ones coming here. I worry about whether or not God wants us to use guns to shoot at people. What do you think?"

"I believe to use a gun to protect yourself is appropriate."

"Grammy Sally says Jesus said in the Bible that if you live by the sword you will die by the sword. I think she believes sword and guns to be pretty much the same thing. Grandpa Jonathan says the Bible says, 'We are to be as wise as serpents and as harmless as doves.' He also mentioned that

Jesus told the disciples to have swords right after the last supper, but then when Peter used his to cut off the man's ear, Jesus put it back on. I think it is confusing. What do you think?"

"I agree that it is confusing, and it is understandable that good Christian people come to differing conclusions on the same issue. How did you feel about your dad having a gun and using it when the cartel men were breaking into this house?"

"I was very, very glad he had it!"

"Yes, I would think so. Our experiences like that color our thinking. From now on you'll have a hard time thinking that to own and use a gun is wrong," Esther responded.

"You haven't rested any," Sissy observed. "I haven't let you. Do you need to rest, or do you want me to take you on a tour of the house and the yard?"

"I'm not sleepy at all," Ester replied. "I'd be glad to see it; let me run a comb through my hair and I'll be ready."

"OK, I'll comb mine too. I do think it will be good to go now rather than after dinner, because then it might be getting dark. Let's go outside first."

Shortly the two were on the back patio with Sissy pointing out the pool, the terraced azalea beds, the freshly planted garden, and the garage and covered two-car carport where Zack with Danny's assistance was finishing airing up his tire.

"So what are you ladies up to?" Zack asked, grinning.

"She's giving me the grand tour," Esther smiled.

"May I go with them?" Danny asked.

"Sure, buddy, we're through here anyway; let's go get cleaned up and you can join them. Let's all go to the other end of the house and you ladies can start with our bedrooms. We can walk through the backyard so as not to spoil the tour through the rest of the house; we'll go in through the door in the back hall," Zack directed.

The house was long, and as they passed the back patio, Esther remarked, "This is a big house. Before you came, did the Dentons live here all by themselves?"

"They did!" Danny answered. "They say they're glad we all came so they're not knocking around here all alone. Grandma Thelma makes certain we all do our part to keep things clean and the work done so we don't wear them out. Pop Pop and Grammy Sally say they don't know now what they'll do if we all leave. I don't think it will be very soon, though, with Dad going to school."

The four of them entered the back door, and Danny showed Esther the bedroom he shared with his father. "See," he said, "the bed is made. We make it every day. Dad says that if the bedroom is neat and tidy, you feel better about yourself. Dad studies at the desk sometimes when we're not here, but more often we study together around the table in the family room. I'm thinking maybe I should move into this bedroom next door so that if he needs to study at night after I've gone to bed, he can keep the lights on," he finished, looking at his father to see his response to this announcement.

"I think we'll need to talk with your grandparents about that," Zack said seriously, "it seems reasonable to me, though. However, I haven't minded you being in there with me."

"Esther, I want you to see these cute arches in this big back bathroom," Sissy stated, resuming the tour. "See, these two bedrooms share this bath. This other bedroom was where Mommy was when she was so sick; it makes me feel sad when I'm here."

"I don't think I feel sad; I think I feel closer to her when I'm here," Danny disagreed.

"I believe either response is understandable," Esther placated. "It's a lovely room with a view of the front yard and this flower bed," she continued as she peered out of the window.

"This is the room where we all came when the cartel men were breaking in," Danny said. "Dad was out in this little hall when he shot the man. We were all very scared!"

"I can imagine!" Esther sympathized. "Where was the man?"

"He was in the family room," Sissy informed.

"You girls go on ahead while Danny and I wash up," Zack said. "Danny will join you again in a bit."

"We like the family room; it has a fireplace and we study here," Sissy explained as they entered.

"I like all these windows that look out on the backyard," Esther added.

"Let's go back into the kitchen where you were when we came in from school," Sissy directed. "This is where we all eat together for most meals. Both sets of grandparents like us all to be together, and we all get to talk about a bunch of very interesting things. Grandma, how soon will we be having dinner?"

Thelma looked up smiling from her task of stirring together a cake. "Sally said she'd like us to eat in about half an hour. You could help by setting the table in about fifteen minutes. Sally thought it would be nice to eat in the dining room since we have company. Do you know where things are to do that?"

"Yes, yes, that will be fun!" Sissy enthused. "Esther had such a pretty table set when we ate with them up there at their house in St. Joe. Now we can do the same. Right now I'm showing Esther around the house; would it be OK to show her your room and come back and get the table set?"

"I'm afraid your grandpa is taking a nap in our room," Thelma relied. "I'm sorry."

"I'll help you with the table," Esther offered. "How many place setting will we need?"

"Maybe we'll be able to see the room later; it's very nice," the mollified Sissy responded. "Let's see, there are normally seven of us plus two more so we'll need nine. Grandma, do you want us to put on salad plates or anything else special?"

"Yes, darling, but just bring them in here to the kitchen. We'll put the salads on the plates before we sit to eat, and that can be the first course. Do put salad forks on the table too," Thelma replied.

Sissy headed into the dining room, pulled out the log tablecloth, handing one end to Esther. "Danny's hoping to get you to fix chicken picatta while you're here. If you leave first thing in the morning, you won't be able to do that. Daddy told us about the symphony orchestra you went to in Kansas City; he was hoping we could all go to a symphonic band concert tomorrow evening. I'd like you to stay longer; do you think you could do that?"

"Let me discuss it with my mother and we'll let you know," Esther answered. "The concert sound's interesting," she finished.

Soon the table setting was finished, the food was brought to the table, and the whole household was gathered. Sally directed the seating arrangements for the family and guests, placing Jonathan and Zack next to Henry at the head of the table, placing Belle and Thelma at her right and left, and leaving the children and Esther to be seated in the center seats. The two children took their seats between the Taylor parents, leaving Esther to sit between her mother and Zack across the table from the children. Zack watched Sissy wink at Danny, wondering how much the two had manipulated to accomplish the seating arrangement. Dr. Denton said grace and the food was passed with the requisite expressions of appreciation and anticipation.

"This roast is Grandma Thelma's crockpot recipe," Sissy announced. "Last time she made, it she showed me how. She uses a liner to make the pot easier to clean. I especially like the celery and carrots cooked with the meat!"

"It's delicious!" Belle agreed, taking her first bite. "You'll learn to be a great cook living with these ladies."

"She'll have to learn a big bunch to be a better cook than Esther!" exclaimed Danny. "All of us should be able to eat some of her chicken picatta!"

"It must be very remarkable as much as you've mentioned it," Sally laughed.

"It is!" Danny continued. "I'm wanting to have her stay until tomorrow and make some for us."

Ether looked at her mother smiling, saying, "I'm game for that if you are. How about it?"

"Oh, please do feel welcome," Sally offered. "If you stay just this one night, your visit will seem too short."

"There's a symphonic band concert tomorrow night we thought you might enjoy too," Zack contributed. "You could then stay tomorrow night at least."

"Could you go to church with us Sunday morning?" Sissy asked.

"We were not planning to make the full trip in one day," Belle commented as she thought. "If we were to leave midday Sunday and traveled six or seven hours, we could make it in good time to St. Joseph on Monday."

"Oh, goody!" Sissy exclaimed. "What else can we plan to do tomorrow?"

"We do not need to be entertained," Belle said. "A quiet day here with friends will be fine."

"The weather is to be warmer again tomorrow; maybe we can go swimming," Danny suggested. "What do you think, Pop Pop?"

"I think it's fine if they're interested," Henry answered.

"We didn't pack swimming outfits," Belle demurred.

"We both need new swimwear, so I could buy some for us in the morning if the weather permits," Esther suggested.

"May I go with you?" Sissy asked.

"Why, certainly," Esther agreed, "maybe all of us ladies could go on a little shopping trip."

"We'd want to include Sally for sure," Thelma added. "She's the one who knows where to go to get the most for your money in this town."

"While you ladies are in the stores, we fellows could all work together to get Henry's yard all shipshape," Jonathan suggested. "Danny, I need to show you the little carrots and radishes that are already coming up. Zack, will you be able to help us or do you have homework?"

"I have several hours of it to do, but I need to help too. I'll work with you an hour or two and then get started on the homework."

"How do you feel the class auditing is going?" Esther asked. "Is it so difficult you're lost, or is it coming together?"

"I'm somewhat surprised about what's easier and what's harder," Zack answered. "Interestingly, the chemistry and chemistry labs are the easiest. Some of the definitions there have changed a bit, but I could pick it up quite rapidly. My advanced algebra is also going well, but I'm feeling a real problem with the physics. I'm not certain if the big challenges are related to my natural aptitude in some areas, the quality of the learning that I did before, or the quality of the teaching that I'm getting now. I'm certainly finding the teachers at LeTourneau to be extremely helpful as I face my difficulties. They're very willing to meet me after class or at scheduled times to review something I don't understand."

"Are these courses you're taking ones you've already had or ones you may take later?" Belle asked.

"Well, your question somewhat applies to the issue of why the physics is so difficult," Zack grinned. "I'd already taken the algebra and chemistry in college. I'd taken honors physics in high school and tested out of the physics course at Normal, but this is now on a college level. I'm hoping with this review I will be able to test out again, but we'll see. Although it is all a lot of work, I'm enjoying it all a lot. The students at Letourneau are for the most part graciously accepting of me, and my chemistry lab partners are so appreciative of my help that it is almost embarrassing. None of the auditing is required, but I thought that since I'd been out of the educational system so long, I'd use this as a time to see how adept I could be moving back into the stream and as a leg up to get restarted in the areas I'm wanting to study. I'm also glad right now that it's keeping me busy."

"So what degree are you working toward?" Esther asked.

"When I was at Normal, I started on a mechanical engineering degree but then thought I'd do civil engineering. However, now I believe I'm going to work on electrical engineering, focusing on electronics. They have a good program in that at LeTourneau."

"He thinks he'll be able to finish in two years," Danny added. "Pop Pop says that he mustn't overdo his schedule and burn himself out."

Henry laughingly looked at his grandson, saying, "Not much gets past you, does it? We just don't want him feeling that he's under the gun to be finished already."

"I think we've talked enough about me; I would like to change the subject," Zack smiled. "How about us all playing a game after dinner and after the dishes are done?"

"Oh, that would be fun!" Sissy exclaimed. "We could play Scrabble, but probably Grandpa would win; it's a lot of fun, though."

"This is a large number of people to play Scrabble," Sally responded. "When you have this number, the game becomes nearly impossible unless you play as teams because technically only four can play at a time. I'd suggest we play charades; it's a game that lends itself to a large group."

"Oh, boy, that will be fun!" Danny exclaimed. "I've read about how people play that, but I've never played it. I know what I want to be!"

"We need to choose a category for all of us before we decide," Sissy corrected.

"Oh, my idea will fit into almost any category," Danny continued undeterred.

The easy conversation flowed on to other topics, and Zack recognized how smoothly Esther and Belle fit into the group. Belle was vivacious but did not dominate the conversation, and Esther's contributions were kind and unfailingly considerate. It was interesting to see how quickly the two children were accepting her comments as important, hanging on to her every word. He noted her attractive appearance but unassuming demeanor, wondering if Danny's suggestion might have a good bit of validity. He put the thought on a back burner, however, as he considered the next two years of school. *I need to admit that I have an attraction here,* he thought, *but for now there's no acting on it. I know I'm heading down the right path, but also know I'm in a trial period. I need to prove to myself and everyone else that I'm on this track to stay.*

Dear reader... look for the continuation of the events in Zack Taylor and his family's life in the sequel entitled 'Zack on Track'. The following first chapter gives an inkling of what is in store.

Sincerely,
Ken Marshall

Chapter One of Zack on Track (sequel to Back on Track)

On an early cool morning in late April Zack sat at the kitchen table in his parent's home drinking coffee and talking with his mother. He'd been out jogging and had stopped in, as was his custom, to drink a cup and chat. Frequently his father joined them, but today it was just the two of them since Jonathan, his father, was in Dallas helping his brother, Evan, reroof his house. "Mom, did you talk with Dad last night?" Zack asked. "Did he say how things were going with the roofing?"

"Yes," she replied, "the weather didn't cooperate the first couple days on Monday and Tuesday, but the last couple days went well. They were able to get all the old shingles off Wednesday and all the tar paper up yesterday as well as starting with the shingles. They think they can finish it by tomorrow."

"I still doubt if Dad should be up there on that roof at his age," Zack commented.

"Well, I'm glad it's an old ranch-style house with minimal slope to the roof," Thelma, his mother, responded. "I cautioned him, but he seemed confident in his ability. I'm certain Evan will keep a close eye on him. They both were looking forward to spending the time together. I felt it was too bad that Evan had to use his vacation time to shingle the roof, but he told me that he had to use the vacation time up or he'd lose it and that he couldn't leave town anyhow because of Alice's advanced pregnancy. I know this is abrupt, but I wish to change the subject before you have to leave. I want to say a couple things with just the two of us here. How soon do you need to go?"

"I need to get on to the house in about twenty minutes," Zack replied. "I trust I haven't done something troublesome that we need to talk about."

"No, nothing like that. First, I want to say once again how delighted I am with what you've been able to accomplish over the past couple years; I know it can't have been easy, but to me it seems you've made it appear easy. Here you are a few weeks away from graduating! Your grades have been enviable, and the children are making steady progress. You are an encouragement to Jonathan and me, and I know you're a blessing to your in-laws as well. Sally was telling me yesterday that Henry's trying not to worry about how he'll handle the household tasks should you find a job elsewhere. The second thing, which may seem a little invasive, is that I'm wondering if you're still having any contact with Esther Jonas. Part of the reason that I'm asking is because your son was asking me a couple days ago if we could invite Belle and Esther down here for your graduation. I would be glad to do that if you'd feel comfortable with it."

With a blushing smile Zack responded, "Mom, you certainly have a knack for mixing complements with solutions to my consternations. I've intentionally avoided any dating or anything similar since Elaine's death, but at this point I'm thinking it may be about time." He stopped while rubbing his stubbled beard and slowly continued, "I do know that Sissy's been keeping up a steady correspondence with Esther and that Sissy eventually shares every letter with her snoopy little brother. A year and a half ago I spoke quite sternly directing Dan not to discuss Esther with me again until I brought the subject up. I told him at that time that I was not able to be starting a new relationship, and that when Esther and I had last met we'd agreed I needed time to validate a different way of life than I'd lived for the past several years. He's been very good to heed my warning. I guess he's circumventing my instructions by talking to you."

"Oh yes, I know all about those stern instructions; Dan's mentioned them several times. He was worried initially that Esther would find someone else. I'd told him we couldn't control that, but he apparently knows via

Sissy's correspondence that there's no one else in the picture. The invitation for a possible visit wouldn't need to come from you; however, even if it comes from Jonathan and me, Esther is likely to suspect it comes with your tacit approval."

"I've actually thought I shouldn't allow any romantic plans to develop until I had a job and was truly on my own and self-supporting."

"Well, you're pretty close to that now. You just told us last week that you have three job offers on the table. Didn't you say there were two in Dallas and one here in Longview as well as another offer here that you were hoping for? Are you any closer to deciding?

"No, I've been praying about it. I know to have several offers is a blessing, but I am still waiting to see if the fourth one comes through; the pay and benefits would be much better than the other local one, however, I know that's not everything. Time's running out. All four would start immediately after graduation."

"Are you able then to give me an OK on the invitation?" Thelma persisted.

"OK, Mom, with the stipulation that you caution little snoopy Dan not to be discussing any romantic overtones of the visit; I don't want any awkward talk for Esther," Zack grinned as he stood and carried his coffee cup to the sink, rinsed it, and placed it in the dishwasher. I need get on back to have breakfast with those two little yokels. Love you!" He gave his mother a hug and a quick peck on the cheek before heading out to jog the two blocks on home where he lived with his children and in-laws.

The Denton household was in full swing as he entered the front door. Sally, his mother-in-law was making breakfast in the kitchen while Henry, his father-in-law was sitting at the head of the table by the raised dinette fireplace reading the morning paper. The dishes set for the morning meal were spread in front of him. Sissy was in the living room pounding out her current lesson on the piano while Dan came rushing into the kitchen from the family room with wet hair awkwardly combed, and an exuberant smile to give his dad a hug.

"You smell clean," Zack commended. "Do you have your homework together in the backpack?"

"No, it's still on the desk in my room."

"Breakfast will be ready in five minutes," Sally informed.

"OK, we'll be right back," Zack responded grabbing the still nearby Dan up and carrying him toward the back of the house through the family room to their bedrooms.

Dan, laughing and struggling vigorously to get free, complained, "Hey, I'm too big to be hauled around! You need to treat me with respect."

"Here I am giving you a free ride and you're agitating for respect," Zack chuckled as he stood his son up by his bedroom door. "You need to be thankful for a ride like this; with you growing so fast it will not be long before I can't provide one. Gather up the homework and come right on back to the dinette for breakfast. I'll get Sissy if I can pry her off that piano bench."

Sissy had shut the French glass doors into the living room but ended a hymn she was playing with a resounding crash as Zack went in to inform her that breakfast was ready. "Hi Dad, did you have a good run?" she asked. "My piano lesson's tonight at 4:30; will you be able to take me? Grammy said she could if you can't. The teacher moved the time forward an hour tonight because her son is in a school play she doesn't want to miss it."

Zack had left the door open to the kitchen and knew Sally could hear their conversation. "Unfortunately, I have a committee meeting then and can't make it. Mom, are you certain you're OK with this?" he asked in a voice with raised volume addressing his mother-in-law.

As soon as Sissy had risen from the piano bench Zack grabbed her in a hug saying, "Your music sounded wonderful; I liked that dramatic ending. How do you think your teacher thinks you're doing?"

"I'm happy to take her," Sally responded to Zack as she brought the food around the island to the table with Sissy and Zack entering the room. "As for your second question, I know the answer. Her teacher compliments Sissy every time I speak with her; she says she's never had a student make such rapid progress."

"You need to take some of the credit, Mom," Zack remarked. "You encourage her to practice every day and help her make certain it happens"

"Thanks, Son, but she's so willing. If I remind her and she starts I almost never have to prod her to fulfil the whole practice time."

Dan had entered the room with his backpack and had placed it by the kitchen door. "I like her practice racket," he announced with a grin. "Are we Democrats or Republicans now? My Social Studies teacher says we need to ask our parents five differences between the two so I'm asking."

"Dad, why don't you field that question," Zack directed as everyone gathered to sit at the table.

"Let's pray first and then I'll talk," Henry responded. The whole group bowed their heads as he thanked God for the day, the meal, and asked for heavenly watch care for those around the table. Finishing, he said, "Let's see, Democrats think we need more government supervision in our businesses and lives and Republicans think we need less. Democrats think we need to tax more to carry out the functions of government while Republicans think taxes are too high and the taxes we have are an unnecessary weight on economic activity. Those are two differences. Does anyone else have more ideas?"

"We generally think of the Democrats being more liberal socially than the Republicans, but I don't know if we can count that since there are a group of Democrat politicians who are more conservative than some Republicans," Sally contributed as she passed the sausage gravy.

"I think it's valid," Zack said serving his plate. "There undoubtedly is a larger percentage of Republican politicians that are conservative than Democrat politicians that are conservative."

"Republicans are elephants and Democrats are donkeys!" Sissy added with a smirk. That makes four. What's the last one we need?"

"Here's something interesting," Henry replied wiping his mouth with his paper napkin. "Numerous counts have shown that there appear to be more Democrats than Republicans, but it is seen that a larger percentage of Republicans vote so elections can go either way depending on who votes. In a way that may count as two differences."

"I think that's enough," Dan laughed. I'm going to have a problem remembering all that already. Dad, what is the date of your graduation and what day of the week is it on?"

Smelling a mouse at the uncharacteristic question Zack asked, "What makes you ask?"

"Grandma asked me," Dan answered looking innocent enough as he polished off his biscuit and gravy.

"Why were discussing that with my mother?" Zack pursued.

"Well, we were talking about plans for the event," Dan hedged now with a furtive glance at Sally and an obvious expression of guilt.

"You need to be aware that I am now in know about your mechanizations, Son," Zack laughed. "Is your sister part of this too?"

"No, I've only talked to Grandma and Grammy," Dan grinned in relief seeing his father did not appear angry.

"What are you two talking about?" Sissy asked. "Is this a secret or something?"

"Your brother has a one-track mind that hasn't deviated in the past two years. You'll need to get him to reveal his plans. Right now, however, we need to be packing up and getting on to school." Zack directed. "Sissy, do you have all you need for today? Will your Grammy need to bring your music lesson books, or will you have them with you?"

"I have them in my backpack," Sissy answered. "I'm ready."

"Dan, do you have your assignments?" Zack continued.

"Yes, Dad."

"Well, then, let's get going," Zack directed.

Both Dan and Sissy hugged their grandparents goodbye before rushing to gather their things and heading for the car. Within five minutes the three were on the drive to the school.

"OK, what was that last conversation at the breakfast table about?" Sissy asked.

"Bud, now's the time to talk," Zack directed.

"Umm," Dan hedged, "I asked the grandmothers if we could invite Belle and Esther Jonas down for Dad's graduation."

"I think that's a wonderful idea!" Sissy enthused. "Why should that be a secret?"

"Because Dad told me after they visited last time that I was not to talk about Esther with him until he gave me permission. He said he needed to focus on school and not on a new marriage while he was going to school and depending on Pop Pop to help him financially to get his college degree. Actually, I haven't disobeyed because I didn't talk to Dad; I talked with the grandmothers. Dad's nearly finished with school and he's about to get a job, so I think it is time for him to deal with this."

Silence prevailed in the vehicle as both Zack and Sissy considered their response to Dan's comment.

"Somehow, I feel that my life is being controlled by my son," Zack responded with a wry chuckle.

"I think Dan means well, and this is something that affects all three of us," Sissy rejoined. "I believe that if Dad remarries the right person it could be good for all of us. He's the one that has to make the decision, but I believe he'll want us to be happy with his choice. We've known Esther for quite some time now, or at least I have through her letters. I think she's superb. Dad hasn't seen her for a long time now, though."

"It's been over two years now that Mommy died," Dan said. "She wasn't with us for about three years before that, so that's at least five years. Dad, if you don't hurry up and get married we'll be grown and ready to go out on our own having missed out on all those years of having a mother!"

Zack again chuckled somewhat uncomfortably as he replied, "Sissy is right; the decision is mine. However, none of what either of you have said seems wrong to me. I like Esther, but she may not be interested in us to the extent that you both seem so willing to plan. When a guy like me made such a mess of the earlier part of his life as I did, there remains a risk in planning to spend the rest of your life with him. I'm not certain Esther knows how I'm doing."

"Oh, she knows! "Sissy exclaimed. "When she writes she asks how you and Dan are doing; I've made certain that whatever has transpired she's aware of it. I've told her about your grades each semester, about the award you won on the engineering project, about the little computer device you've gotten the patent on, and a bunch of other stuff including that you haven't touched alcohol once. She knows it all."

"See, Dad? Sissy certainly has your number!" Dan added. "You just need to do your part now."

Zack couldn't help but laugh, "OK, OK I'll step right up to the plate. I'll make myself vulnerable and see if she's interested. However, at some point you both need to let us be adults and proceed with this discreetly. I may be able to handle such openness, but she may not, at least initially. We're here at the school now. Both of you have a great day and I'll see Sissy at super and I'll pick Dan up at four thirty."

CPSIA information can be obtained
at www.ICGtesting.com
Printed in the USA
LVHW052158170419
614598LV00006B/29/P